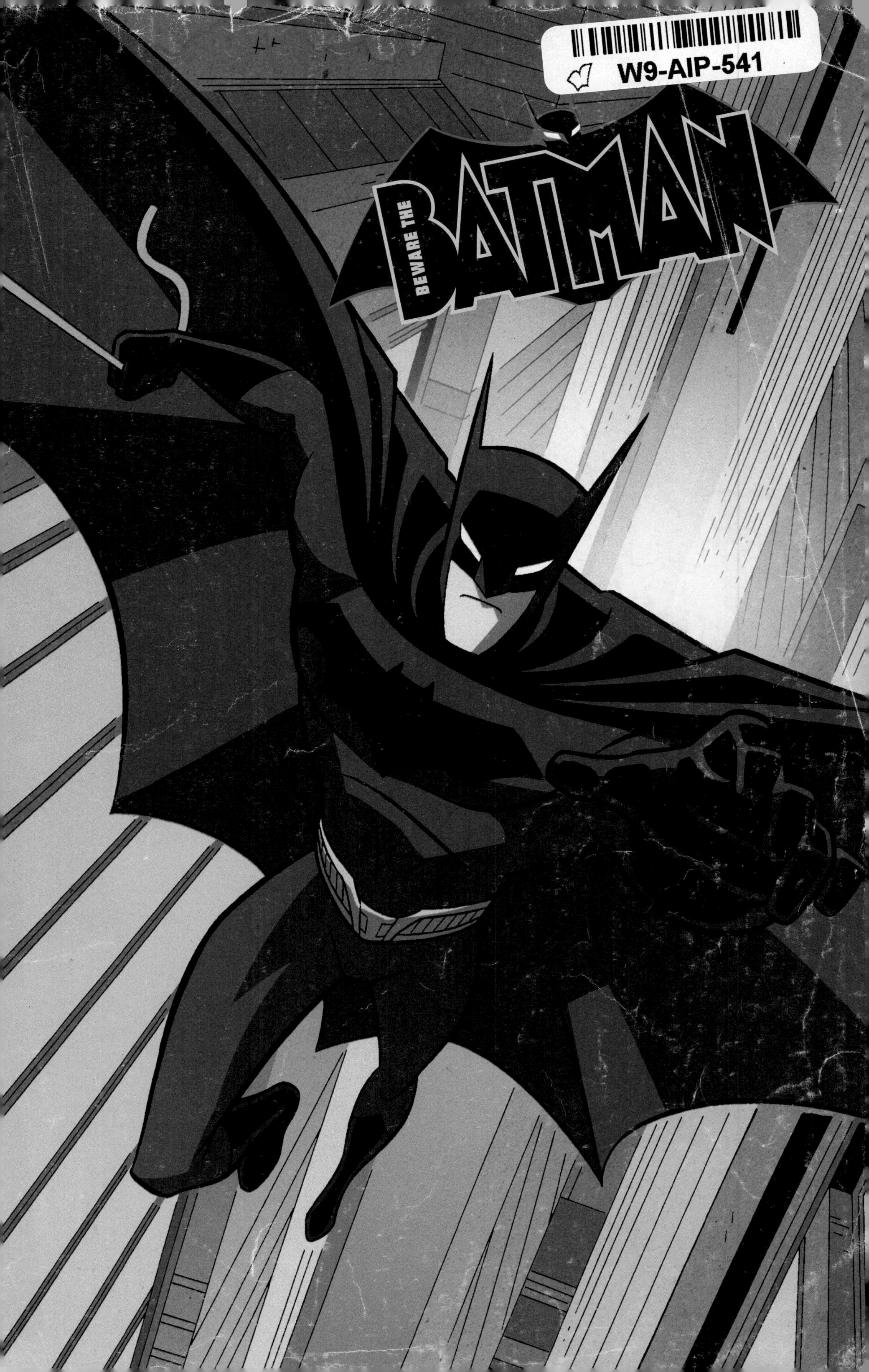
BEWARE THE
BATMAN

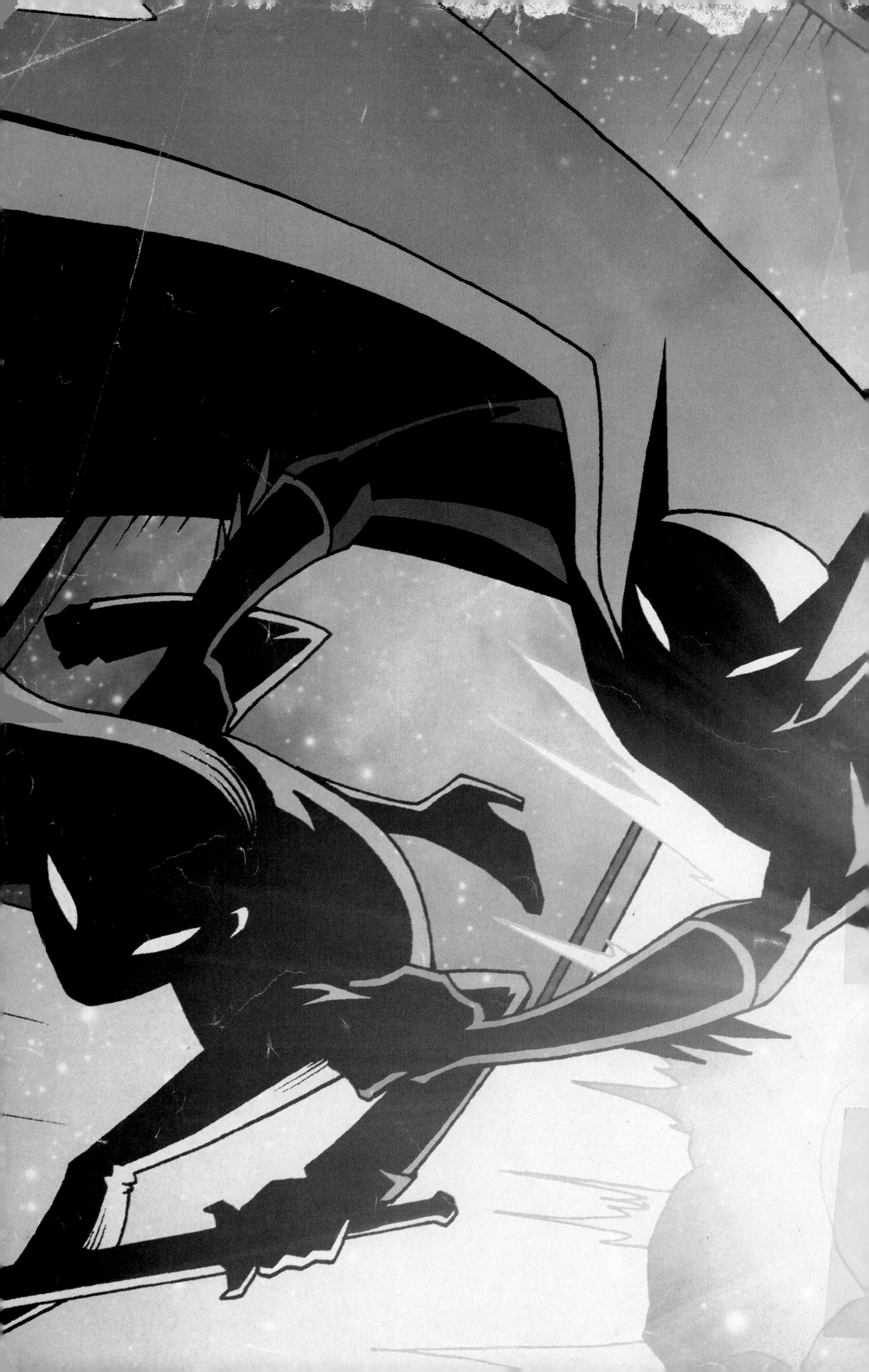

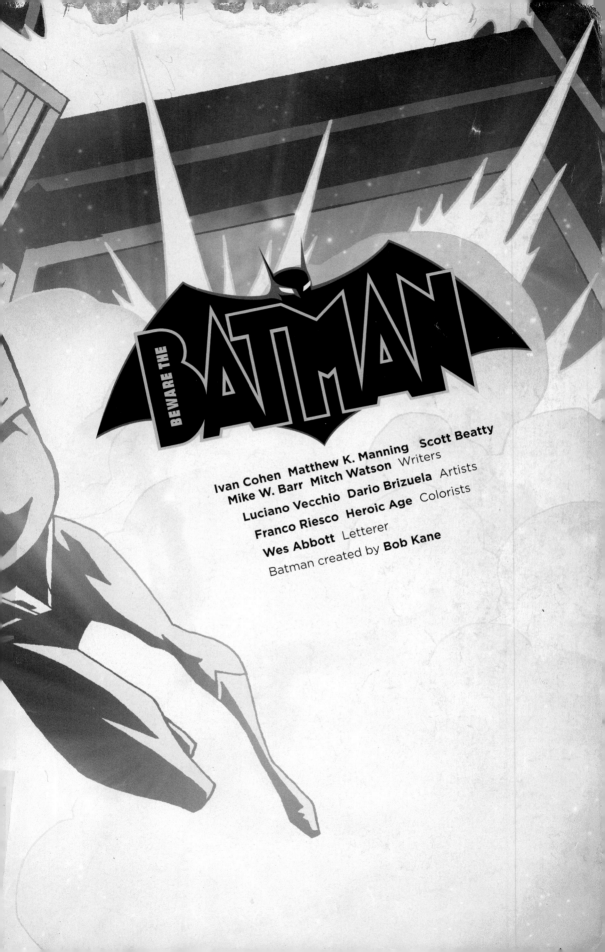

BEWARE THE BATMAN

Ivan Cohen Matthew K. Manning Scott Beatty
Mike W. Barr Mitch Watson Writers
Luciano Vecchio Dario Brizuela Artists
Franco Riesco Heroic Age Colorists
Wes Abbott Letterer
Batman created by Bob Kane

Alex Antone Kristy Quinn Sarah Gaydos Editors– Original Series
Jessica Chen Assistant Editor – Original Series
Liz Erickson Editor
Robbin Brosterman Design Director – Books
Louis Prandi Publication Design

Hank Kanalz Senior VP – Vertigo & Integrated Publishing

Diane Nelson President
Dan DiDio and **Jim Lee** Co-Publishers
Geoff Johns Chief Creative Officer
Amit Desai Senior VP – Marketing & Franchise Management
Amy Genkins Senior VP – Business & Legal Affairs
Nairi Gardiner Senior VP – Finance
Jeff Boison VP – Publishing Planning
Mark Chiarello VP – Art Direction & Design
John Cunningham VP – Marketing
Terri Cunningham VP – Editorial Administration
Larry Ganem VP – Talent Relations & Services
Alison Gill Senior VP – Manufacturing & Operations
Jay Kogan VP – Business & Legal Affairs, Publishing
Jack Mahan VP – Business Affairs, Talent
Nick Napolitano VP – Manufacturing Administration
Sue Pohja VP – Book Sales
Fred Ruiz VP – Manufacturing Operations
Courtney Simmons Senior VP – Publicity
Bob Wayne Senior VP – Sales

BEWARE THE BATMAN

Published by DC Comics. Cover and compilation Copyright
© 2015 DC Comics. All Rights Reserved.

Originally published in single magazine form in
DC NATION SUPER SAMPLER 1, BEWARE THE BATMAN 1-6
© 2013, 2014 DC Comics. All Rights Reserved. All characters,
their distinctive likenesses and related elements featured in
this publication are trademarks of DC Comics. The stories,
characters and incidents featured in this publication are
entirely fictional. DC Comics does not read or accept
unsolicited ideas, stories or artwork.

DC Comics, 1700 Broadway, New York, NY 10019
A Warner Bros. Entertainment Company.
Printed by RR Donnelley, Owensville, MO, USA. 12/19/14.
First Printing. ISBN: 978-1-4012-4936-6

Library of Congress Cataloging-in-Publication Data
is Available.

SUSTAINABLE
FORESTRY
INITIATIVE

Certified Chain of Custody
20% Certified Forest Content,
80% Certified Sourcing
www.sfiprogram.org
SFI-01042
APPLIES TO TEXT STOCK ONLY

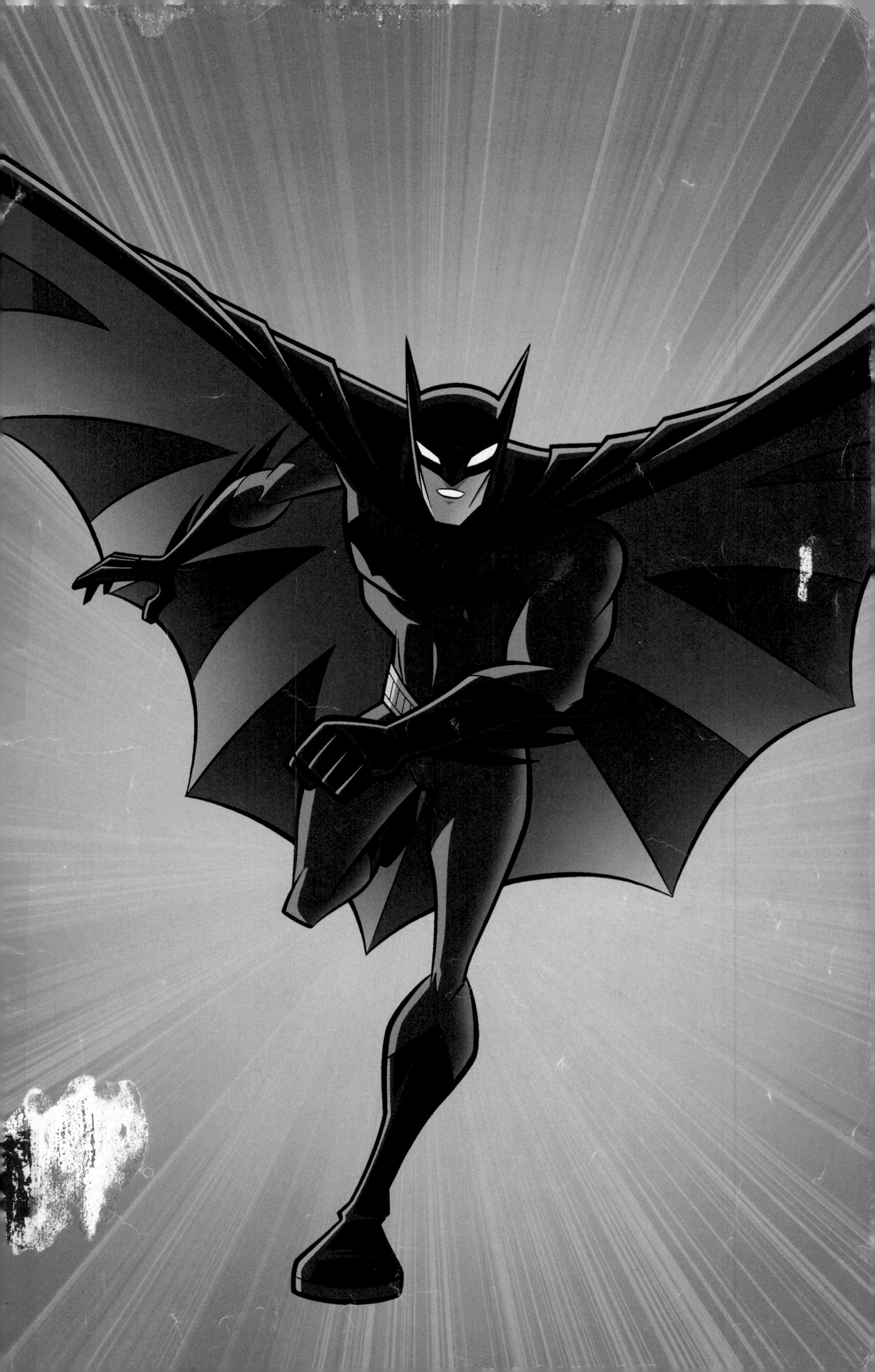

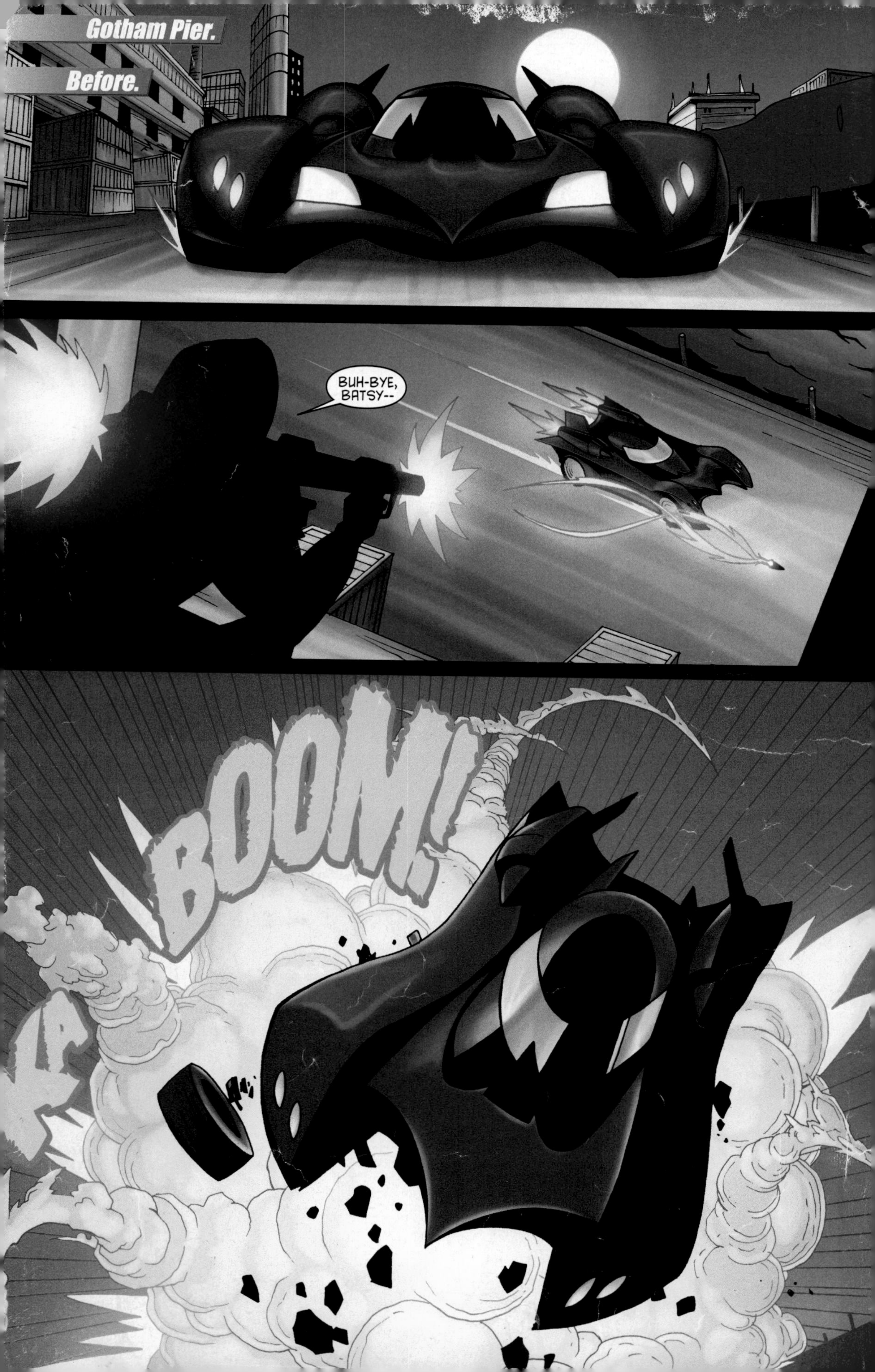
Gotham Pier.
Before.
BUH-BYE, BATSY--
BOOM!

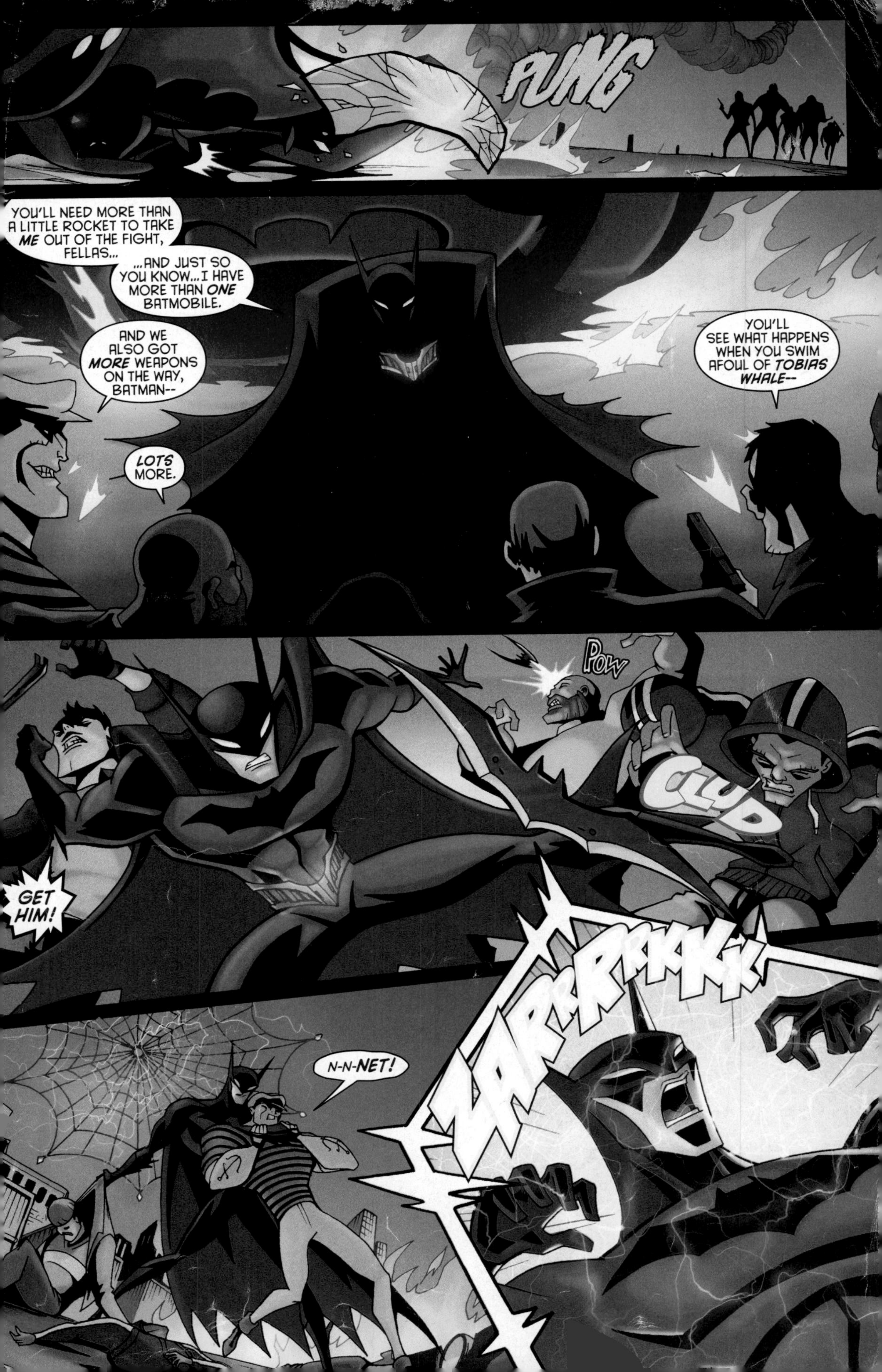
PUNG
YOU'LL NEED MORE THAN A LITTLE ROCKET TO TAKE ME OUT OF THE FIGHT, FELLAS...
...AND JUST SO YOU KNOW...I HAVE MORE THAN ONE BATMOBILE.
AND WE ALSO GOT MORE WEAPONS ON THE WAY, BATMAN--
LOTS MORE.
YOU'LL SEE WHAT HAPPENS WHEN YOU SWIM AFOUL OF TOBIAS WHALE--
POW
CLUD
GET HIM!
N-N-NET!

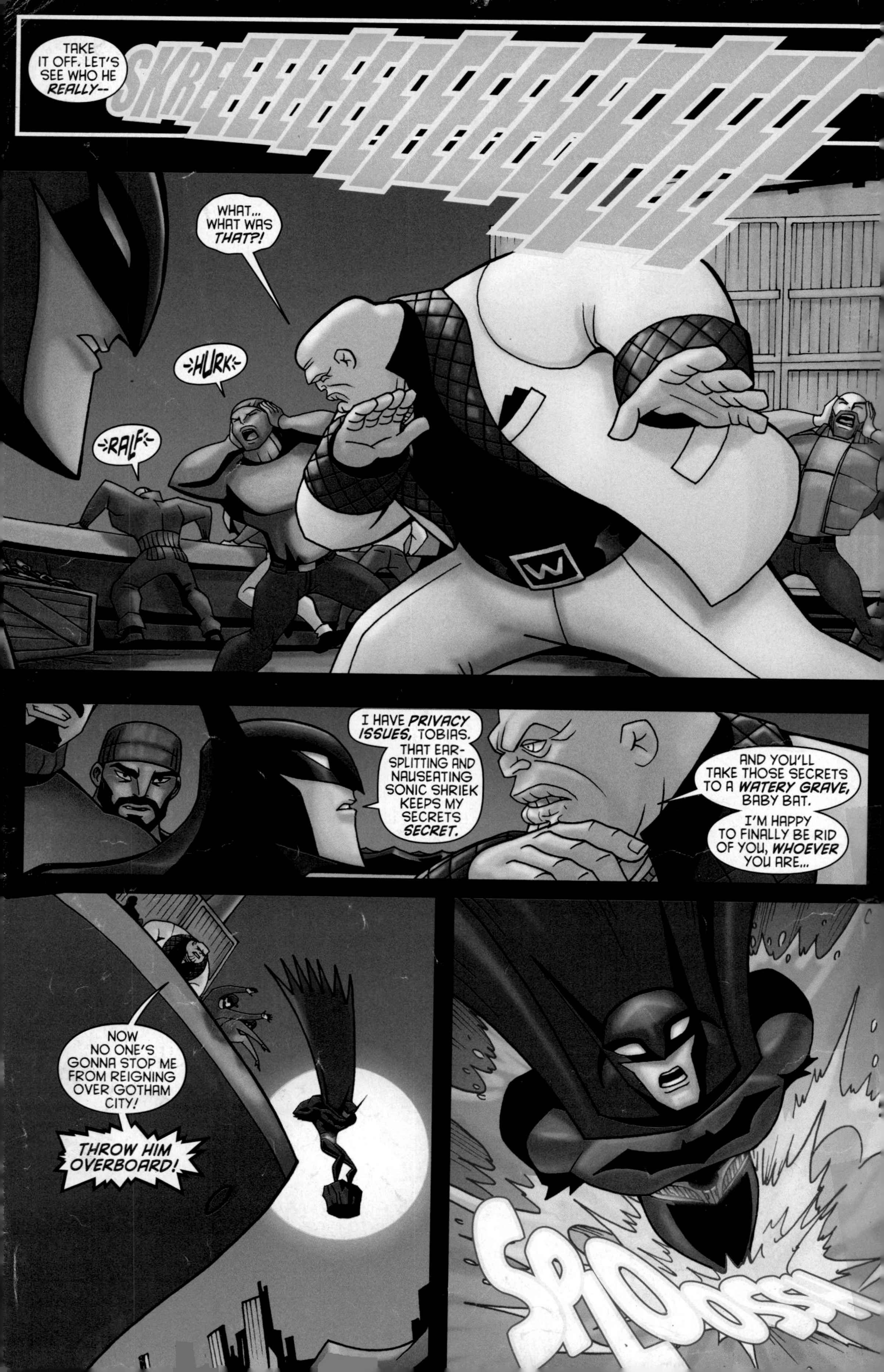
TAKE IT OFF. LET'S SEE WHO HE *REALLY*--
SKREEEEEEEEEEEEEEEEEEEEEEEEEEEEET
WHAT... WHAT WAS *THAT?!*
HURK
RALF
I HAVE *PRIVACY ISSUES,* TOBIAS. THAT EAR-SPLITTING AND NAUSEATING SONIC SHRIEK KEEPS MY SECRETS *SECRET.*
AND YOU'LL TAKE THOSE SECRETS TO A *WATERY GRAVE,* BABY BAT.
I'M HAPPY TO FINALLY BE RID OF YOU, *WHOEVER* YOU ARE...
NOW NO ONE'S GONNA STOP ME FROM REIGNING OVER GOTHAM CITY!
THROW HIM OVERBOARD!
SPLOOSH

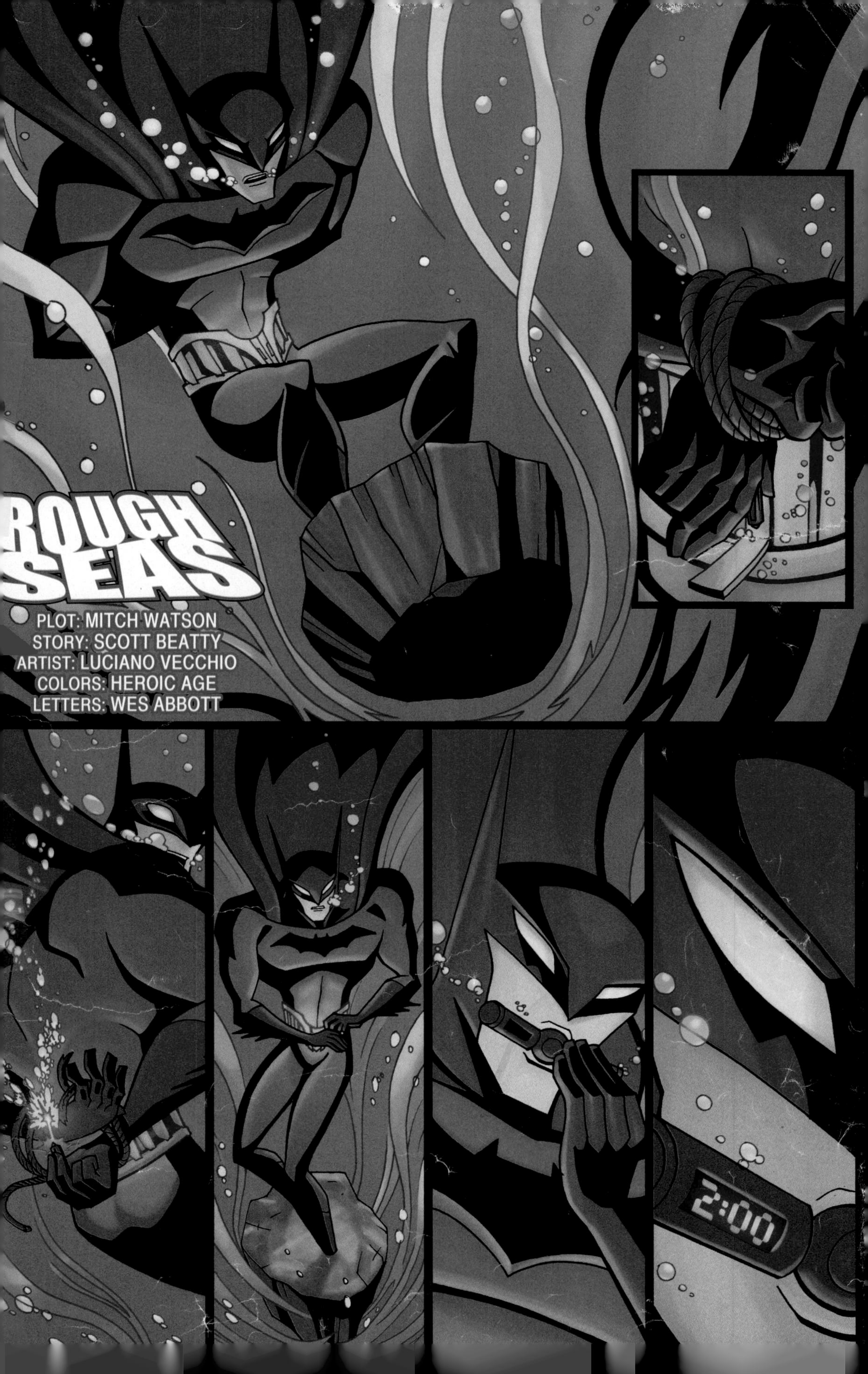
ROUGH SEAS
PLOT: MITCH WATSON
STORY: SCOTT BEATTY
ARTIST: LUCIANO VECCHIO
COLORS: HEROIC AGE
LETTERS: WES ABBOTT
2:00

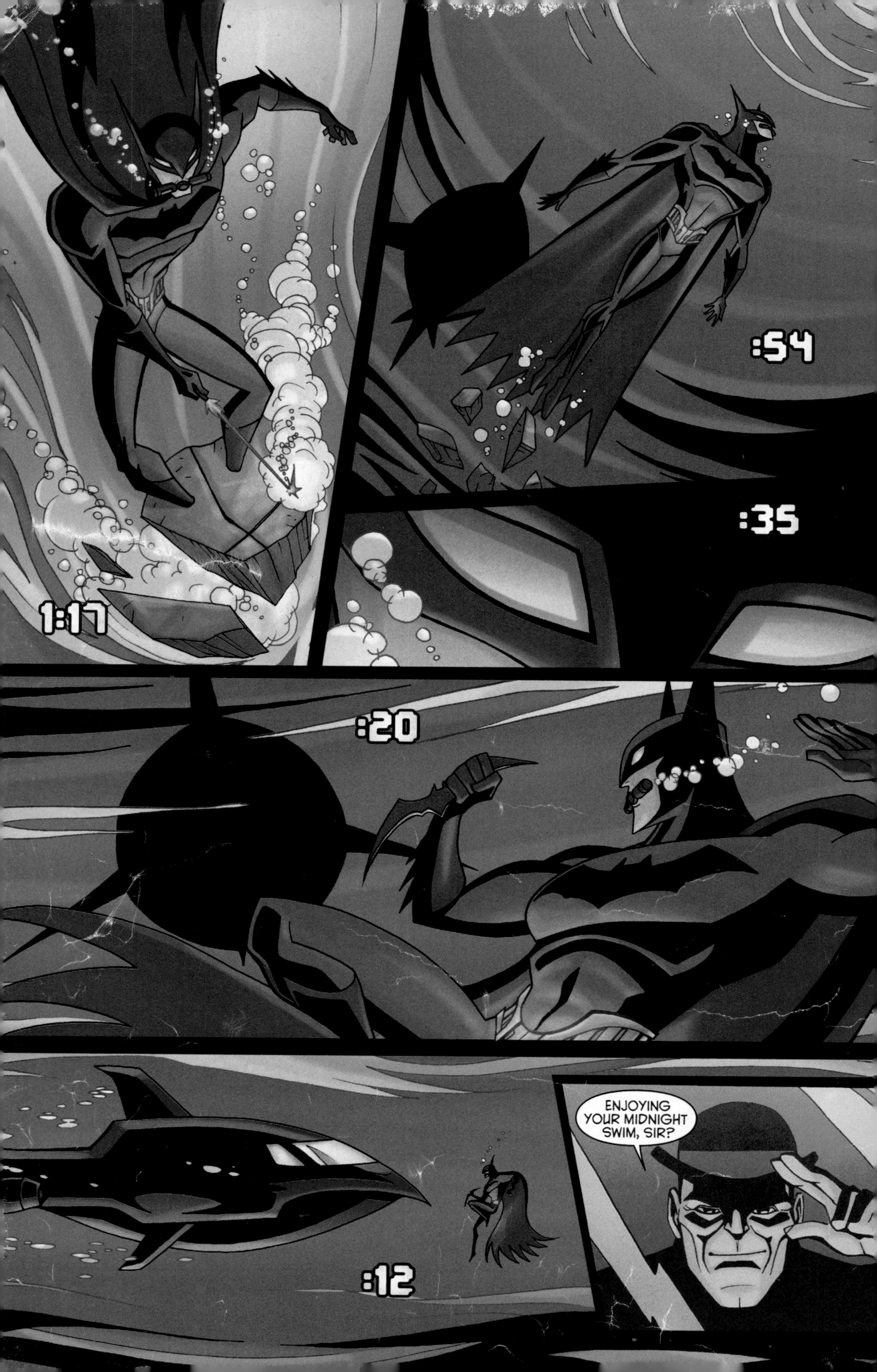
1:17
:54
:35
:20
:12
ENJOYING YOUR MIDNIGHT SWIM, SIR?

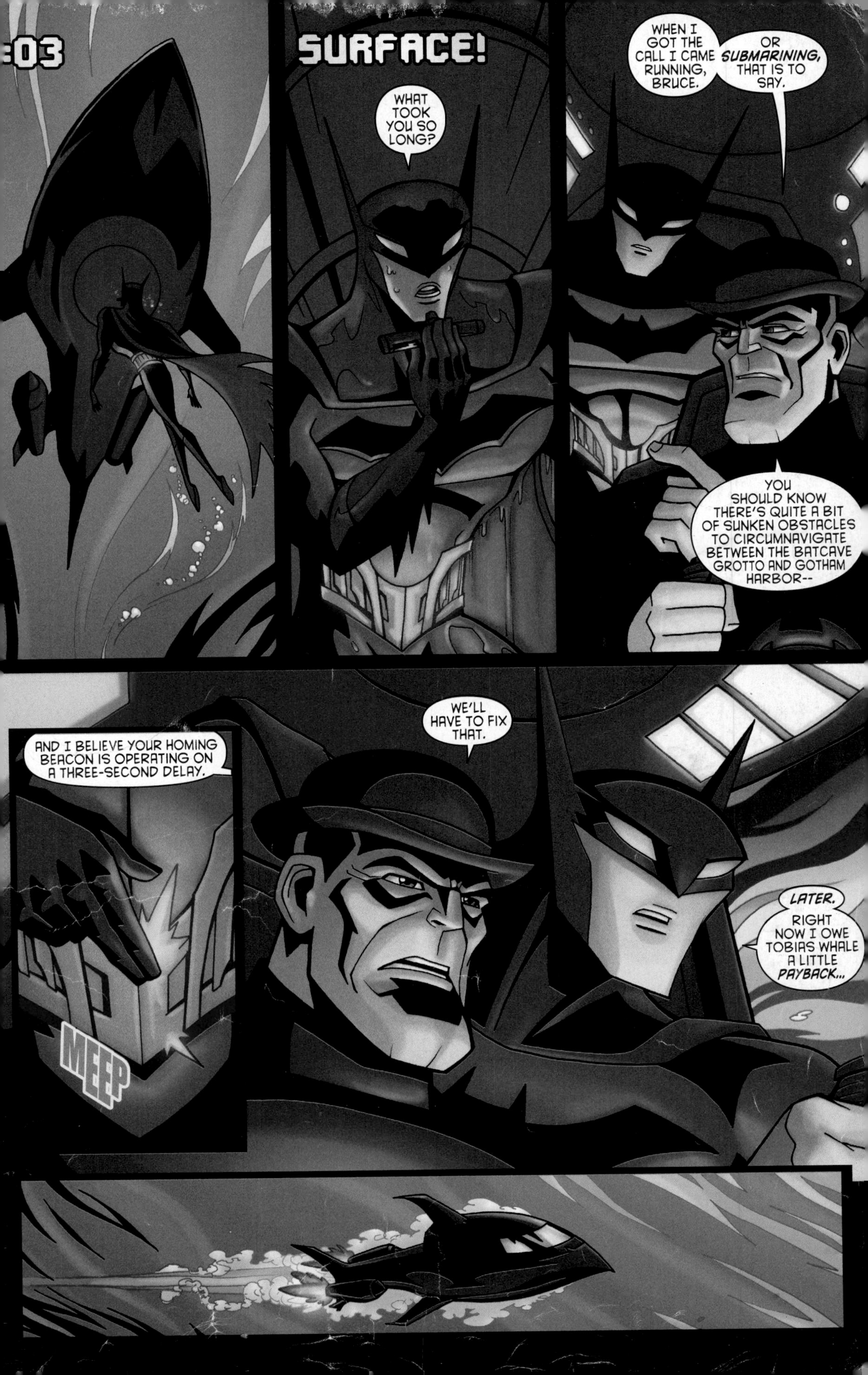
:03
SURFACE!
WHAT TOOK YOU SO LONG?
WHEN I GOT THE CALL I CAME RUNNING, BRUCE.
OR *SUBMARINING,* THAT IS TO SAY.
YOU SHOULD KNOW THERE'S QUITE A BIT OF SUNKEN OBSTACLES TO CIRCUMNAVIGATE BETWEEN THE BATCAVE GROTTO AND GOTHAM HARBOR--
AND I BELIEVE YOUR HOMING BEACON IS OPERATING ON A THREE-SECOND DELAY.
MEEP
WE'LL HAVE TO FIX THAT.
LATER. RIGHT NOW I OWE TOBIAS WHALE A LITTLE *PAYBACK...*

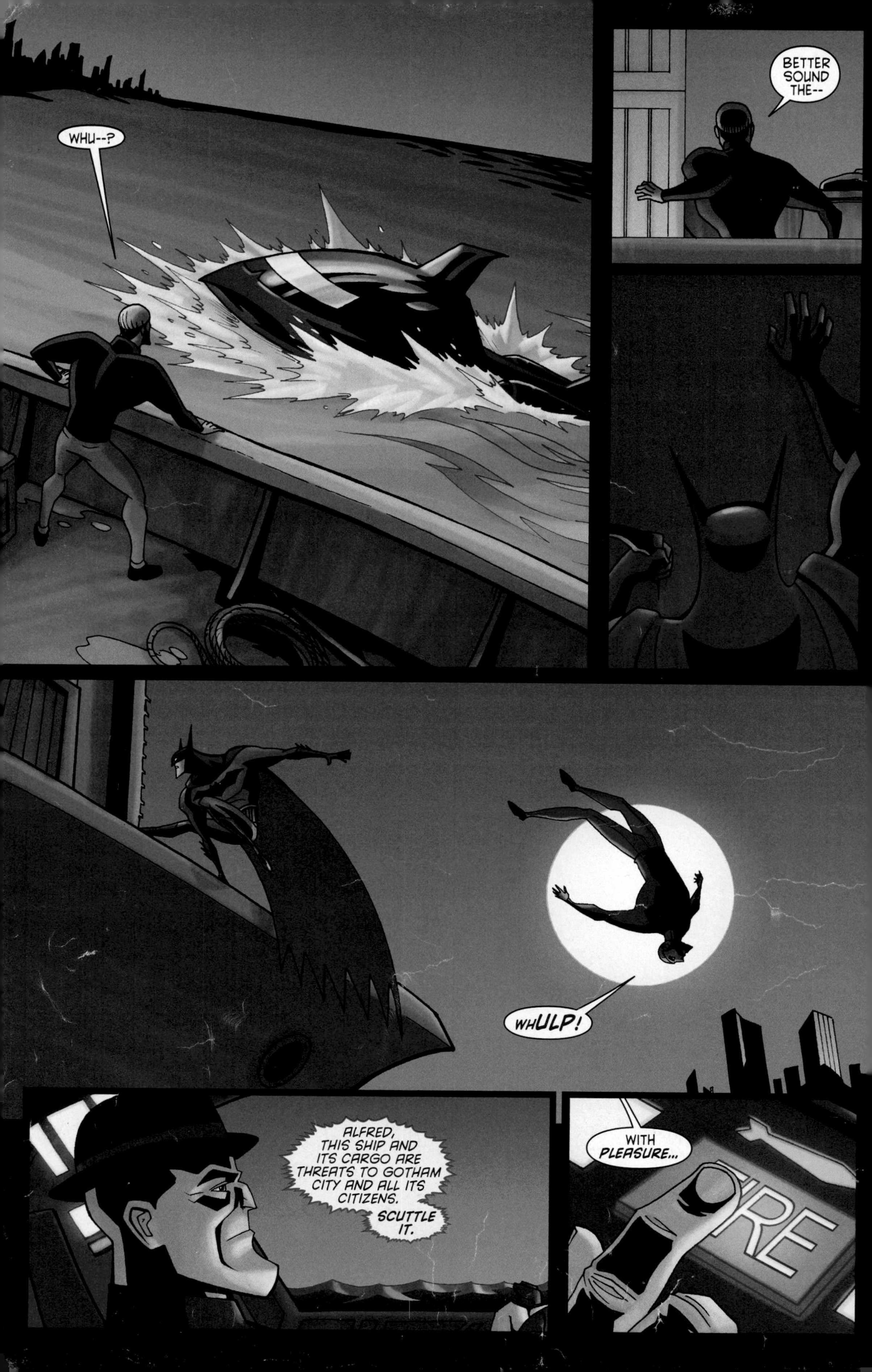
WHU--?
BETTER SOUND THE--
WHULP!
ALFRED, THIS SHIP AND ITS CARGO ARE THREATS TO GOTHAM CITY AND ALL ITS CITIZENS.
SCUTTLE IT.
WITH PLEASURE...
FIRE

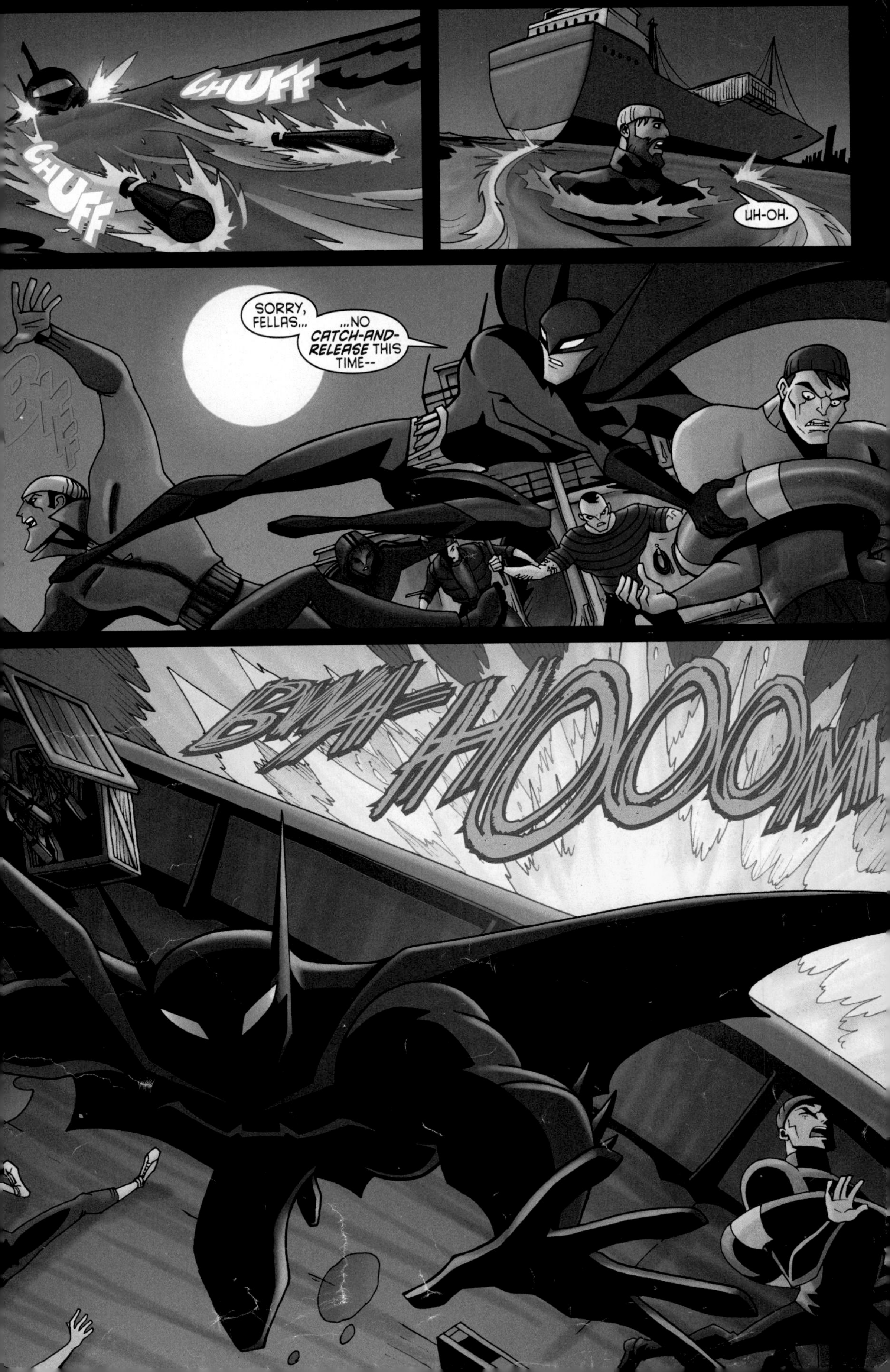
CHUFF
CHUFF
UH-OH.
SORRY, FELLAS...
...NO CATCH-AND-RELEASE THIS TIME--
BFFF
BWAH-HOOOM

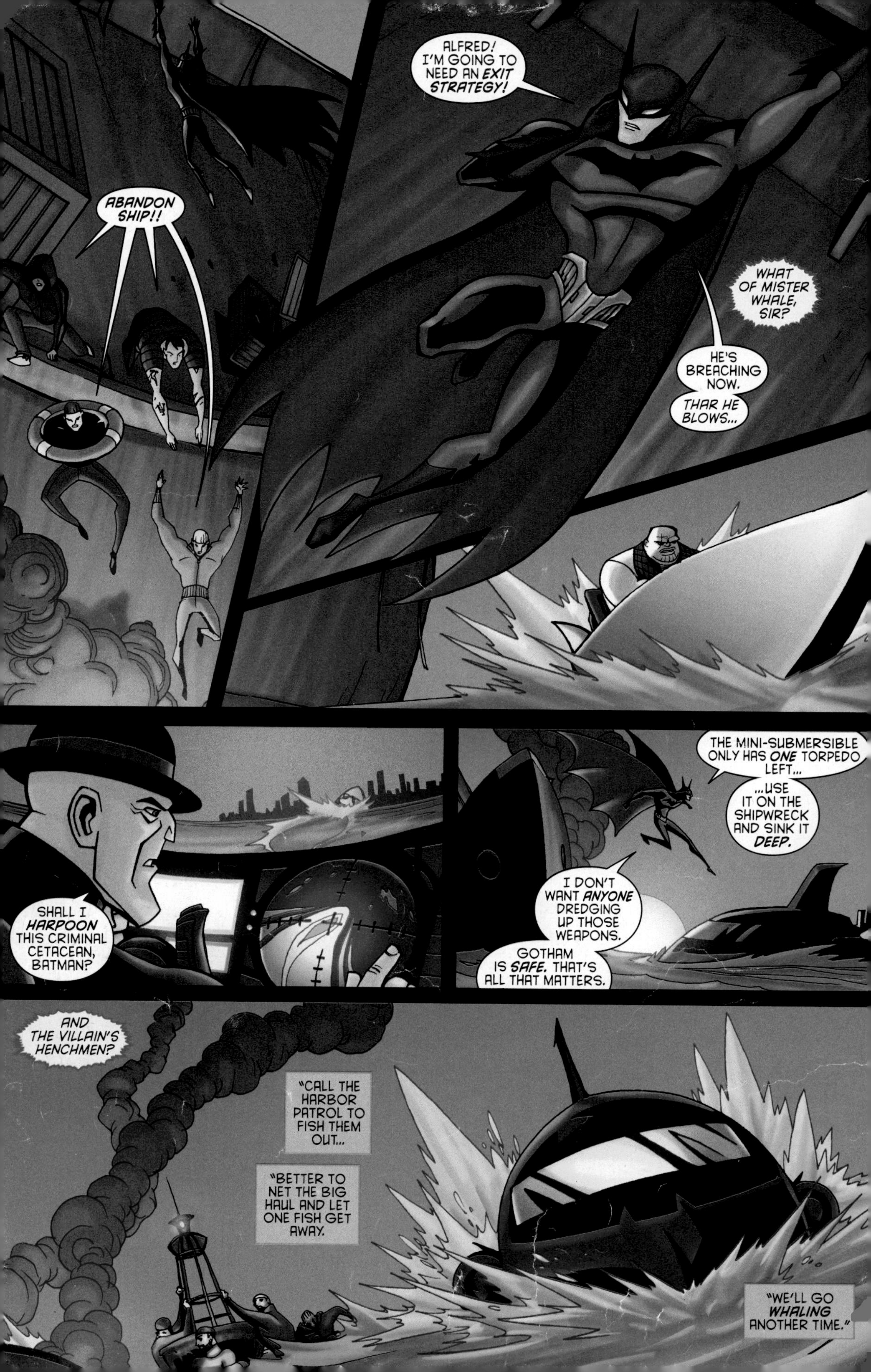
ALFRED! I'M GOING TO NEED AN EXIT STRATEGY!
ABANDON SHIP!!
WHAT OF MISTER WHALE, SIR?
HE'S BREACHING NOW.
THAR HE BLOWS...
SHALL I HARPOON THIS CRIMINAL CETACEAN, BATMAN?
THE MINI-SUBMERSIBLE ONLY HAS ONE TORPEDO LEFT...
...USE IT ON THE SHIPWRECK AND SINK IT DEEP.
I DON'T WANT ANYONE DREDGING UP THOSE WEAPONS.
GOTHAM IS SAFE. THAT'S ALL THAT MATTERS.
AND THE VILLAIN'S HENCHMEN?
"CALL THE HARBOR PATROL TO FISH THEM OUT...
"BETTER TO NET THE BIG HAUL AND LET ONE FISH GET AWAY.
"WE'LL GO WHALING ANOTHER TIME."

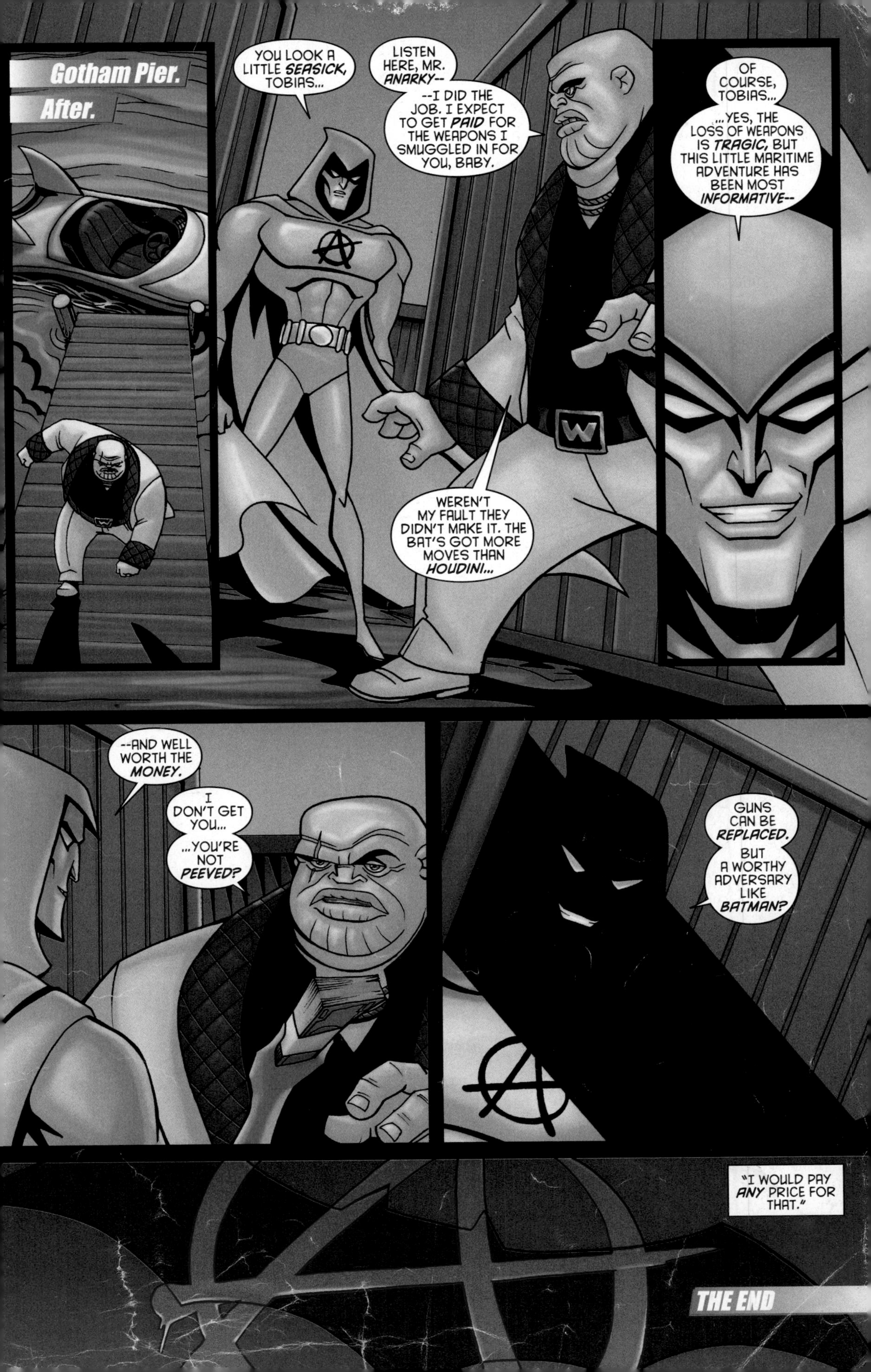
Gotham Pier.
After.
YOU LOOK A LITTLE SEASICK, TOBIAS...
LISTEN HERE, MR. ANARKY--
--I DID THE JOB. I EXPECT TO GET PAID FOR THE WEAPONS I SMUGGLED IN FOR YOU, BABY.
OF COURSE, TOBIAS...
...YES, THE LOSS OF WEAPONS IS TRAGIC, BUT THIS LITTLE MARITIME ADVENTURE HAS BEEN MOST INFORMATIVE--
WEREN'T MY FAULT THEY DIDN'T MAKE IT. THE BAT'S GOT MORE MOVES THAN HOUDINI...
--AND WELL WORTH THE MONEY.
I DON'T GET YOU...
...YOU'RE NOT PEEVED?
GUNS CAN BE REPLACED.
BUT A WORTHY ADVERSARY LIKE BATMAN?
"I WOULD PAY ANY PRICE FOR THAT."
THE END

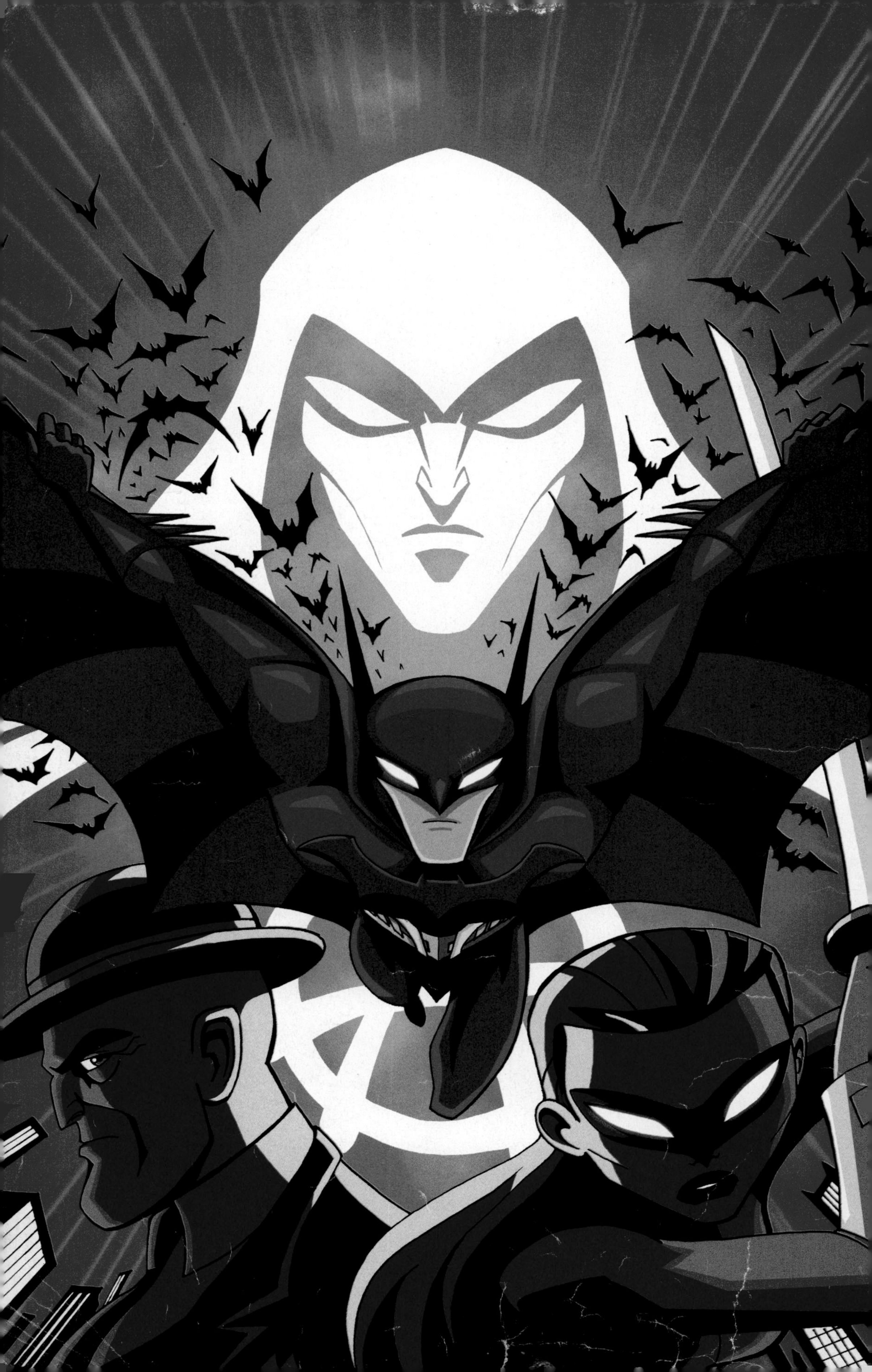

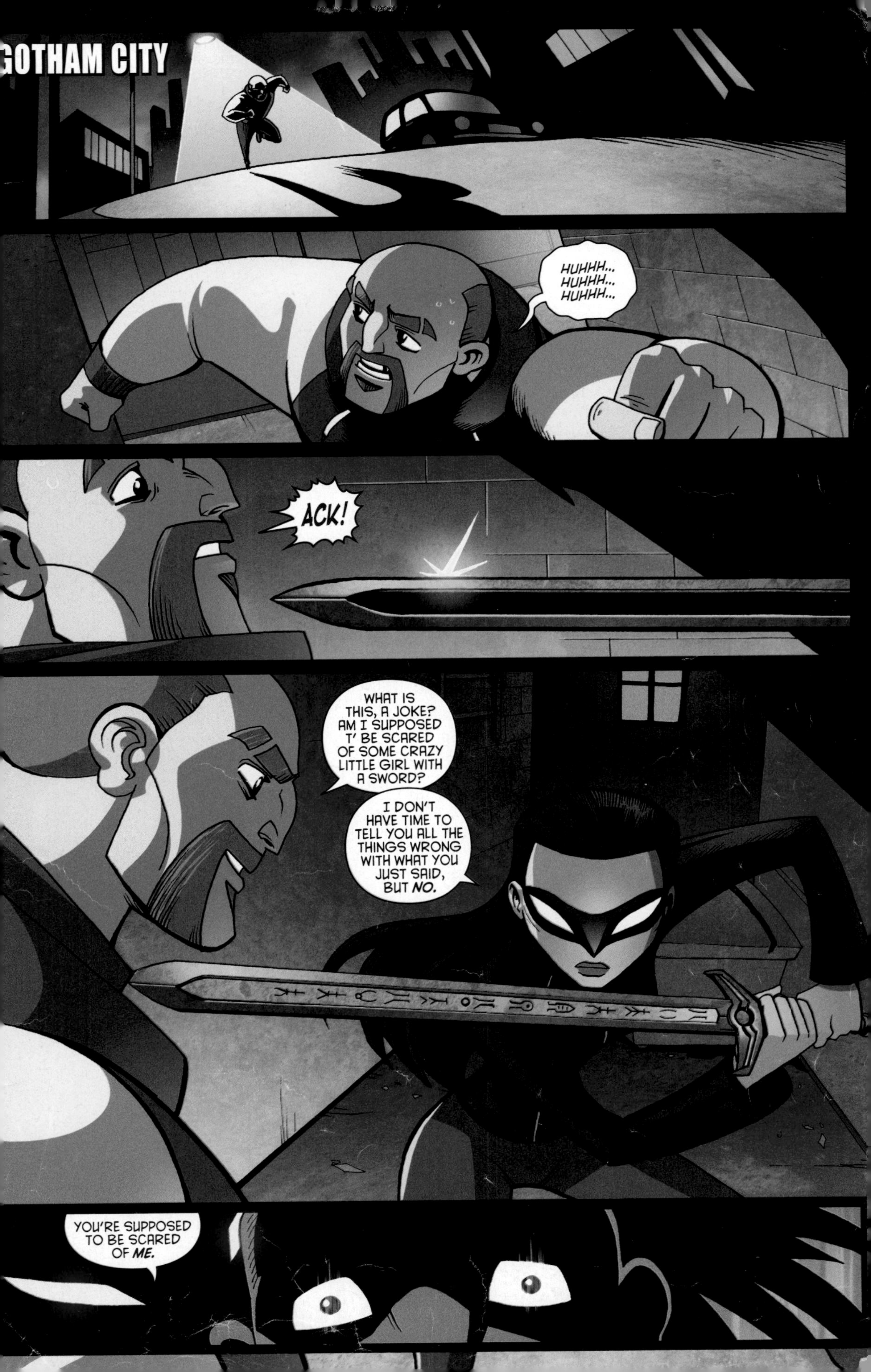
GOTHAM CITY
HUHHH... HUHHH... HUHHH...
ACK!
WHAT IS THIS, A JOKE? AM I SUPPOSED T' BE SCARED OF SOME CRAZY LITTLE GIRL WITH A SWORD?
I DON'T HAVE TIME TO TELL YOU ALL THE THINGS WRONG WITH WHAT YOU JUST SAID, BUT NO.
YOU'RE SUPPOSED TO BE SCARED OF ME.

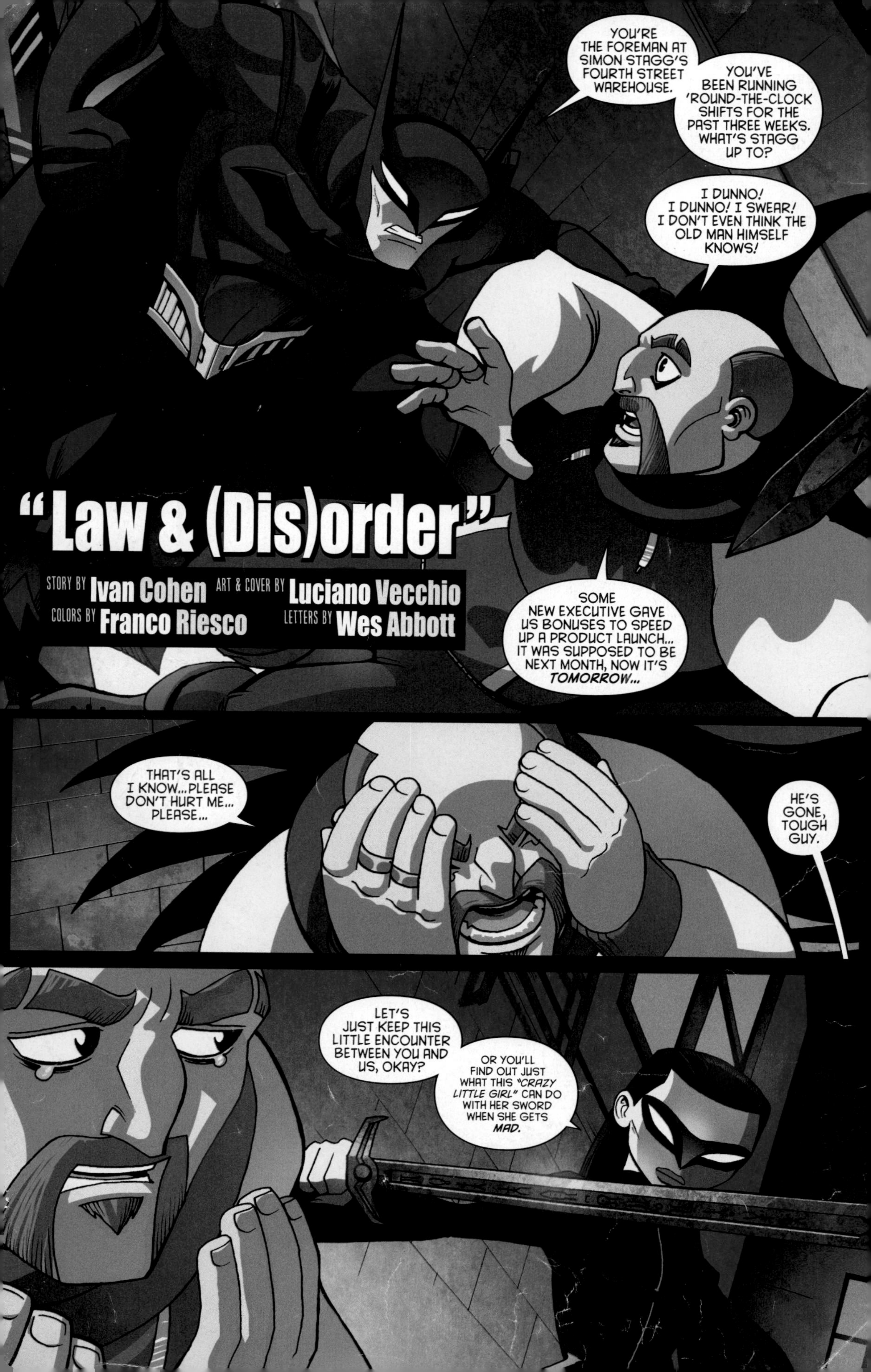
YOU'RE THE FOREMAN AT SIMON STAGG'S FOURTH STREET WAREHOUSE.
YOU'VE BEEN RUNNING 'ROUND-THE-CLOCK SHIFTS FOR THE PAST THREE WEEKS. WHAT'S STAGG UP TO?
I DUNNO! I DUNNO! I SWEAR! I DON'T EVEN THINK THE OLD MAN HIMSELF KNOWS!
"Law & (Dis)order"
STORY BY Ivan Cohen ART & COVER BY Luciano Vecchio
COLORS BY Franco Riesco LETTERS BY Wes Abbott
SOME NEW EXECUTIVE GAVE US BONUSES TO SPEED UP A PRODUCT LAUNCH... IT WAS SUPPOSED TO BE NEXT MONTH, NOW IT'S TOMORROW...
THAT'S ALL I KNOW...PLEASE DON'T HURT ME... PLEASE...
HE'S GONE, TOUGH GUY.
LET'S JUST KEEP THIS LITTLE ENCOUNTER BETWEEN YOU AND US, OKAY?
OR YOU'LL FIND OUT JUST WHAT THIS "CRAZY LITTLE GIRL" CAN DO WITH HER SWORD WHEN SHE GETS MAD.

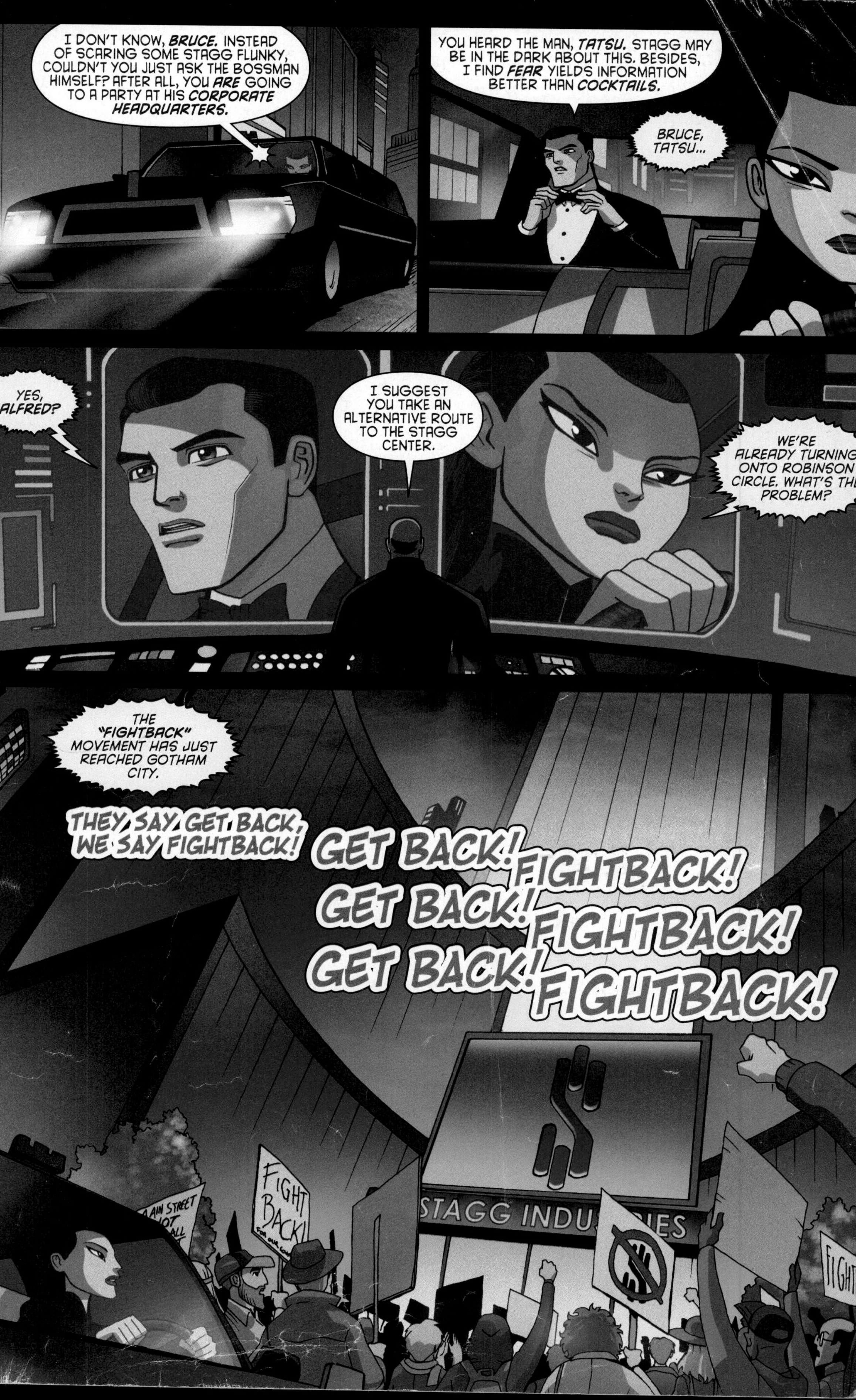
I DON'T KNOW, BRUCE. INSTEAD OF SCARING SOME STAGG FLUNKY, COULDN'T YOU JUST ASK THE BOSSMAN HIMSELF? AFTER ALL, YOU ARE GOING TO A PARTY AT HIS CORPORATE HEADQUARTERS.
YOU HEARD THE MAN, TATSU. STAGG MAY BE IN THE DARK ABOUT THIS. BESIDES, I FIND FEAR YIELDS INFORMATION BETTER THAN COCKTAILS.
BRUCE, TATSU...
YES, ALFRED?
I SUGGEST YOU TAKE AN ALTERNATIVE ROUTE TO THE STAGG CENTER.
WE'RE ALREADY TURNING ONTO ROBINSON CIRCLE. WHAT'S THE PROBLEM?
THE "FIGHTBACK" MOVEMENT HAS JUST REACHED GOTHAM CITY.
THEY SAY GET BACK, WE SAY FIGHTBACK!
GET BACK! FIGHTBACK!
GET BACK! FIGHTBACK!
GET BACK! FIGHTBACK!
FIGHT BACK!
STAGG INDUS IES

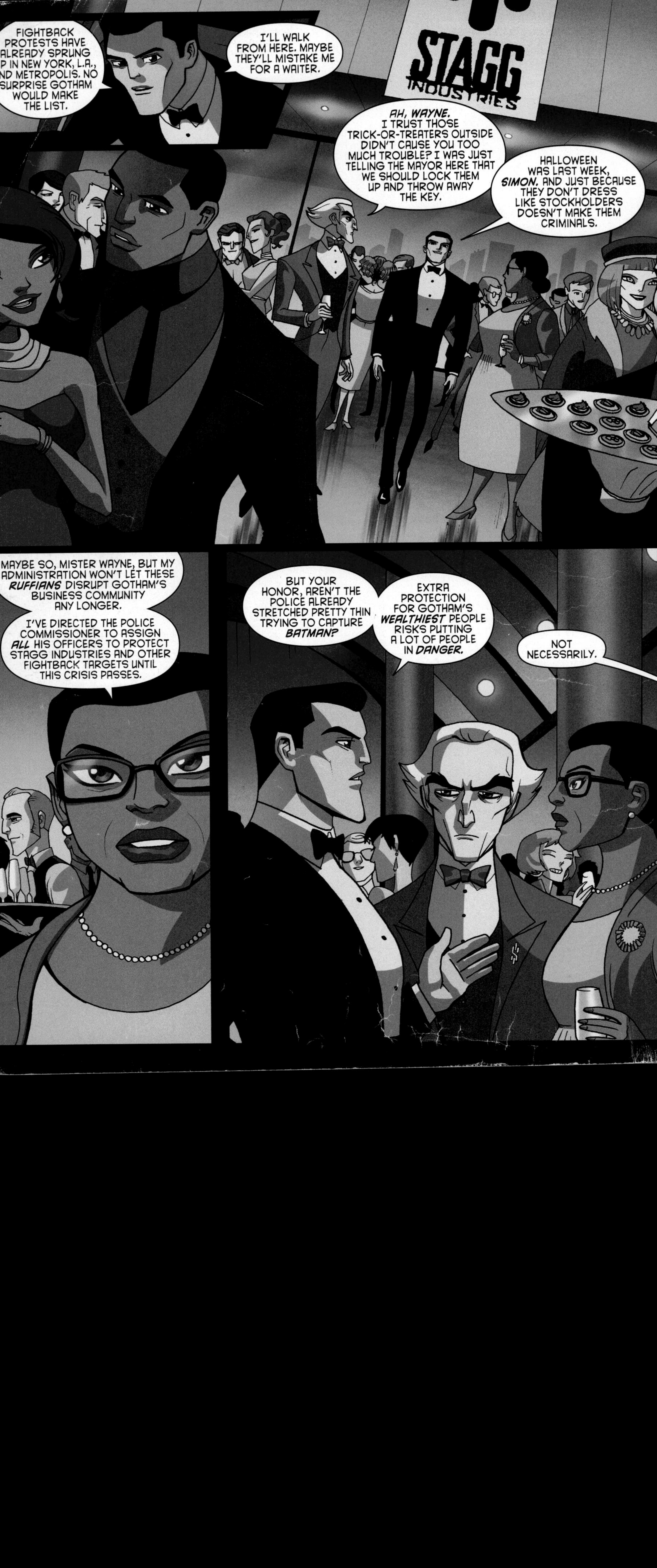
FIGHTBACK PROTESTS HAVE ALREADY SPRUNG P IN NEW YORK, L.A., ND METROPOLIS. NO SURPRISE GOTHAM WOULD MAKE THE LIST.
I'LL WALK FROM HERE. MAYBE THEY'LL MISTAKE ME FOR A WAITER.
STAGG INDUSTRIES
AH, WAYNE. I TRUST THOSE TRICK-OR-TREATERS OUTSIDE DIDN'T CAUSE YOU TOO MUCH TROUBLE? I WAS JUST TELLING THE MAYOR HERE THAT WE SHOULD LOCK THEM UP AND THROW AWAY THE KEY.
HALLOWEEN WAS LAST WEEK, SIMON. AND JUST BECAUSE THEY DON'T DRESS LIKE STOCKHOLDERS DOESN'T MAKE THEM CRIMINALS.
MAYBE SO, MISTER WAYNE, BUT MY ADMINISTRATION WON'T LET THESE RUFFIANS DISRUPT GOTHAM'S BUSINESS COMMUNITY ANY LONGER.
I'VE DIRECTED THE POLICE COMMISSIONER TO ASSIGN ALL HIS OFFICERS TO PROTECT STAGG INDUSTRIES AND OTHER FIGHTBACK TARGETS UNTIL THIS CRISIS PASSES.
BUT YOUR HONOR, AREN'T THE POLICE ALREADY STRETCHED PRETTY THIN TRYING TO CAPTURE BATMAN?
EXTRA PROTECTION FOR GOTHAM'S WEALTHIEST PEOPLE RISKS PUTTING A LOT OF PEOPLE IN DANGER.
NOT NECESSARILY.

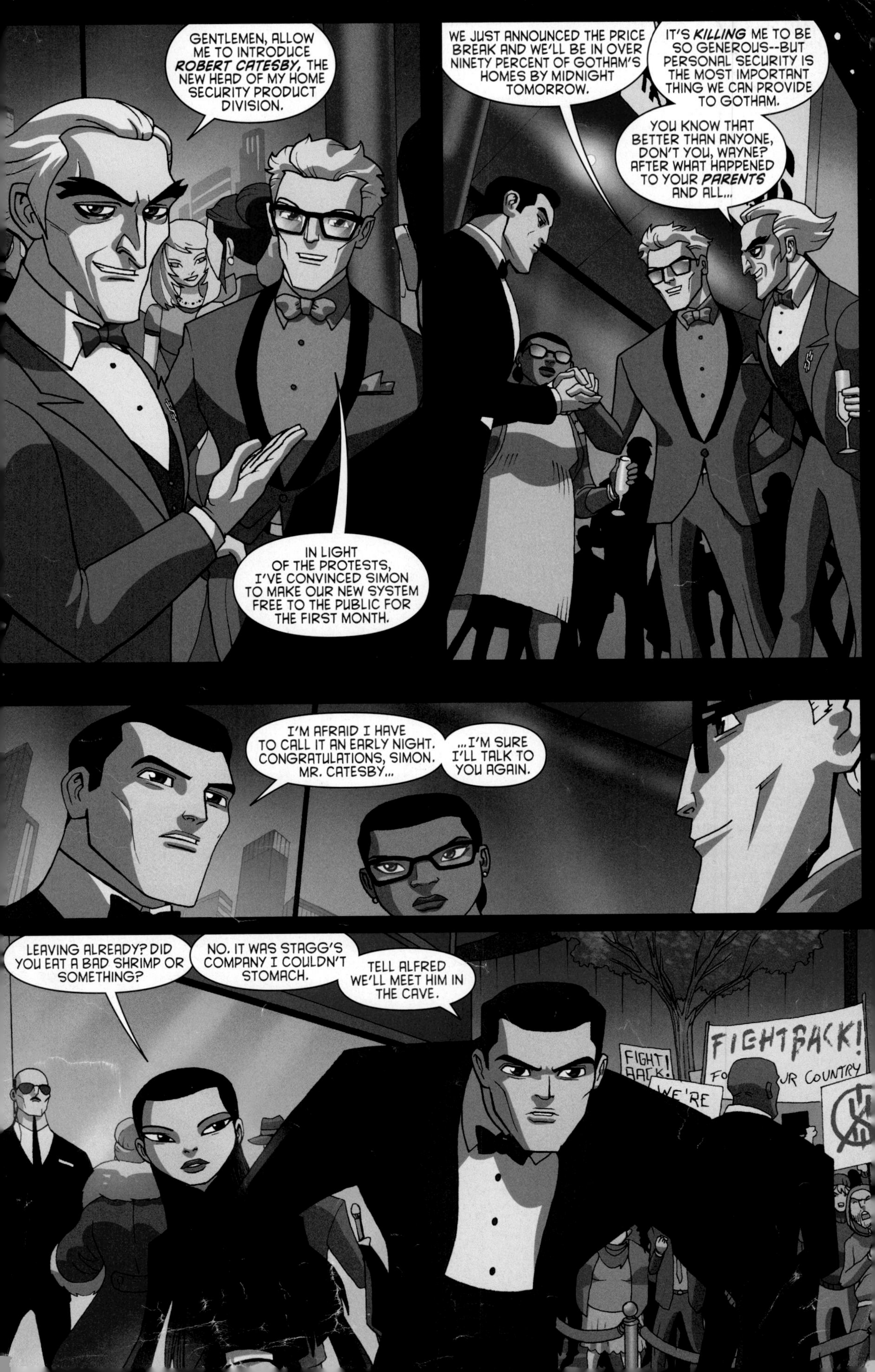
GENTLEMEN, ALLOW ME TO INTRODUCE ROBERT CATESBY, THE NEW HEAD OF MY HOME SECURITY PRODUCT DIVISION.
IN LIGHT OF THE PROTESTS, I'VE CONVINCED SIMON TO MAKE OUR NEW SYSTEM FREE TO THE PUBLIC FOR THE FIRST MONTH.
WE JUST ANNOUNCED THE PRICE BREAK AND WE'LL BE IN OVER NINETY PERCENT OF GOTHAM'S HOMES BY MIDNIGHT TOMORROW.
IT'S KILLING ME TO BE SO GENEROUS--BUT PERSONAL SECURITY IS THE MOST IMPORTANT THING WE CAN PROVIDE TO GOTHAM.
YOU KNOW THAT BETTER THAN ANYONE, DON'T YOU, WAYNE? AFTER WHAT HAPPENED TO YOUR PARENTS AND ALL...
I'M AFRAID I HAVE TO CALL IT AN EARLY NIGHT. CONGRATULATIONS, SIMON. MR. CATESBY...
...I'M SURE I'LL TALK TO YOU AGAIN.
LEAVING ALREADY? DID YOU EAT A BAD SHRIMP OR SOMETHING?
NO. IT WAS STAGG'S COMPANY I COULDN'T STOMACH.
TELL ALFRED WE'LL MEET HIM IN THE CAVE.
FIGHTBACK!
FIGHT!
WE'RE

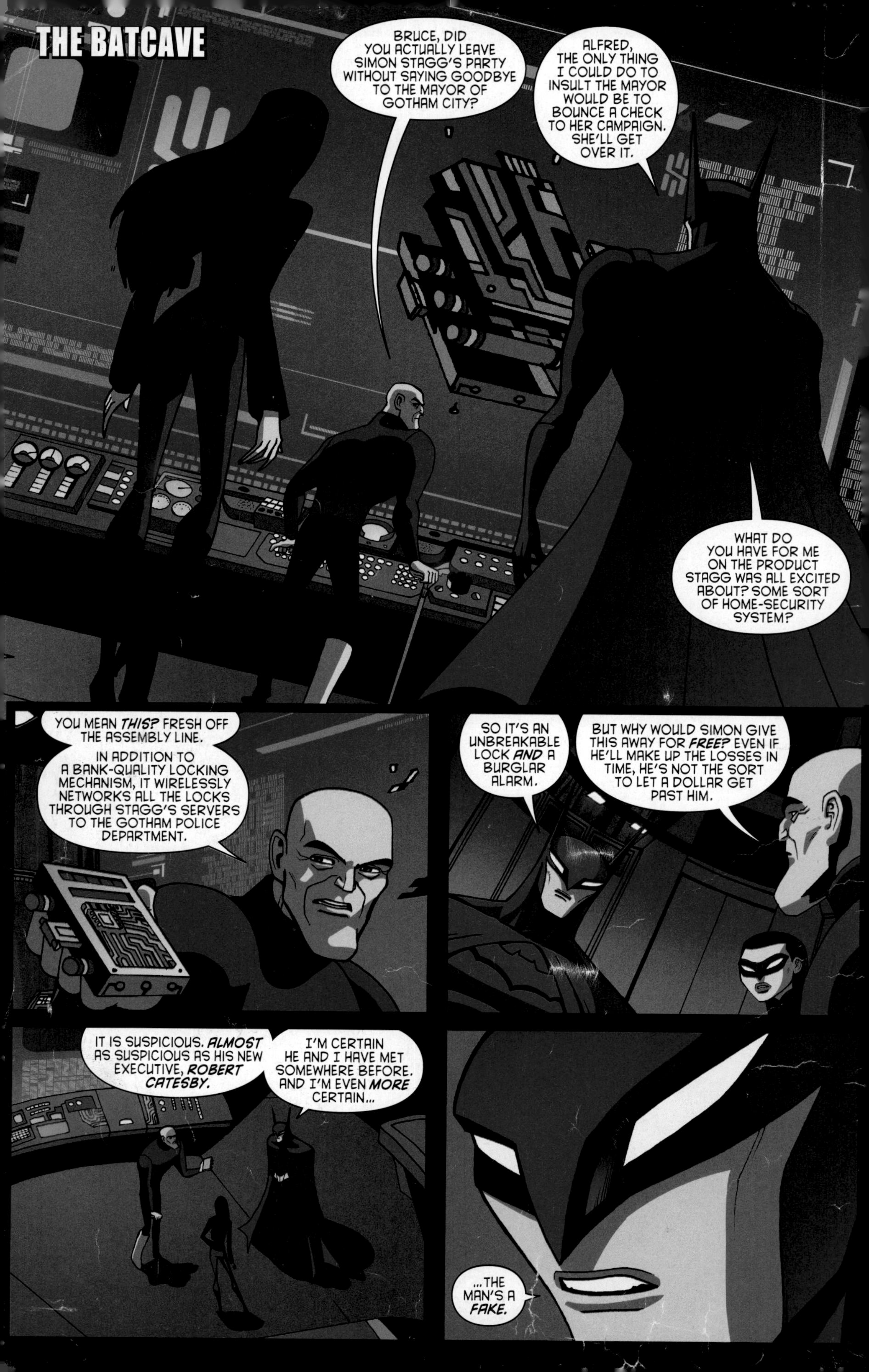
THE BATCAVE
BRUCE, DID YOU ACTUALLY LEAVE SIMON STAGG'S PARTY WITHOUT SAYING GOODBYE TO THE MAYOR OF GOTHAM CITY?
ALFRED, THE ONLY THING I COULD DO TO INSULT THE MAYOR WOULD BE TO BOUNCE A CHECK TO HER CAMPAIGN. SHE'LL GET OVER IT.
WHAT DO YOU HAVE FOR ME ON THE PRODUCT STAGG WAS ALL EXCITED ABOUT? SOME SORT OF HOME-SECURITY SYSTEM?
YOU MEAN THIS? FRESH OFF THE ASSEMBLY LINE.
IN ADDITION TO A BANK-QUALITY LOCKING MECHANISM, IT WIRELESSLY NETWORKS ALL THE LOCKS THROUGH STAGG'S SERVERS TO THE GOTHAM POLICE DEPARTMENT.
SO IT'S AN UNBREAKABLE LOCK AND A BURGLAR ALARM.
BUT WHY WOULD SIMON GIVE THIS AWAY FOR FREE? EVEN IF HE'LL MAKE UP THE LOSSES IN TIME, HE'S NOT THE SORT TO LET A DOLLAR GET PAST HIM.
IT IS SUSPICIOUS. ALMOST AS SUSPICIOUS AS HIS NEW EXECUTIVE, ROBERT CATESBY.
I'M CERTAIN HE AND I HAVE MET SOMEWHERE BEFORE. AND I'M EVEN MORE CERTAIN...
...THE MAN'S A FAKE.

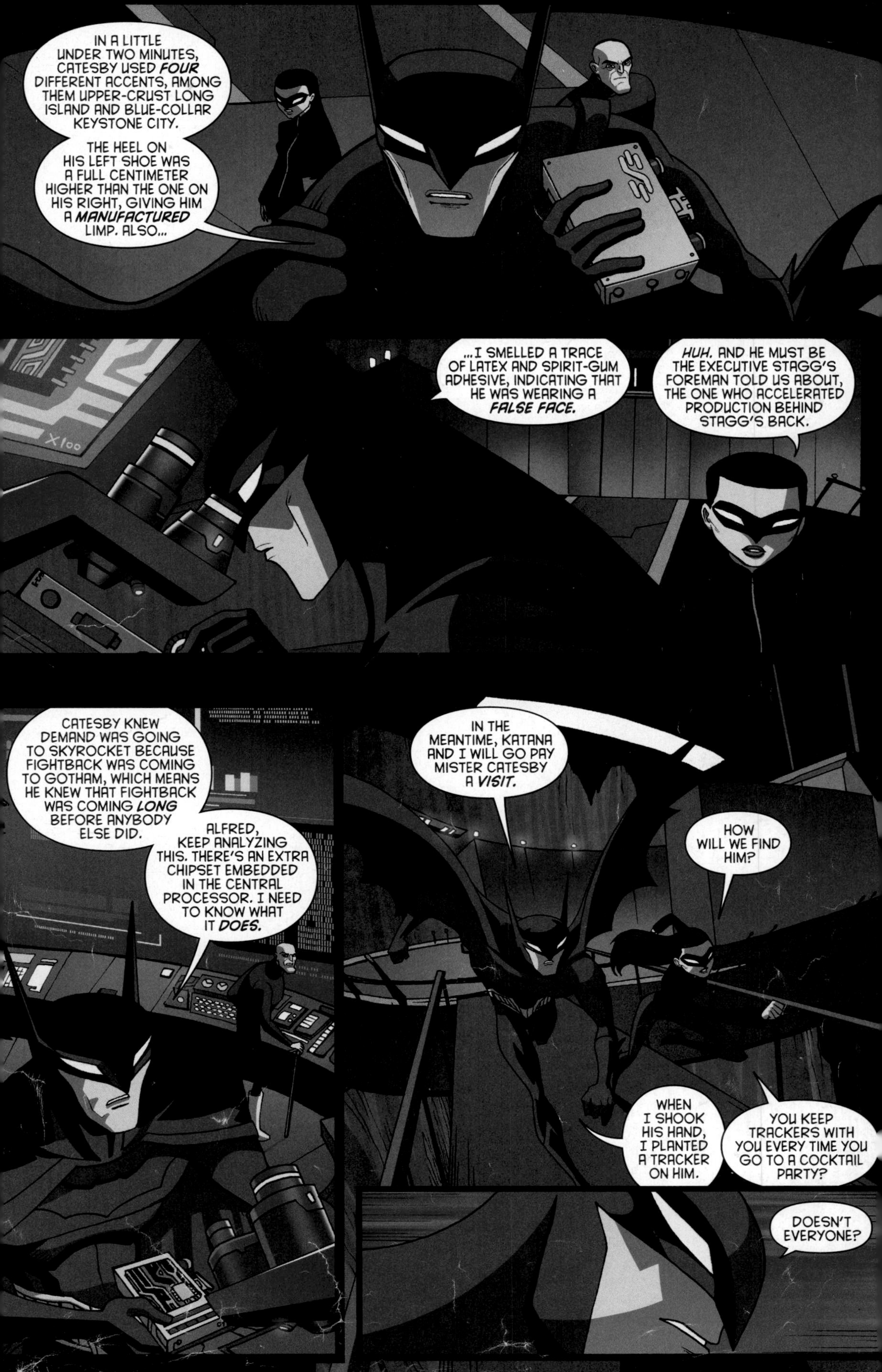
IN A LITTLE UNDER TWO MINUTES, CATESBY USED FOUR DIFFERENT ACCENTS, AMONG THEM UPPER-CRUST LONG ISLAND AND BLUE-COLLAR KEYSTONE CITY.
THE HEEL ON HIS LEFT SHOE WAS A FULL CENTIMETER HIGHER THAN THE ONE ON HIS RIGHT, GIVING HIM A MANUFACTURED LIMP. ALSO...
...I SMELLED A TRACE OF LATEX AND SPIRIT-GUM ADHESIVE, INDICATING THAT HE WAS WEARING A FALSE FACE.
HUH. AND HE MUST BE THE EXECUTIVE STAGG'S FOREMAN TOLD US ABOUT, THE ONE WHO ACCELERATED PRODUCTION BEHIND STAGG'S BACK.
X100
CATESBY KNEW DEMAND WAS GOING TO SKYROCKET BECAUSE FIGHTBACK WAS COMING TO GOTHAM, WHICH MEANS HE KNEW THAT FIGHTBACK WAS COMING LONG BEFORE ANYBODY ELSE DID.
ALFRED, KEEP ANALYZING THIS. THERE'S AN EXTRA CHIPSET EMBEDDED IN THE CENTRAL PROCESSOR. I NEED TO KNOW WHAT IT DOES.
IN THE MEANTIME, KATANA AND I WILL GO PAY MISTER CATESBY A VISIT.
HOW WILL WE FIND HIM?
WHEN I SHOOK HIS HAND, I PLANTED A TRACKER ON HIM.
YOU KEEP TRACKERS WITH YOU EVERY TIME YOU GO TO A COCKTAIL PARTY?
DOESN'T EVERYONE?

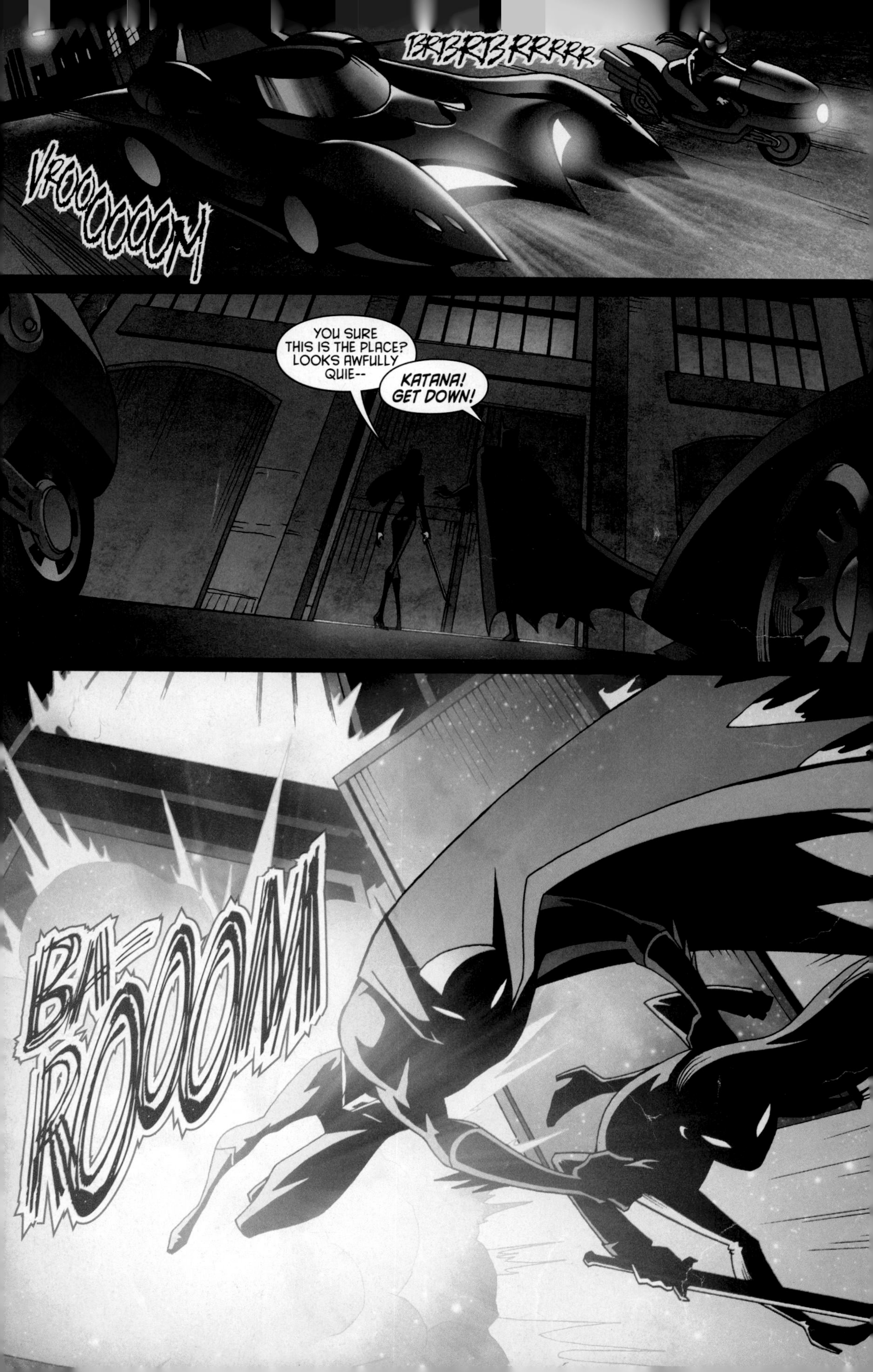
BRBRBRRRRRR
VROOOOOOOM
YOU SURE THIS IS THE PLACE? LOOKS AWFULLY QUIE--
KATANA! GET DOWN!
BA-ROOOOM

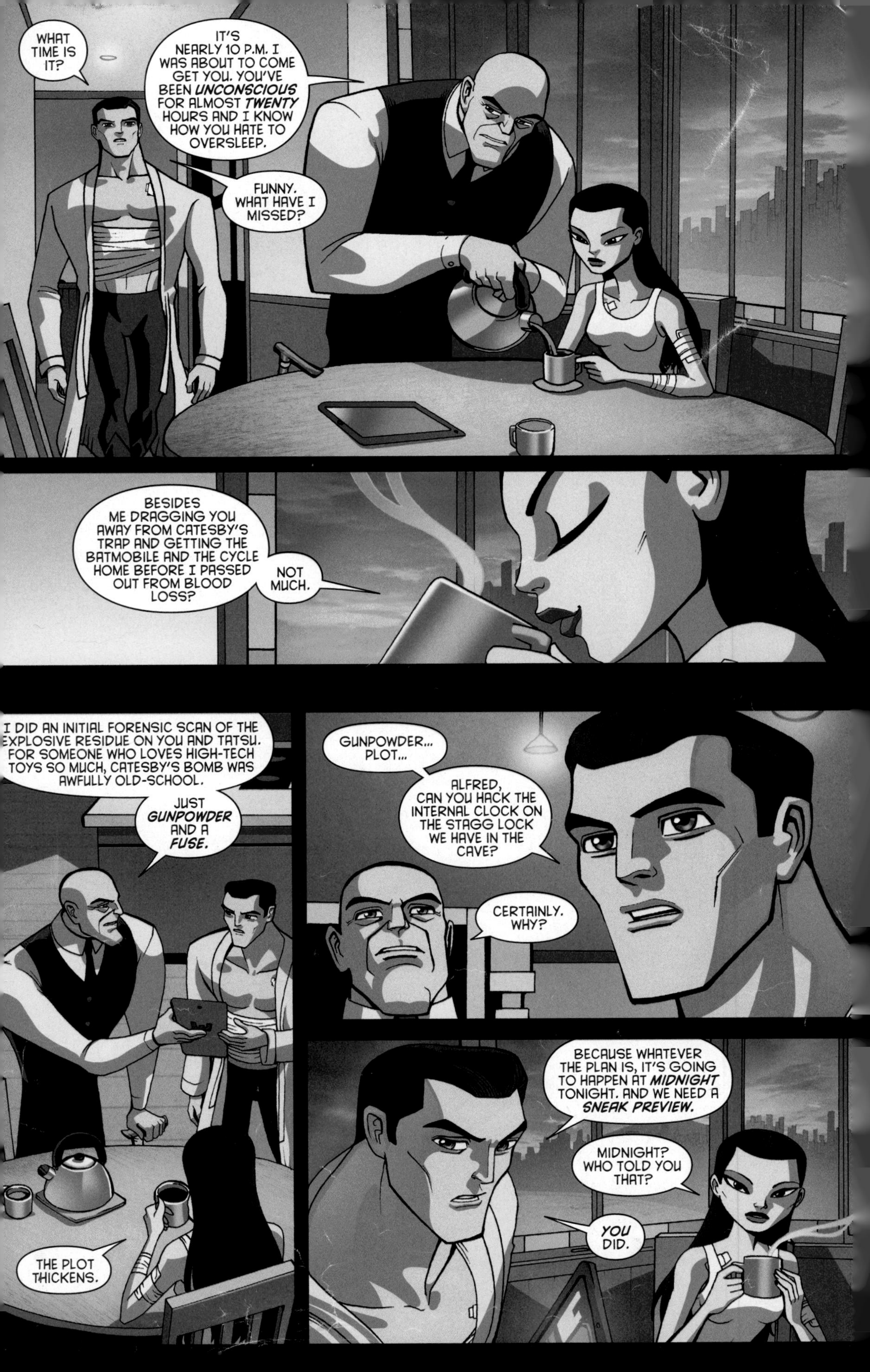
WHAT TIME IS IT?
IT'S NEARLY 10 P.M. I WAS ABOUT TO COME GET YOU. YOU'VE BEEN UNCONSCIOUS FOR ALMOST TWENTY HOURS AND I KNOW HOW YOU HATE TO OVERSLEEP.
FUNNY. WHAT HAVE I MISSED?
BESIDES ME DRAGGING YOU AWAY FROM CATESBY'S TRAP AND GETTING THE BATMOBILE AND THE CYCLE HOME BEFORE I PASSED OUT FROM BLOOD LOSS?
NOT MUCH.
I DID AN INITIAL FORENSIC SCAN OF THE EXPLOSIVE RESIDUE ON YOU AND TATSU. FOR SOMEONE WHO LOVES HIGH-TECH TOYS SO MUCH, CATESBY'S BOMB WAS AWFULLY OLD-SCHOOL.
JUST GUNPOWDER AND A FUSE.
THE PLOT THICKENS.
GUNPOWDER... PLOT...
ALFRED, CAN YOU HACK THE INTERNAL CLOCK ON THE STAGG LOCK WE HAVE IN THE CAVE?
CERTAINLY. WHY?
BECAUSE WHATEVER THE PLAN IS, IT'S GOING TO HAPPEN AT MIDNIGHT TONIGHT. AND WE NEED A SNEAK PREVIEW.
MIDNIGHT? WHO TOLD YOU THAT?
YOU DID.

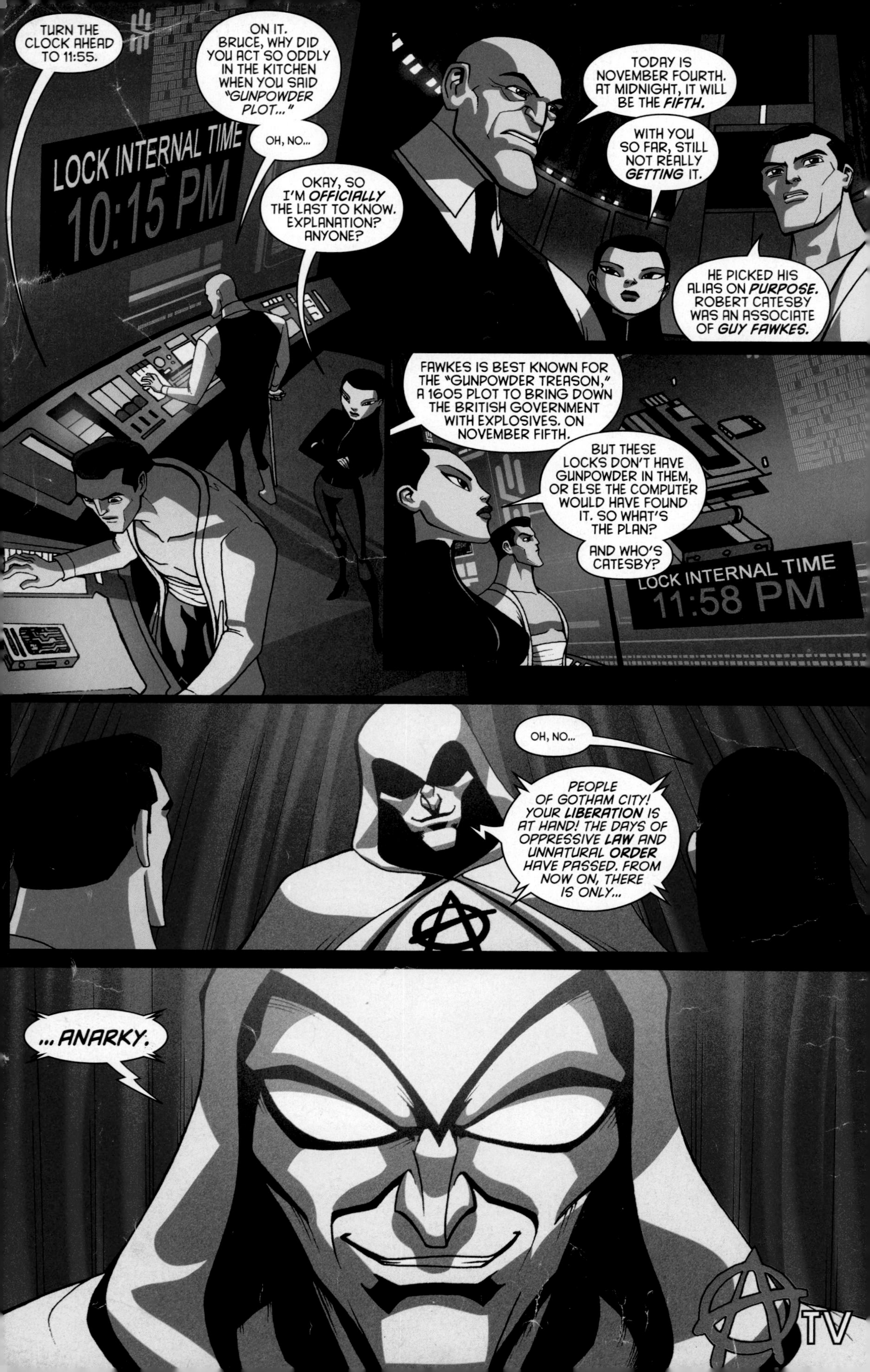
TURN THE CLOCK AHEAD TO 11:55.
ON IT. BRUCE, WHY DID YOU ACT SO ODDLY IN THE KITCHEN WHEN YOU SAID "GUNPOWDER PLOT..."
LOCK INTERNAL TIME
10:15 PM
OH, NO...
OKAY, SO I'M OFFICIALLY THE LAST TO KNOW. EXPLANATION? ANYONE?
TODAY IS NOVEMBER FOURTH. AT MIDNIGHT, IT WILL BE THE FIFTH.
WITH YOU SO FAR, STILL NOT REALLY GETTING IT.
HE PICKED HIS ALIAS ON PURPOSE. ROBERT CATESBY WAS AN ASSOCIATE OF GUY FAWKES.
FAWKES IS BEST KNOWN FOR THE "GUNPOWDER TREASON," A 1605 PLOT TO BRING DOWN THE BRITISH GOVERNMENT WITH EXPLOSIVES. ON NOVEMBER FIFTH.
BUT THESE LOCKS DON'T HAVE GUNPOWDER IN THEM, OR ELSE THE COMPUTER WOULD HAVE FOUND IT. SO WHAT'S THE PLAN?
AND WHO'S CATESBY?
LOCK INTERNAL TIME
11:58 PM
OH, NO...
PEOPLE OF GOTHAM CITY! YOUR LIBERATION IS AT HAND! THE DAYS OF OPPRESSIVE LAW AND UNNATURAL ORDER HAVE PASSED. FROM NOW ON, THERE IS ONLY...
...ANARKY.
TV

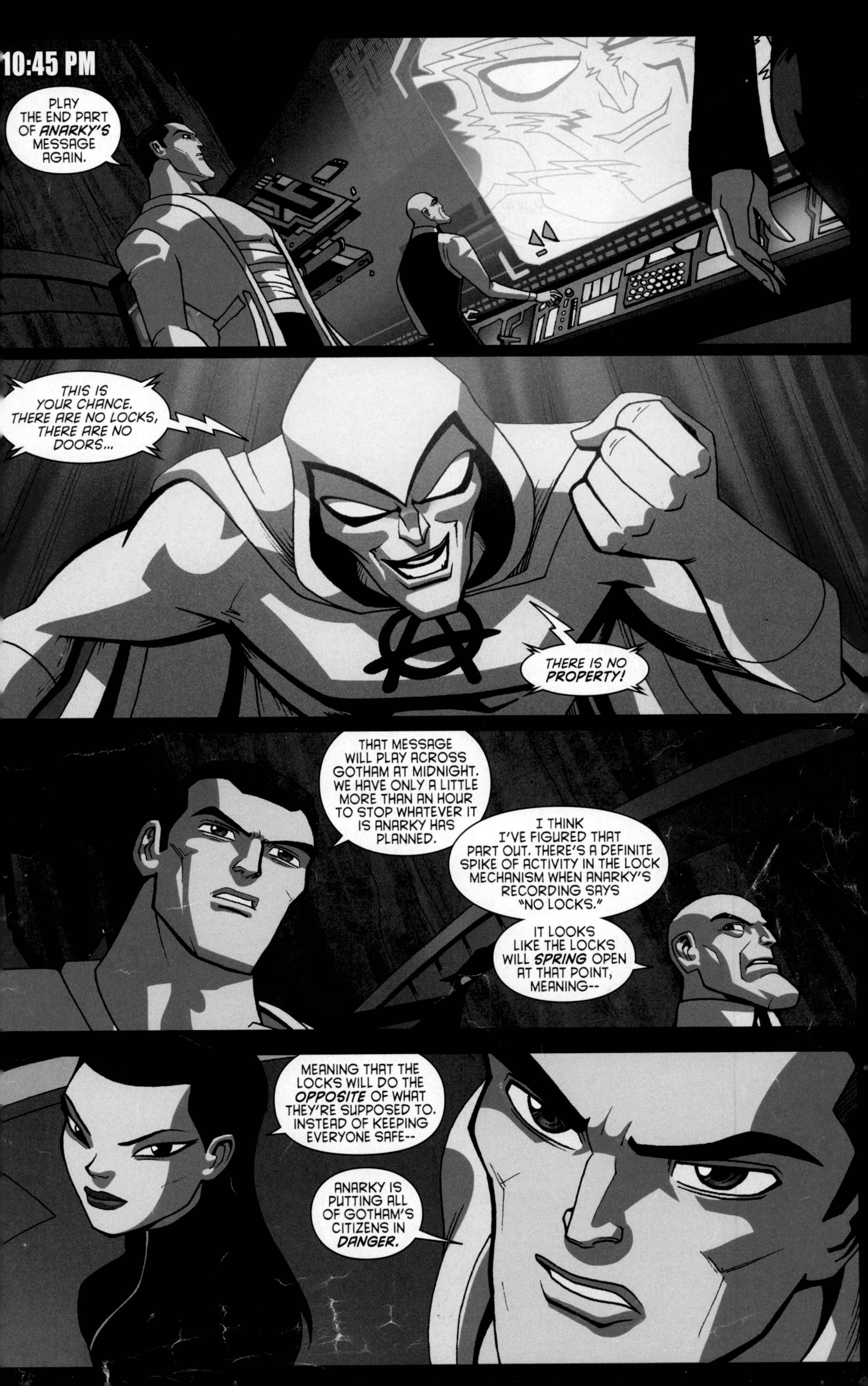
10:45 PM
PLAY THE END PART OF ANARKY'S MESSAGE AGAIN.
THIS IS YOUR CHANCE. THERE ARE NO LOCKS, THERE ARE NO DOORS...
THERE IS NO PROPERTY!
THAT MESSAGE WILL PLAY ACROSS GOTHAM AT MIDNIGHT. WE HAVE ONLY A LITTLE MORE THAN AN HOUR TO STOP WHATEVER IT IS ANARKY HAS PLANNED.
I THINK I'VE FIGURED THAT PART OUT. THERE'S A DEFINITE SPIKE OF ACTIVITY IN THE LOCK MECHANISM WHEN ANARKY'S RECORDING SAYS "NO LOCKS."
IT LOOKS LIKE THE LOCKS WILL SPRING OPEN AT THAT POINT, MEANING--
MEANING THAT THE LOCKS WILL DO THE OPPOSITE OF WHAT THEY'RE SUPPOSED TO. INSTEAD OF KEEPING EVERYONE SAFE--
ANARKY IS PUTTING ALL OF GOTHAM'S CITIZENS IN DANGER.

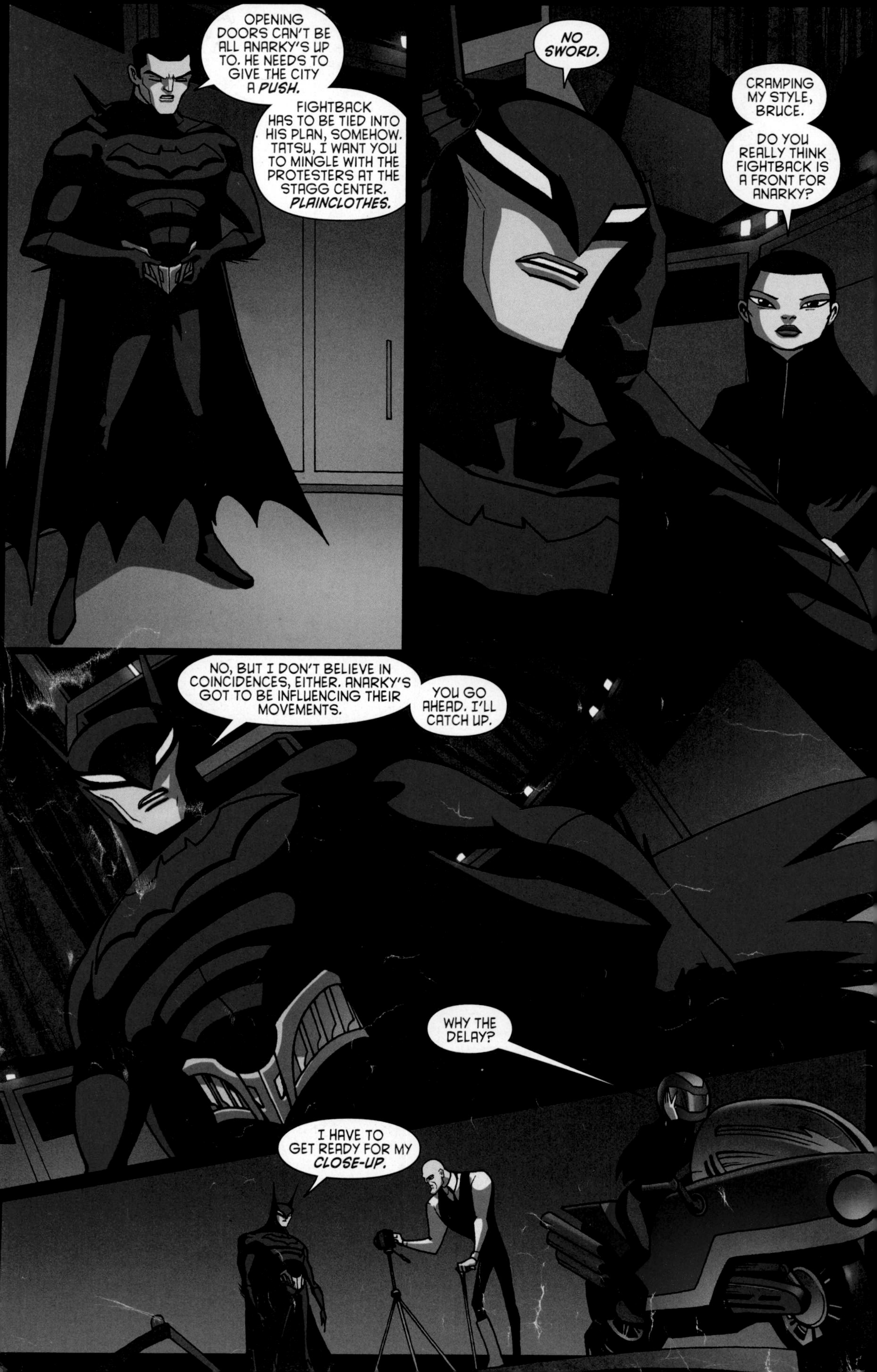
OPENING DOORS CAN'T BE ALL ANARKY'S UP TO. HE NEEDS TO GIVE THE CITY A *PUSH.*
FIGHTBACK HAS TO BE TIED INTO HIS PLAN, SOMEHOW. TATSU, I WANT YOU TO MINGLE WITH THE PROTESTERS AT THE STAGG CENTER. *PLAINCLOTHES.*
NO SWORD.
CRAMPING MY STYLE, BRUCE.
DO YOU REALLY THINK FIGHTBACK IS A FRONT FOR ANARKY?
NO, BUT I DON'T BELIEVE IN COINCIDENCES, EITHER. ANARKY'S GOT TO BE INFLUENCING THEIR MOVEMENTS.
YOU GO AHEAD. I'LL CATCH UP.
WHY THE DELAY?
I HAVE TO GET READY FOR MY *CLOSE-UP.*

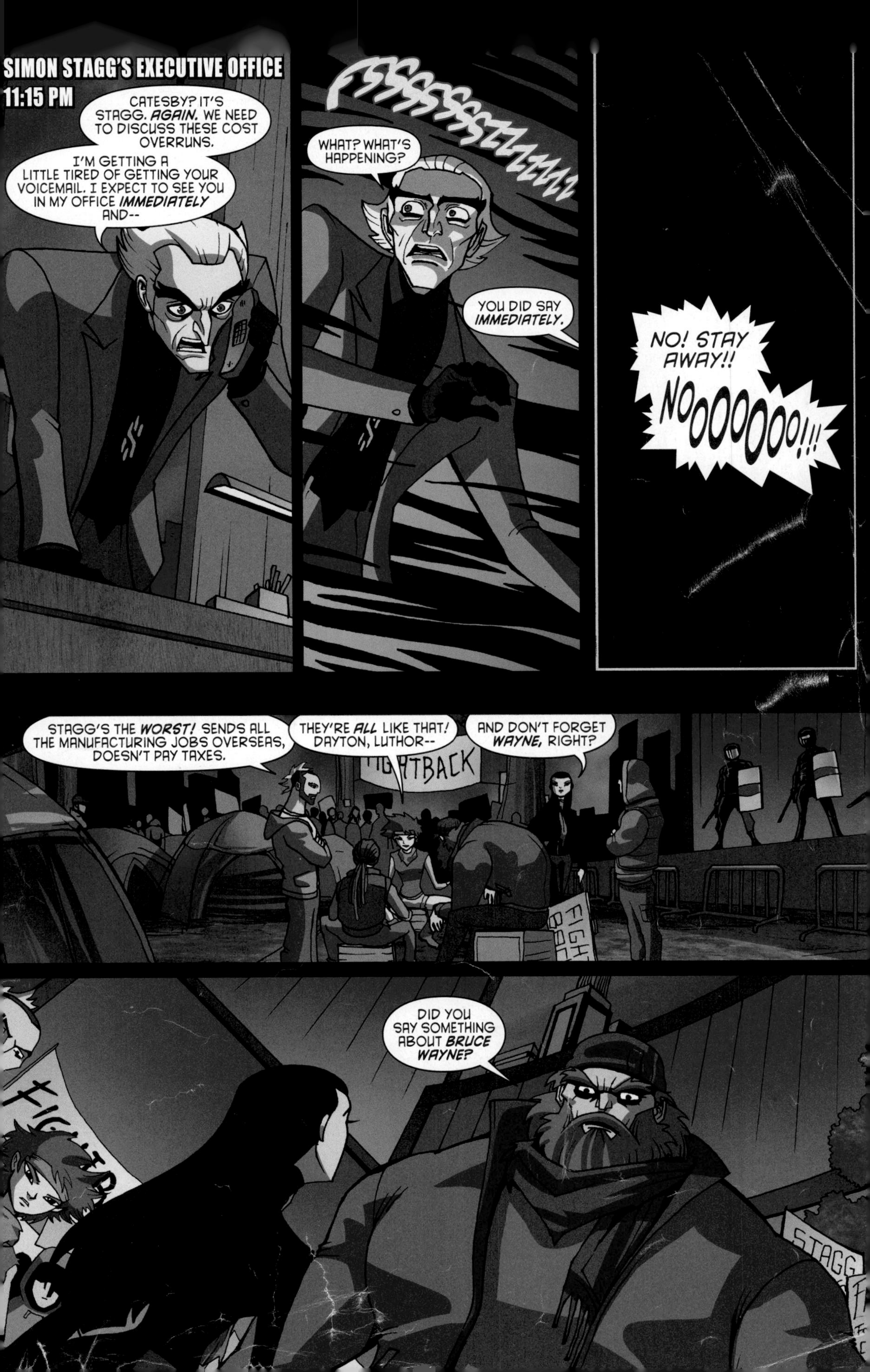
SIMON STAGG'S EXECUTIVE OFFICE
11:15 PM
CATESBY? IT'S STAGG. AGAIN. WE NEED TO DISCUSS THESE COST OVERRUNS.
I'M GETTING A LITTLE TIRED OF GETTING YOUR VOICEMAIL. I EXPECT TO SEE YOU IN MY OFFICE IMMEDIATELY AND--
FSSSSSSZZZZZZZZ
WHAT? WHAT'S HAPPENING?
YOU DID SAY IMMEDIATELY.
NO! STAY AWAY!!
NOOOOOOO!!!
STAGG'S THE WORST! SENDS ALL THE MANUFACTURING JOBS OVERSEAS, DOESN'T PAY TAXES.
THEY'RE ALL LIKE THAT! DAYTON, LUTHOR--
AND DON'T FORGET WAYNE, RIGHT?
FIGHTBACK
DID YOU SAY SOMETHING ABOUT BRUCE WAYNE?
STAGG

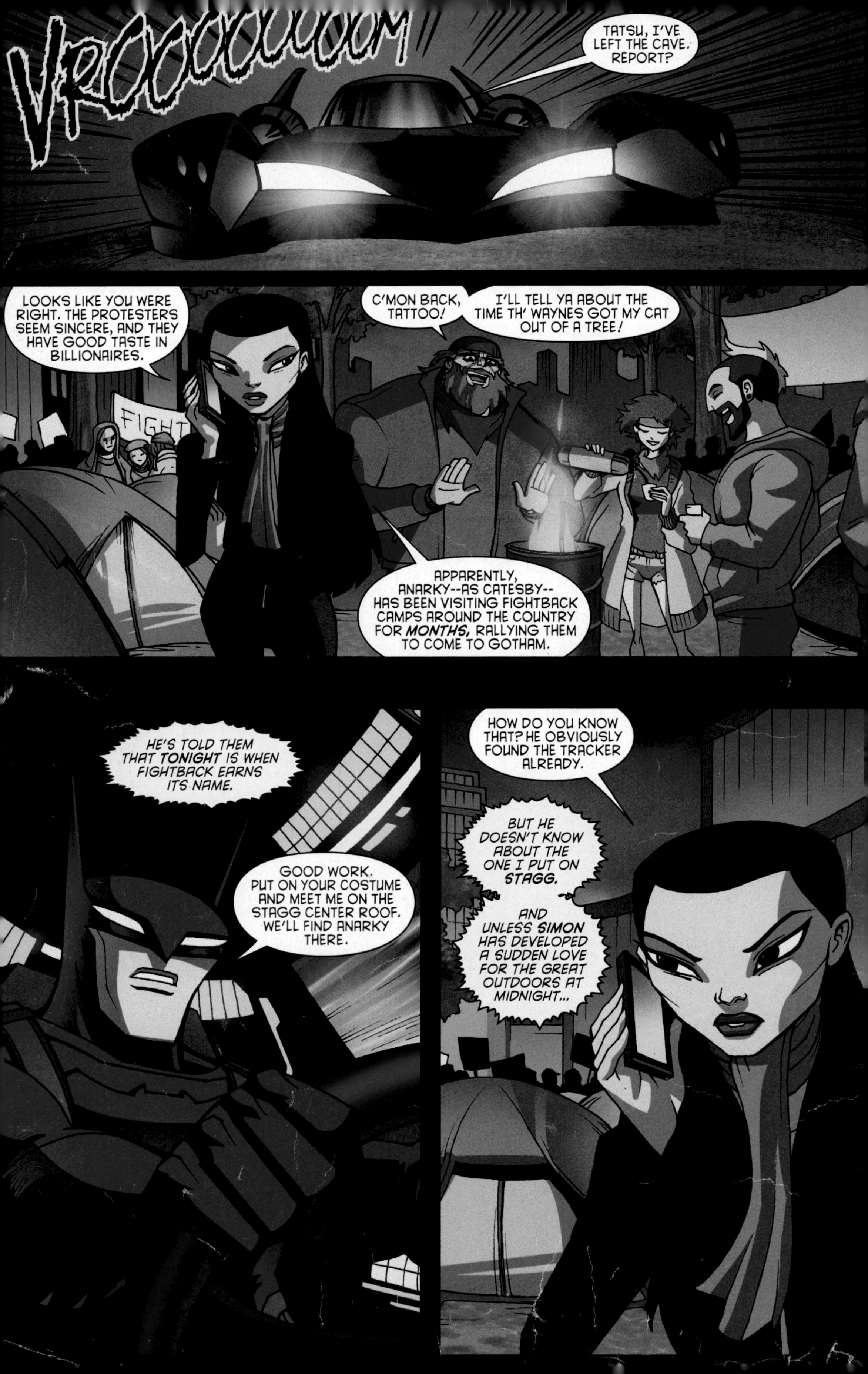
VROOOOOOOOM
TATSU, I'VE LEFT THE CAVE. REPORT?
LOOKS LIKE YOU WERE RIGHT. THE PROTESTERS SEEM SINCERE, AND THEY HAVE GOOD TASTE IN BILLIONAIRES.
FIGHT
C'MON BACK, TATTOO!
I'LL TELL YA ABOUT THE TIME TH' WAYNES GOT MY CAT OUT OF A TREE!
APPARENTLY, ANARKY--AS CATESBY--HAS BEEN VISITING FIGHTBACK CAMPS AROUND THE COUNTRY FOR **MONTHS,** RALLYING THEM TO COME TO GOTHAM.
HE'S TOLD THEM THAT **TONIGHT** IS WHEN FIGHTBACK EARNS ITS NAME.
GOOD WORK. PUT ON YOUR COSTUME AND MEET ME ON THE STAGG CENTER ROOF. WE'LL FIND ANARKY THERE.
HOW DO YOU KNOW THAT? HE OBVIOUSLY FOUND THE TRACKER ALREADY.
BUT HE DOESN'T KNOW ABOUT THE ONE I PUT ON **STAGG.**
AND UNLESS **SIMON** HAS DEVELOPED A SUDDEN LOVE FOR THE GREAT OUTDOORS AT MIDNIGHT...

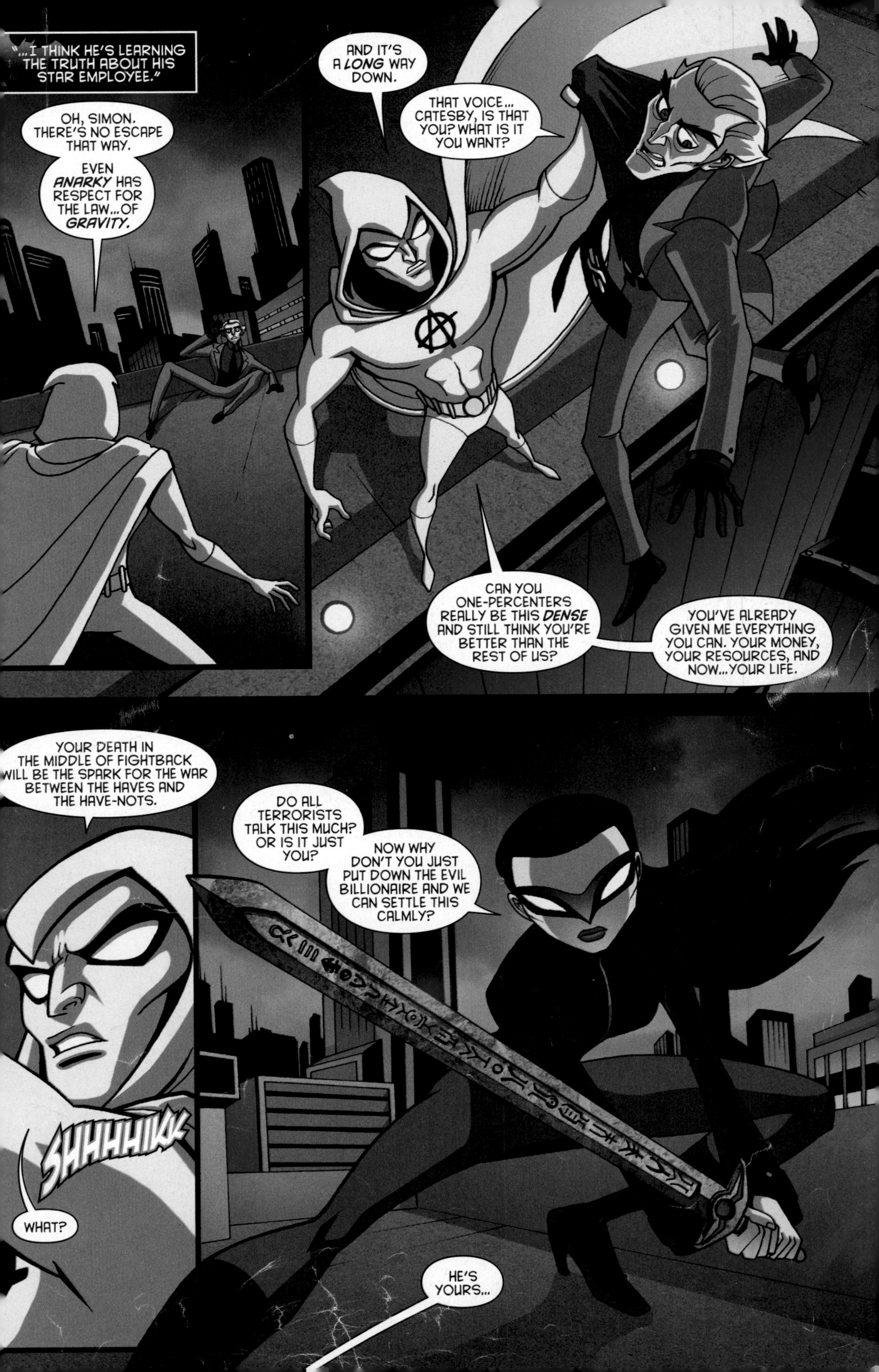
"...I THINK HE'S LEARNING THE TRUTH ABOUT HIS STAR EMPLOYEE."
OH, SIMON. THERE'S NO ESCAPE THAT WAY.
EVEN ANARKY HAS RESPECT FOR THE LAW...OF GRAVITY.
AND IT'S A LONG WAY DOWN.
THAT VOICE... CATESBY, IS THAT YOU? WHAT IS IT YOU WANT?
CAN YOU ONE-PERCENTERS REALLY BE THIS DENSE AND STILL THINK YOU'RE BETTER THAN THE REST OF US?
YOU'VE ALREADY GIVEN ME EVERYTHING YOU CAN. YOUR MONEY, YOUR RESOURCES, AND NOW...YOUR LIFE.
YOUR DEATH IN THE MIDDLE OF FIGHTBACK WILL BE THE SPARK FOR THE WAR BETWEEN THE HAVES AND THE HAVE-NOTS.
DO ALL TERRORISTS TALK THIS MUCH? OR IS IT JUST YOU?
NOW WHY DON'T YOU JUST PUT DOWN THE EVIL BILLIONAIRE AND WE CAN SETTLE THIS CALMLY?
SHHHHIKK
WHAT?
HE'S YOURS...

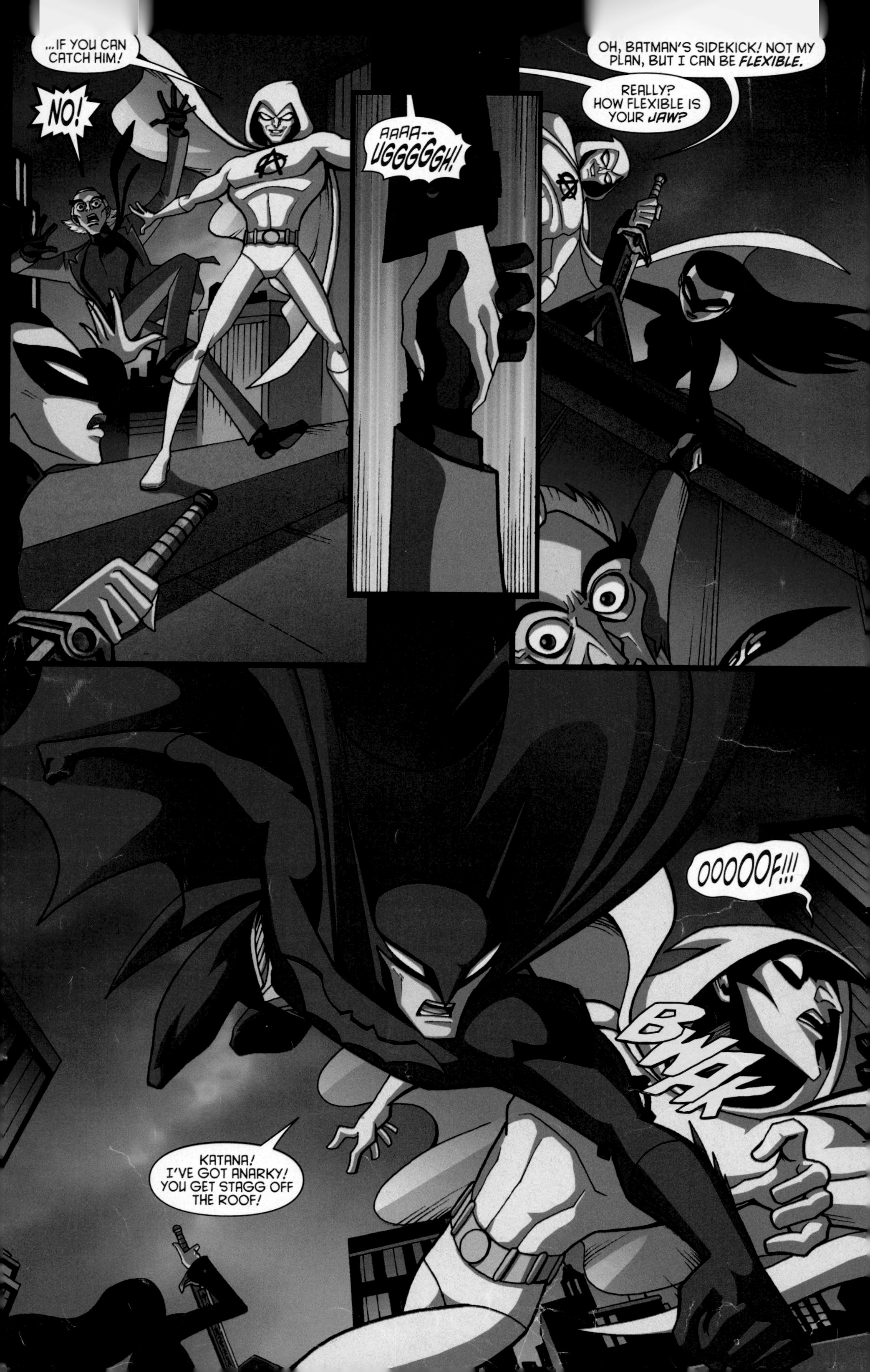
...IF YOU CAN CATCH HIM!
NO!
AAAA-- UGGGGGH!
OH, BATMAN'S SIDEKICK! NOT MY PLAN, BUT I CAN BE *FLEXIBLE.*
REALLY? HOW FLEXIBLE IS YOUR *JAW?*
OOOOOF!!!
BWAK
KATANA! I'VE GOT ANARKY! YOU GET STAGG OFF THE ROOF!

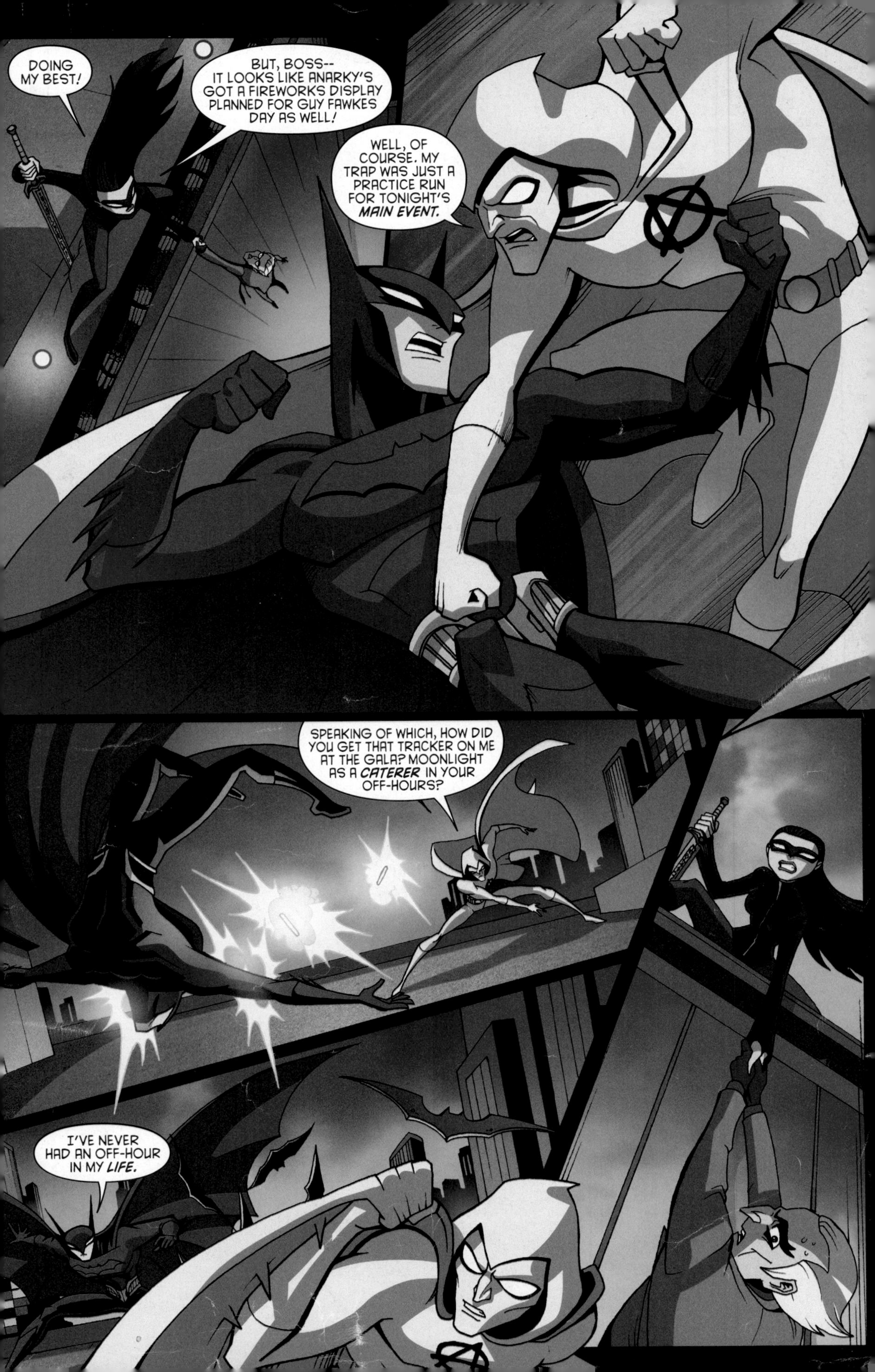
DOING MY BEST!
BUT, BOSS-- IT LOOKS LIKE ANARKY'S GOT A FIREWORKS DISPLAY PLANNED FOR GUY FAWKES DAY AS WELL!
WELL, OF COURSE. MY TRAP WAS JUST A PRACTICE RUN FOR TONIGHT'S MAIN EVENT.
SPEAKING OF WHICH, HOW DID YOU GET THAT TRACKER ON ME AT THE GALA? MOONLIGHT AS A CATERER IN YOUR OFF-HOURS?
I'VE NEVER HAD AN OFF-HOUR IN MY LIFE.

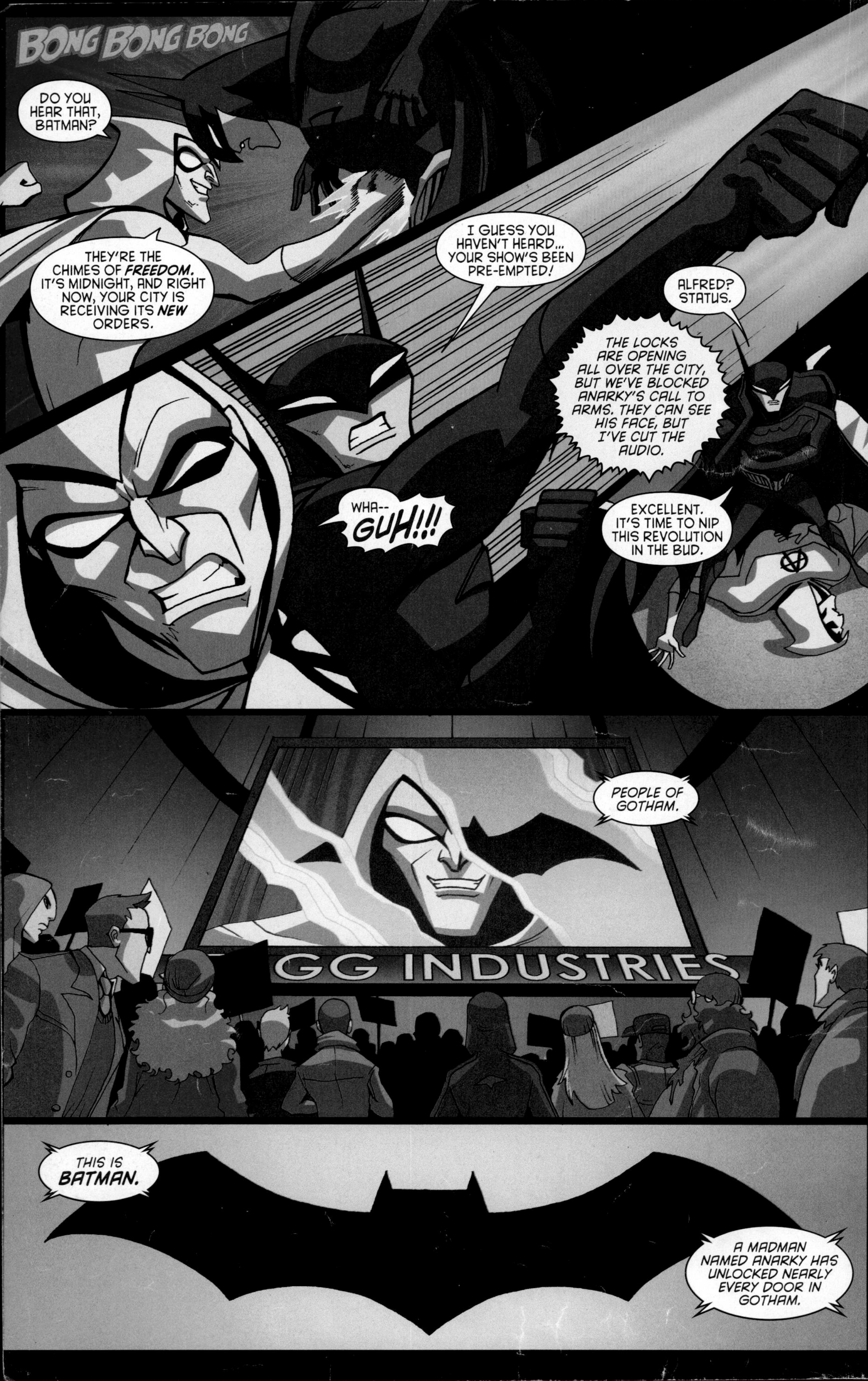
BONG BONG BONG
DO YOU HEAR THAT, BATMAN?
THEY'RE THE CHIMES OF FREEDOM. IT'S MIDNIGHT, AND RIGHT NOW, YOUR CITY IS RECEIVING ITS NEW ORDERS.
I GUESS YOU HAVEN'T HEARD... YOUR SHOW'S BEEN PRE-EMPTED!
WHA-- GUH!!!
ALFRED? STATUS.
THE LOCKS ARE OPENING ALL OVER THE CITY, BUT WE'VE BLOCKED ANARKY'S CALL TO ARMS. THEY CAN SEE HIS FACE, BUT I'VE CUT THE AUDIO.
EXCELLENT. IT'S TIME TO NIP THIS REVOLUTION IN THE BUD.
PEOPLE OF GOTHAM.
GG INDUSTRIES
THIS IS BATMAN.
A MADMAN NAMED ANARKY HAS UNLOCKED NEARLY EVERY DOOR IN GOTHAM.

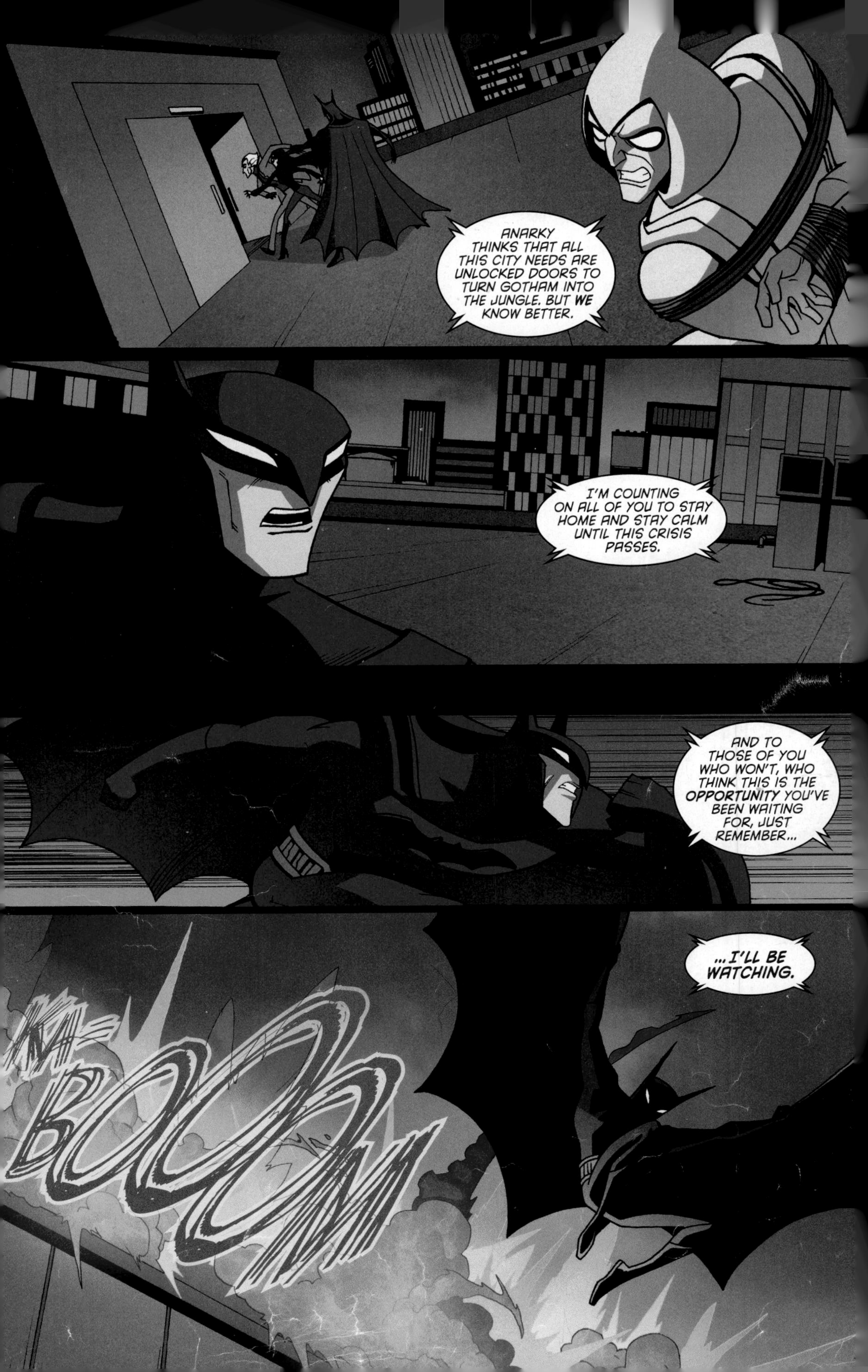
ANARKY THINKS THAT ALL THIS CITY NEEDS ARE UNLOCKED DOORS TO TURN GOTHAM INTO THE JUNGLE. BUT WE KNOW BETTER.
I'M COUNTING ON ALL OF YOU TO STAY HOME AND STAY CALM UNTIL THIS CRISIS PASSES.
AND TO THOSE OF YOU WHO WON'T, WHO THINK THIS IS THE OPPORTUNITY YOU'VE BEEN WAITING FOR, JUST REMEMBER...
...I'LL BE WATCHING.
KA-BOOOM

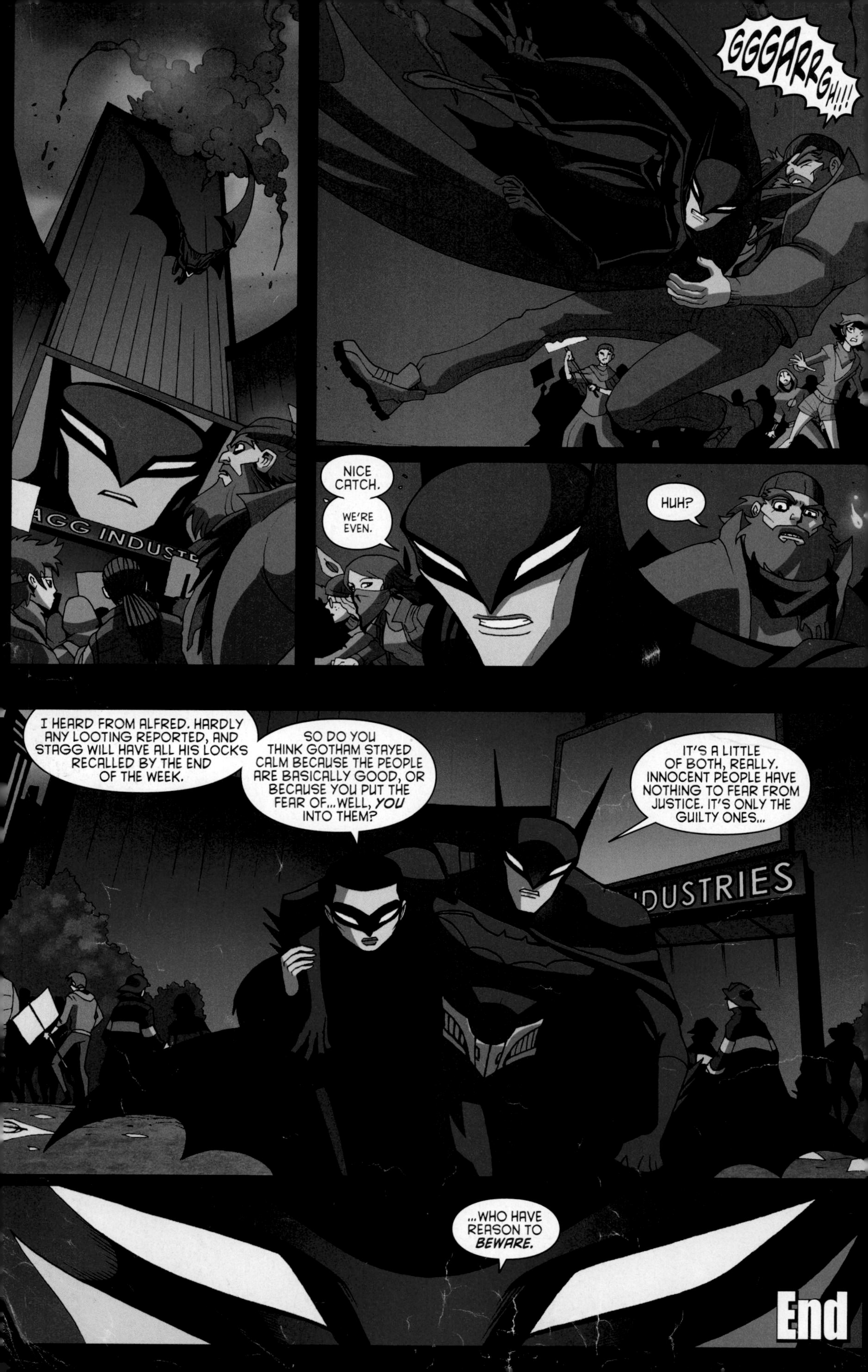

GGGARRGH!!!
AGG INDUST
NICE CATCH.
WE'RE EVEN.
HUH?
I HEARD FROM ALFRED. HARDLY ANY LOOTING REPORTED, AND STAGG WILL HAVE ALL HIS LOCKS RECALLED BY THE END OF THE WEEK.
SO DO YOU THINK GOTHAM STAYED CALM BECAUSE THE PEOPLE ARE BASICALLY GOOD, OR BECAUSE YOU PUT THE FEAR OF... WELL, *YOU* INTO THEM?
IT'S A LITTLE OF BOTH, REALLY. INNOCENT PEOPLE HAVE NOTHING TO FEAR FROM JUSTICE. IT'S ONLY THE GUILTY ONES...
NDUSTRIES
...WHO HAVE REASON TO *BEWARE.*
End

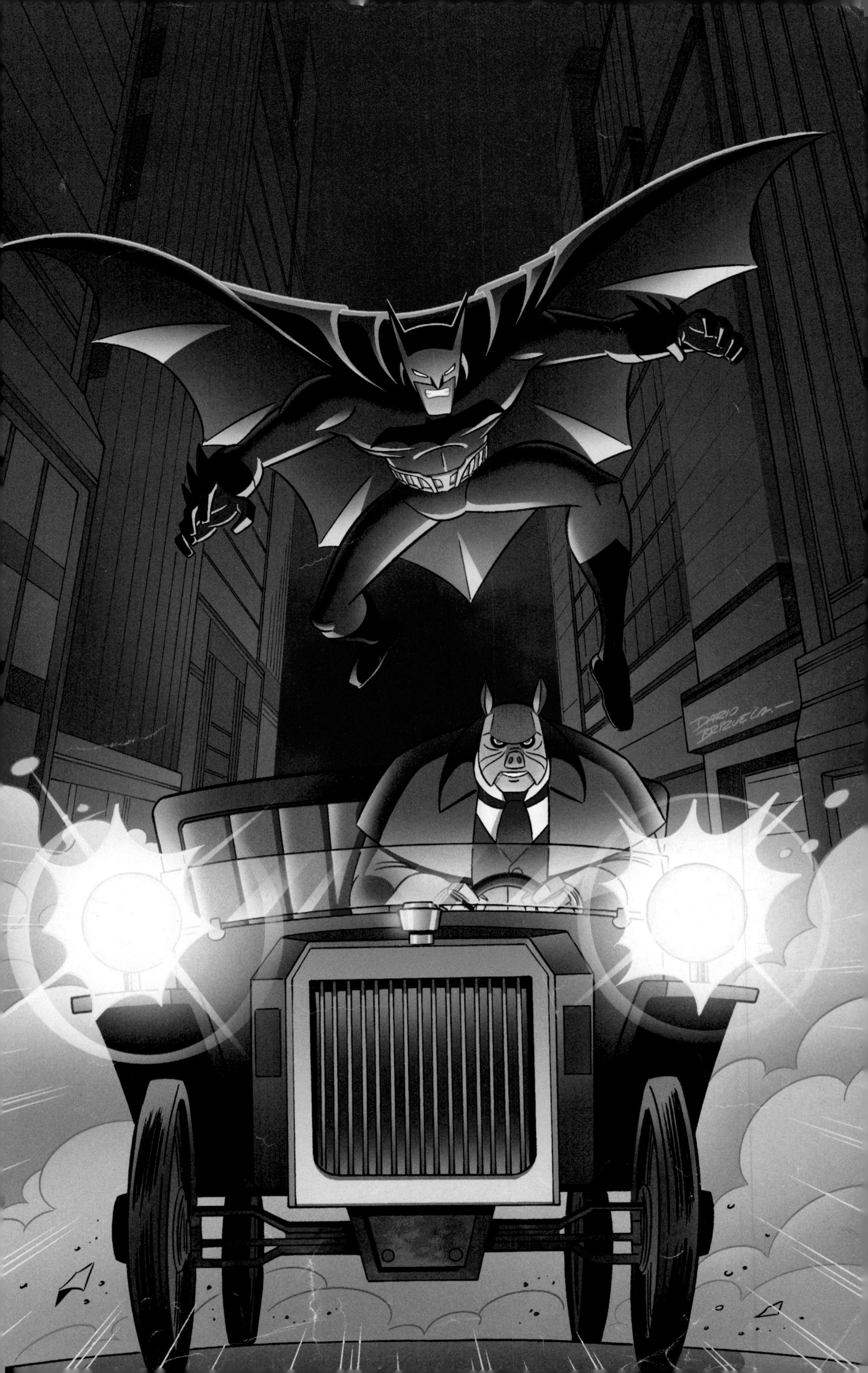
DARIO BRIZUELA

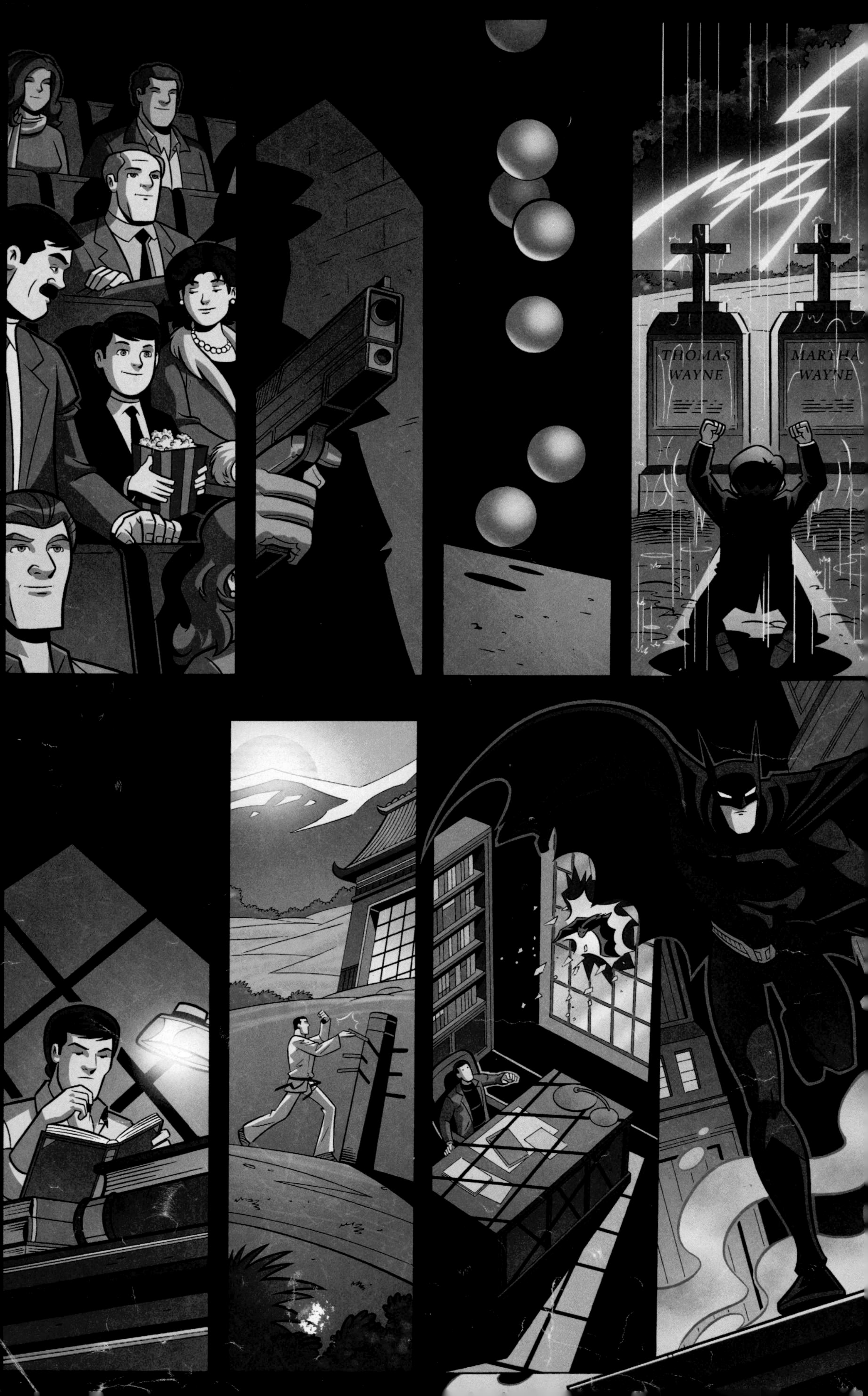
THOMAS WAYNE
MARTHA WAYNE

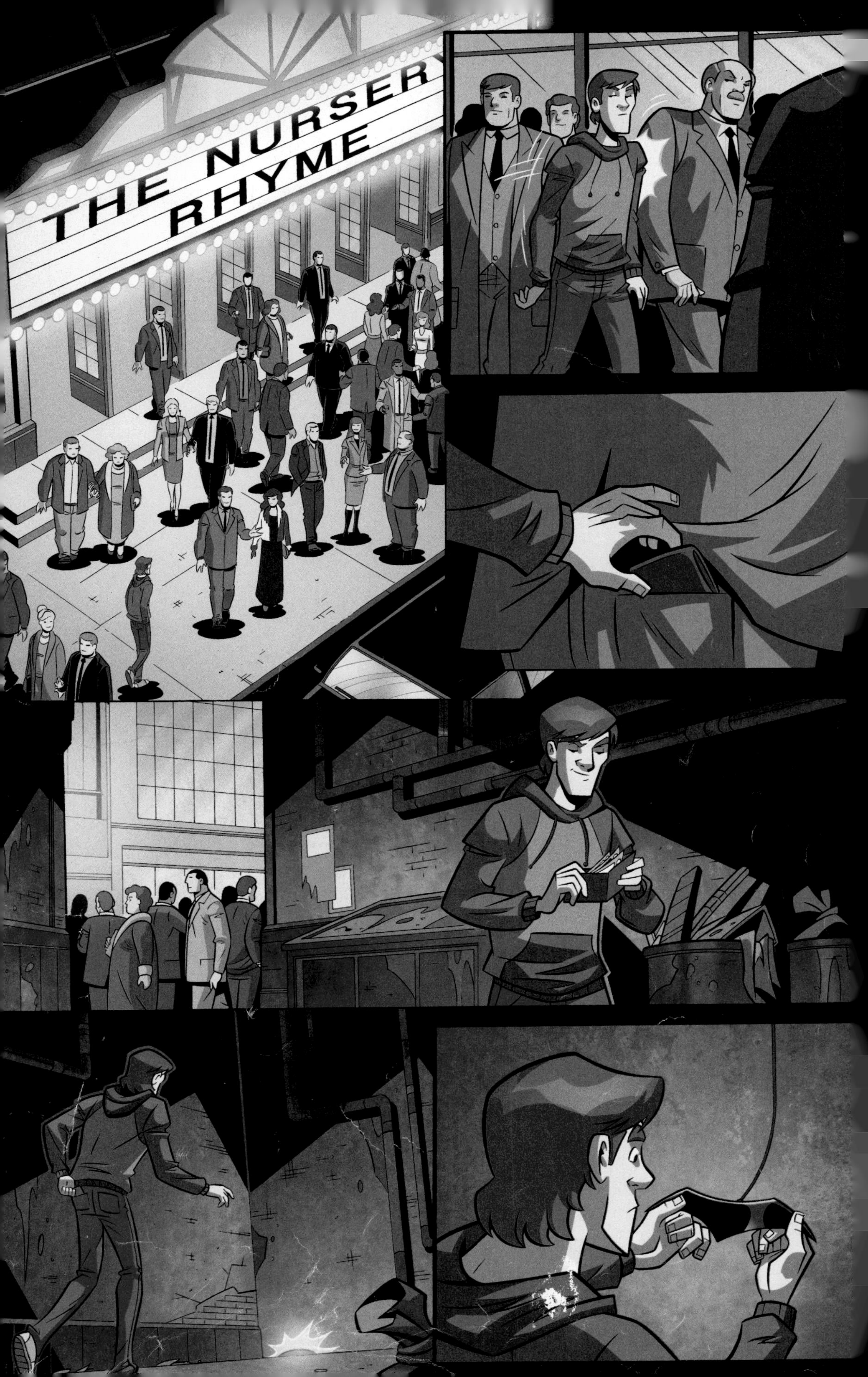

THE NURSERY
RHYME

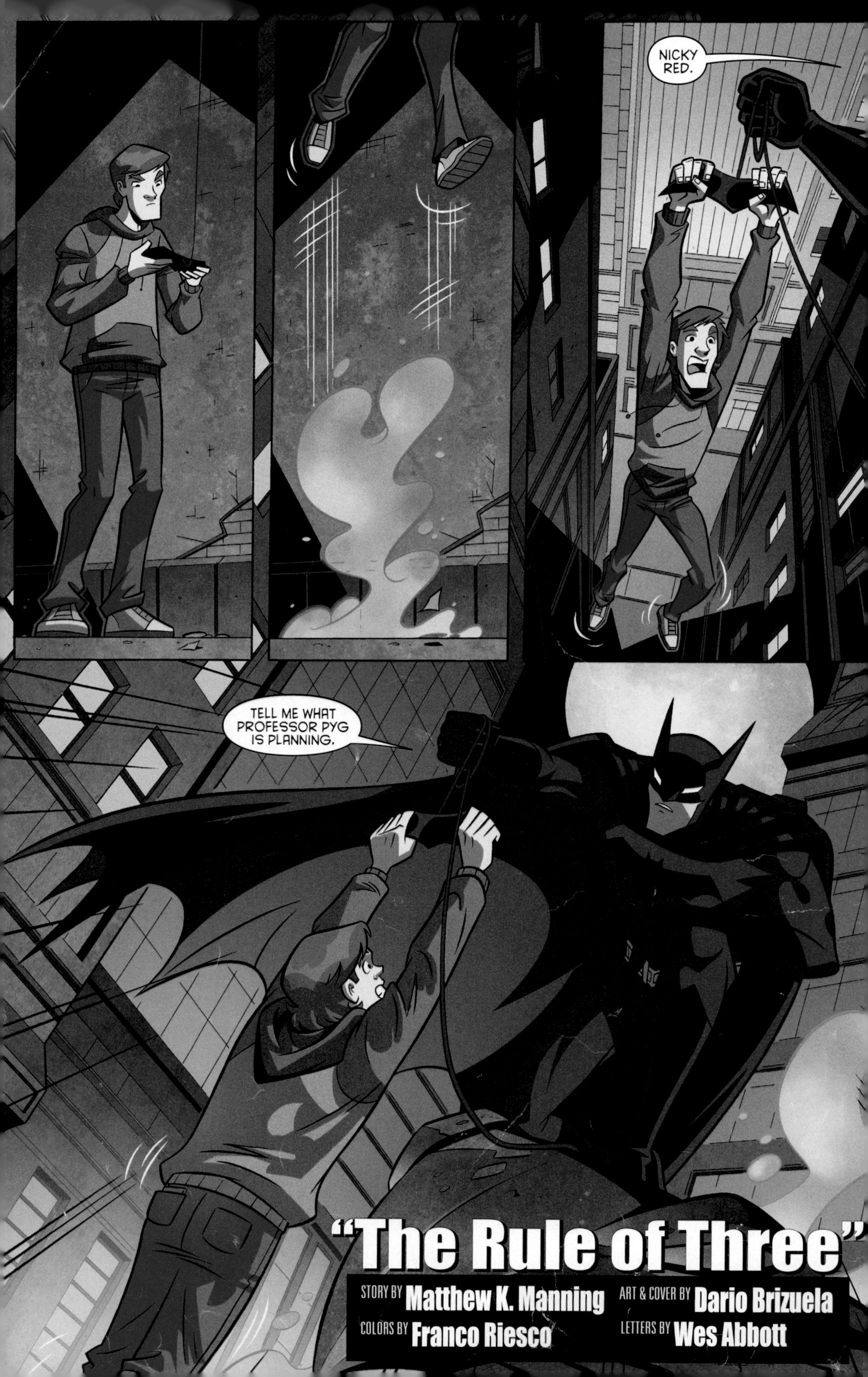
NICKY RED.
TELL ME WHAT PROFESSOR PYG IS PLANNING.
"The Rule of Three"
STORY BY Matthew K. Manning
ART & COVER BY Dario Brizuela
COLORS BY Franco Riesco
LETTERS BY Wes Abbott

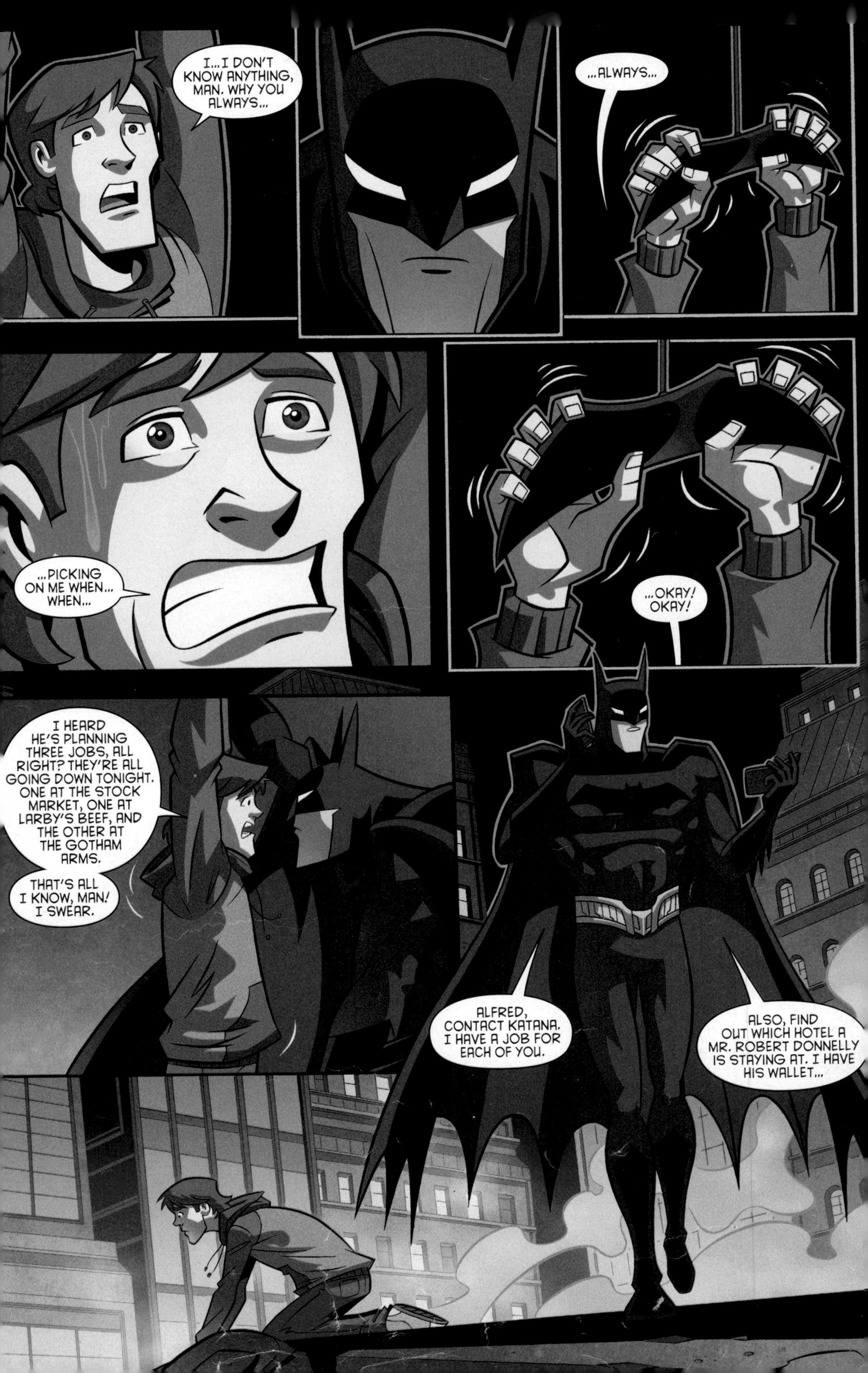
I...I DON'T KNOW ANYTHING, MAN. WHY YOU ALWAYS...
...ALWAYS...
...PICKING ON ME WHEN... WHEN...
...OKAY! OKAY!
I HEARD HE'S PLANNING THREE JOBS, ALL RIGHT? THEY'RE ALL GOING DOWN TONIGHT. ONE AT THE STOCK MARKET, ONE AT LARBY'S BEEF, AND THE OTHER AT THE GOTHAM ARMS.
THAT'S ALL I KNOW, MAN! I SWEAR.
ALFRED, CONTACT KATANA. I HAVE A JOB FOR EACH OF YOU.
ALSO, FIND OUT WHICH HOTEL A MR. ROBERT DONNELLY IS STAYING AT. I HAVE HIS WALLET...

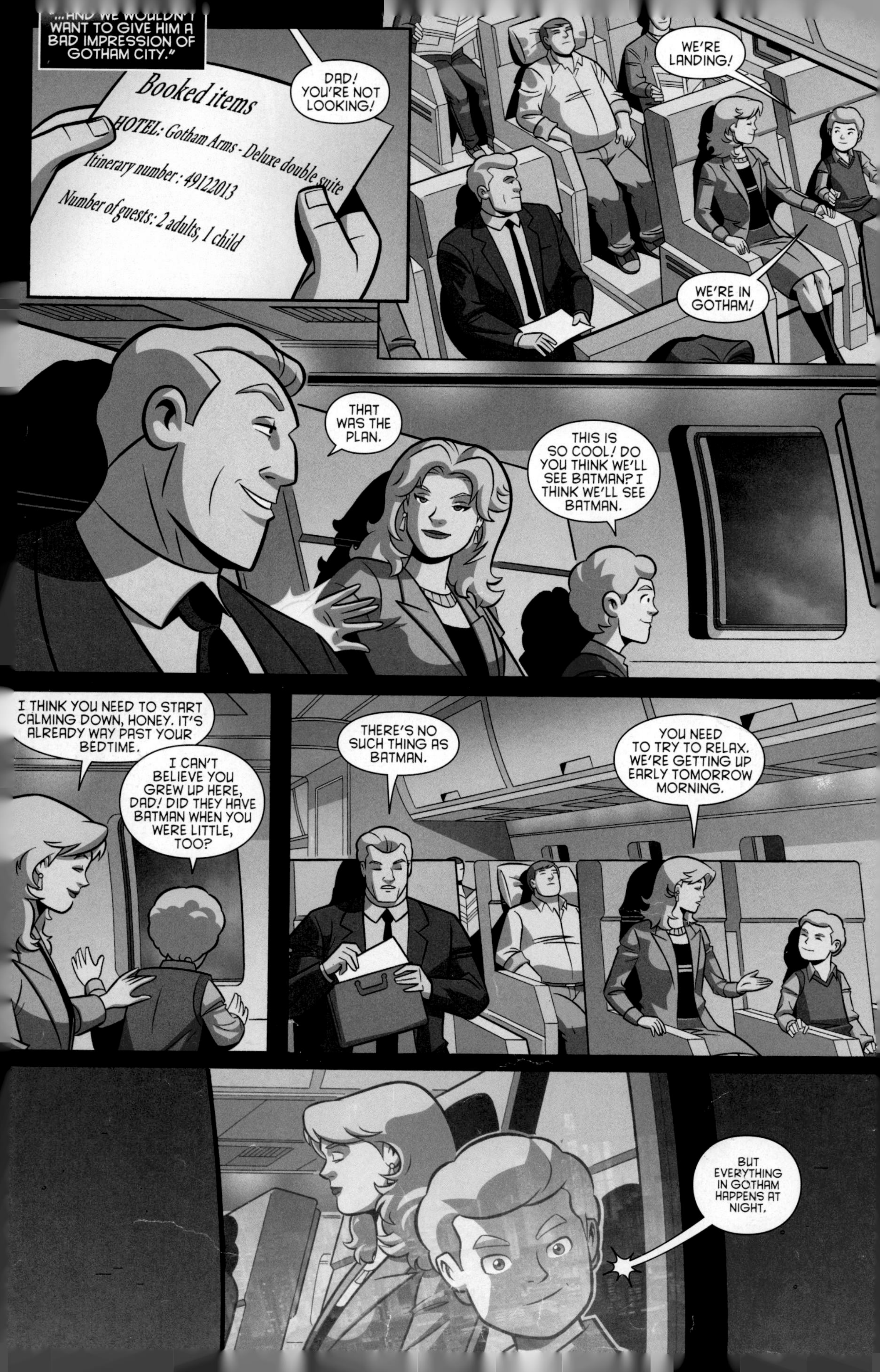
"...AND WE WOULDN'T WANT TO GIVE HIM A BAD IMPRESSION OF GOTHAM CITY."
Booked items
HOTEL: Gotham Arms - Deluxe double suite
Itinerary number: 49122013
Number of guests: 2 adults, 1 child
DAD! YOU'RE NOT LOOKING!
WE'RE LANDING!
WE'RE IN GOTHAM!
THAT WAS THE PLAN.
THIS IS SO COOL! DO YOU THINK WE'LL SEE BATMAN? I THINK WE'LL SEE BATMAN.
I THINK YOU NEED TO START CALMING DOWN, HONEY. IT'S ALREADY WAY PAST YOUR BEDTIME.
I CAN'T BELIEVE YOU GREW UP HERE, DAD! DID THEY HAVE BATMAN WHEN YOU WERE LITTLE, TOO?
THERE'S NO SUCH THING AS BATMAN.
YOU NEED TO TRY TO RELAX. WE'RE GETTING UP EARLY TOMORROW MORNING.
BUT EVERYTHING IN GOTHAM HAPPENS AT NIGHT.

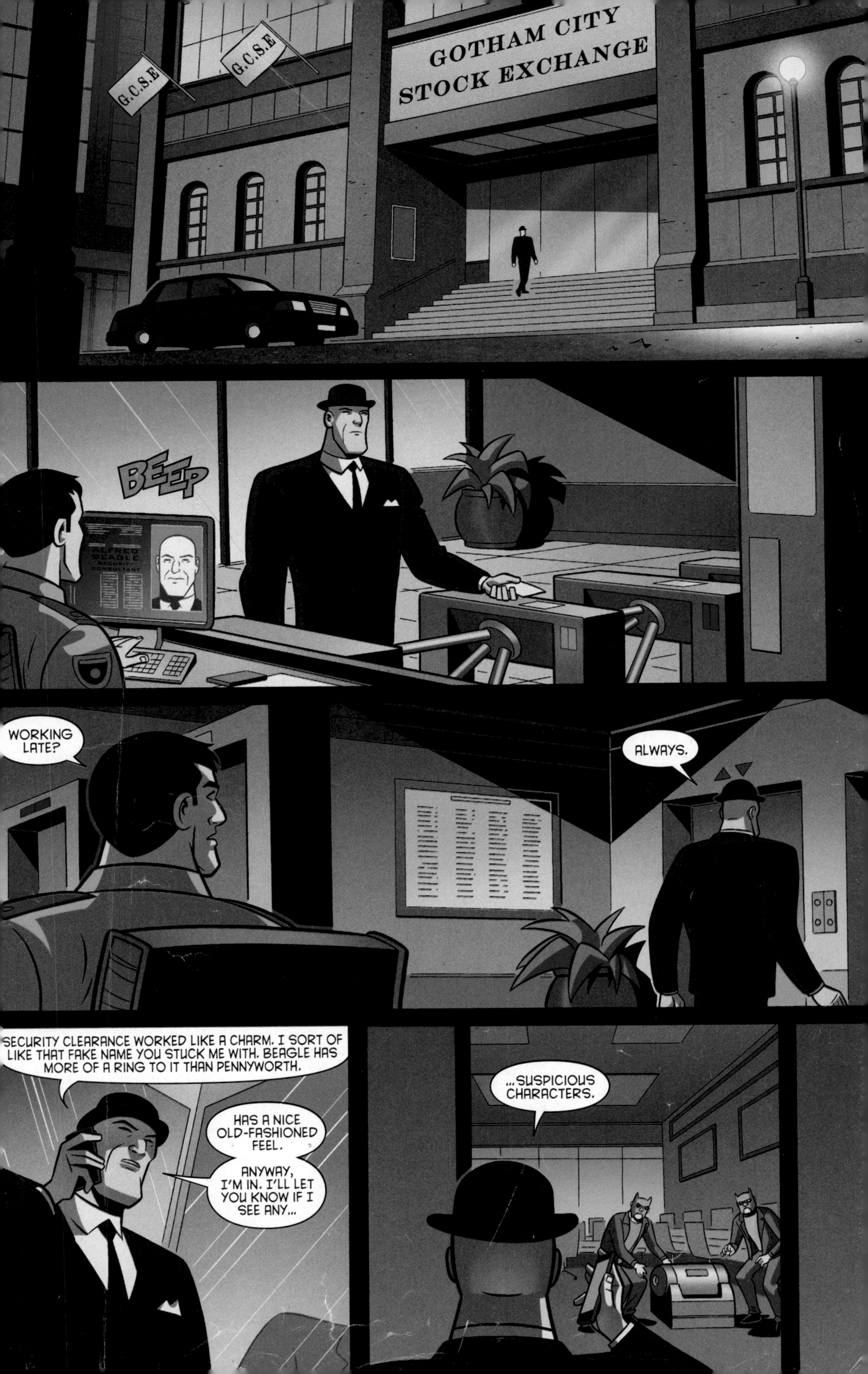
GOTHAM CITY STOCK EXCHANGE
G.C.S.E
G.C.S.E
BEEP
ALFRED BEAGLE SECURITY CONSULTANT
WORKING LATE?
ALWAYS.
SECURITY CLEARANCE WORKED LIKE A CHARM. I SORT OF LIKE THAT FAKE NAME YOU STUCK ME WITH. BEAGLE HAS MORE OF A RING TO IT THAN PENNYWORTH.
HAS A NICE OLD-FASHIONED FEEL.
ANYWAY, I'M IN. I'LL LET YOU KNOW IF I SEE ANY...
...SUSPICIOUS CHARACTERS.

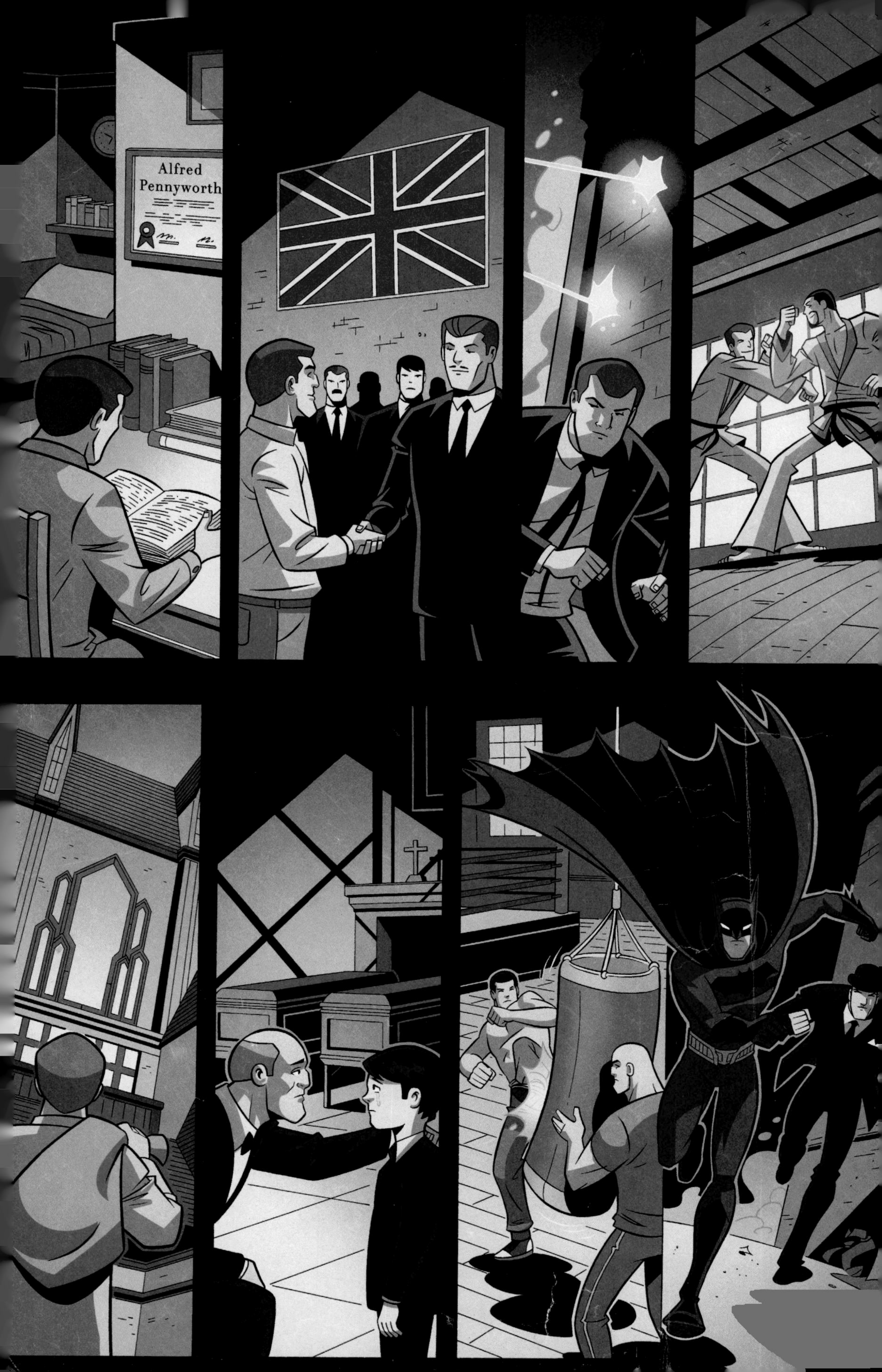
Alfred
Pennyworth

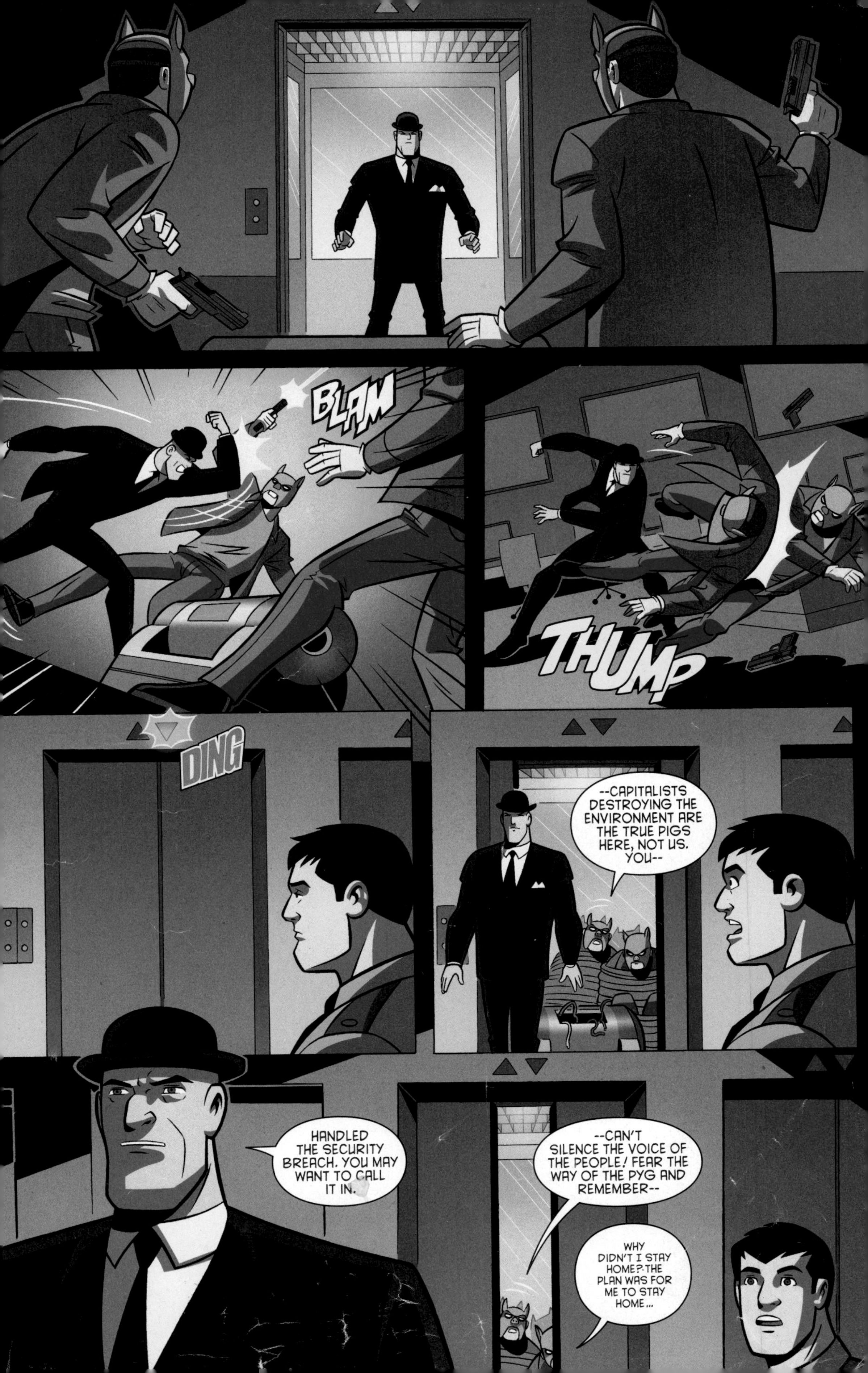

BLAM
THUMP
DING
--CAPITALISTS DESTROYING THE ENVIRONMENT ARE THE TRUE PIGS HERE, NOT US. YOU--
HANDLED THE SECURITY BREACH. YOU MAY WANT TO CALL IT IN.
--CAN'T SILENCE THE VOICE OF THE PEOPLE! FEAR THE WAY OF THE PYG AND REMEMBER--
WHY DIDN'T I STAY HOME? THE PLAN WAS FOR ME TO STAY HOME...

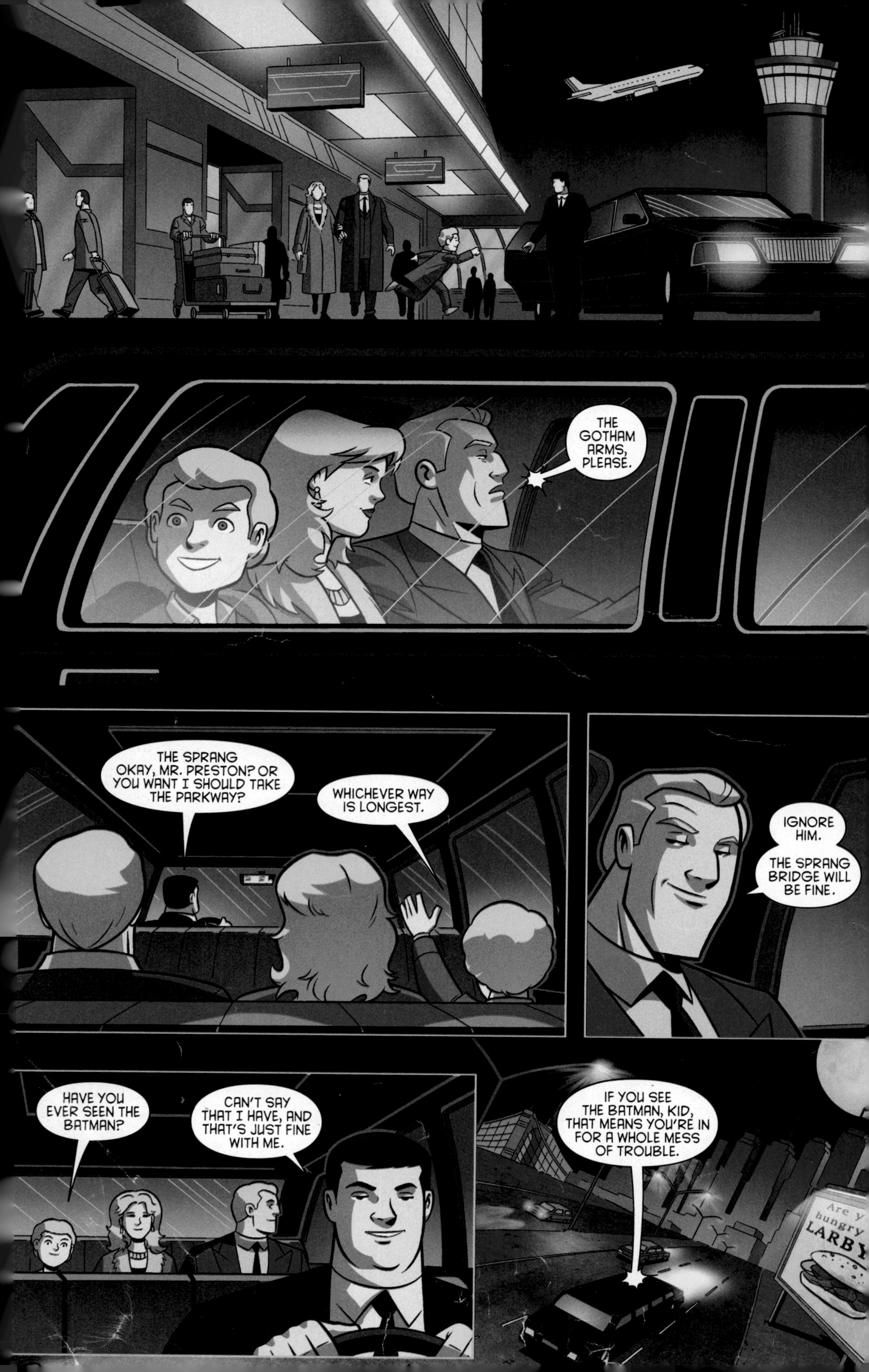
THE GOTHAM ARMS, PLEASE.
THE SPRANG OKAY, MR. PRESTON? OR YOU WANT I SHOULD TAKE THE PARKWAY?
WHICHEVER WAY IS LONGEST.
IGNORE HIM.
THE SPRANG BRIDGE WILL BE FINE.
HAVE YOU EVER SEEN THE BATMAN?
CAN'T SAY THAT I HAVE, AND THAT'S JUST FINE WITH ME.
IF YOU SEE THE BATMAN, KID, THAT MEANS YOU'RE IN FOR A WHOLE MESS OF TROUBLE.
Are
hungry

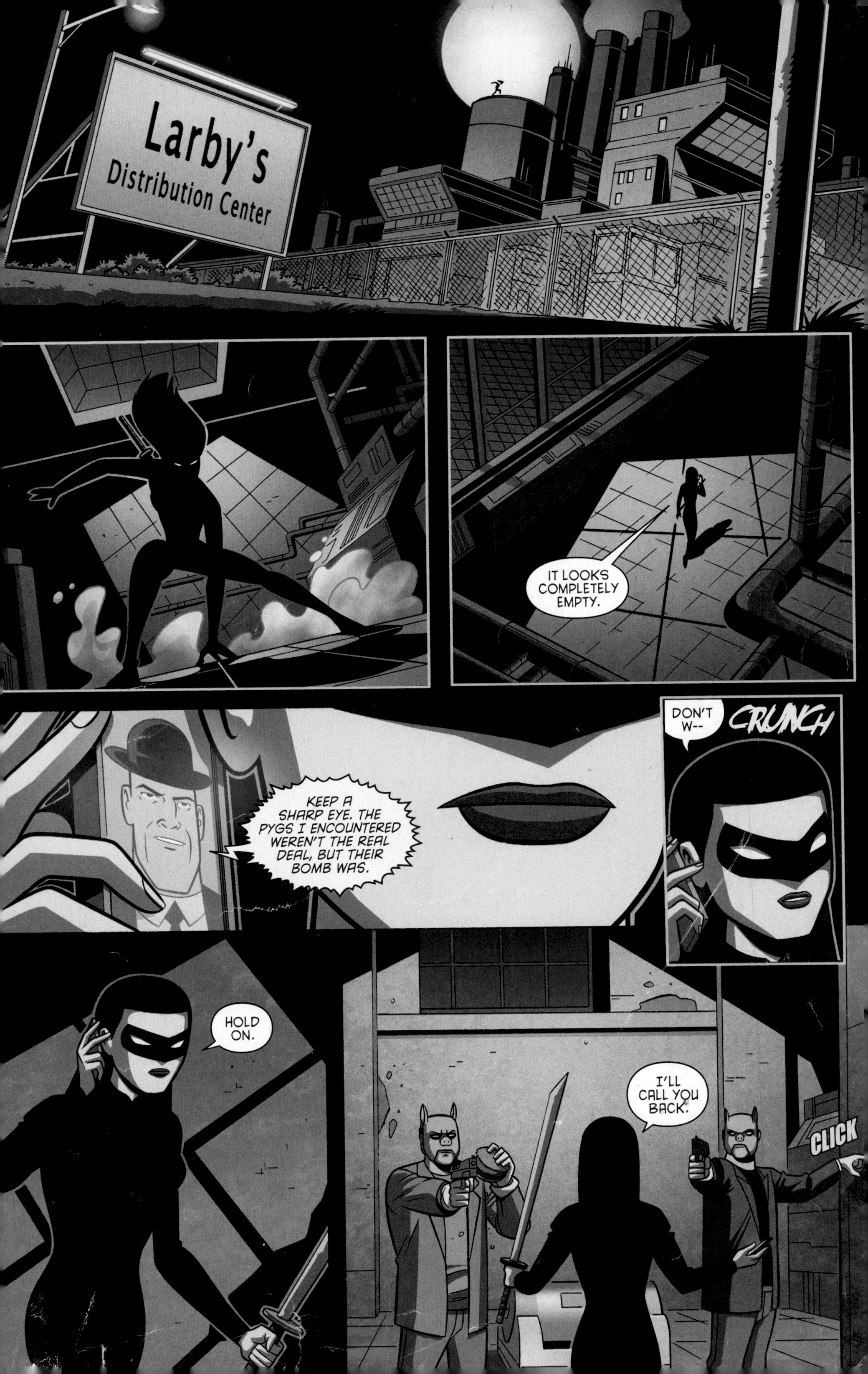
Larby's
Distribution Center
IT LOOKS COMPLETELY EMPTY.
KEEP A SHARP EYE. THE PYGS I ENCOUNTERED WEREN'T THE REAL DEAL, BUT THEIR BOMB WAS.
DON'T W--
CRUNCH
HOLD ON.
I'LL CALL YOU BACK.
CLICK

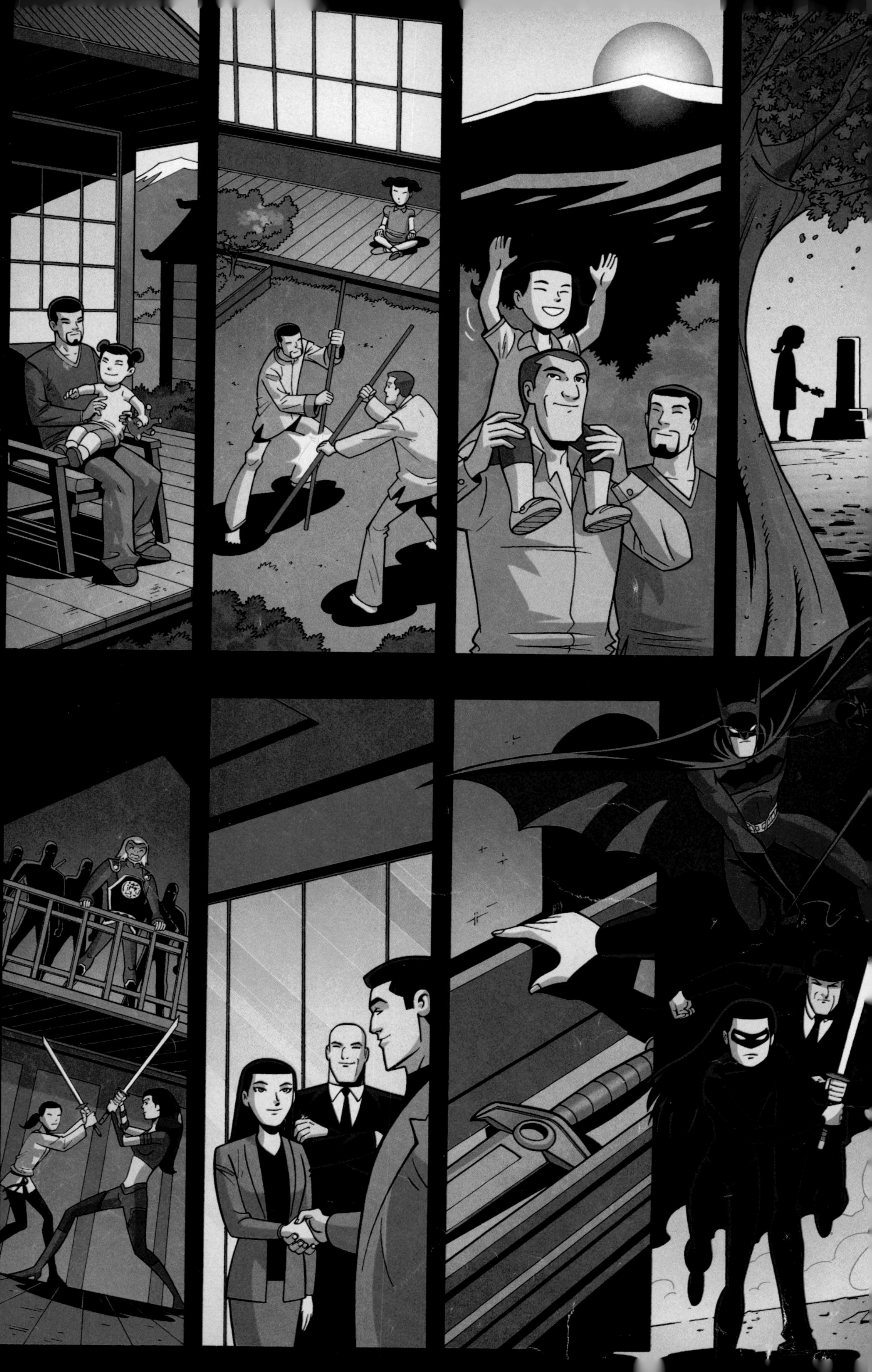

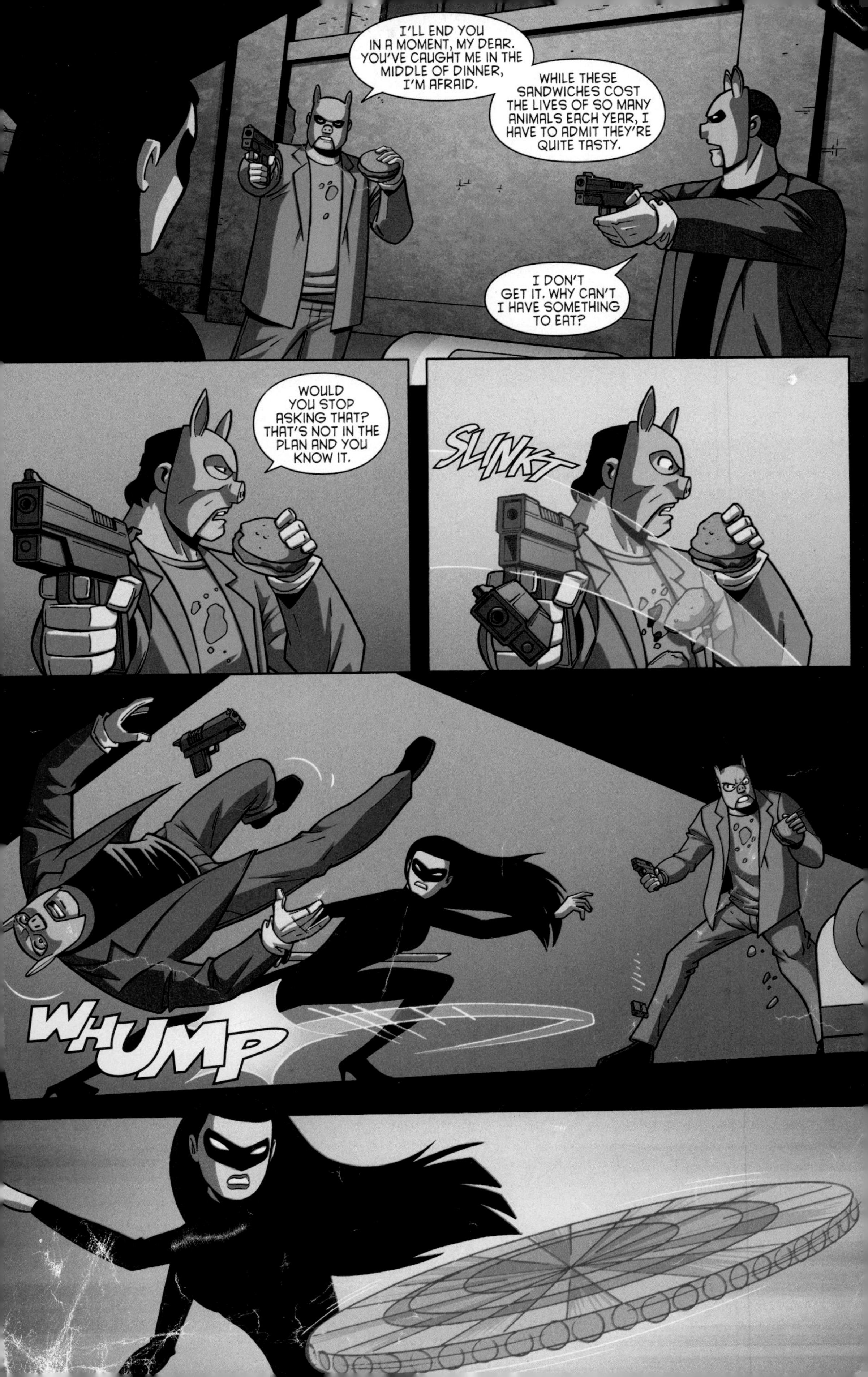
I'LL END YOU IN A MOMENT, MY DEAR. YOU'VE CAUGHT ME IN THE MIDDLE OF DINNER, I'M AFRAID.
WHILE THESE SANDWICHES COST THE LIVES OF SO MANY ANIMALS EACH YEAR, I HAVE TO ADMIT THEY'RE QUITE TASTY.
I DON'T GET IT. WHY CAN'T I HAVE SOMETHING TO EAT?
WOULD YOU STOP ASKING THAT? THAT'S NOT IN THE PLAN AND YOU KNOW IT.
SLINKT
WHUMP

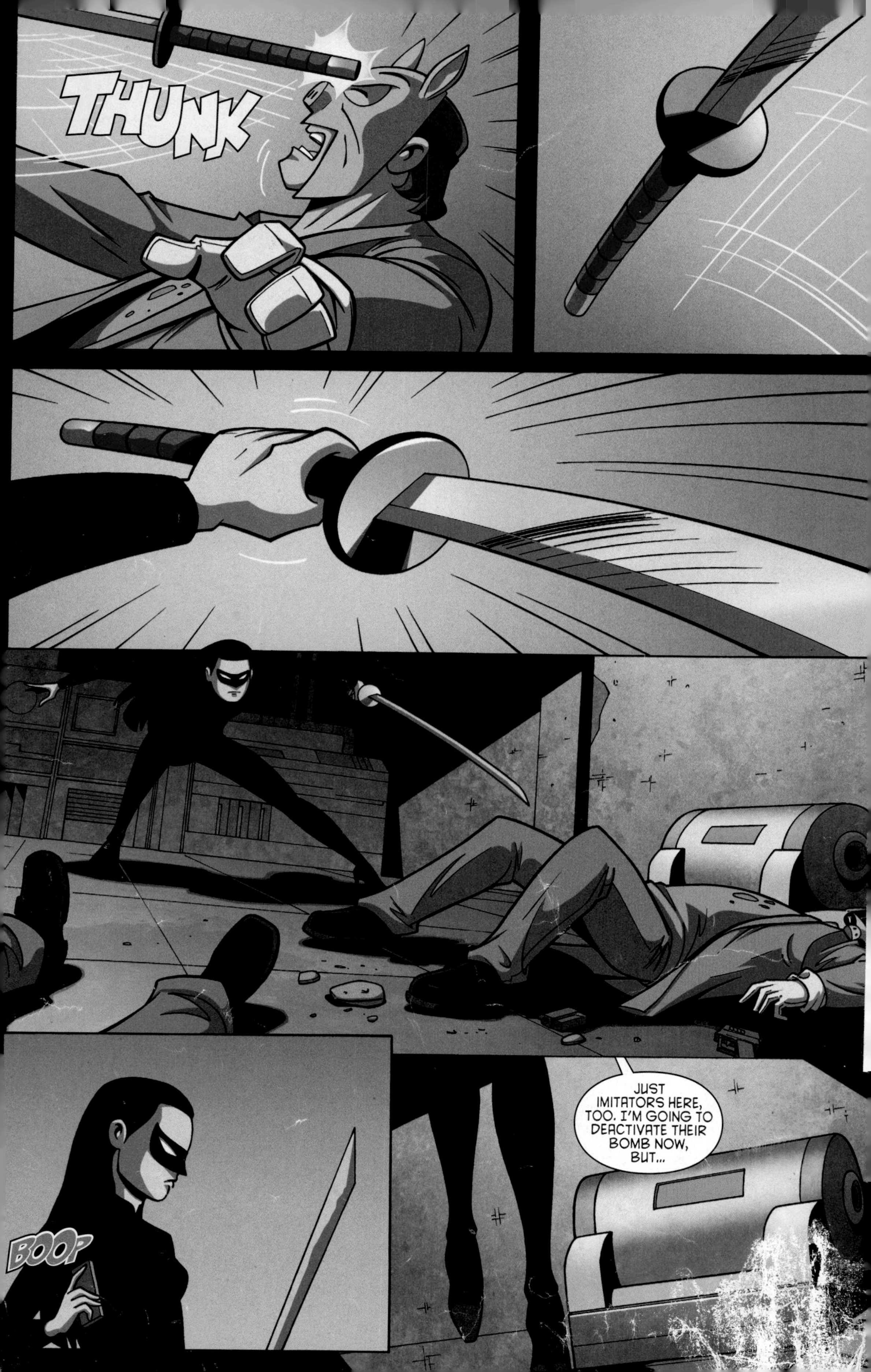
THUNK
JUST IMITATORS HERE, TOO. I'M GOING TO DEACTIVATE THEIR BOMB NOW, BUT...
BOOP

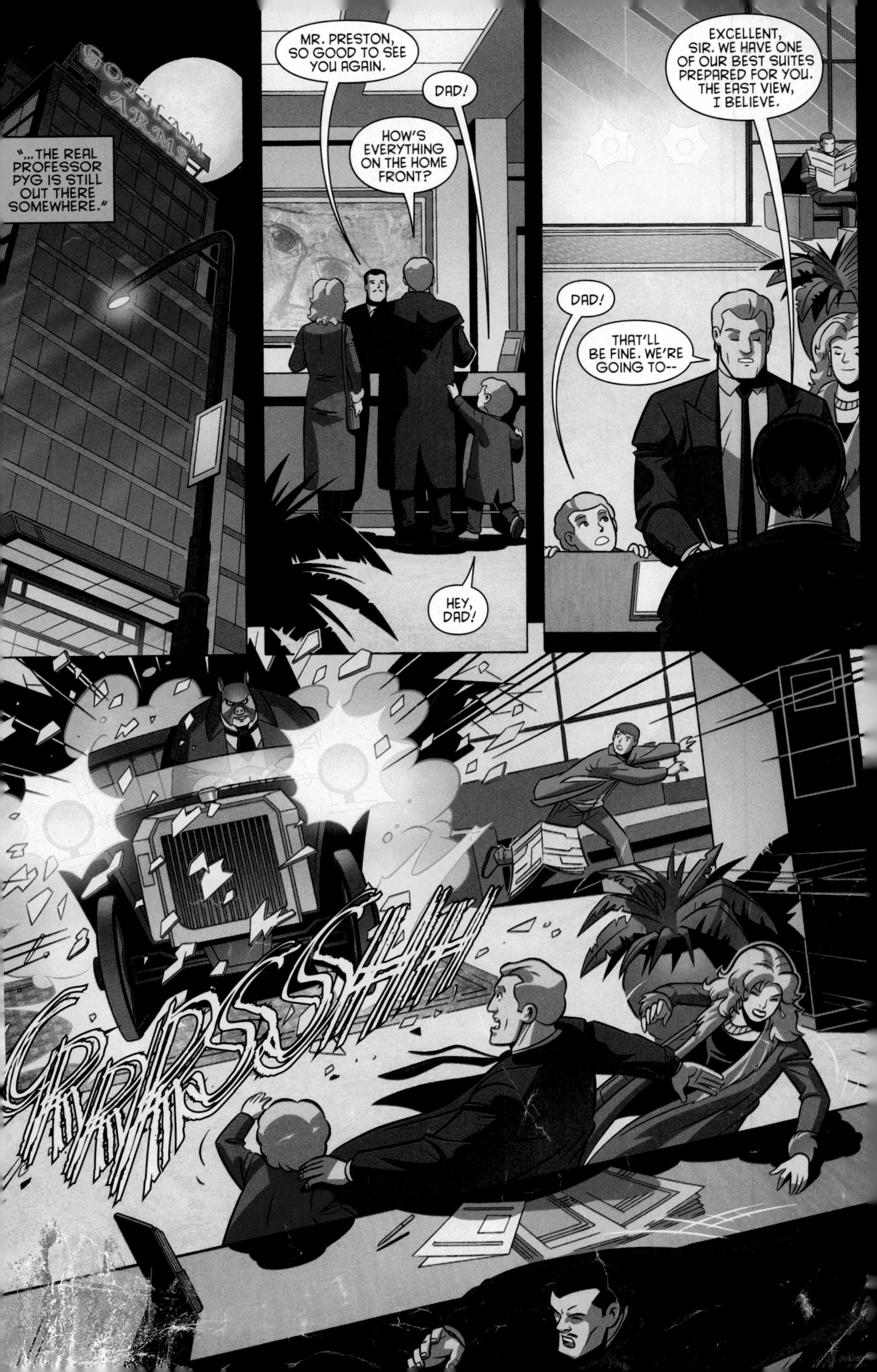
GOTHAM ARMS
"...THE REAL PROFESSOR PYG IS STILL OUT THERE SOMEWHERE."
MR. PRESTON, SO GOOD TO SEE YOU AGAIN.
DAD!
HOW'S EVERYTHING ON THE HOME FRONT?
HEY, DAD!
EXCELLENT, SIR. WE HAVE ONE OF OUR BEST SUITES PREPARED FOR YOU. THE EAST VIEW, I BELIEVE.
DAD!
THAT'LL BE FINE. WE'RE GOING TO--
GRRRSSSHHH

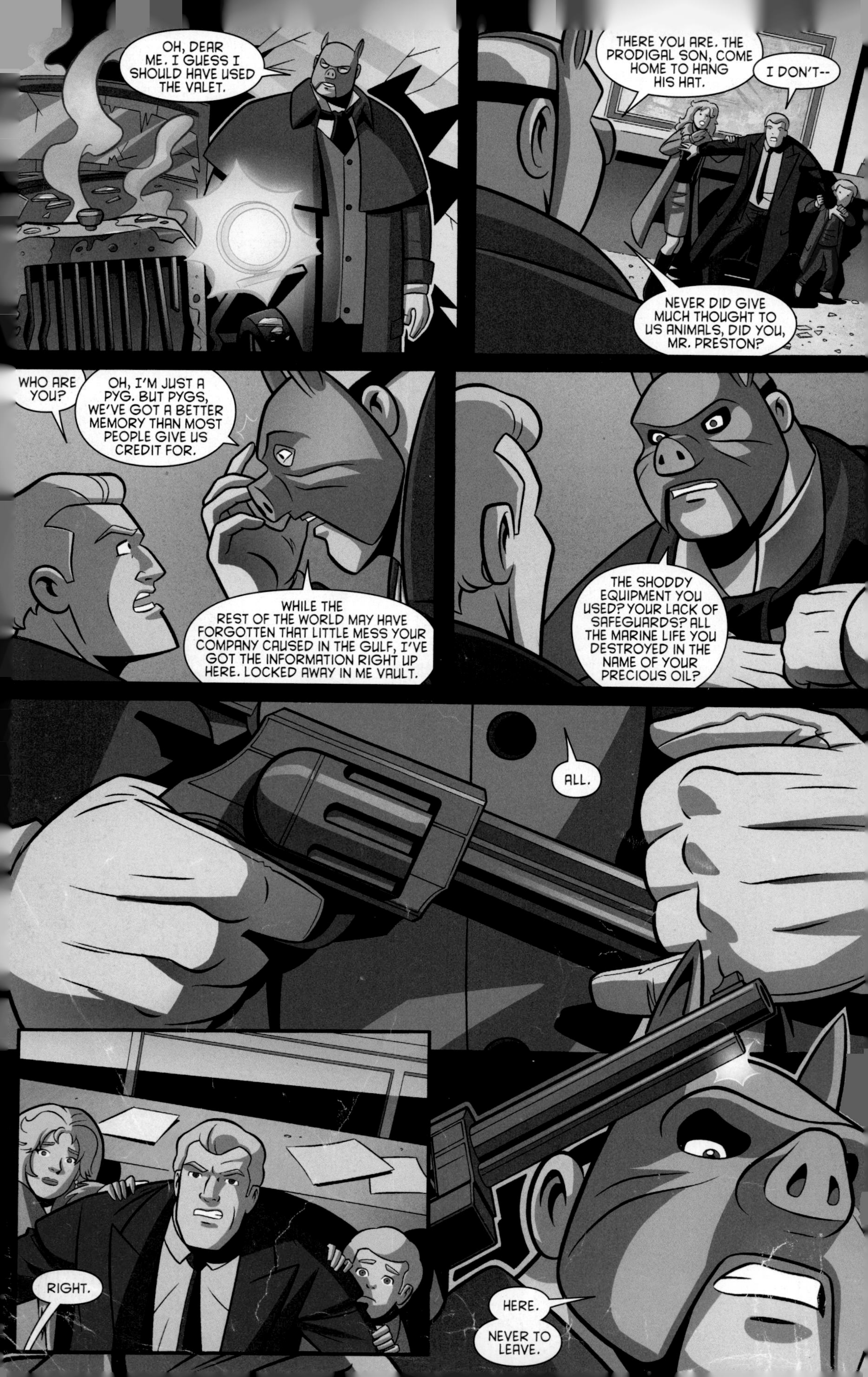

OH, DEAR ME. I GUESS I SHOULD HAVE USED THE VALET.
THERE YOU ARE. THE PRODIGAL SON, COME HOME TO HANG HIS HAT.
I DON'T--
NEVER DID GIVE MUCH THOUGHT TO US ANIMALS, DID YOU, MR. PRESTON?
WHO ARE YOU?
OH, I'M JUST A PYG. BUT PYGS, WE'VE GOT A BETTER MEMORY THAN MOST PEOPLE GIVE US CREDIT FOR.
WHILE THE REST OF THE WORLD MAY HAVE FORGOTTEN THAT LITTLE MESS YOUR COMPANY CAUSED IN THE GULF, I'VE GOT THE INFORMATION RIGHT UP HERE. LOCKED AWAY IN ME VAULT.
THE SHODDY EQUIPMENT YOU USED? YOUR LACK OF SAFEGUARDS? ALL THE MARINE LIFE YOU DESTROYED IN THE NAME OF YOUR PRECIOUS OIL?
ALL.
RIGHT.
HERE.
NEVER TO LEAVE.

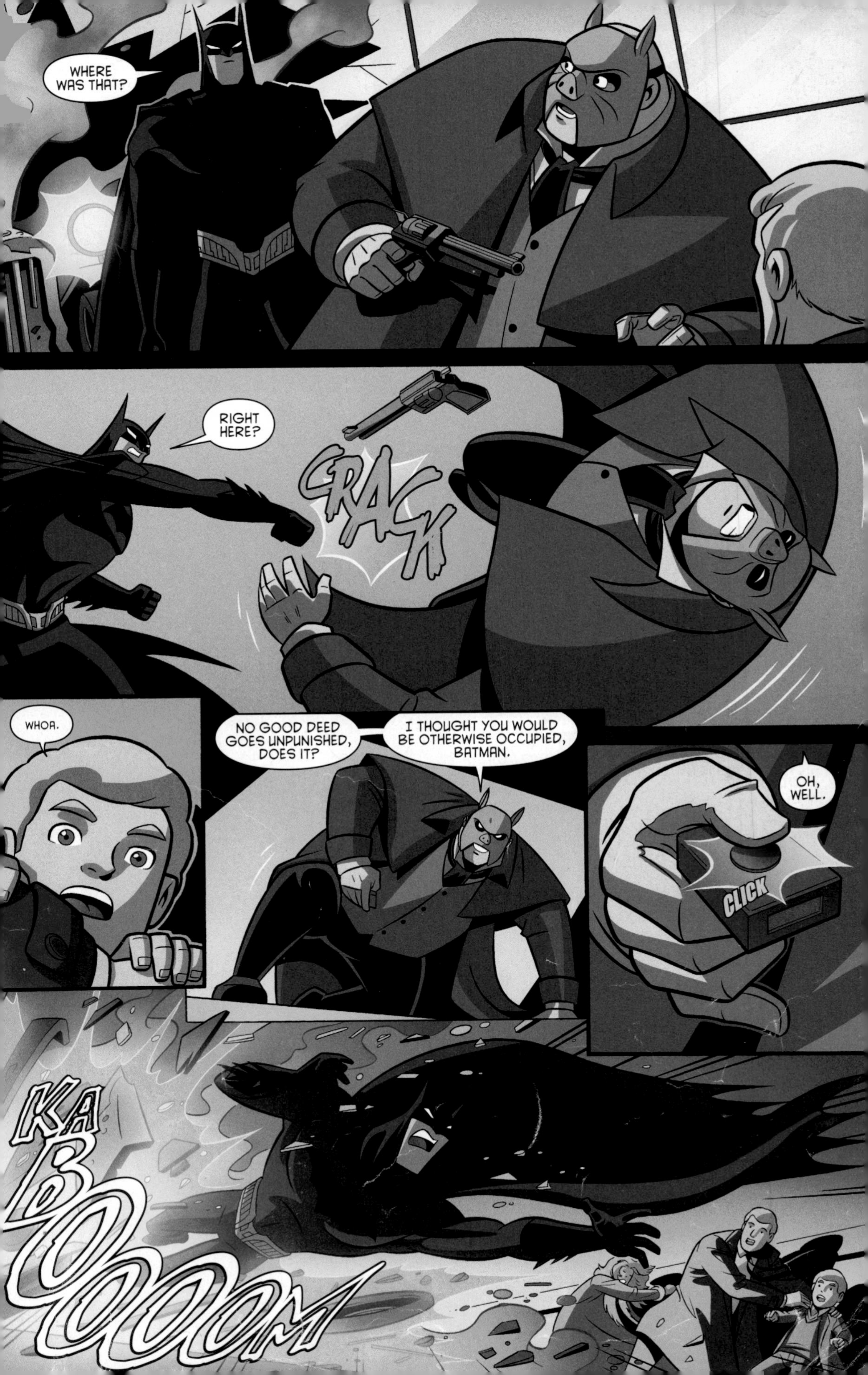
WHERE WAS THAT?
RIGHT HERE?
CRACK
WHOA.
NO GOOD DEED GOES UNPUNISHED, DOES IT?
I THOUGHT YOU WOULD BE OTHERWISE OCCUPIED, BATMAN.
OH, WELL.
CLICK
KABOOOOM

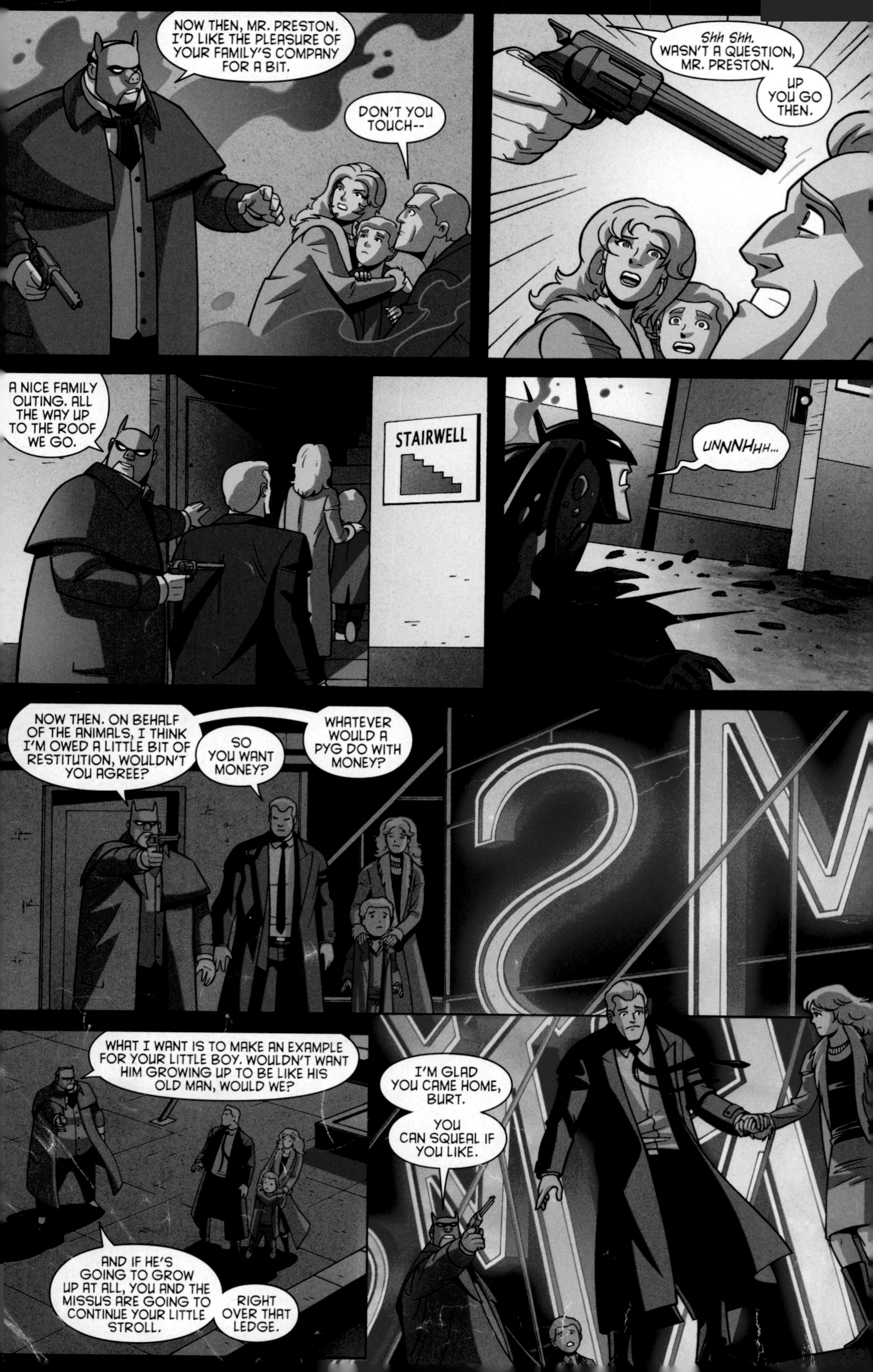
NOW THEN, MR. PRESTON. I'D LIKE THE PLEASURE OF YOUR FAMILY'S COMPANY FOR A BIT.
DON'T YOU TOUCH--
Shh Shh. WASN'T A QUESTION, MR. PRESTON.
UP YOU GO THEN.
A NICE FAMILY OUTING. ALL THE WAY UP TO THE ROOF WE GO.
STAIRWELL
UNNNHHH...
NOW THEN. ON BEHALF OF THE ANIMALS, I THINK I'M OWED A LITTLE BIT OF RESTITUTION, WOULDN'T YOU AGREE?
SO YOU WANT MONEY?
WHATEVER WOULD A PYG DO WITH MONEY?
WHAT I WANT IS TO MAKE AN EXAMPLE FOR YOUR LITTLE BOY. WOULDN'T WANT HIM GROWING UP TO BE LIKE HIS OLD MAN, WOULD WE?
AND IF HE'S GOING TO GROW UP AT ALL, YOU AND THE MISSUS ARE GOING TO CONTINUE YOUR LITTLE STROLL.
RIGHT OVER THAT LEDGE.
I'M GLAD YOU CAME HOME, BURT.
YOU CAN SQUEAL IF YOU LIKE.

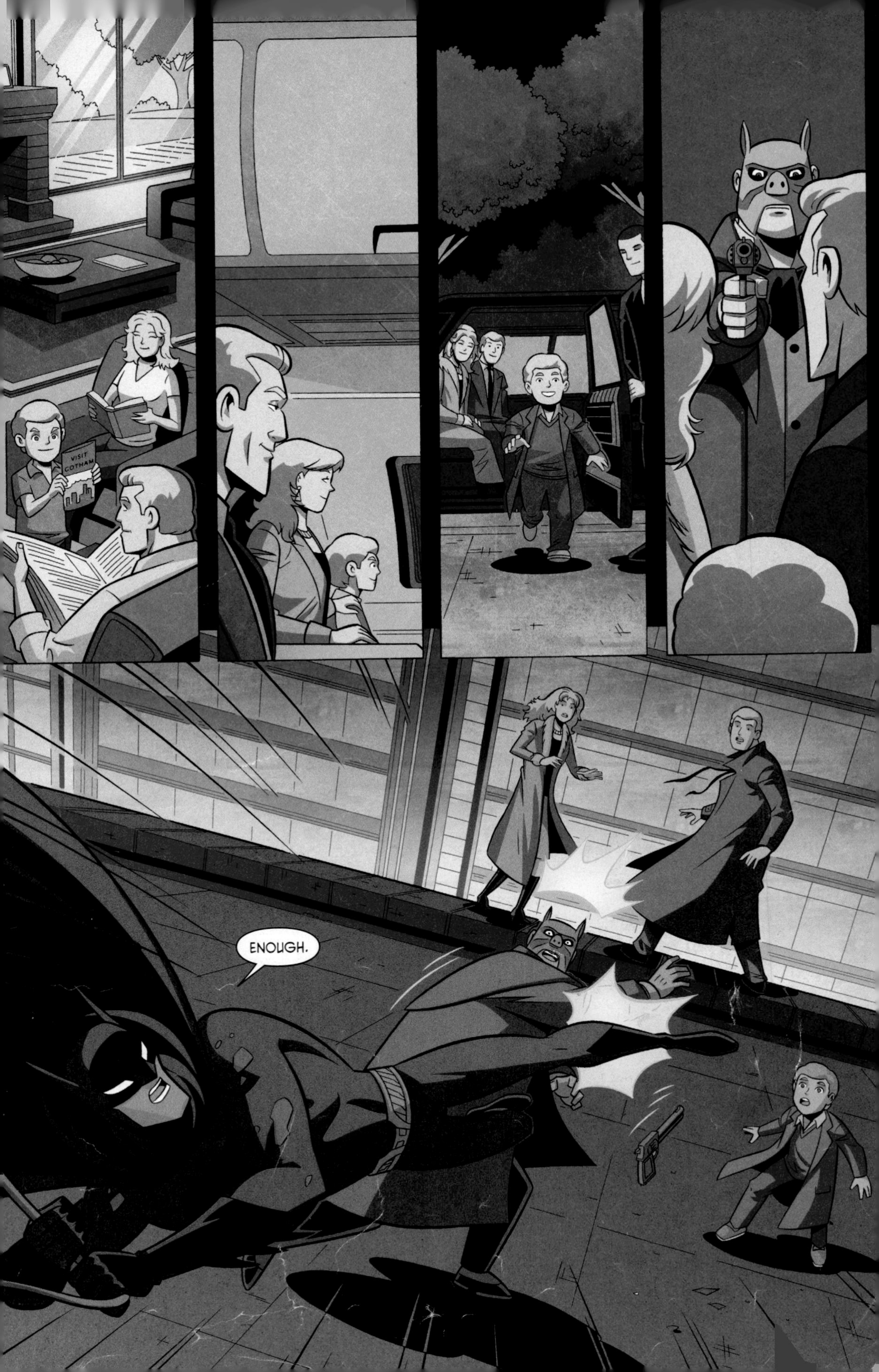
VISIT GOTHAM
ENOUGH.

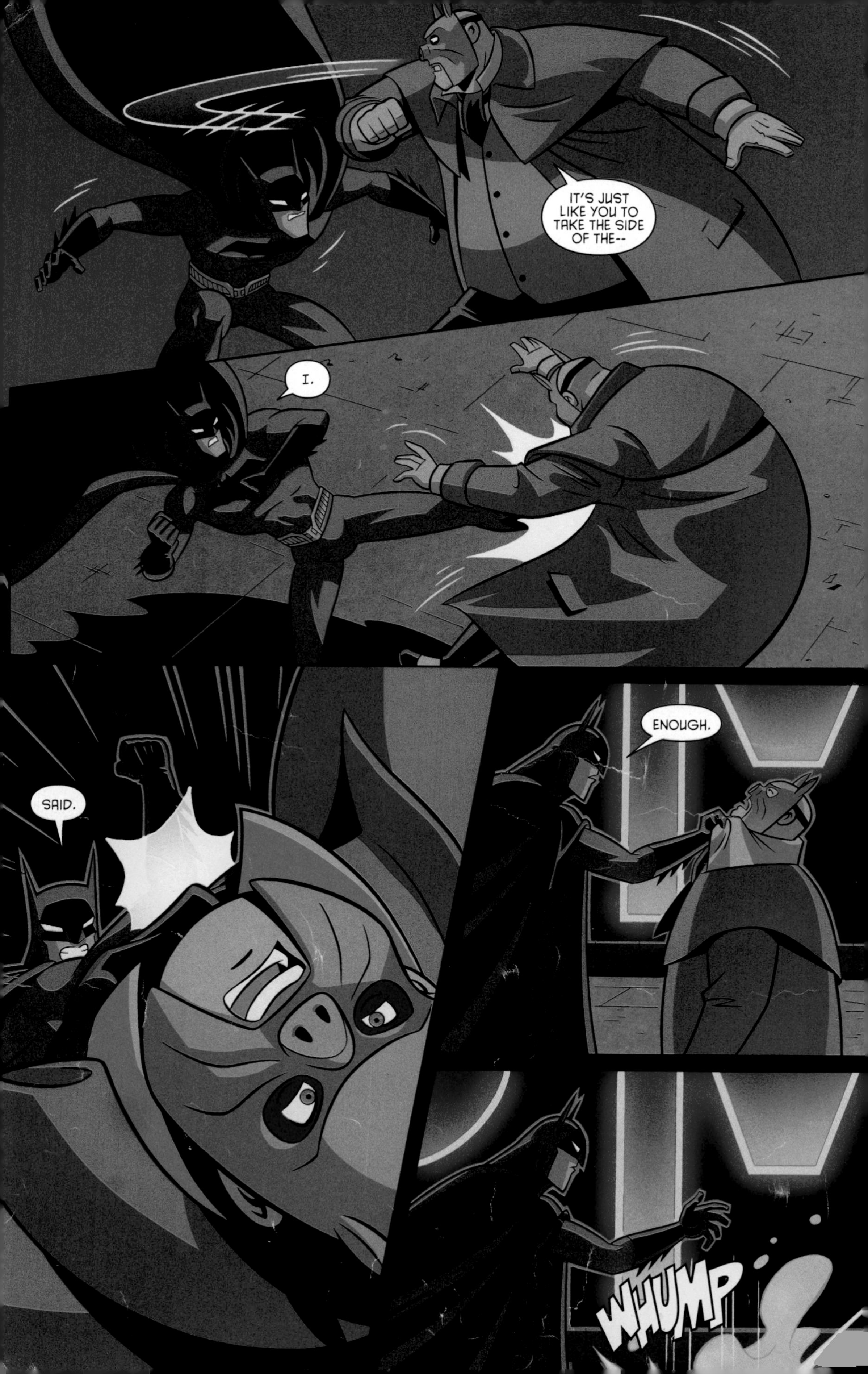
IT'S JUST LIKE YOU TO TAKE THE SIDE OF THE--
I.
SAID.
ENOUGH.
WHUMP

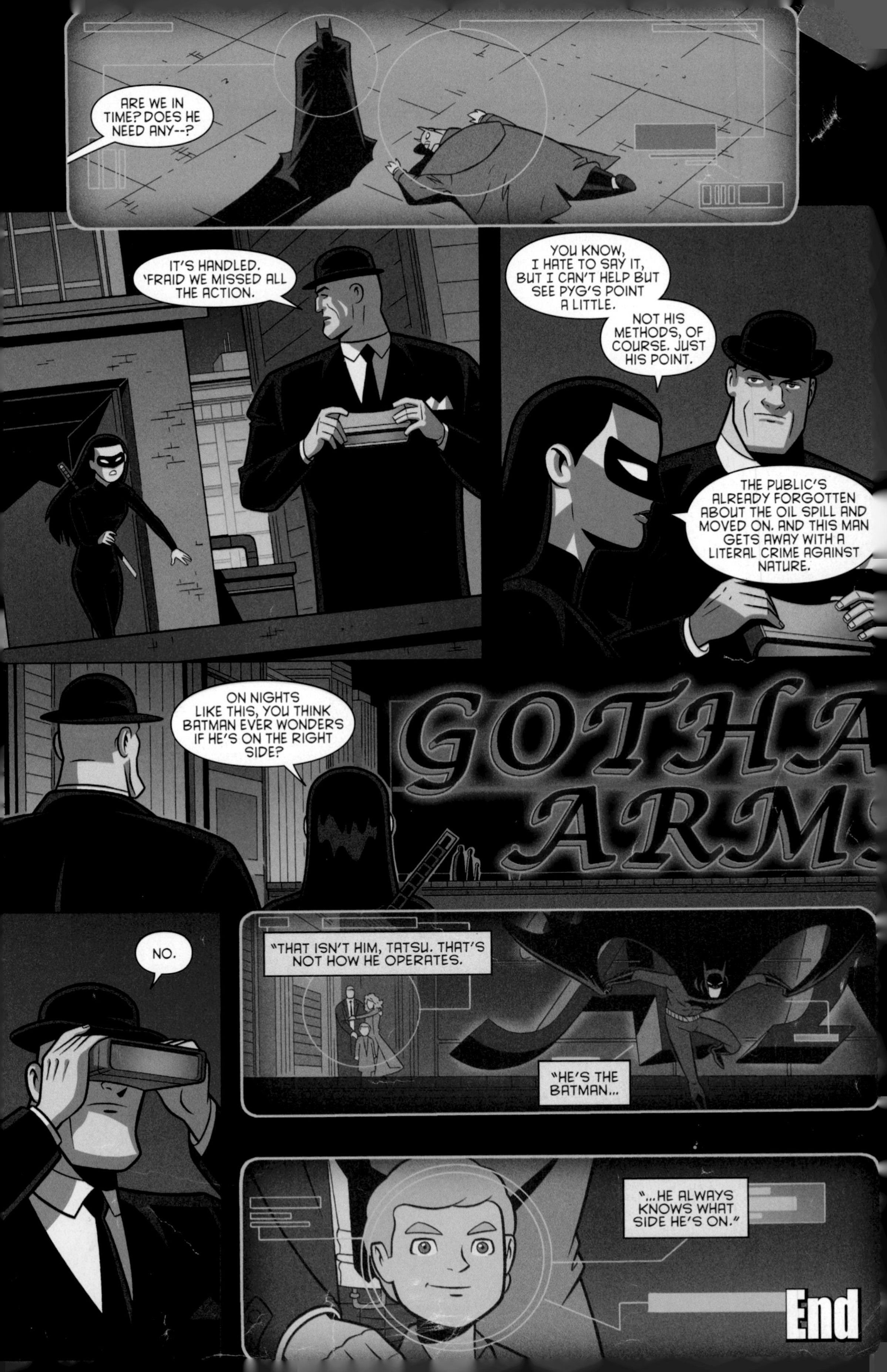
ARE WE IN TIME? DOES HE NEED ANY--?
IT'S HANDLED. 'FRAID WE MISSED ALL THE ACTION.
YOU KNOW, I HATE TO SAY IT, BUT I CAN'T HELP BUT SEE PYG'S POINT A LITTLE.
NOT HIS METHODS, OF COURSE. JUST HIS POINT.
THE PUBLIC'S ALREADY FORGOTTEN ABOUT THE OIL SPILL AND MOVED ON. AND THIS MAN GETS AWAY WITH A LITERAL CRIME AGAINST NATURE.
ON NIGHTS LIKE THIS, YOU THINK BATMAN EVER WONDERS IF HE'S ON THE RIGHT SIDE?
GOTHA
ARMS
NO.
"THAT ISN'T HIM, TATSU. THAT'S NOT HOW HE OPERATES.
"HE'S THE BATMAN...
"...HE ALWAYS KNOWS WHAT SIDE HE'S ON."
End

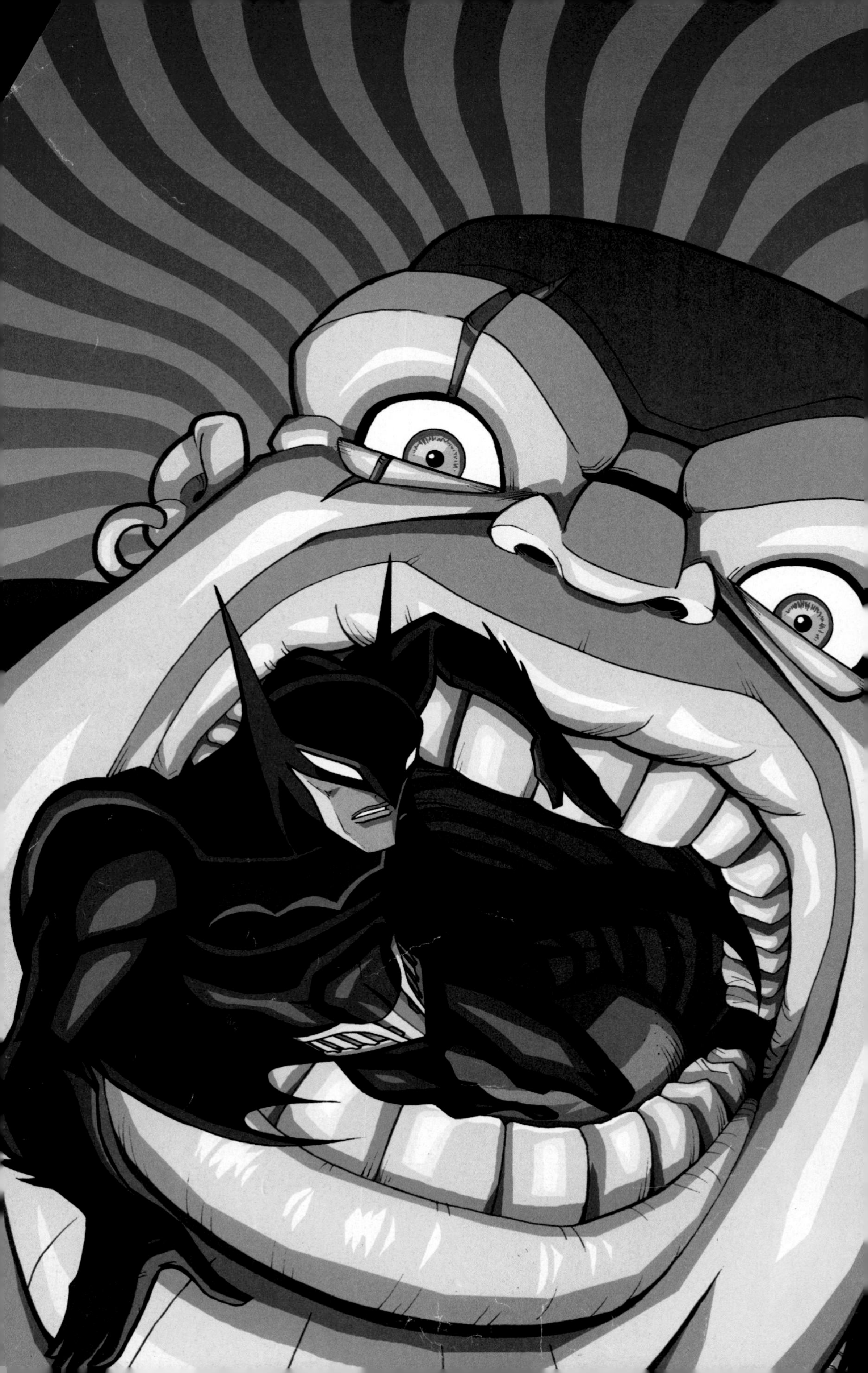

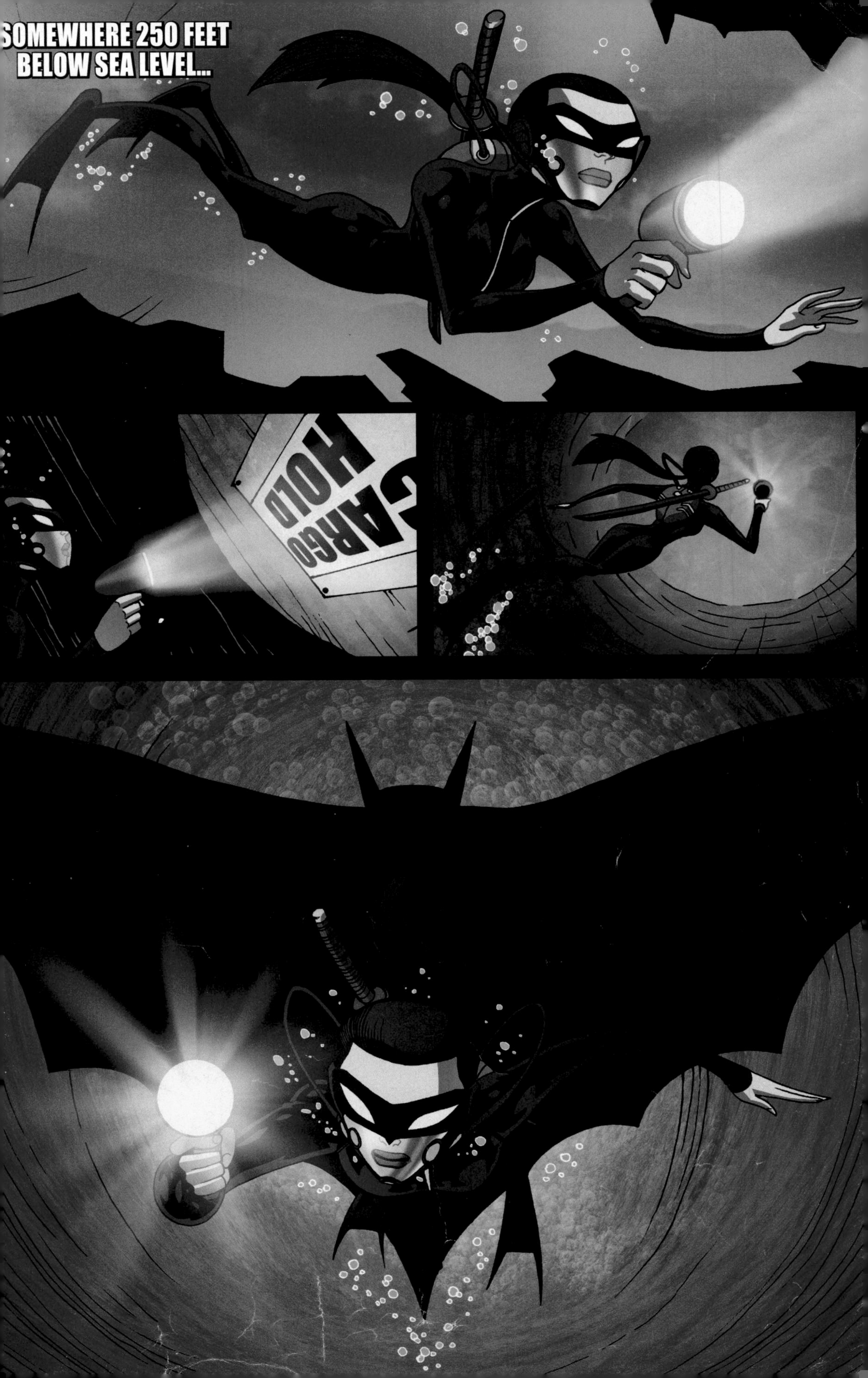
SOMEWHERE 250 FEET BELOW SEA LEVEL...
CARGO HOLD

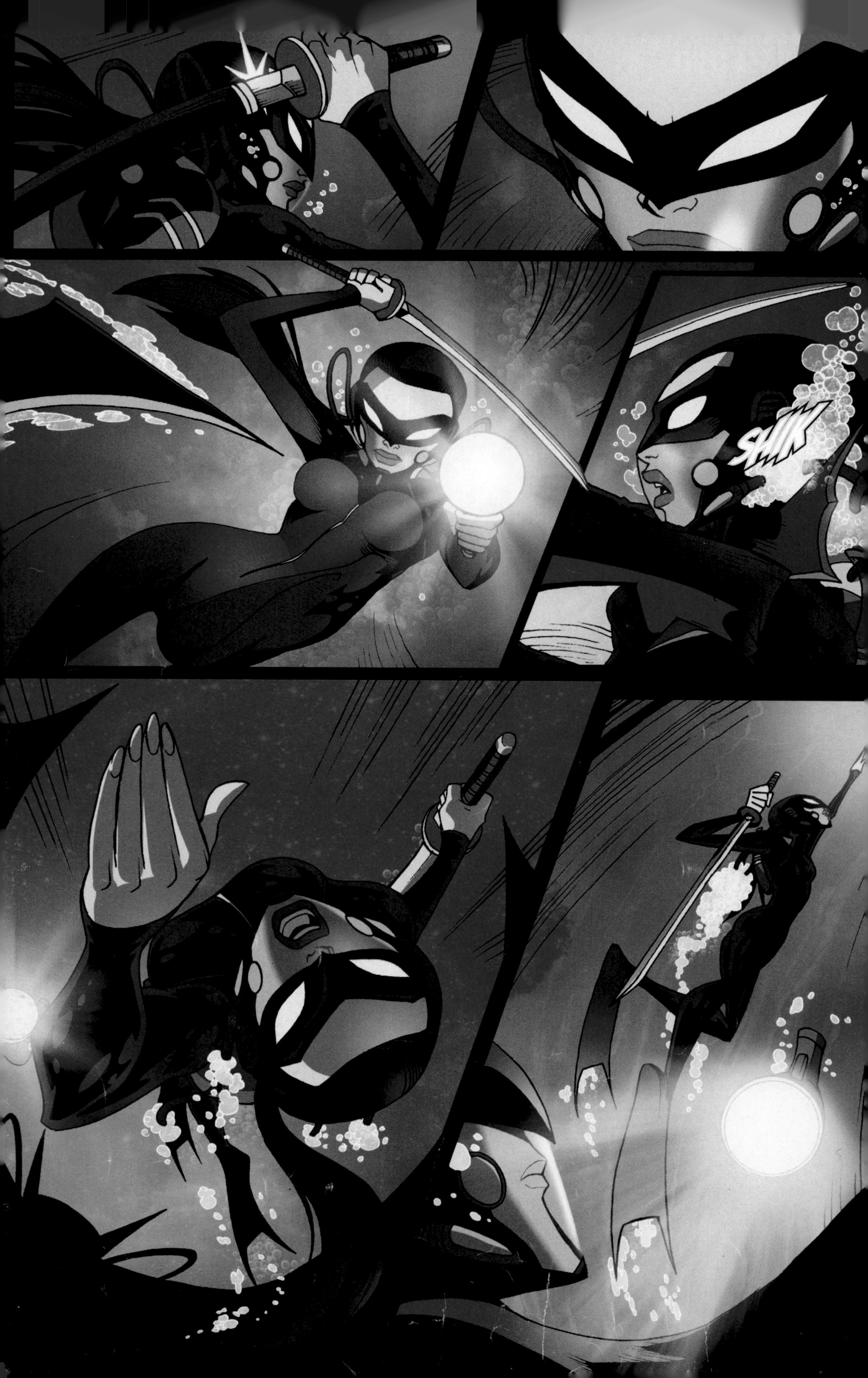
SHIK

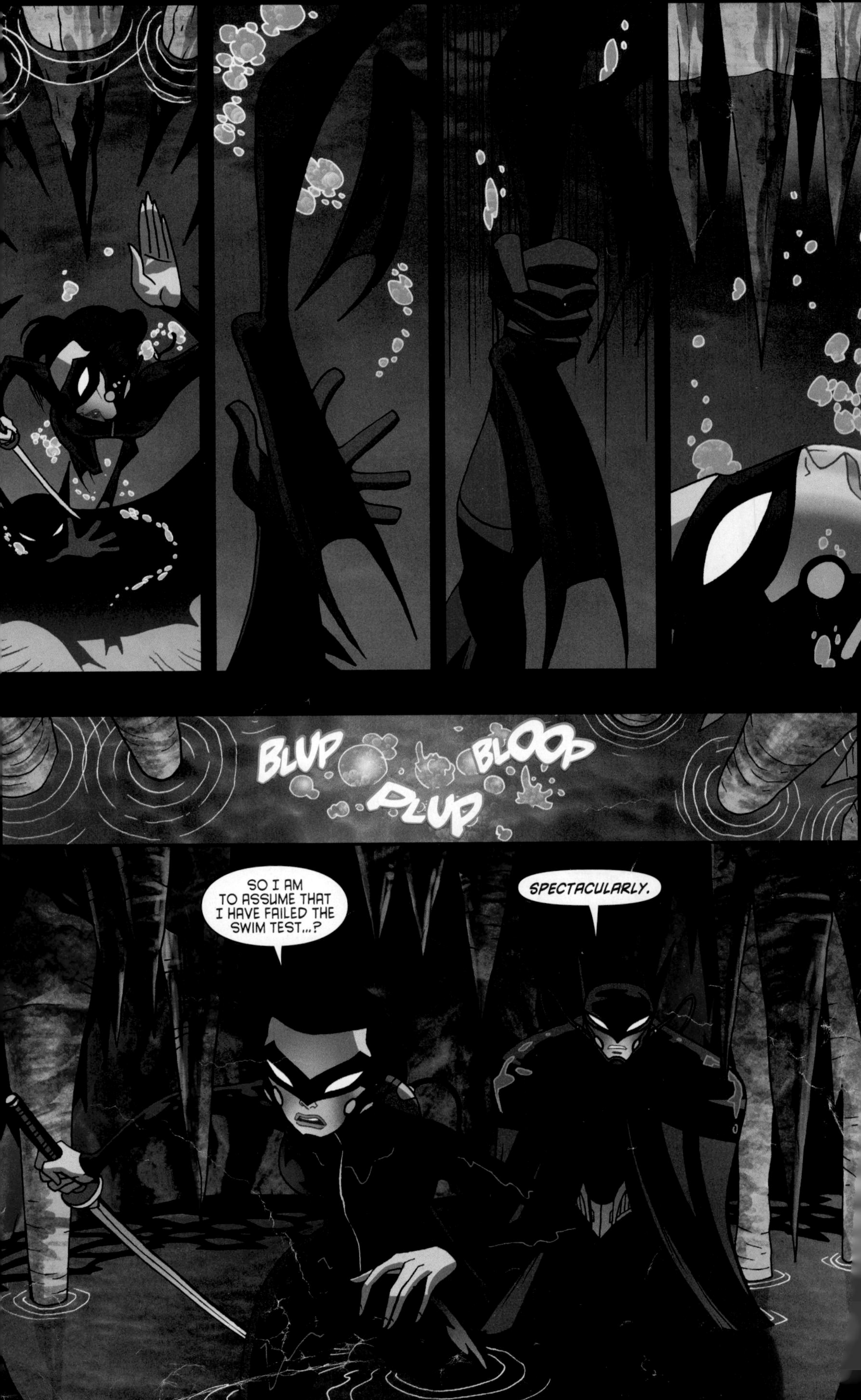
BLUP
PLUP
BLOOP
SO I AM TO ASSUME THAT I HAVE FAILED THE SWIM TEST...?
SPECTACULARLY.

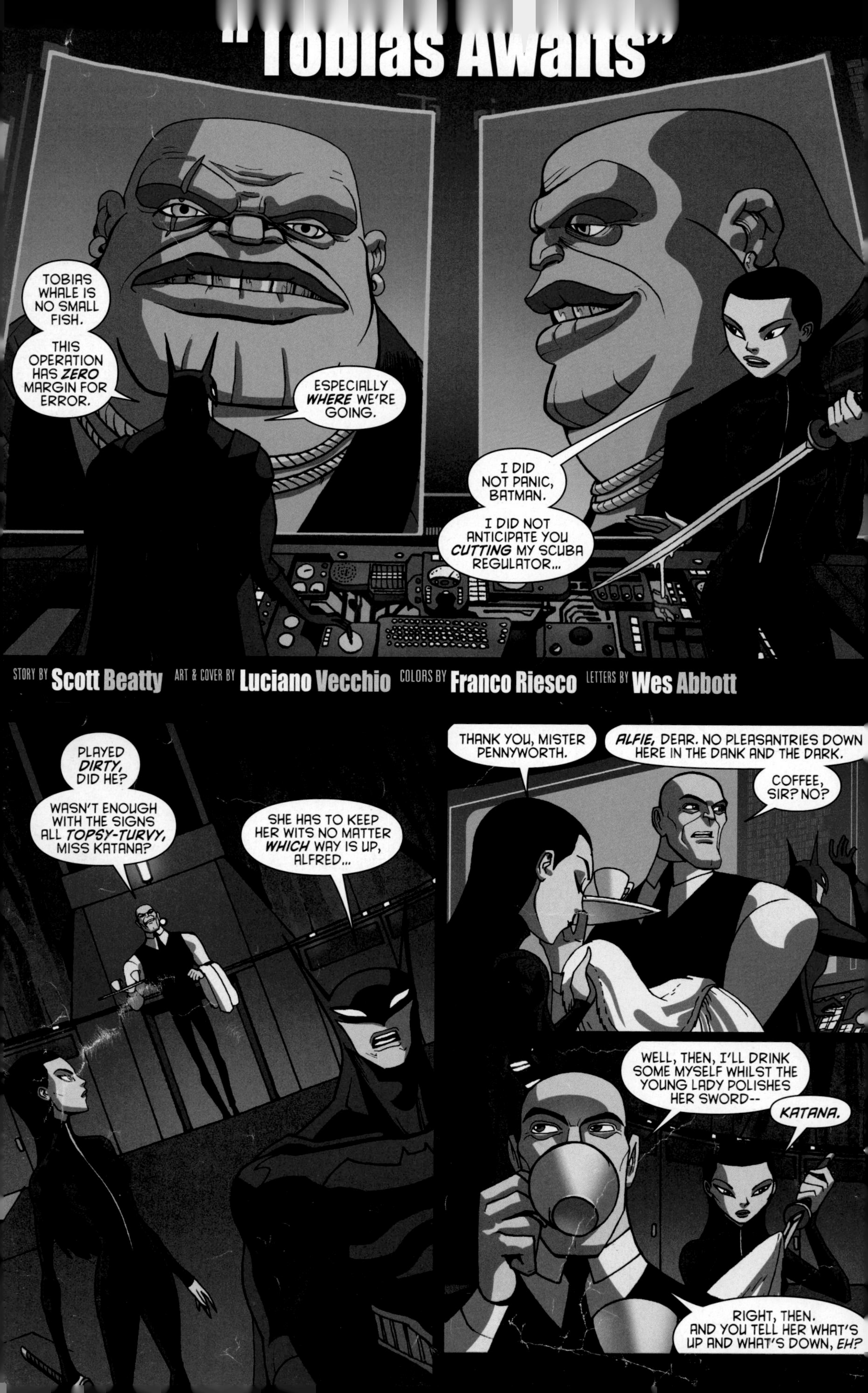
"Tobias Awaits"
TOBIAS WHALE IS NO SMALL FISH.
THIS OPERATION HAS ZERO MARGIN FOR ERROR.
ESPECIALLY WHERE WE'RE GOING.
I DID NOT PANIC, BATMAN.
I DID NOT ANTICIPATE YOU CUTTING MY SCUBA REGULATOR...
STORY BY Scott Beatty ART & COVER BY Luciano Vecchio COLORS BY Franco Riesco LETTERS BY Wes Abbott
PLAYED DIRTY, DID HE?
WASN'T ENOUGH WITH THE SIGNS ALL TOPSY-TURVY, MISS KATANA?
SHE HAS TO KEEP HER WITS NO MATTER WHICH WAY IS UP, ALFRED...
THANK YOU, MISTER PENNYWORTH.
ALFIE, DEAR. NO PLEASANTRIES DOWN HERE IN THE DANK AND THE DARK.
COFFEE, SIR? NO?
WELL, THEN, I'LL DRINK SOME MYSELF WHILST THE YOUNG LADY POLISHES HER SWORD--
KATANA.
RIGHT, THEN. AND YOU TELL HER WHAT'S UP AND WHAT'S DOWN, EH?

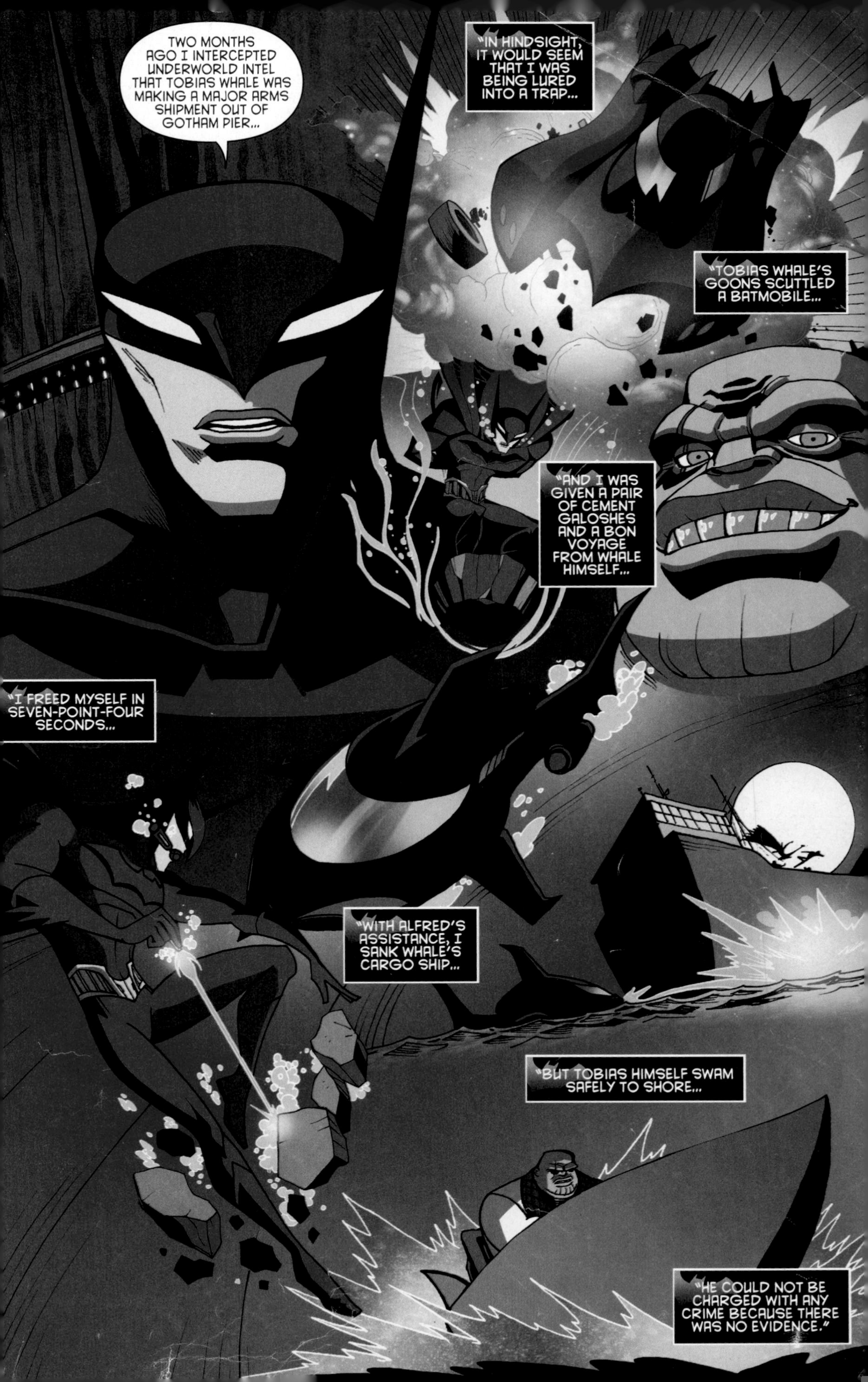
TWO MONTHS AGO I INTERCEPTED UNDERWORLD INTEL THAT TOBIAS WHALE WAS MAKING A MAJOR ARMS SHIPMENT OUT OF GOTHAM PIER...
"IN HINDSIGHT, IT WOULD SEEM THAT I WAS BEING LURED INTO A TRAP...
"TOBIAS WHALE'S GOONS SCUTTLED A BATMOBILE...
"AND I WAS GIVEN A PAIR OF CEMENT GALOSHES AND A BON VOYAGE FROM WHALE HIMSELF...
"I FREED MYSELF IN SEVEN-POINT-FOUR SECONDS...
"WITH ALFRED'S ASSISTANCE, I SANK WHALE'S CARGO SHIP...
"BUT TOBIAS HIMSELF SWAM SAFELY TO SHORE...
"HE COULD NOT BE CHARGED WITH ANY CRIME BECAUSE THERE WAS NO EVIDENCE."

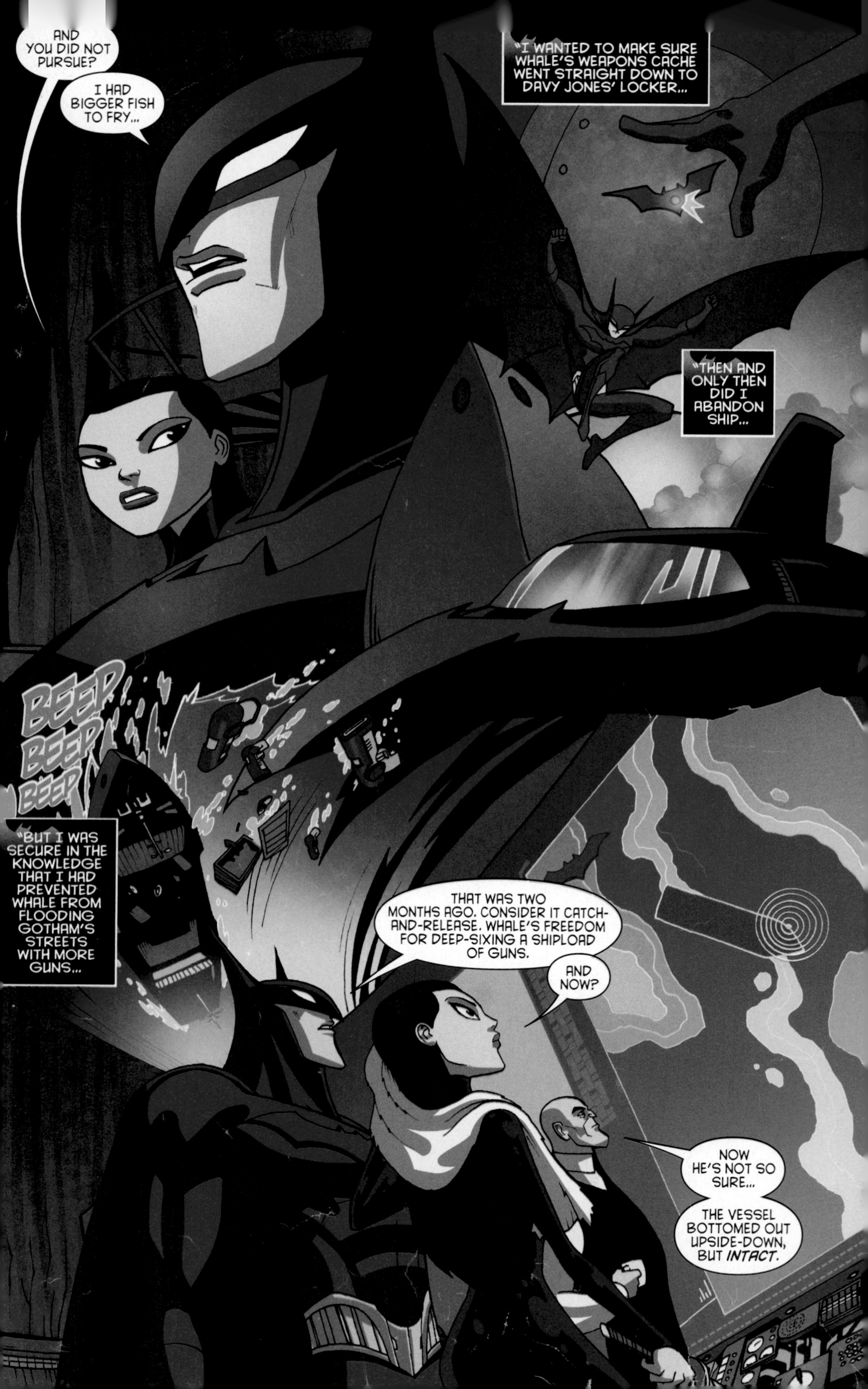
AND YOU DID NOT PURSUE?
I HAD BIGGER FISH TO FRY...
"I WANTED TO MAKE SURE WHALE'S WEAPONS CACHE WENT STRAIGHT DOWN TO DAVY JONES' LOCKER...
"THEN AND ONLY THEN DID I ABANDON SHIP...
BEEP BEEP BEEP
"BUT I WAS SECURE IN THE KNOWLEDGE THAT I HAD PREVENTED WHALE FROM FLOODING GOTHAM'S STREETS WITH MORE GUNS...
THAT WAS TWO MONTHS AGO. CONSIDER IT CATCH-AND-RELEASE. WHALE'S FREEDOM FOR DEEP-SIXING A SHIPLOAD OF GUNS.
AND NOW?
NOW HE'S NOT SO SURE...
THE VESSEL BOTTOMED OUT UPSIDE-DOWN, BUT *INTACT*.

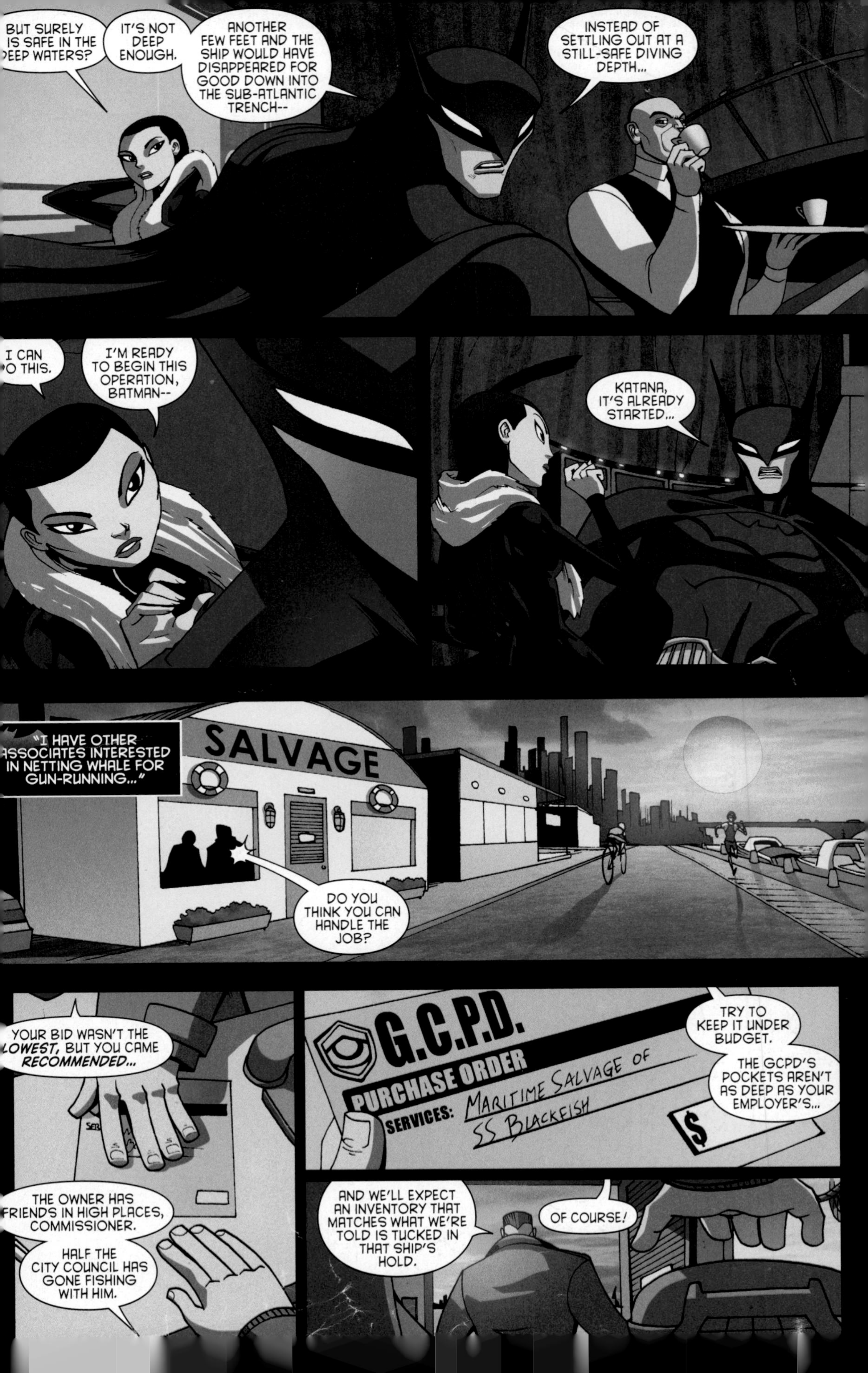
BUT SURELY IS SAFE IN THE DEEP WATERS?
IT'S NOT DEEP ENOUGH.
ANOTHER FEW FEET AND THE SHIP WOULD HAVE DISAPPEARED FOR GOOD DOWN INTO THE SUB-ATLANTIC TRENCH--
INSTEAD OF SETTLING OUT AT A STILL-SAFE DIVING DEPTH...
I CAN DO THIS.
I'M READY TO BEGIN THIS OPERATION, BATMAN--
KATANA, IT'S ALREADY STARTED...
"I HAVE OTHER ASSOCIATES INTERESTED IN NETTING WHALE FOR GUN-RUNNING..."
SALVAGE
DO YOU THINK YOU CAN HANDLE THE JOB?
YOUR BID WASN'T THE LOWEST, BUT YOU CAME RECOMMENDED...
THE OWNER HAS FRIENDS IN HIGH PLACES, COMMISSIONER.
HALF THE CITY COUNCIL HAS GONE FISHING WITH HIM.
G.C.P.D.
PURCHASE ORDER
SERVICES: MARITIME SALVAGE OF SS BLACKFISH
$
TRY TO KEEP IT UNDER BUDGET.
THE GCPD'S POCKETS AREN'T AS DEEP AS YOUR EMPLOYER'S...
AND WE'LL EXPECT AN INVENTORY THAT MATCHES WHAT WE'RE TOLD IS TUCKED IN THAT SHIP'S HOLD.
OF COURSE!

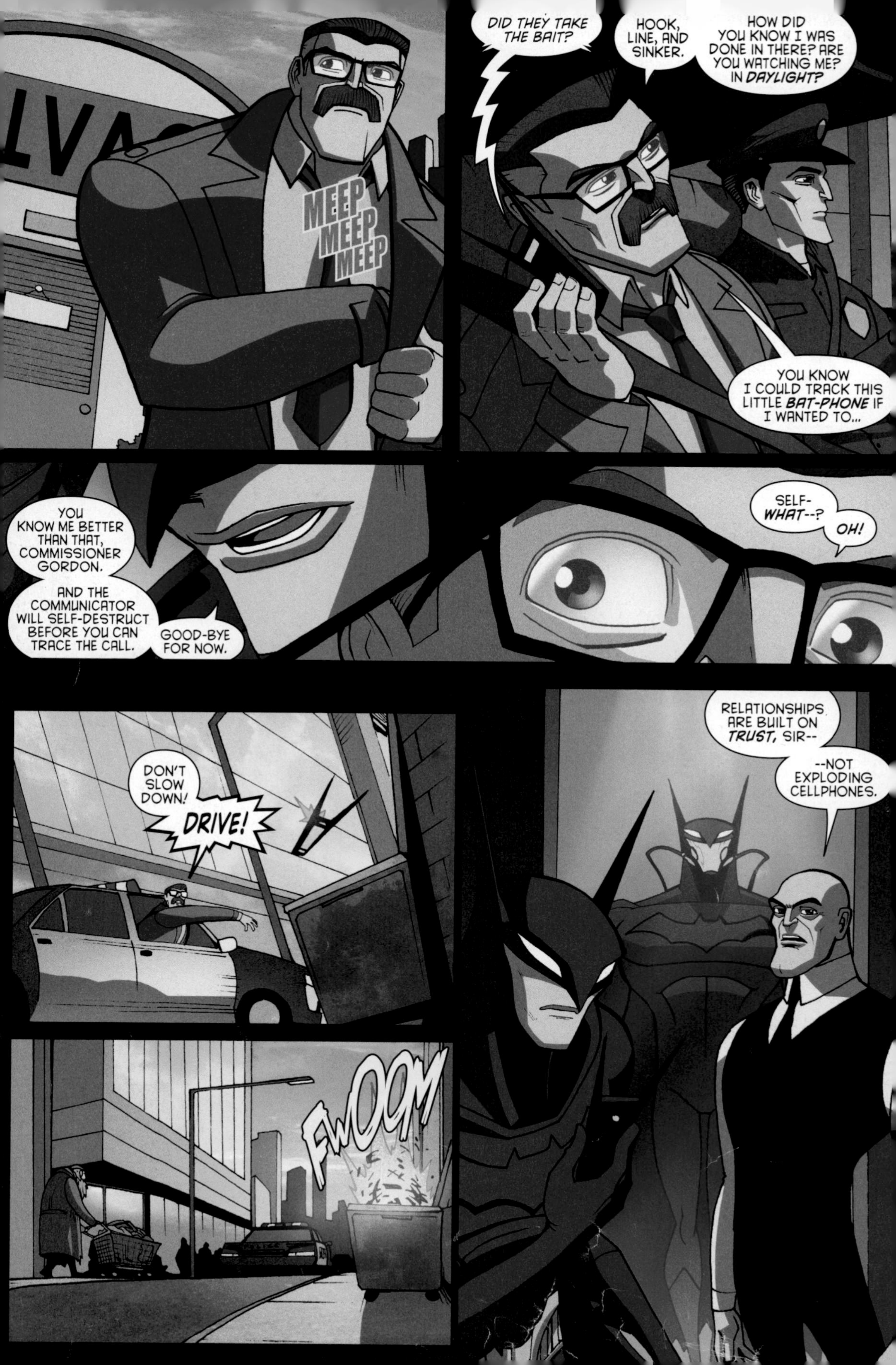
MEEP
MEEP
MEEP
DID THEY TAKE THE BAIT?
HOOK, LINE, AND SINKER.
HOW DID YOU KNOW I WAS DONE IN THERE? ARE YOU WATCHING ME? IN DAYLIGHT?
YOU KNOW I COULD TRACK THIS LITTLE BAT-PHONE IF I WANTED TO...
YOU KNOW ME BETTER THAN THAT, COMMISSIONER GORDON.
AND THE COMMUNICATOR WILL SELF-DESTRUCT BEFORE YOU CAN TRACE THE CALL.
GOOD-BYE FOR NOW.
SELF-WHAT--?
OH!
DON'T SLOW DOWN!
DRIVE!
FWOOM
RELATIONSHIPS ARE BUILT ON TRUST, SIR--
--NOT EXPLODING CELLPHONES.

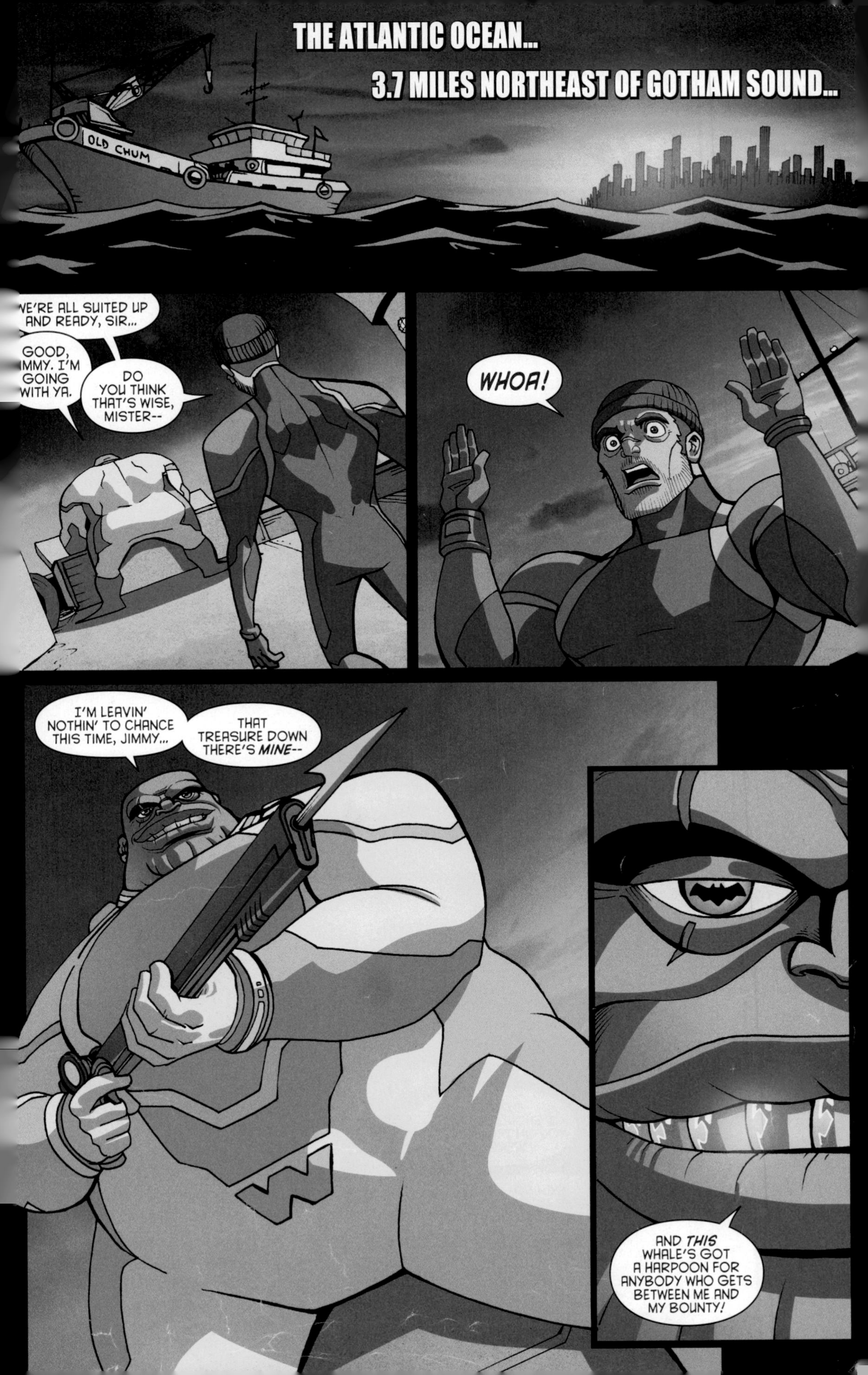
THE ATLANTIC OCEAN...
3.7 MILES NORTHEAST OF GOTHAM SOUND...
OLD CHUM
WE'RE ALL SUITED UP AND READY, SIR...
GOOD, JIMMY. I'M GOING WITH YA.
DO YOU THINK THAT'S WISE, MISTER--
WHOA!
I'M LEAVIN' NOTHIN' TO CHANCE THIS TIME, JIMMY...
THAT TREASURE DOWN THERE'S MINE--
AND THIS WHALE'S GOT A HARPOON FOR ANYBODY WHO GETS BETWEEN ME AND MY BOUNTY!

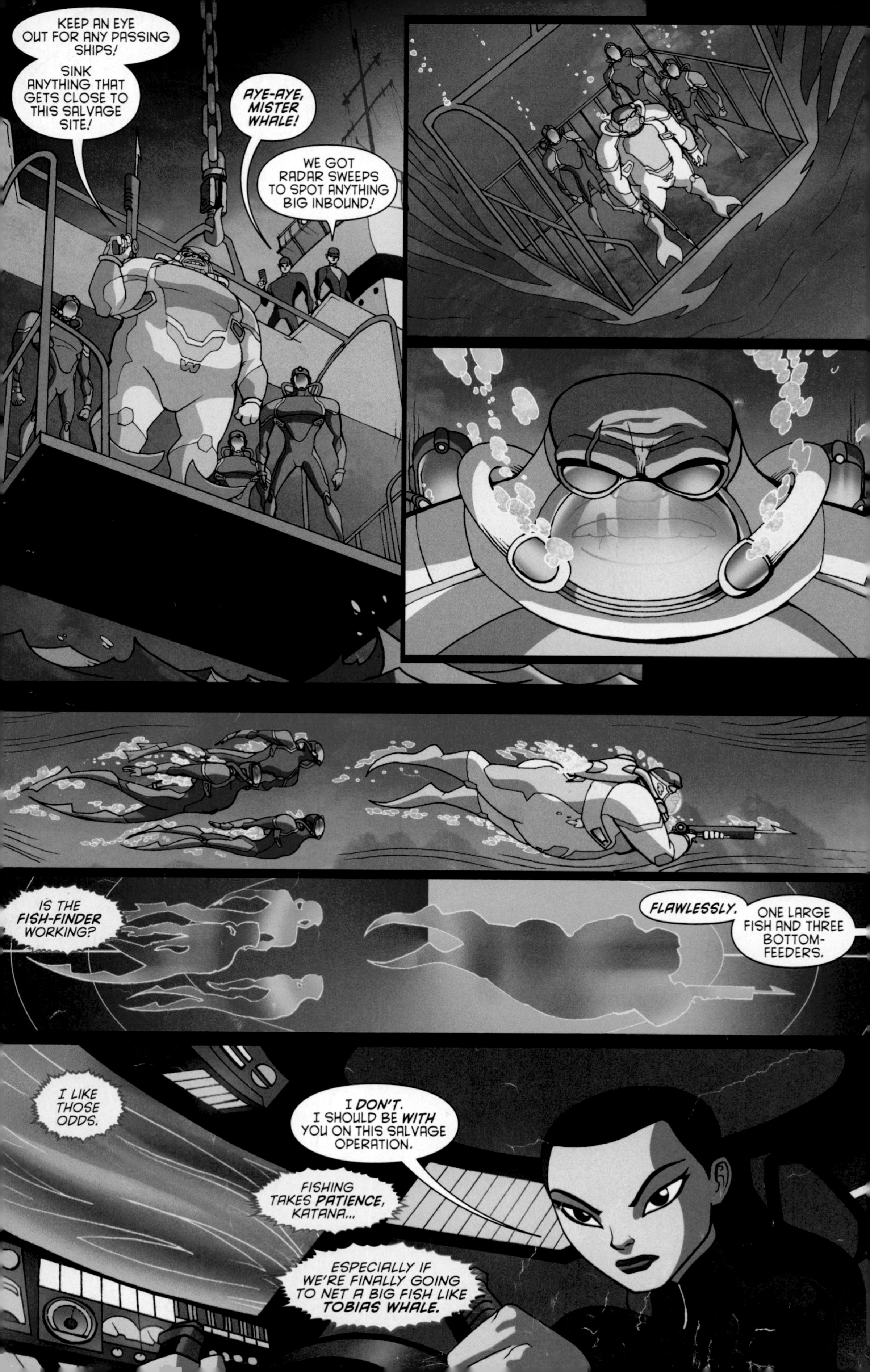
KEEP AN EYE OUT FOR ANY PASSING SHIPS!
SINK ANYTHING THAT GETS CLOSE TO THIS SALVAGE SITE!
AYE-AYE, MISTER WHALE!
WE GOT RADAR SWEEPS TO SPOT ANYTHING BIG INBOUND!
IS THE FISH-FINDER WORKING?
FLAWLESSLY.
ONE LARGE FISH AND THREE BOTTOM-FEEDERS.
I LIKE THOSE ODDS.
I DON'T. I SHOULD BE WITH YOU ON THIS SALVAGE OPERATION.
FISHING TAKES PATIENCE, KATANA...
ESPECIALLY IF WE'RE FINALLY GOING TO NET A BIG FISH LIKE TOBIAS WHALE.

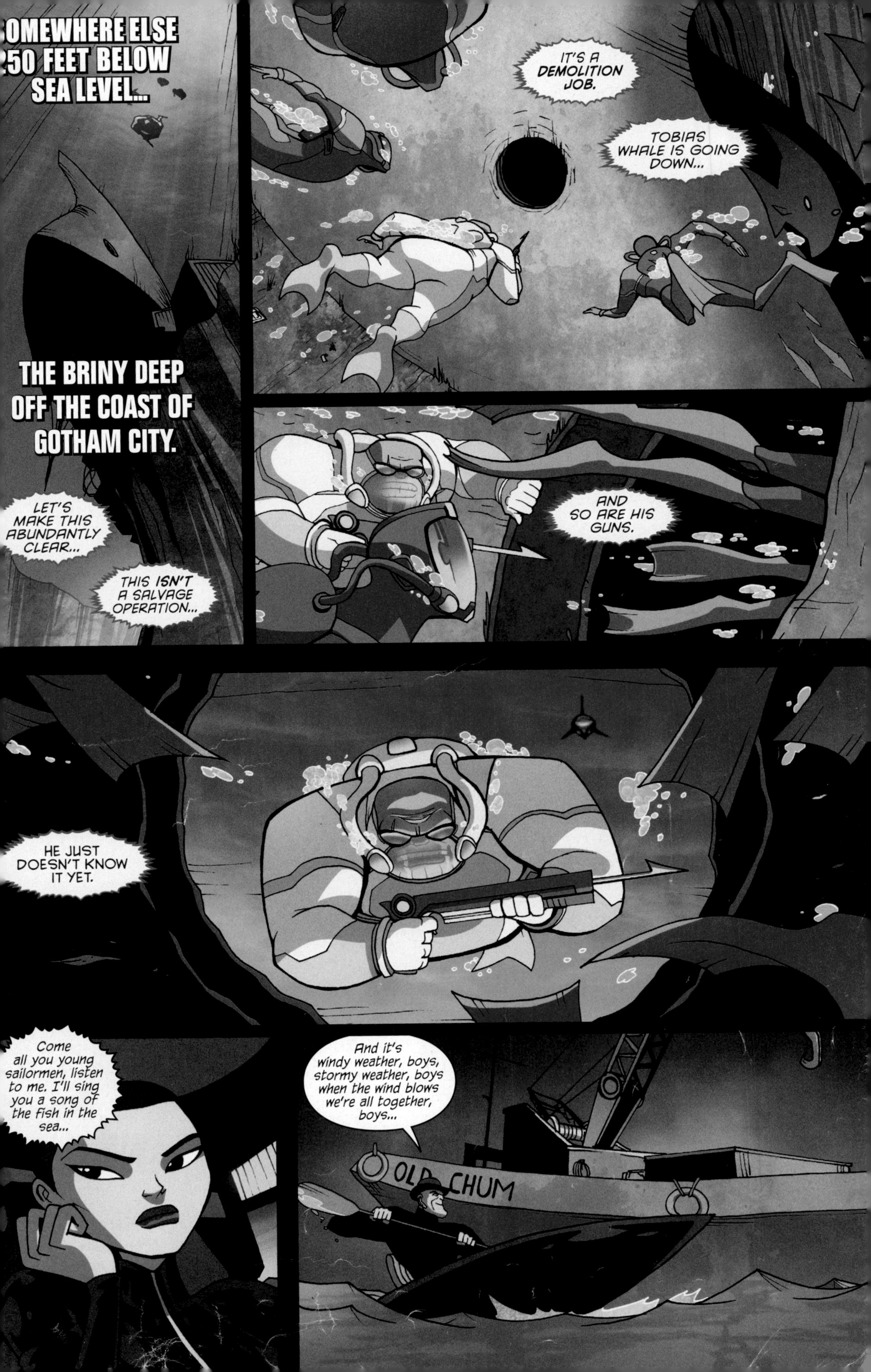
OMEWHERE ELSE 50 FEET BELOW SEA LEVEL...
THE BRINY DEEP OFF THE COAST OF GOTHAM CITY.
IT'S A DEMOLITION JOB.
TOBIAS WHALE IS GOING DOWN...
LET'S MAKE THIS ABUNDANTLY CLEAR...
THIS ISN'T A SALVAGE OPERATION...
AND SO ARE HIS GUNS.
HE JUST DOESN'T KNOW IT YET.
Come all you young sailormen, listen to me. I'll sing you a song of the fish in the sea...
And it's windy weather, boys, stormy weather, boys when the wind blows we're all together, boys...
OLD CHUM

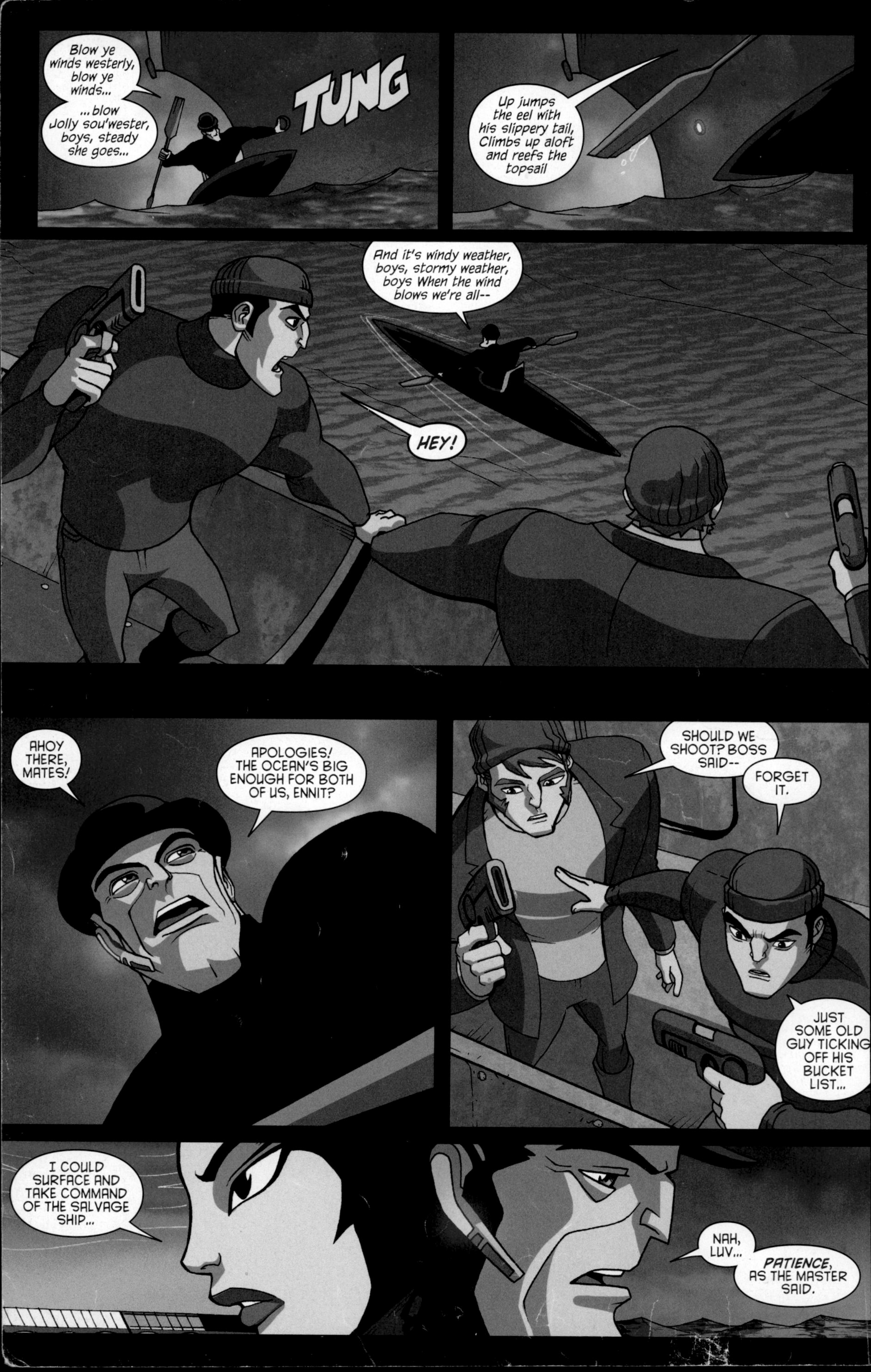
Blow ye winds westerly, blow ye winds...
...blow Jolly sou'wester, boys, steady she goes...
TUNG
Up jumps the eel with his slippery tail, Climbs up aloft and reefs the topsail
And it's windy weather, boys, stormy weather, boys When the wind blows we're all--
HEY!
AHOY THERE, MATES!
APOLOGIES! THE OCEAN'S BIG ENOUGH FOR BOTH OF US, ENNIT?
SHOULD WE SHOOT? BOSS SAID--
FORGET IT.
JUST SOME OLD GUY TICKING OFF HIS BUCKET LIST...
I COULD SURFACE AND TAKE COMMAND OF THE SALVAGE SHIP...
NAH, LUV... PATIENCE, AS THE MASTER SAID.

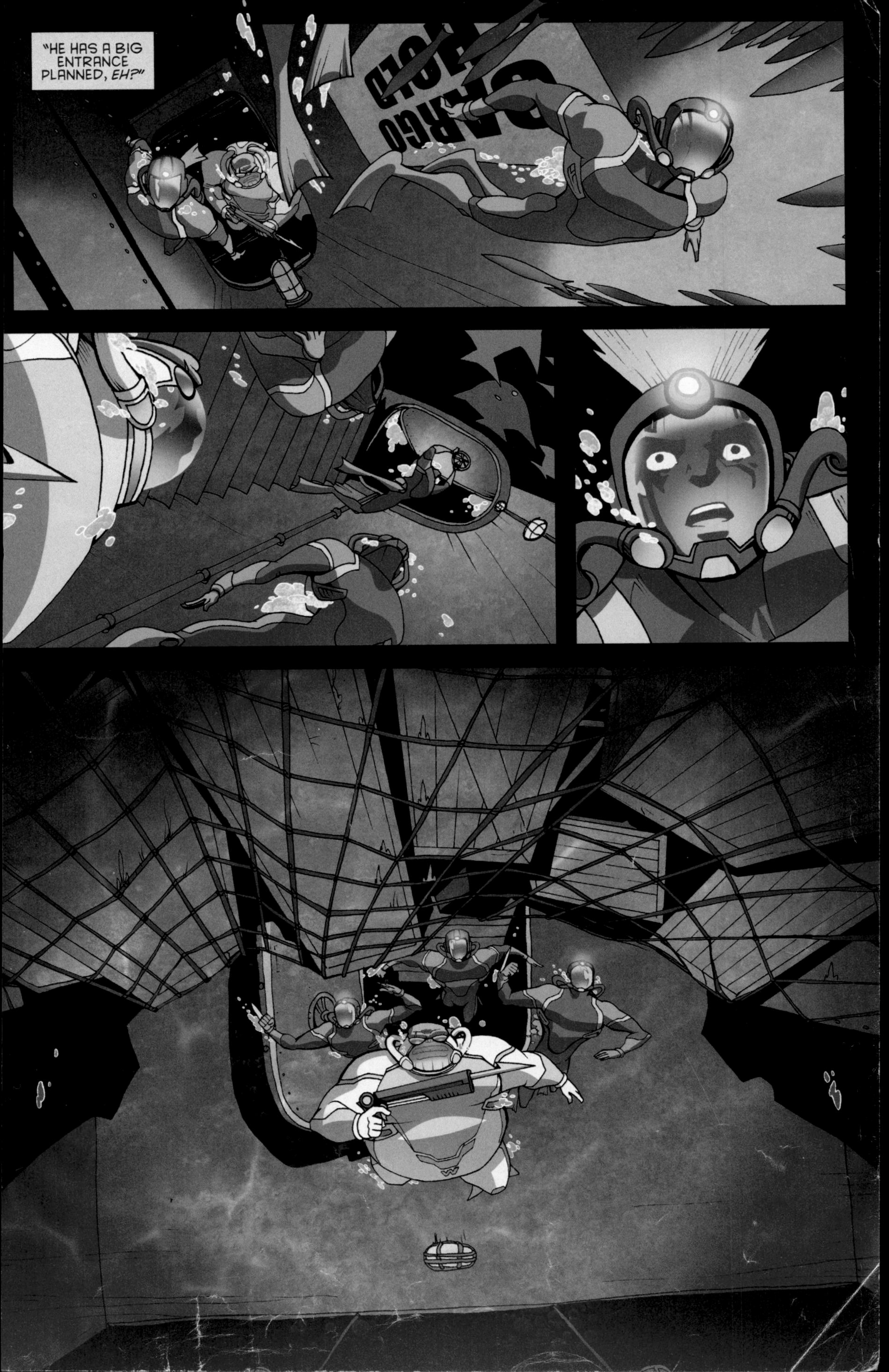
"HE HAS A BIG ENTRANCE PLANNED, EH?"
CARGO HOLD

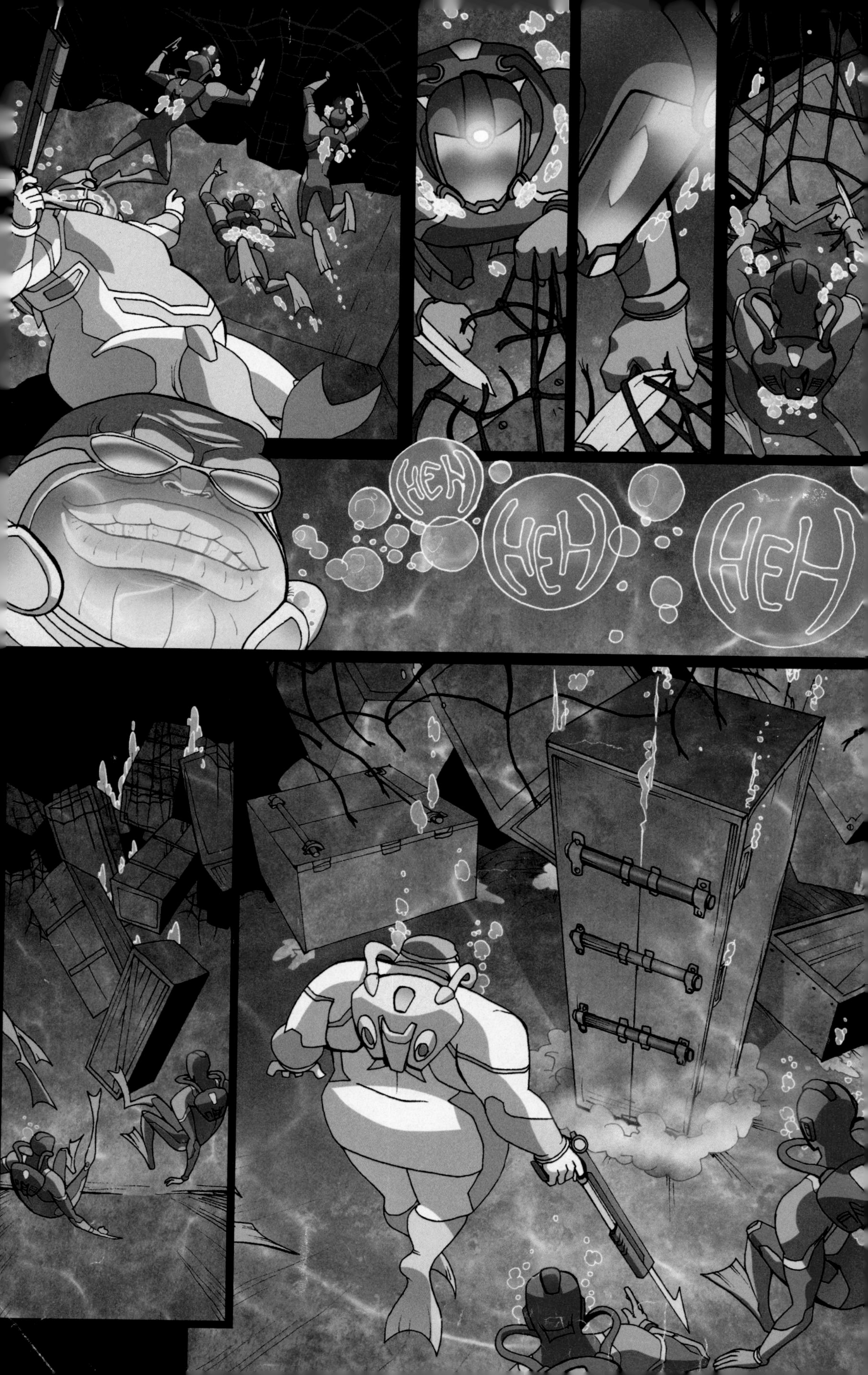
HEH
HEH
HEH

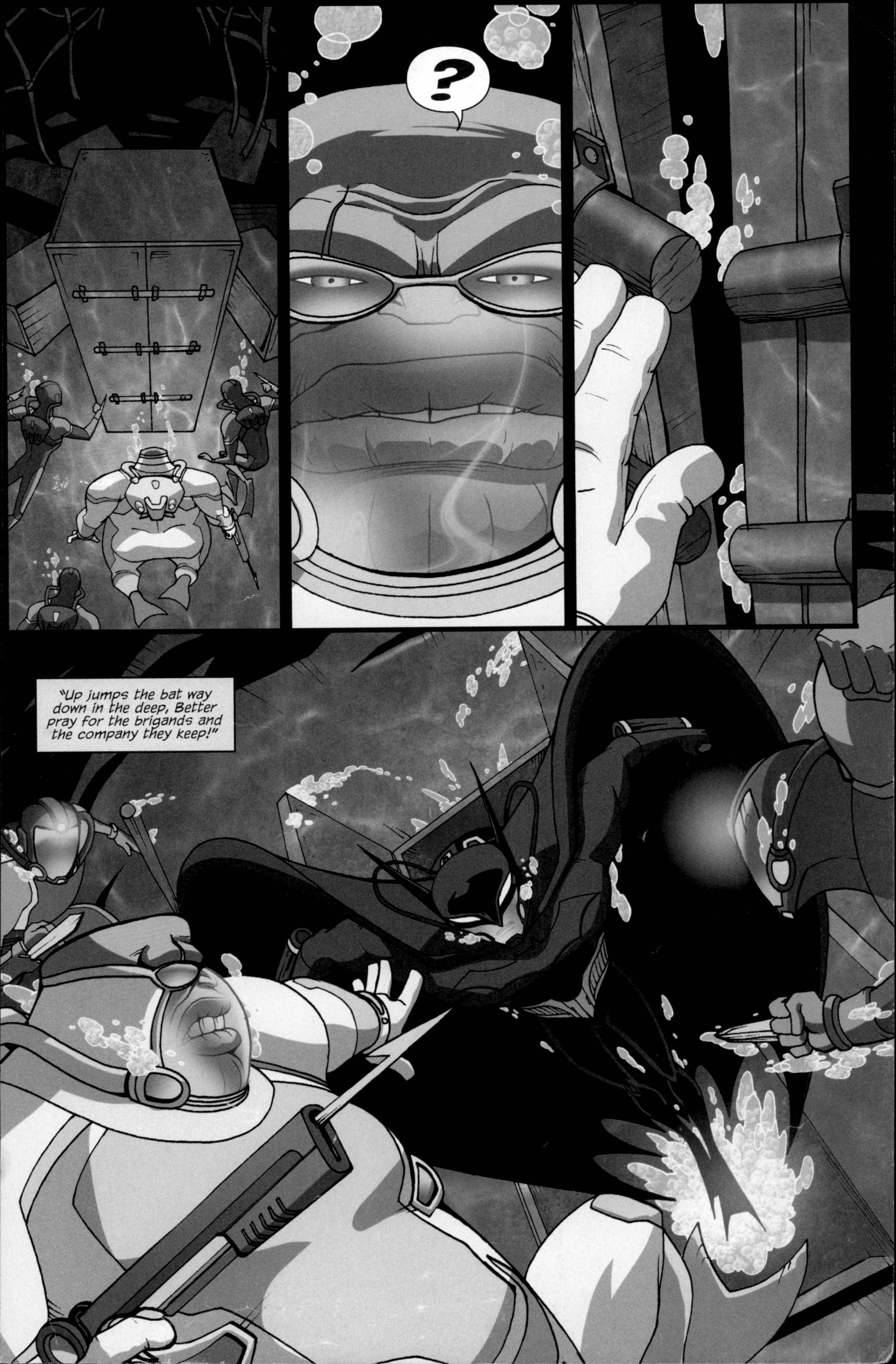
?
"Up jumps the bat way down in the deep, Better pray for the brigands and the company they keep!"

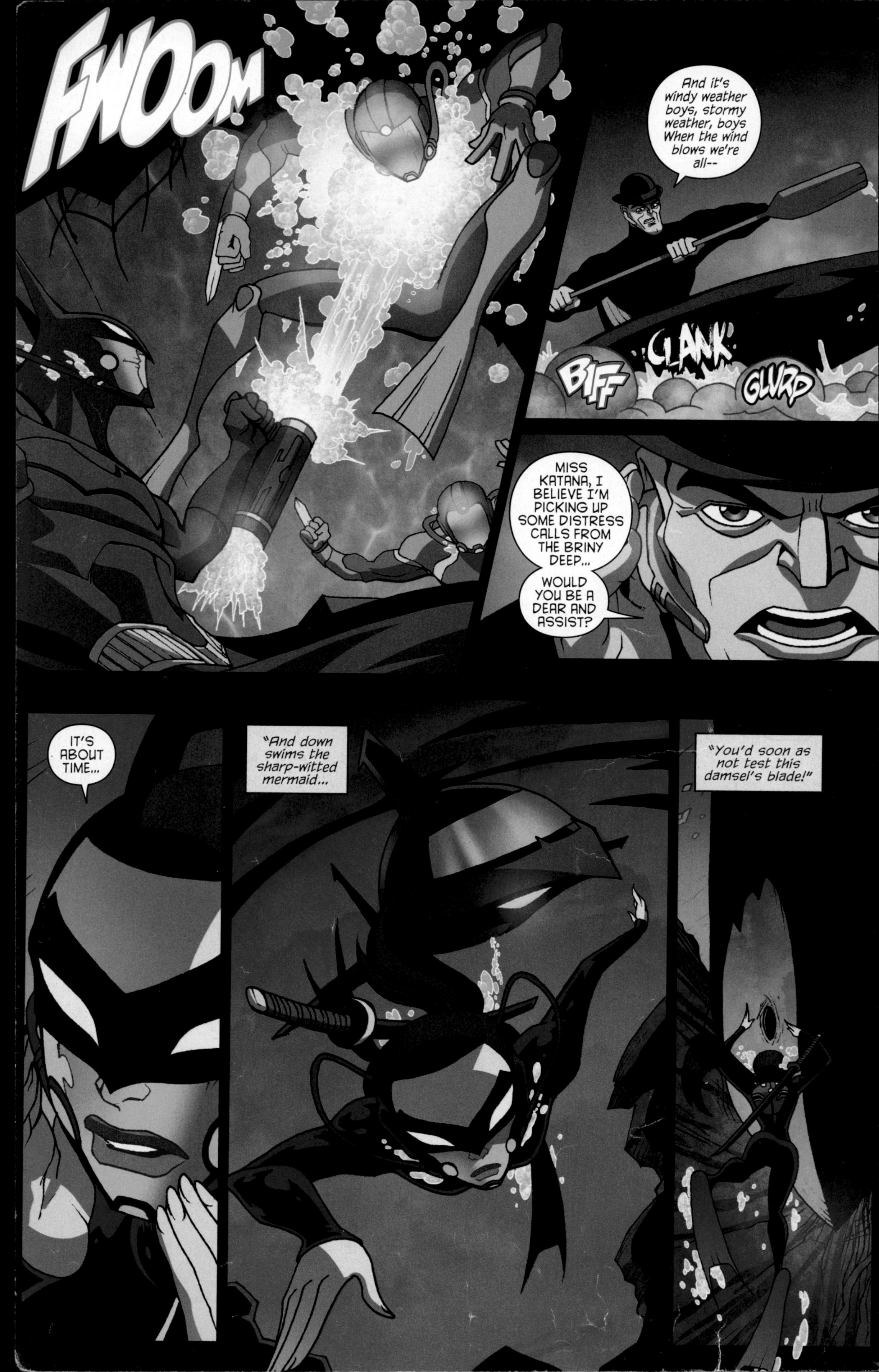
FWOOM
And it's windy weather boys, stormy weather, boys When the wind blows we're all--
BIFF
CLANK
GLURP
MISS KATANA, I BELIEVE I'M PICKING UP SOME DISTRESS CALLS FROM THE BRINY DEEP...
WOULD YOU BE A DEAR AND ASSIST?
IT'S ABOUT TIME...
"And down swims the sharp-witted mermaid...
"You'd soon as not test this damsel's blade!"

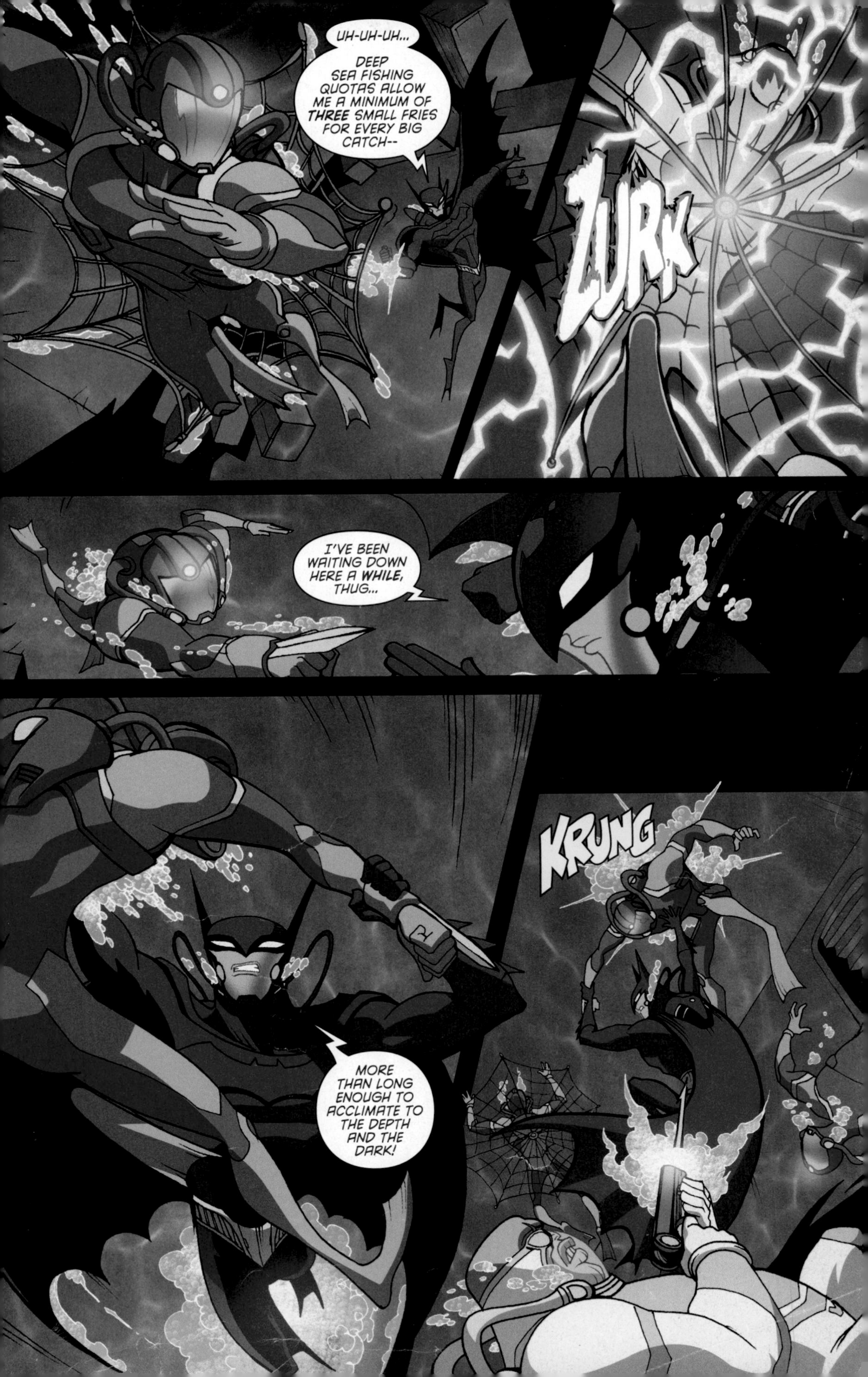
UH-UH-UH...
DEEP SEA FISHING QUOTAS ALLOW ME A MINIMUM OF THREE SMALL FRIES FOR EVERY BIG CATCH--
ZURK
I'VE BEEN WAITING DOWN HERE A WHILE, THUG...
MORE THAN LONG ENOUGH TO ACCLIMATE TO THE DEPTH AND THE DARK!
KRUNG

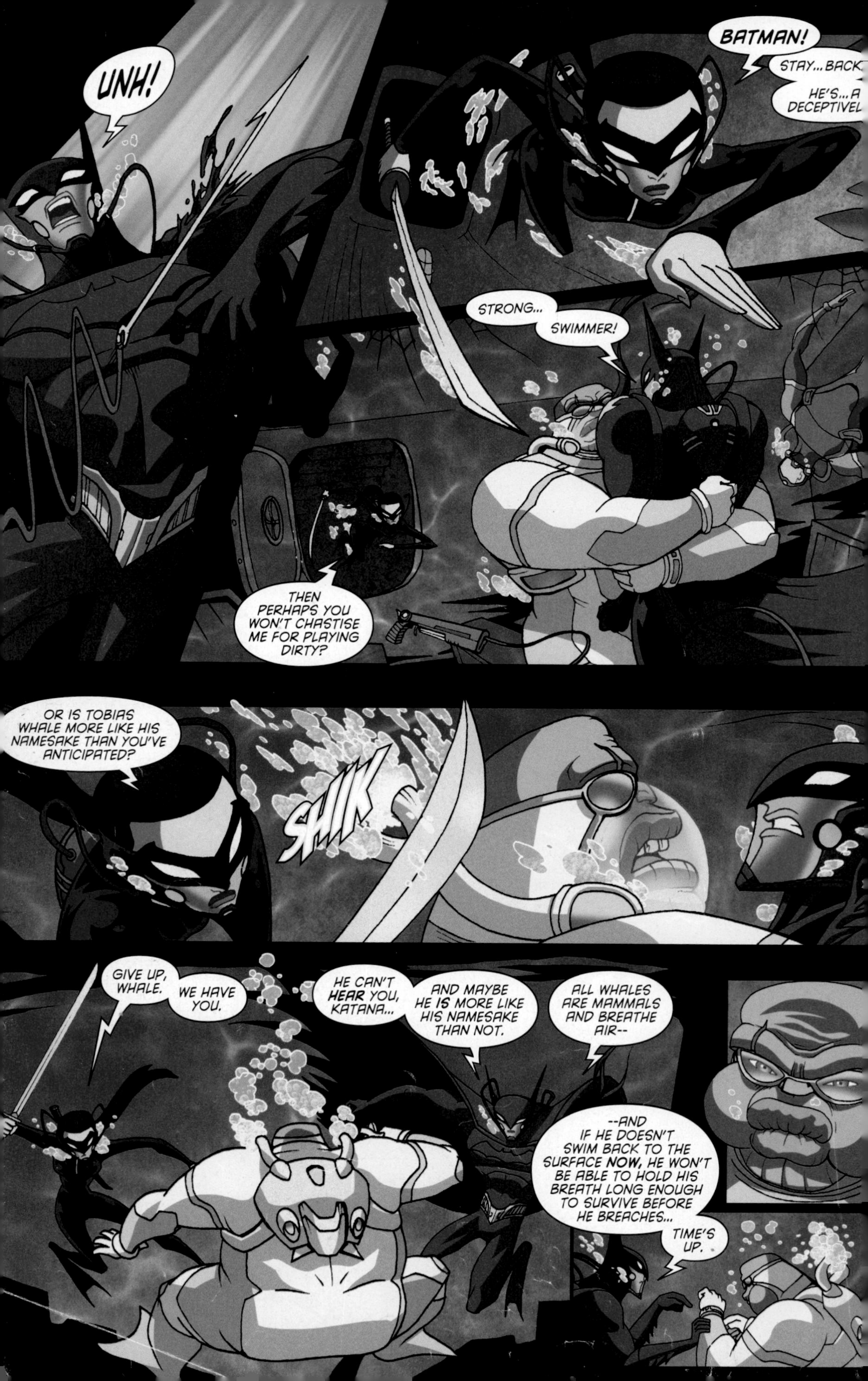
UNH!
BATMAN!
STAY... BACK.
HE'S... A DECEPTIVEL
STRONG...
SWIMMER!
THEN PERHAPS YOU WON'T CHASTISE ME FOR PLAYING DIRTY?
OR IS TOBIAS WHALE MORE LIKE HIS NAMESAKE THAN YOU'VE ANTICIPATED?
SHIK
GIVE UP, WHALE.
WE HAVE YOU.
HE CAN'T HEAR YOU, KATANA...
AND MAYBE HE IS MORE LIKE HIS NAMESAKE THAN NOT.
ALL WHALES ARE MAMMALS AND BREATHE AIR--
--AND IF HE DOESN'T SWIM BACK TO THE SURFACE NOW, HE WON'T BE ABLE TO HOLD HIS BREATH LONG ENOUGH TO SURVIVE BEFORE HE BREACHES...
TIME'S UP.

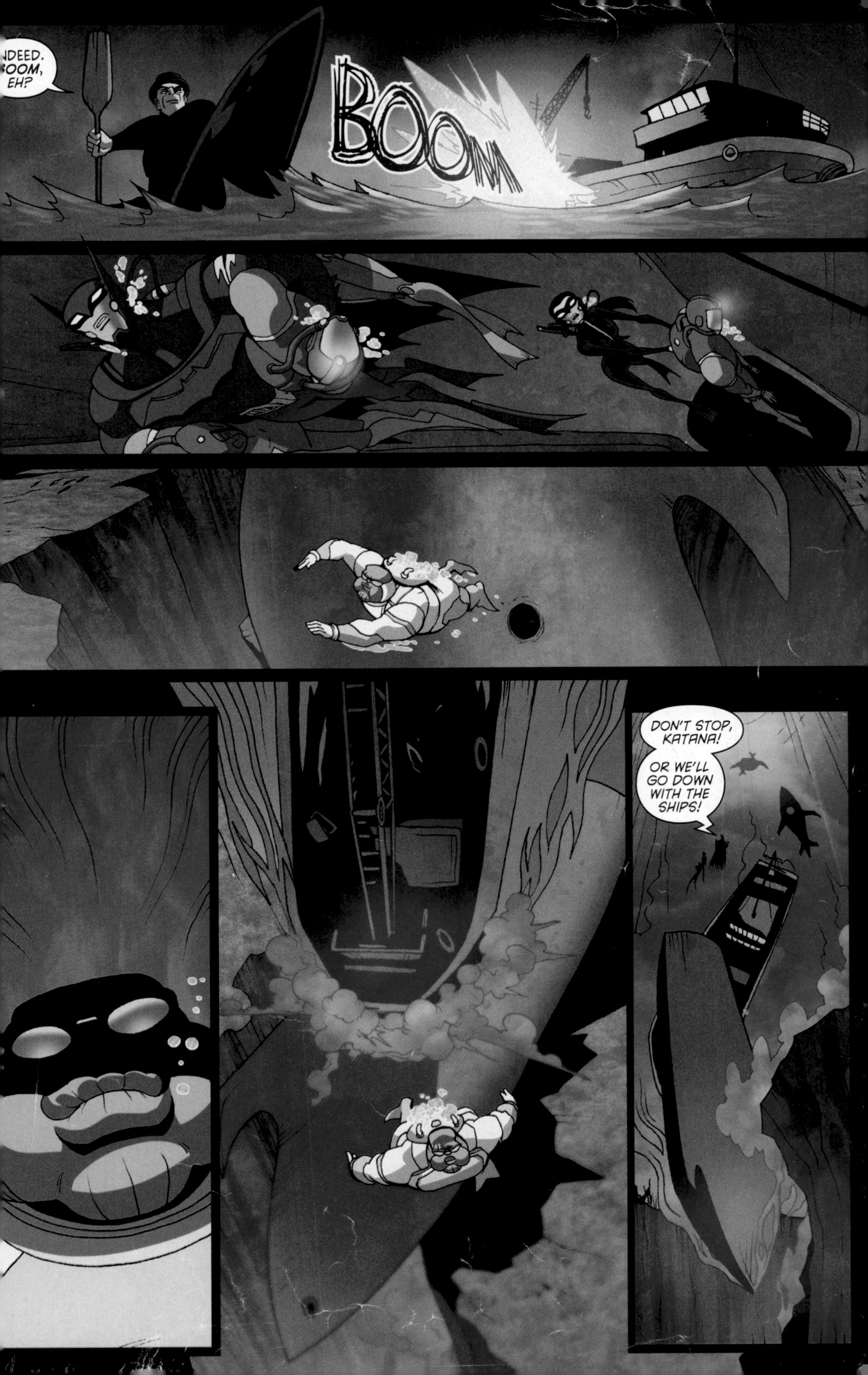
NDEED. BOOM, EH?
BOOM
DON'T STOP, KATANA!
OR WE'LL GO DOWN WITH THE SHIPS!

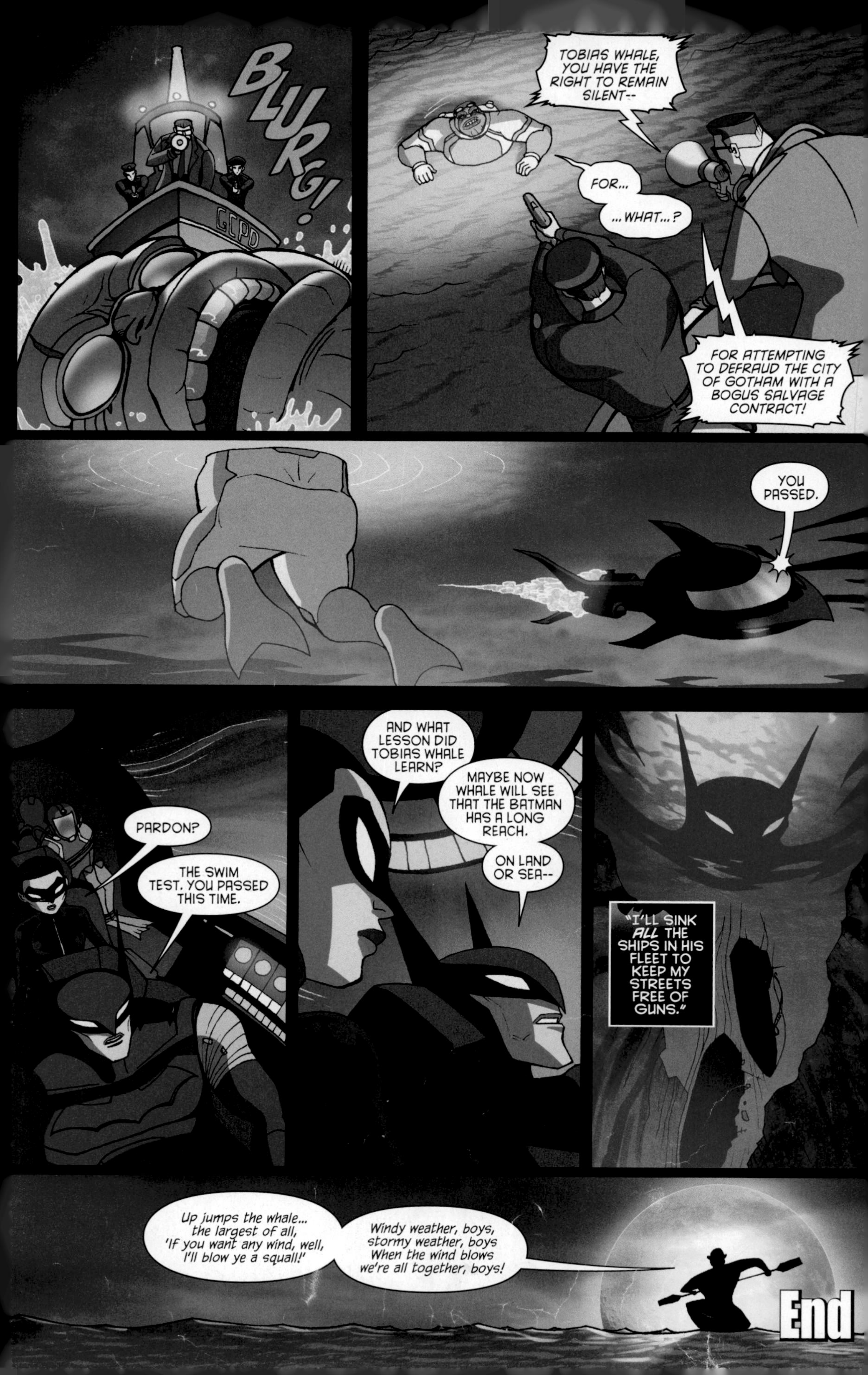
BLURG!
GCPD
TOBIAS WHALE, YOU HAVE THE RIGHT TO REMAIN SILENT--
FOR...
...WHAT...?
FOR ATTEMPTING TO DEFRAUD THE CITY OF GOTHAM WITH A BOGUS SALVAGE CONTRACT!
YOU PASSED.
PARDON?
THE SWIM TEST. YOU PASSED THIS TIME.
AND WHAT LESSON DID TOBIAS WHALE LEARN?
MAYBE NOW WHALE WILL SEE THAT THE BATMAN HAS A LONG REACH.
ON LAND OR SEA--
"I'LL SINK ALL THE SHIPS IN HIS FLEET TO KEEP MY STREETS FREE OF GUNS."
Up jumps the whale... the largest of all, 'If you want any wind, well, I'll blow ye a squall!'
Windy weather, boys, stormy weather, boys When the wind blows we're all together, boys!
End

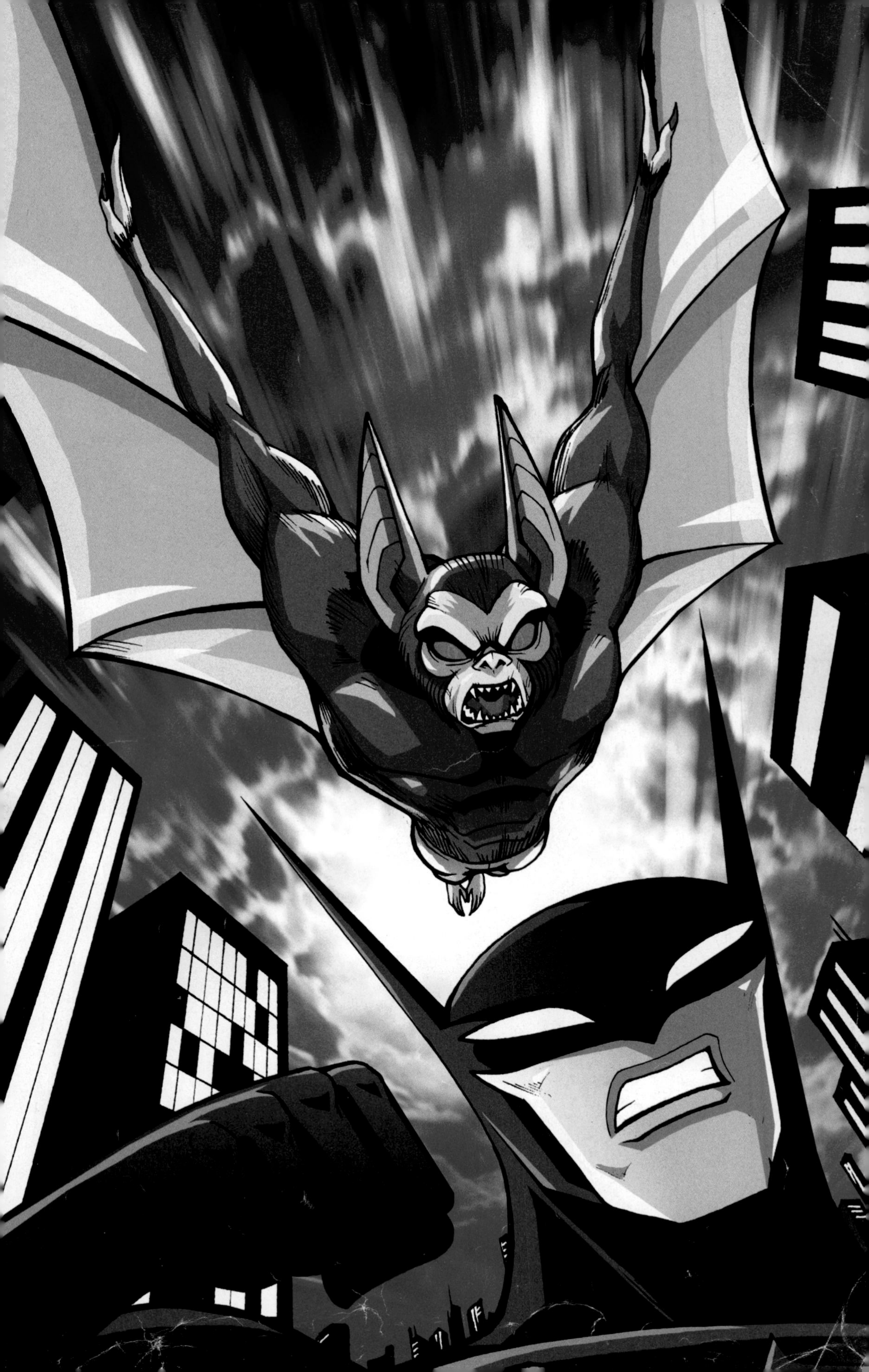

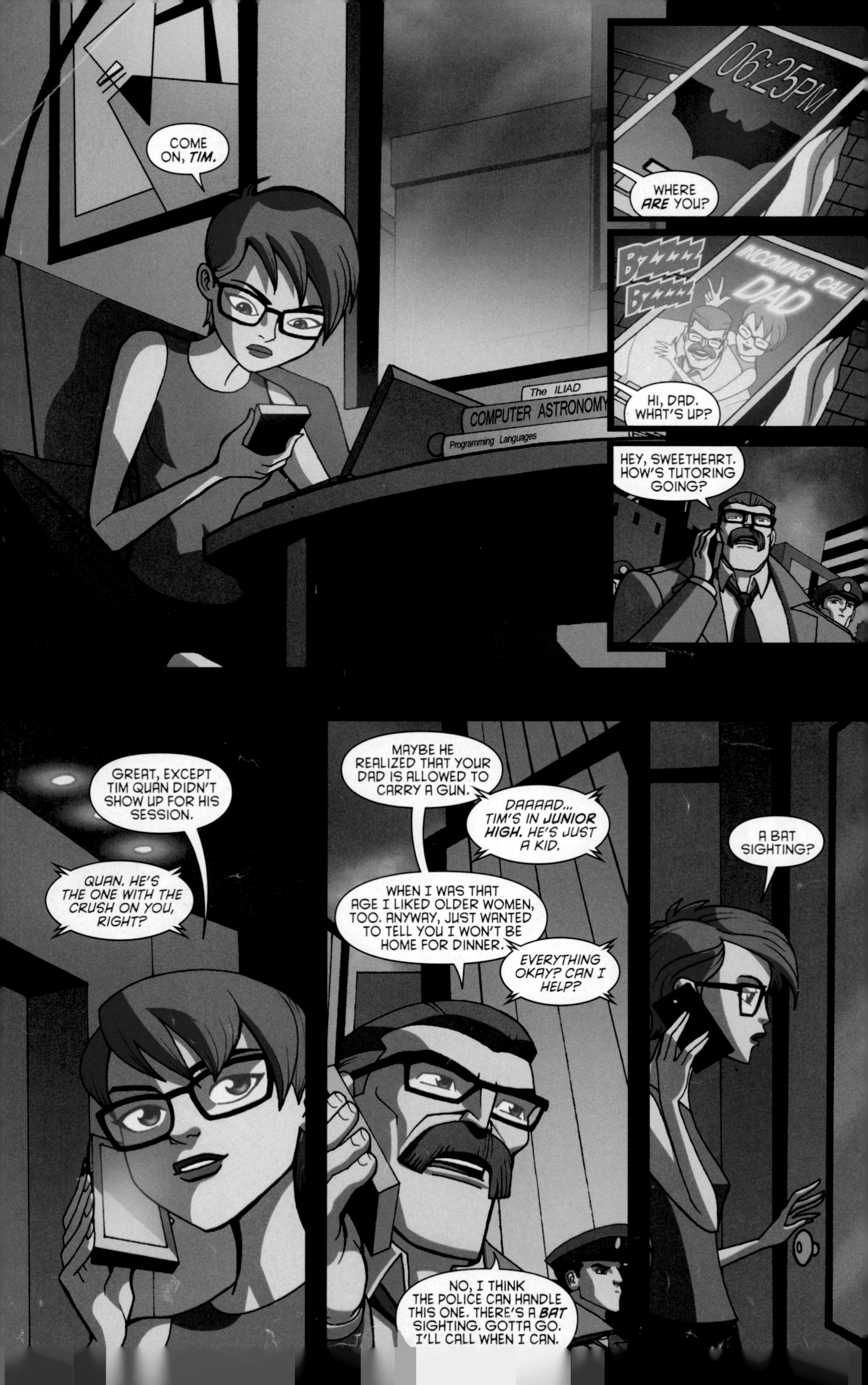
COME ON, TIM.
The ILIAD
COMPUTER ASTRONOMY
Programming Languages
06:25PM
WHERE ARE YOU?
BZZZ BZZZ
INCOMING CALL DAD
HI, DAD. WHAT'S UP?
HEY, SWEETHEART. HOW'S TUTORING GOING?
GREAT, EXCEPT TIM QUAN DIDN'T SHOW UP FOR HIS SESSION.
QUAN. HE'S THE ONE WITH THE CRUSH ON YOU, RIGHT?
MAYBE HE REALIZED THAT YOUR DAD IS ALLOWED TO CARRY A GUN.
DAAAAD... TIM'S IN JUNIOR HIGH. HE'S JUST A KID.
WHEN I WAS THAT AGE I LIKED OLDER WOMEN, TOO. ANYWAY, JUST WANTED TO TELL YOU I WON'T BE HOME FOR DINNER.
EVERYTHING OKAY? CAN I HELP?
NO, I THINK THE POLICE CAN HANDLE THIS ONE. THERE'S A BAT SIGHTING. GOTTA GO. I'LL CALL WHEN I CAN.
A BAT SIGHTING?

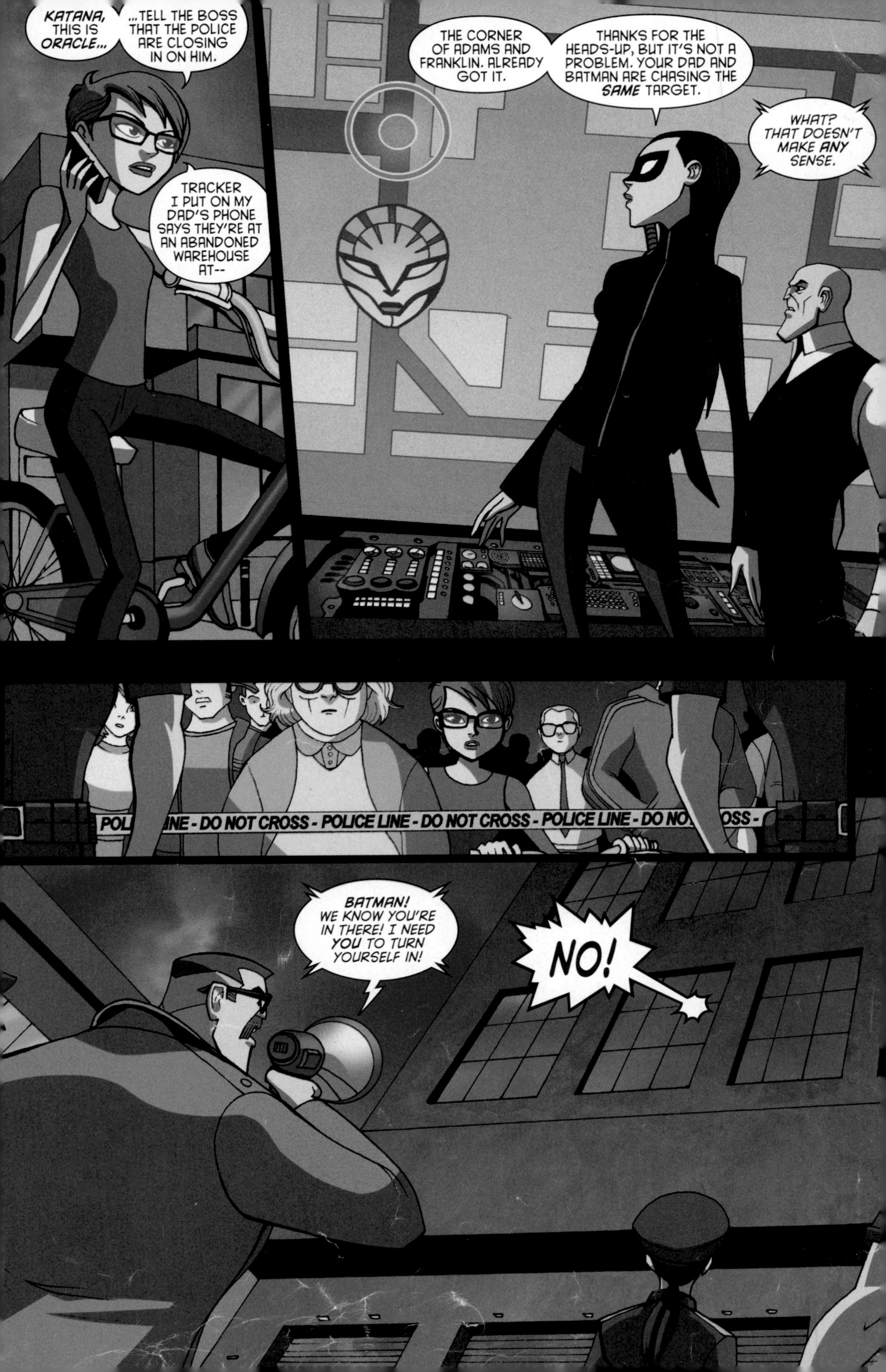
KATANA, THIS IS ORACLE...
...TELL THE BOSS THAT THE POLICE ARE CLOSING IN ON HIM.
TRACKER I PUT ON MY DAD'S PHONE SAYS THEY'RE AT AN ABANDONED WAREHOUSE AT--
THE CORNER OF ADAMS AND FRANKLIN. ALREADY GOT IT.
THANKS FOR THE HEADS-UP, BUT IT'S NOT A PROBLEM. YOUR DAD AND BATMAN ARE CHASING THE SAME TARGET.
WHAT? THAT DOESN'T MAKE ANY SENSE.
POLI INE - DO NOT CROSS - POLICE LINE - DO NOT CROSS - POLICE LINE - DO NO OSS -
BATMAN! WE KNOW YOU'RE IN THERE! I NEED YOU TO TURN YOURSELF IN!
NO!

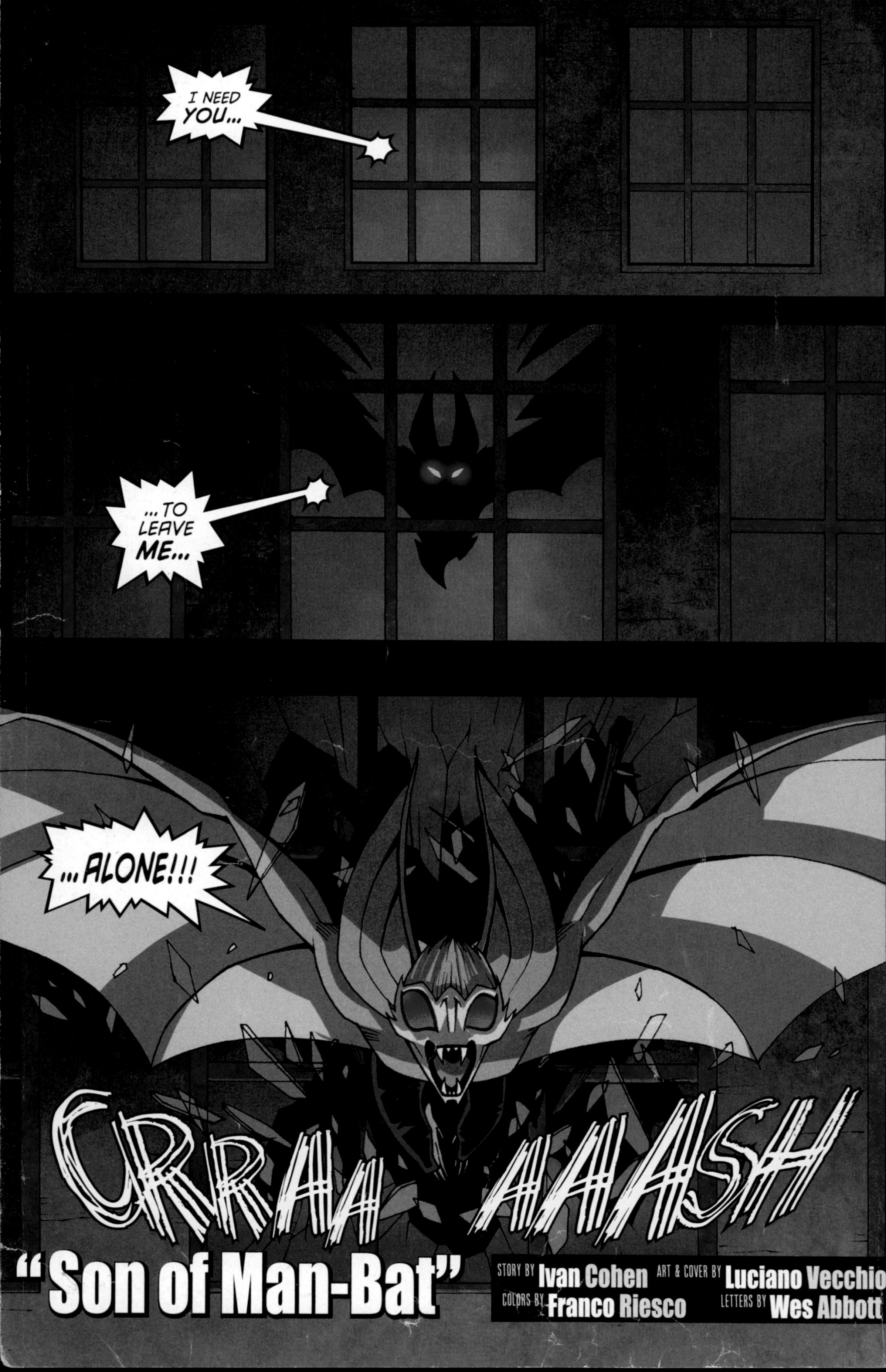
I NEED YOU...
...TO LEAVE ME...
...ALONE!!!
CRRAAAAASH
"Son of Man-Bat"
STORY BY Ivan Cohen ART & COVER BY Luciano Vecchio
COLORS BY Franco Riesco LETTERS BY Wes Abbott

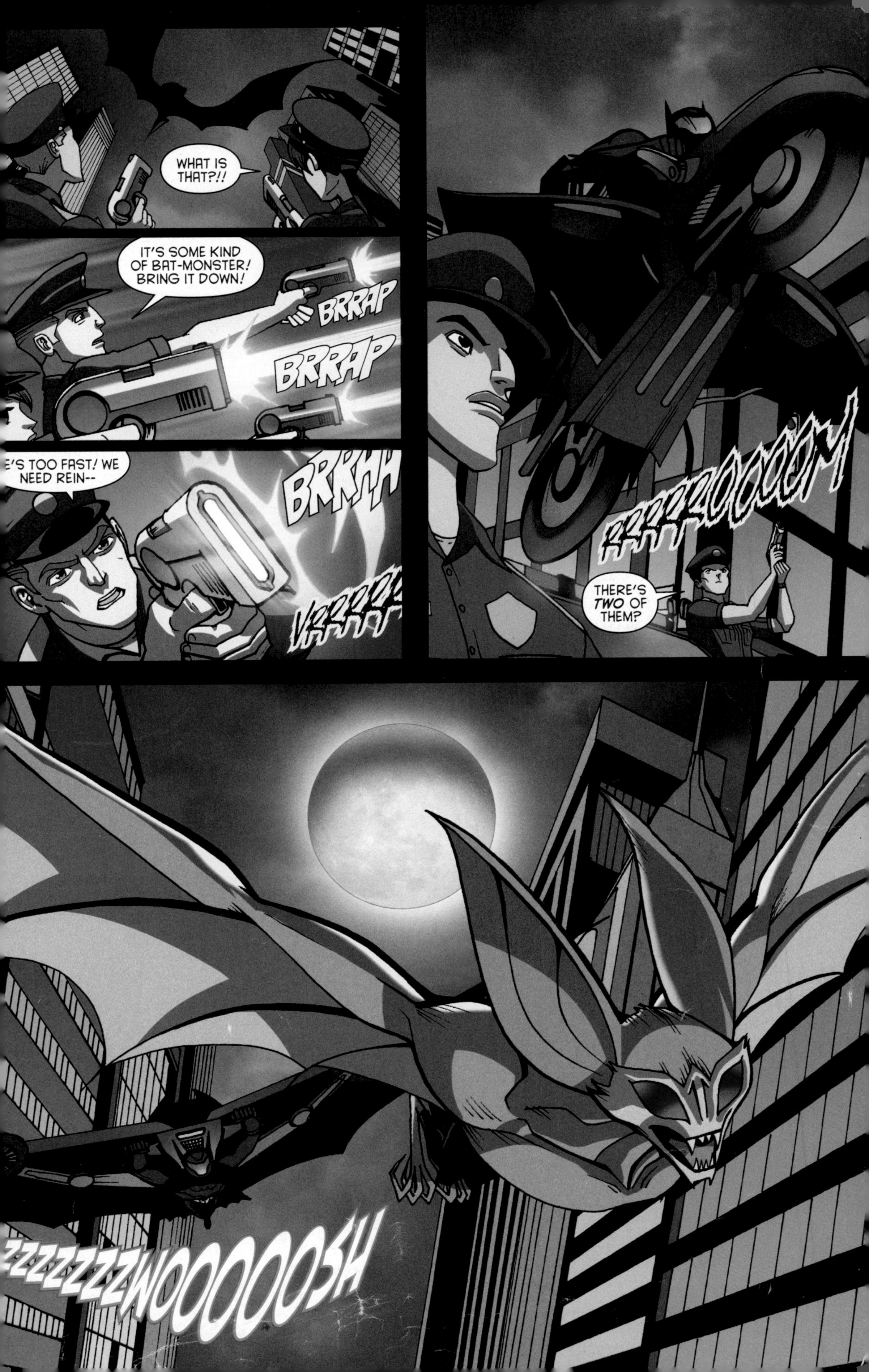
WHAT IS THAT?!!
IT'S SOME KIND OF BAT-MONSTER! BRING IT DOWN!
BRRAP
BRRAP
E'S TOO FAST! WE NEED REIN--
RRRRROOOOOM
THERE'S TWO OF THEM?
ZZZZZZZWOOOOOOSH

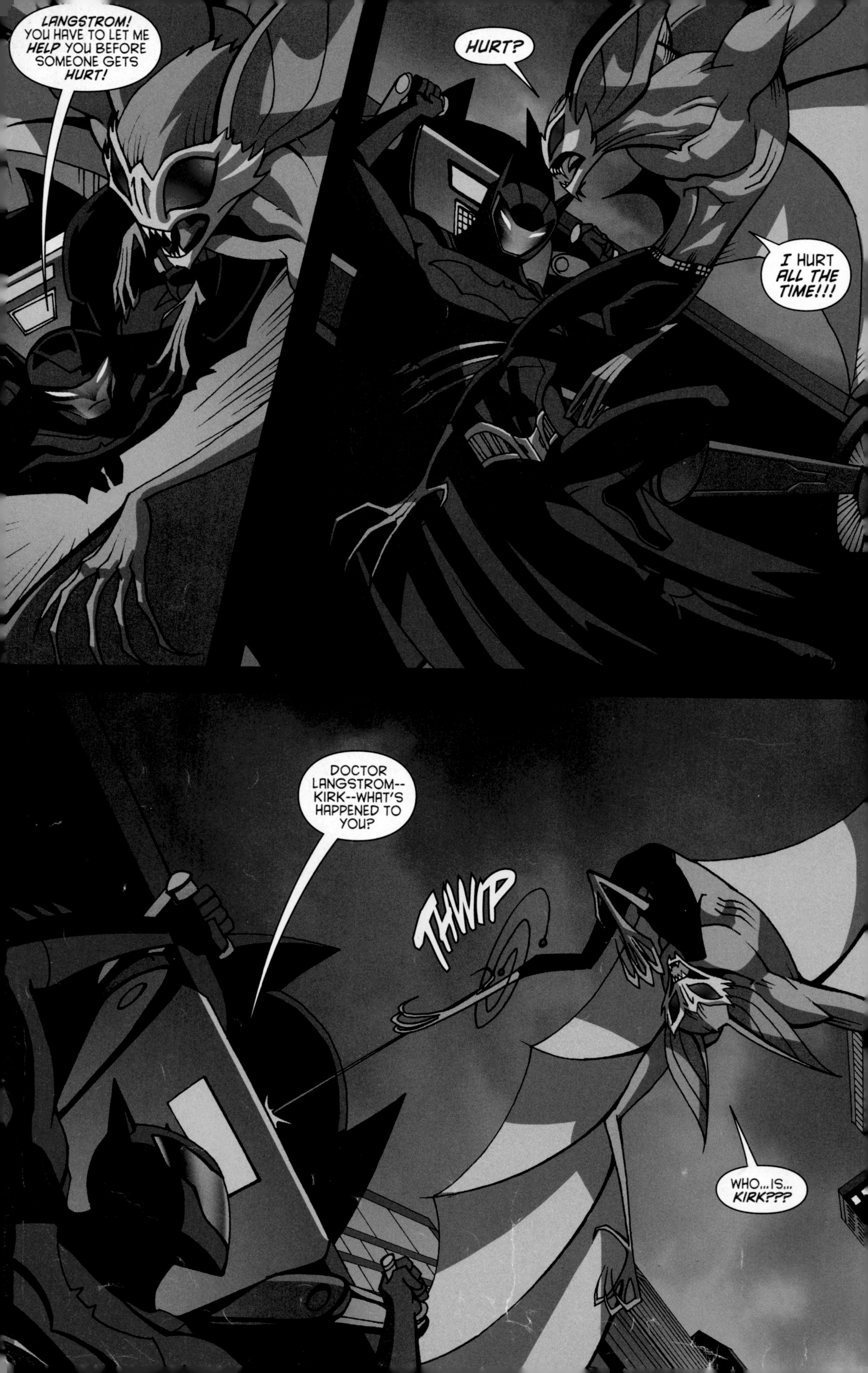
LANGSTROM! YOU HAVE TO LET ME HELP YOU BEFORE SOMEONE GETS HURT!
HURT?
I HURT ALL THE TIME!!!
DOCTOR LANGSTROM--KIRK--WHAT'S HAPPENED TO YOU?
THWIP
WHO...IS... KIRK???

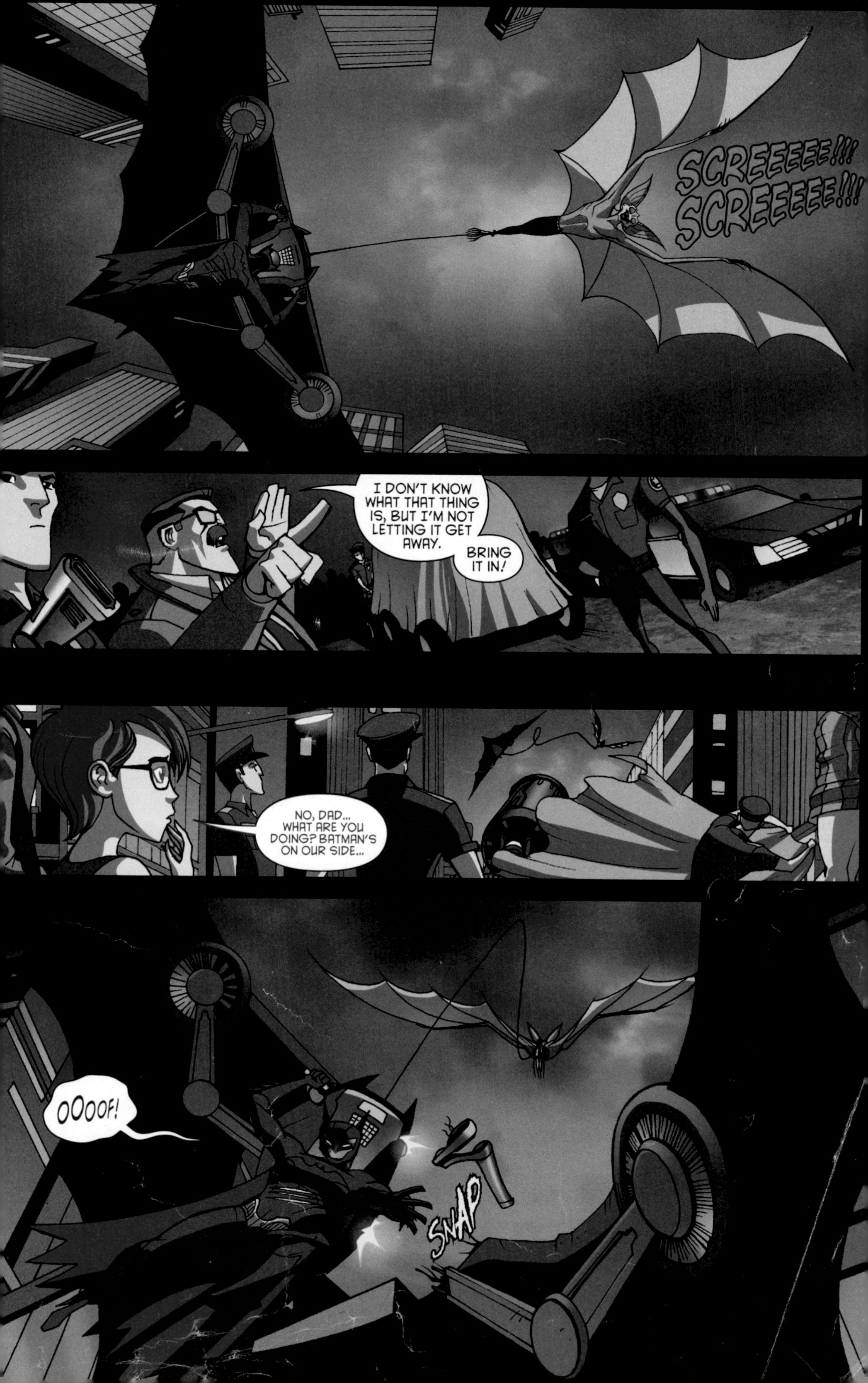
SCREEEEEE!!!
SCREEEEEE!!!
I DON'T KNOW WHAT THAT THING IS, BUT I'M NOT LETTING IT GET AWAY.
BRING IT IN!
NO, DAD... WHAT ARE YOU DOING? BATMAN'S ON OUR SIDE...
OOOOF!
SNAP

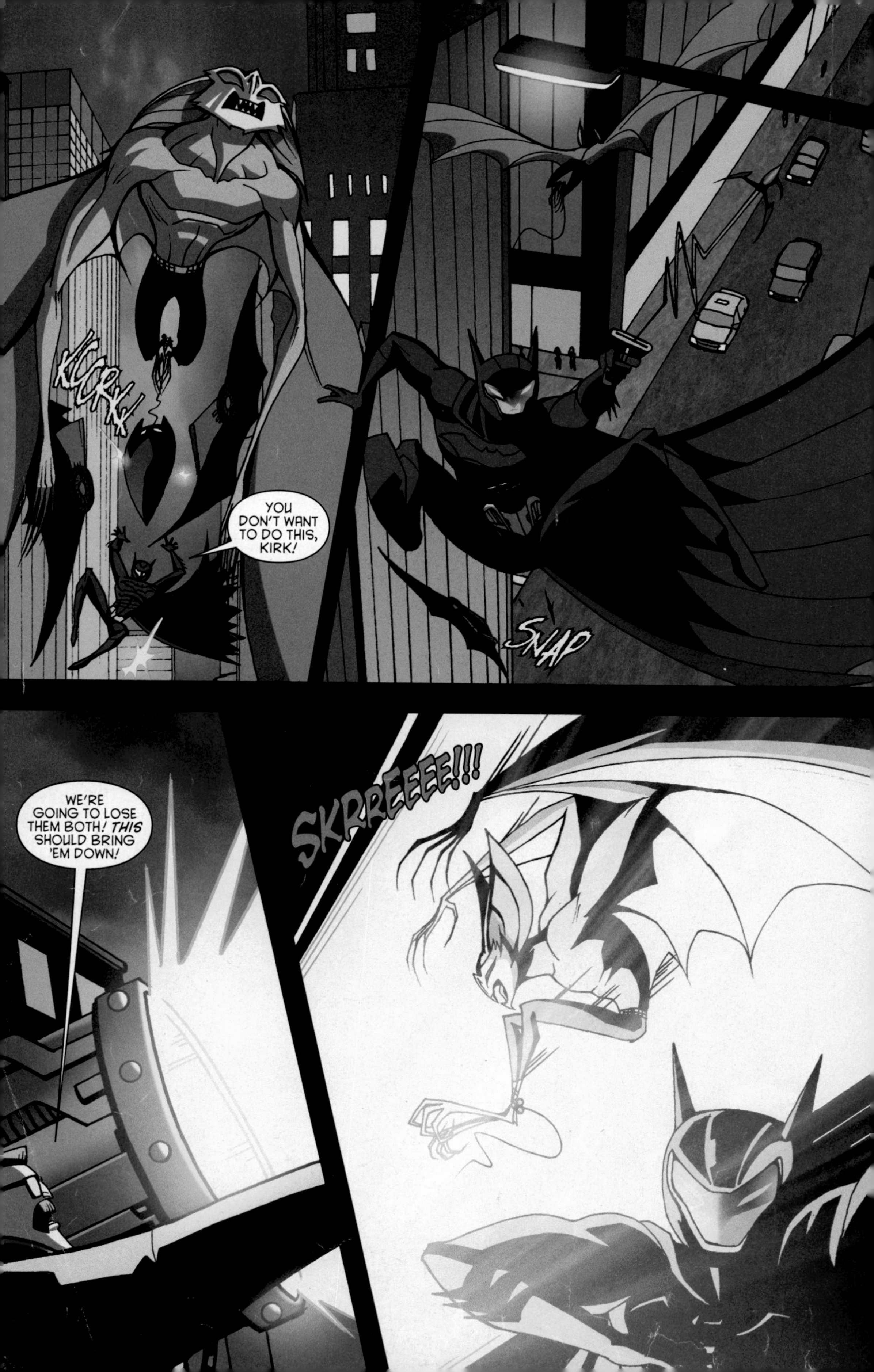
KKCCRKK
YOU DON'T WANT TO DO THIS, KIRK!
SNAP
WE'RE GOING TO LOSE THEM BOTH! THIS SHOULD BRING 'EM DOWN!
SKRREEEE!!!

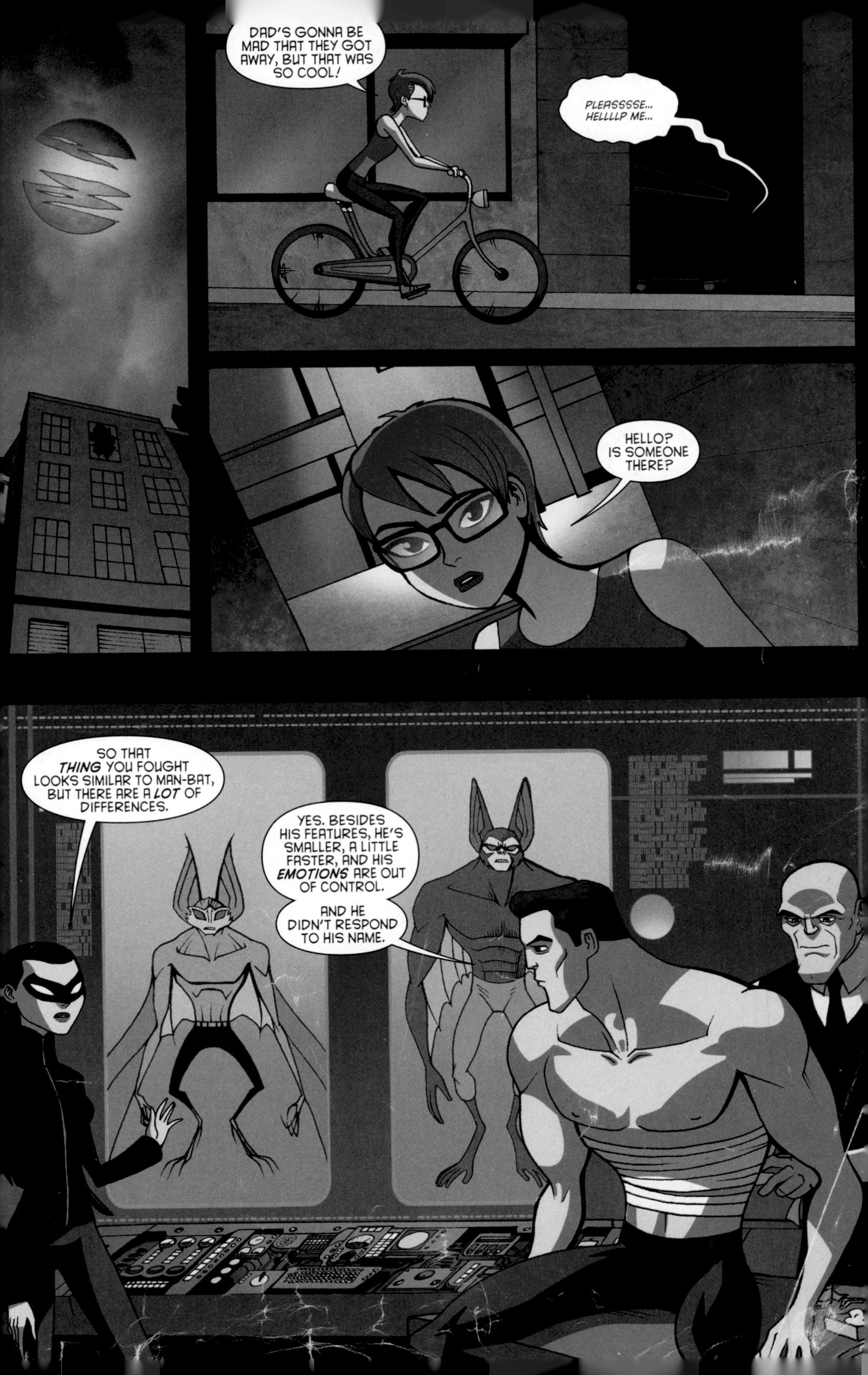
DAD'S GONNA BE MAD THAT THEY GOT AWAY, BUT THAT WAS SO COOL!
PLEASSSSE... HELLLLP ME...
HELLO? IS SOMEONE THERE?
SO THAT *THING* YOU FOUGHT LOOKS SIMILAR TO MAN-BAT, BUT THERE ARE A *LOT* OF DIFFERENCES.
YES. BESIDES HIS FEATURES, HE'S SMALLER, A LITTLE FASTER, AND HIS *EMOTIONS* ARE OUT OF CONTROL.
AND HE DIDN'T RESPOND TO HIS NAME.

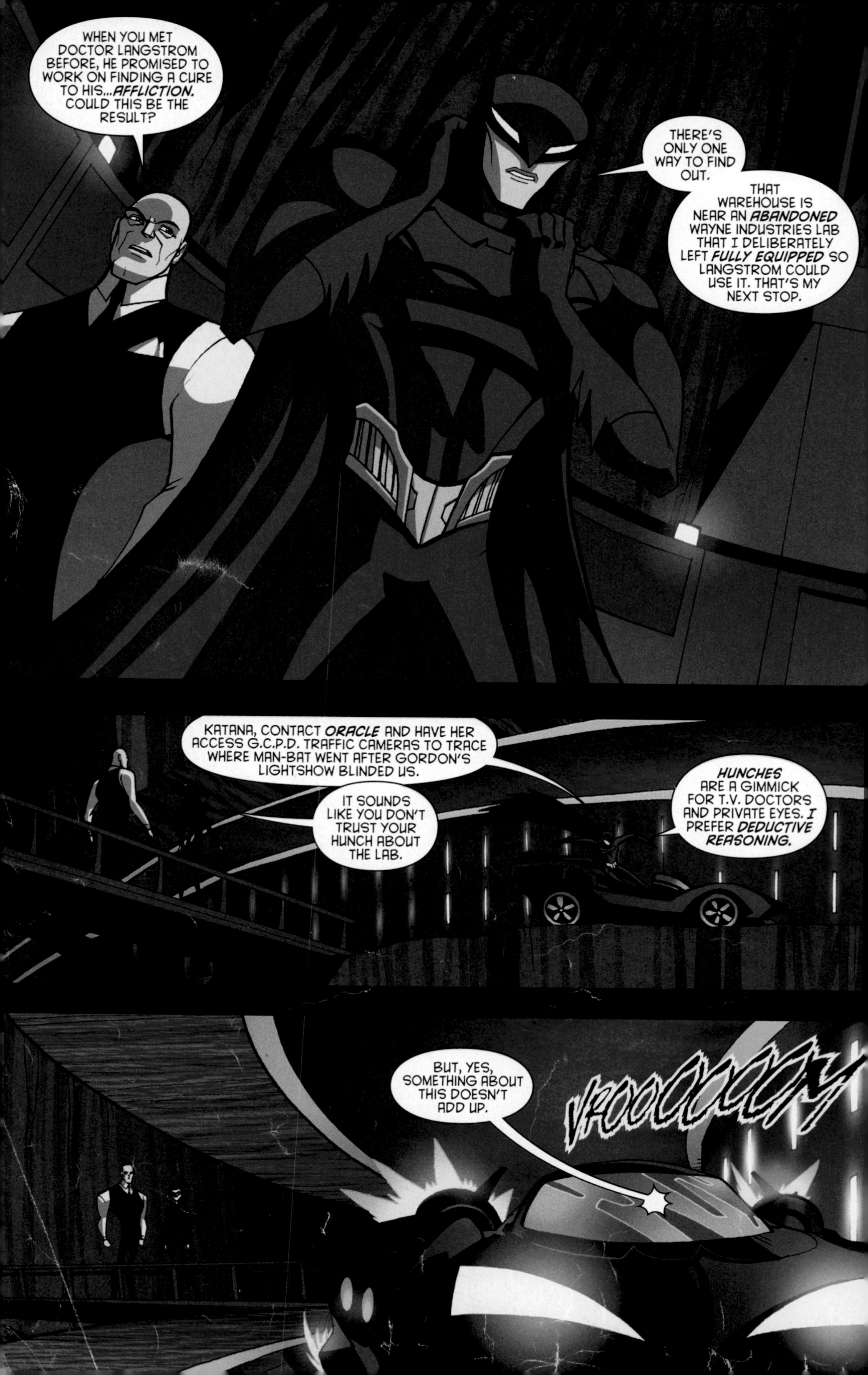
WHEN YOU MET DOCTOR LANGSTROM BEFORE, HE PROMISED TO WORK ON FINDING A CURE TO HIS...AFFLICTION. COULD THIS BE THE RESULT?
THERE'S ONLY ONE WAY TO FIND OUT.
THAT WAREHOUSE IS NEAR AN ABANDONED WAYNE INDUSTRIES LAB THAT I DELIBERATELY LEFT FULLY EQUIPPED SO LANGSTROM COULD USE IT. THAT'S MY NEXT STOP.
KATANA, CONTACT ORACLE AND HAVE HER ACCESS G.C.P.D. TRAFFIC CAMERAS TO TRACE WHERE MAN-BAT WENT AFTER GORDON'S LIGHTSHOW BLINDED US.
IT SOUNDS LIKE YOU DON'T TRUST YOUR HUNCH ABOUT THE LAB.
HUNCHES ARE A GIMMICK FOR T.V. DOCTORS AND PRIVATE EYES. I PREFER DEDUCTIVE REASONING.
BUT, YES, SOMETHING ABOUT THIS DOESN'T ADD UP.
VROOOOOOOM

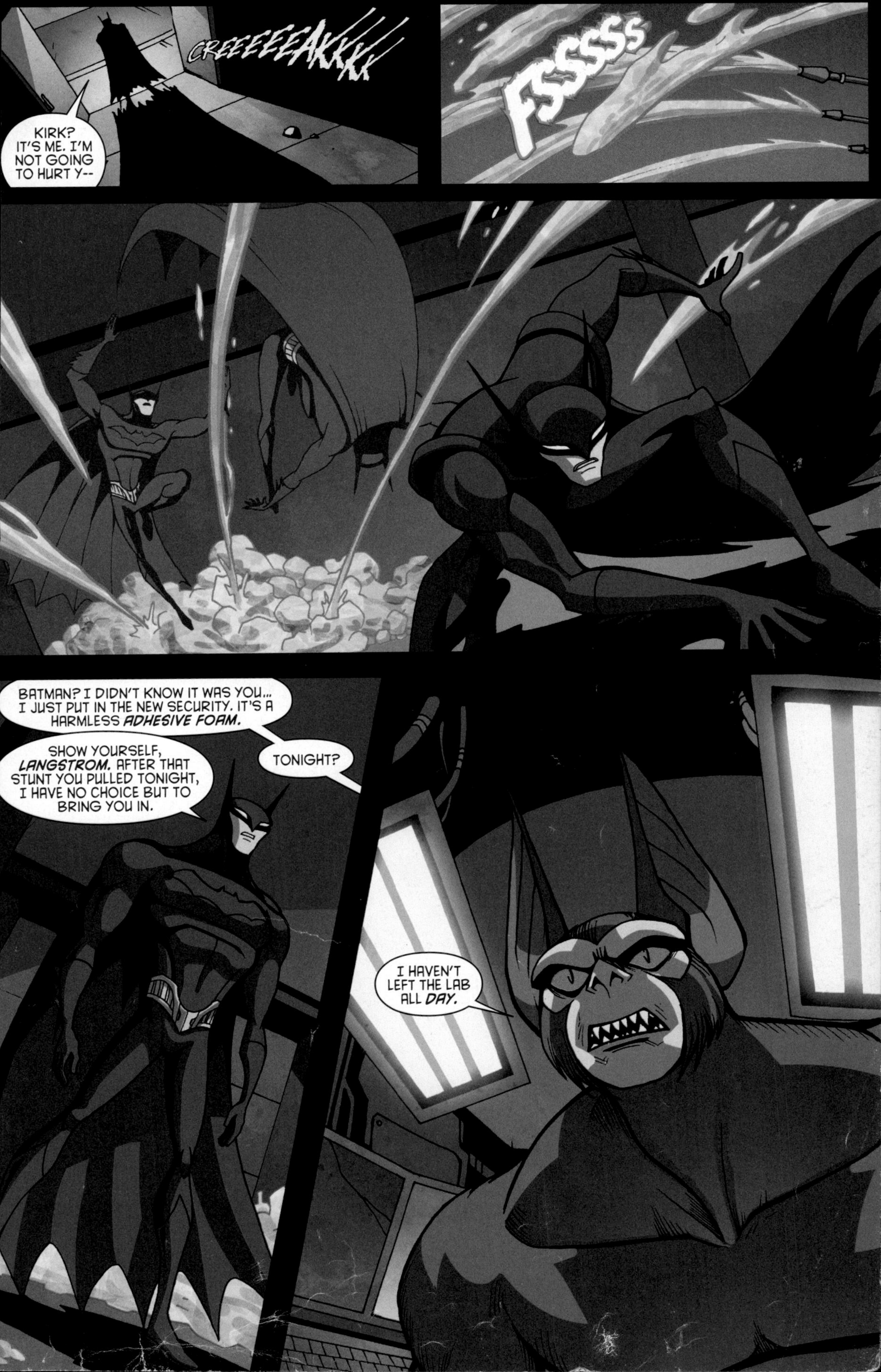
CREEEEEEAKKKK
KIRK? IT'S ME. I'M NOT GOING TO HURT Y--
FSSSSS
BATMAN? I DIDN'T KNOW IT WAS YOU... I JUST PUT IN THE NEW SECURITY. IT'S A HARMLESS ADHESIVE FOAM.
SHOW YOURSELF, LANGSTROM. AFTER THAT STUNT YOU PULLED TONIGHT, I HAVE NO CHOICE BUT TO BRING YOU IN.
TONIGHT?
I HAVEN'T LEFT THE LAB ALL DAY.

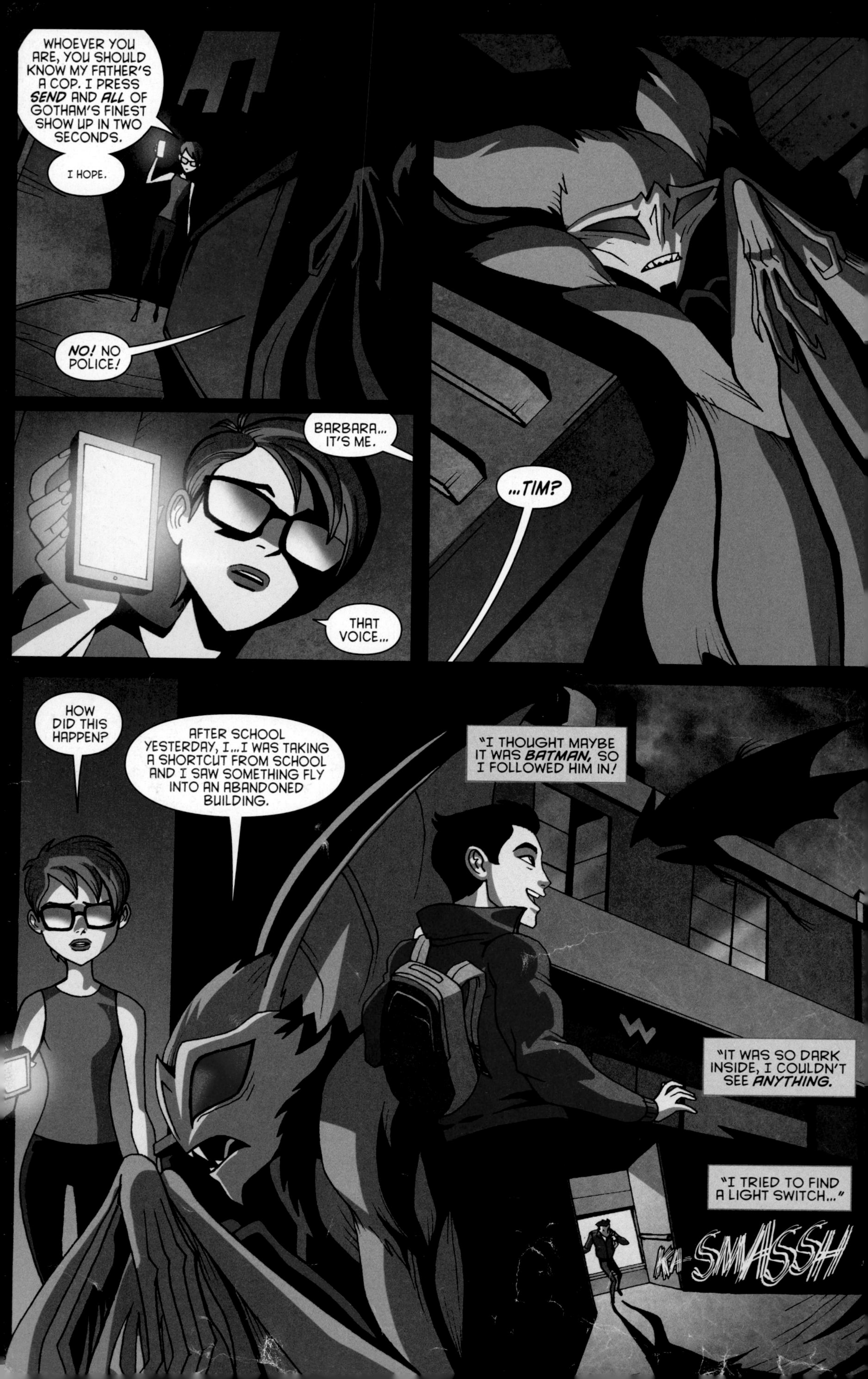

WHOEVER YOU ARE, YOU SHOULD KNOW MY FATHER'S A COP. I PRESS SEND AND ALL OF GOTHAM'S FINEST SHOW UP IN TWO SECONDS.
I HOPE.
NO! NO POLICE!
...TIM?
BARBARA... IT'S ME.
THAT VOICE...
HOW DID THIS HAPPEN?
AFTER SCHOOL YESTERDAY, I...I WAS TAKING A SHORTCUT FROM SCHOOL AND I SAW SOMETHING FLY INTO AN ABANDONED BUILDING.
"I THOUGHT MAYBE IT WAS BATMAN, SO I FOLLOWED HIM IN!
"IT WAS SO DARK INSIDE, I COULDN'T SEE ANYTHING.
"I TRIED TO FIND A LIGHT SWITCH..."
KA-SMASSH

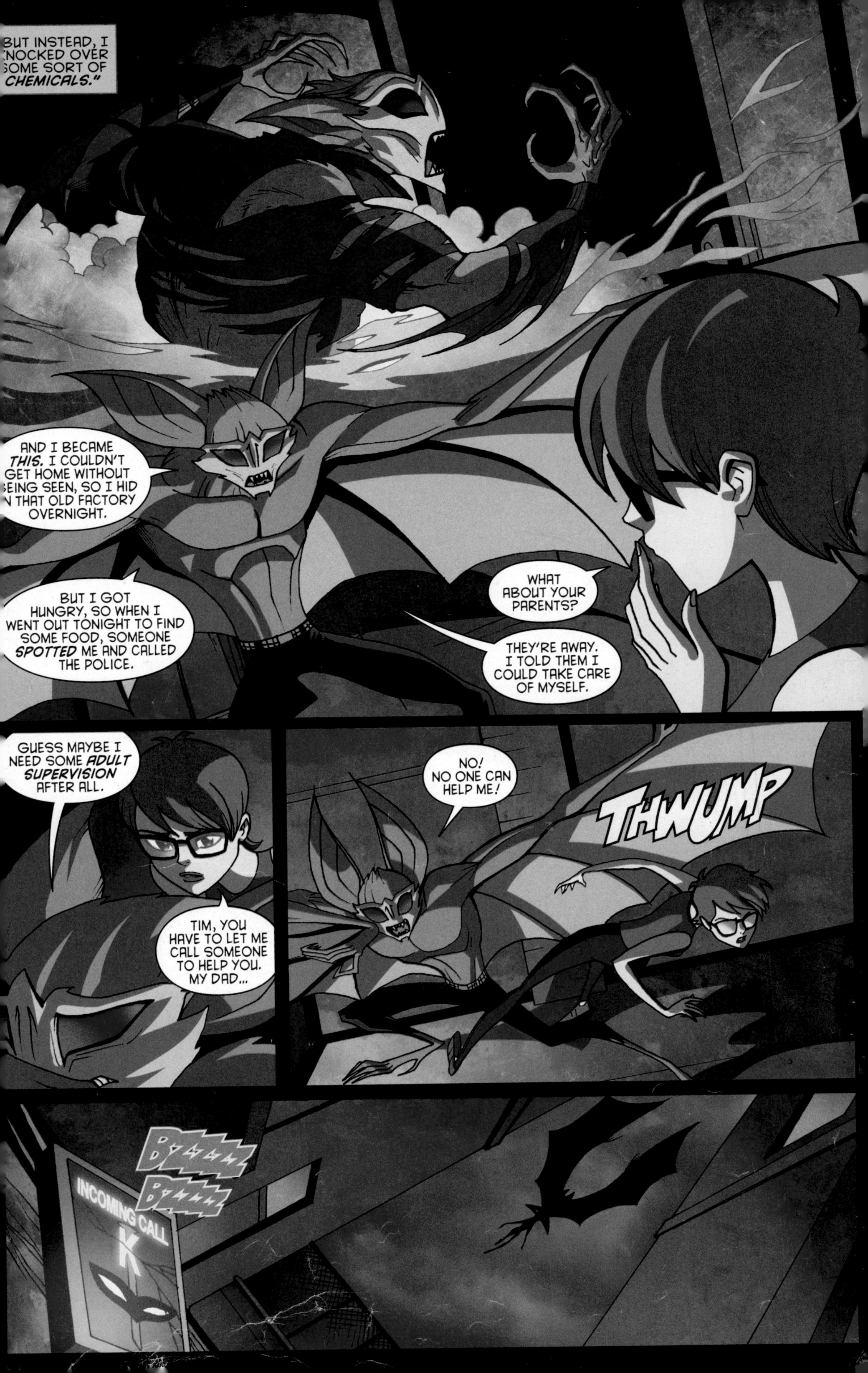
BUT INSTEAD, I KNOCKED OVER SOME SORT OF CHEMICALS."
AND I BECAME THIS. I COULDN'T GET HOME WITHOUT BEING SEEN, SO I HID IN THAT OLD FACTORY OVERNIGHT.
BUT I GOT HUNGRY, SO WHEN I WENT OUT TONIGHT TO FIND SOME FOOD, SOMEONE SPOTTED ME AND CALLED THE POLICE.
WHAT ABOUT YOUR PARENTS?
THEY'RE AWAY. I TOLD THEM I COULD TAKE CARE OF MYSELF.
GUESS MAYBE I NEED SOME ADULT SUPERVISION AFTER ALL.
TIM, YOU HAVE TO LET ME CALL SOMEONE TO HELP YOU. MY DAD...
NO! NO ONE CAN HELP ME!
THWUMP
BZZZ BZZZ
INCOMING CALL
K

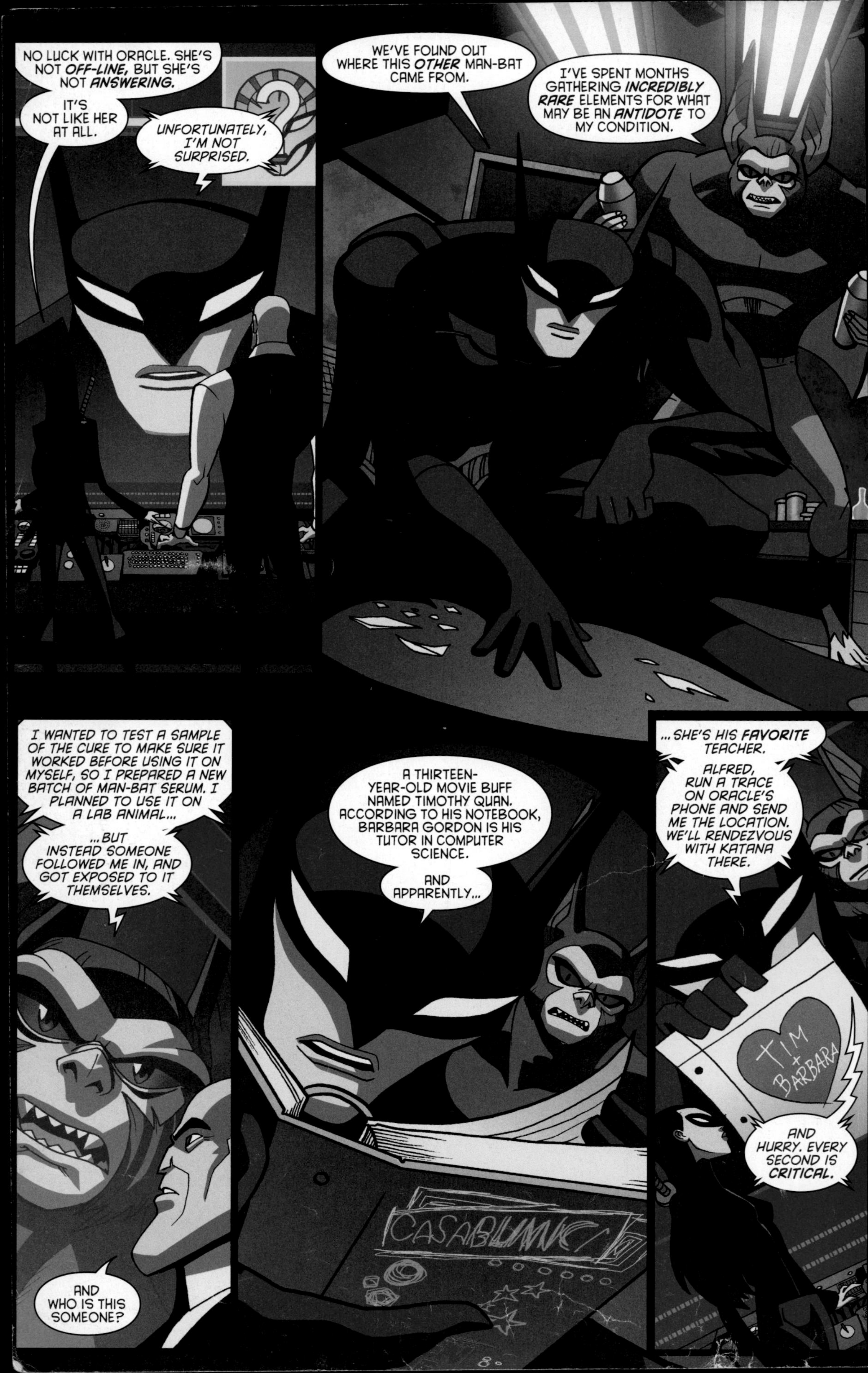

NO LUCK WITH ORACLE. SHE'S NOT OFF-LINE, BUT SHE'S NOT ANSWERING.
IT'S NOT LIKE HER AT ALL.
UNFORTUNATELY, I'M NOT SURPRISED.
WE'VE FOUND OUT WHERE THIS OTHER MAN-BAT CAME FROM.
I'VE SPENT MONTHS GATHERING INCREDIBLY RARE ELEMENTS FOR WHAT MAY BE AN ANTIDOTE TO MY CONDITION.
I WANTED TO TEST A SAMPLE OF THE CURE TO MAKE SURE IT WORKED BEFORE USING IT ON MYSELF, SO I PREPARED A NEW BATCH OF MAN-BAT SERUM. I PLANNED TO USE IT ON A LAB ANIMAL...
...BUT INSTEAD SOMEONE FOLLOWED ME IN, AND GOT EXPOSED TO IT THEMSELVES.
AND WHO IS THIS SOMEONE?
A THIRTEEN-YEAR-OLD MOVIE BUFF NAMED TIMOTHY QUAN. ACCORDING TO HIS NOTEBOOK, BARBARA GORDON IS HIS TUTOR IN COMPUTER SCIENCE.
AND APPARENTLY...
CASABLANCA
...SHE'S HIS FAVORITE TEACHER.
ALFRED, RUN A TRACE ON ORACLE'S PHONE AND SEND ME THE LOCATION. WE'LL RENDEZVOUS WITH KATANA THERE.
TIM + BARBARA
AND HURRY. EVERY SECOND IS CRITICAL.

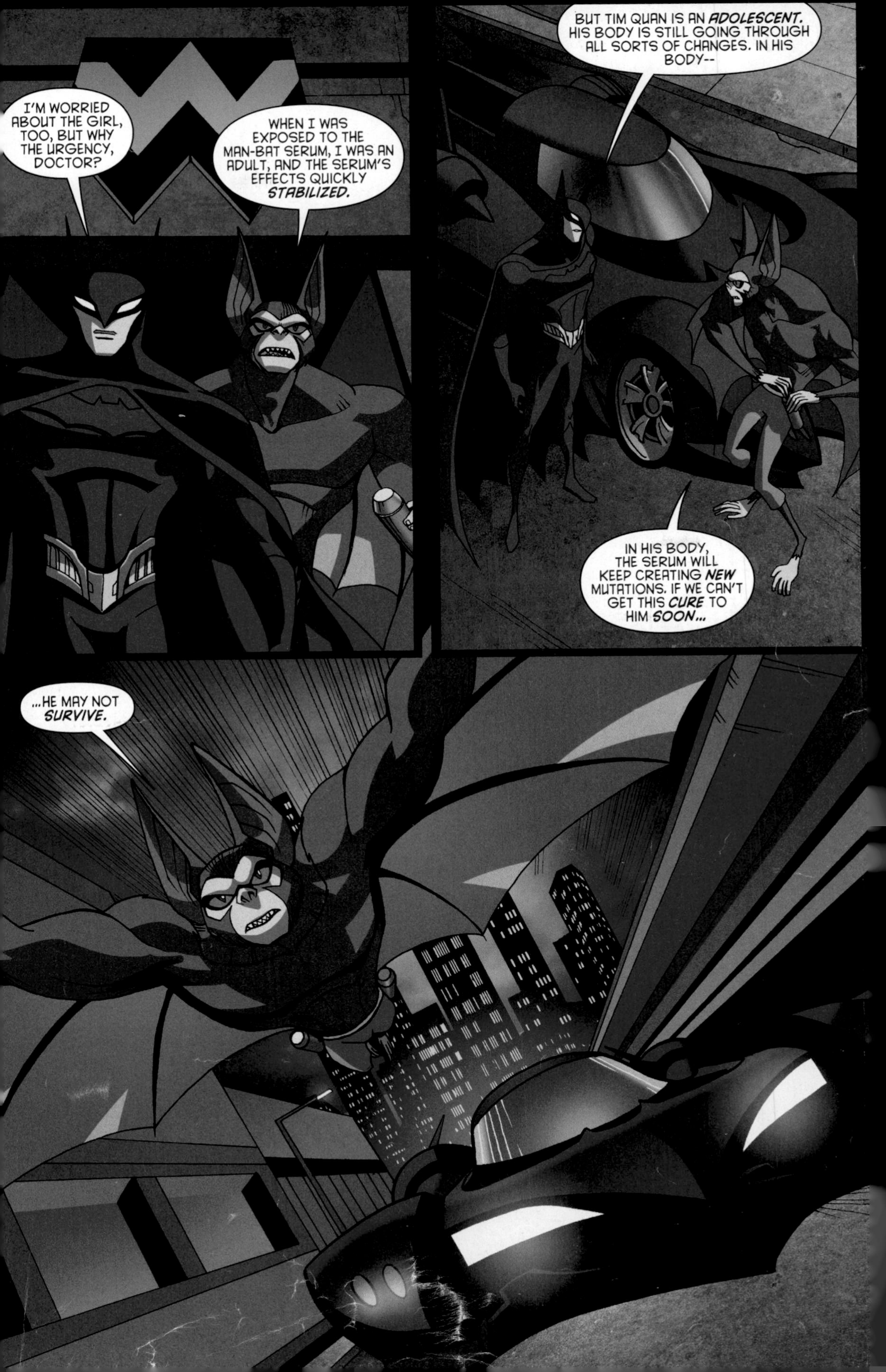
I'M WORRIED ABOUT THE GIRL, TOO, BUT WHY THE URGENCY, DOCTOR?
WHEN I WAS EXPOSED TO THE MAN-BAT SERUM, I WAS AN ADULT, AND THE SERUM'S EFFECTS QUICKLY *STABILIZED.*
BUT TIM QUAN IS AN *ADOLESCENT.* HIS BODY IS STILL GOING THROUGH ALL SORTS OF CHANGES. IN HIS BODY--
IN HIS BODY, THE SERUM WILL KEEP CREATING *NEW* MUTATIONS. IF WE CAN'T GET THIS *CURE* TO HIM *SOON...*
...HE MAY NOT *SURVIVE.*

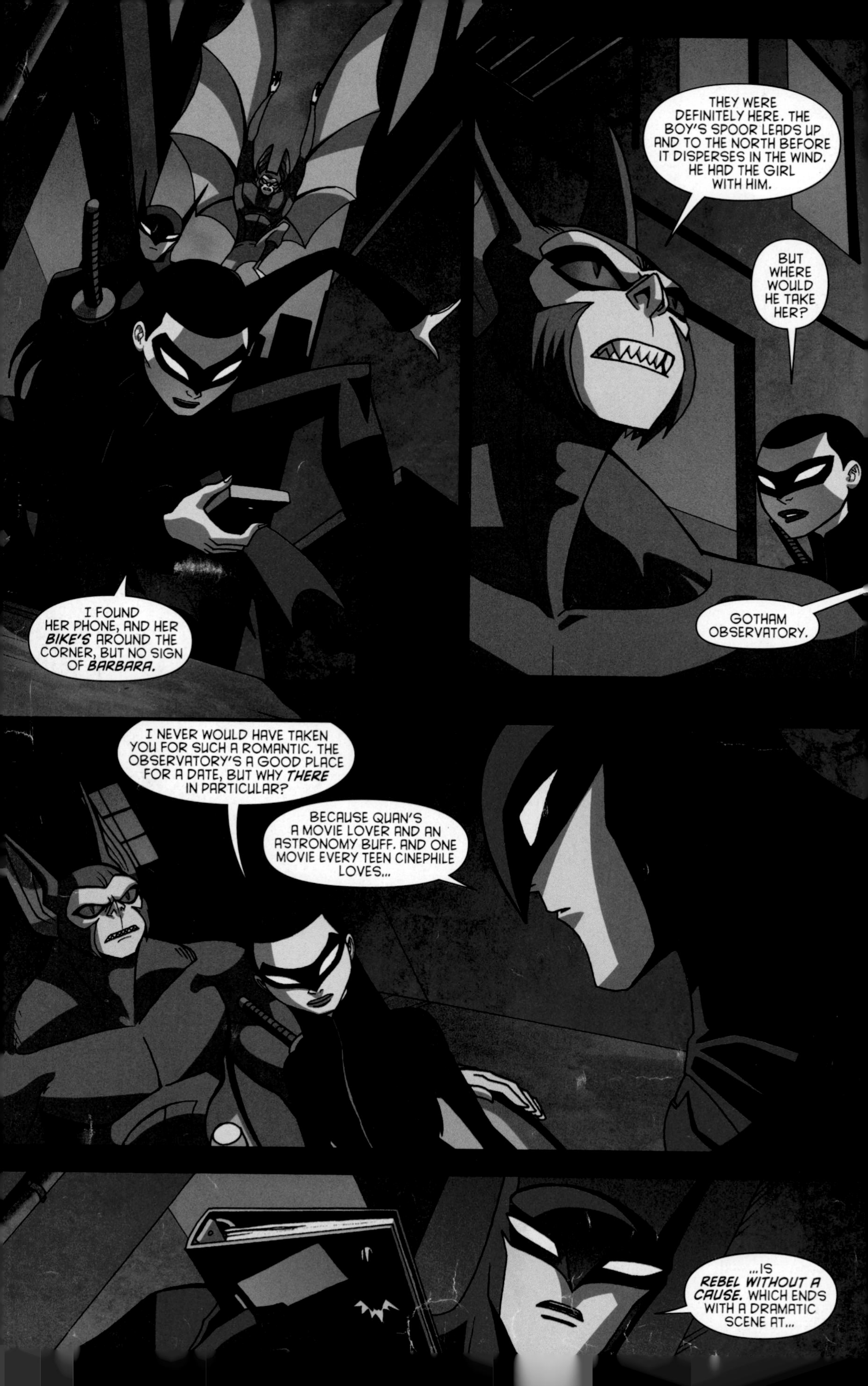
I FOUND HER PHONE, AND HER BIKE'S AROUND THE CORNER, BUT NO SIGN OF BARBARA.
THEY WERE DEFINITELY HERE. THE BOY'S SPOOR LEADS UP AND TO THE NORTH BEFORE IT DISPERSES IN THE WIND. HE HAD THE GIRL WITH HIM.
BUT WHERE WOULD HE TAKE HER?
GOTHAM OBSERVATORY.
I NEVER WOULD HAVE TAKEN YOU FOR SUCH A ROMANTIC. THE OBSERVATORY'S A GOOD PLACE FOR A DATE, BUT WHY THERE IN PARTICULAR?
BECAUSE QUAN'S A MOVIE LOVER AND AN ASTRONOMY BUFF. AND ONE MOVIE EVERY TEEN CINEPHILE LOVES...
...IS REBEL WITHOUT A CAUSE. WHICH ENDS WITH A DRAMATIC SCENE AT...

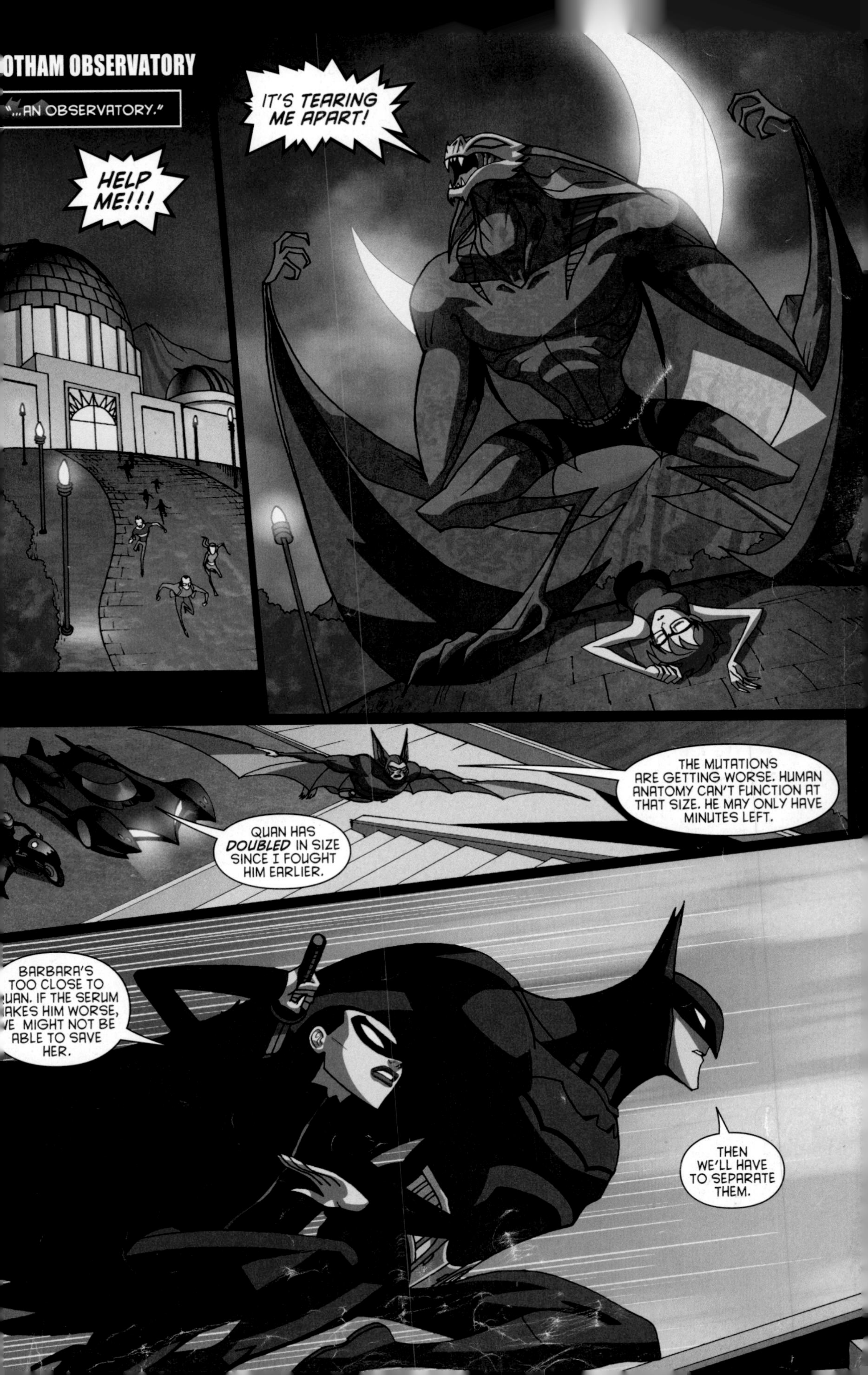
OTHAM OBSERVATORY
"...AN OBSERVATORY."
HELP ME!!!
IT'S TEARING ME APART!
QUAN HAS DOUBLED IN SIZE SINCE I FOUGHT HIM EARLIER.
THE MUTATIONS ARE GETTING WORSE. HUMAN ANATOMY CAN'T FUNCTION AT THAT SIZE. HE MAY ONLY HAVE MINUTES LEFT.
BARBARA'S TOO CLOSE TO UAN. IF THE SERUM AKES HIM WORSE, E MIGHT NOT BE ABLE TO SAVE HER.
THEN WE'LL HAVE TO SEPARATE THEM.

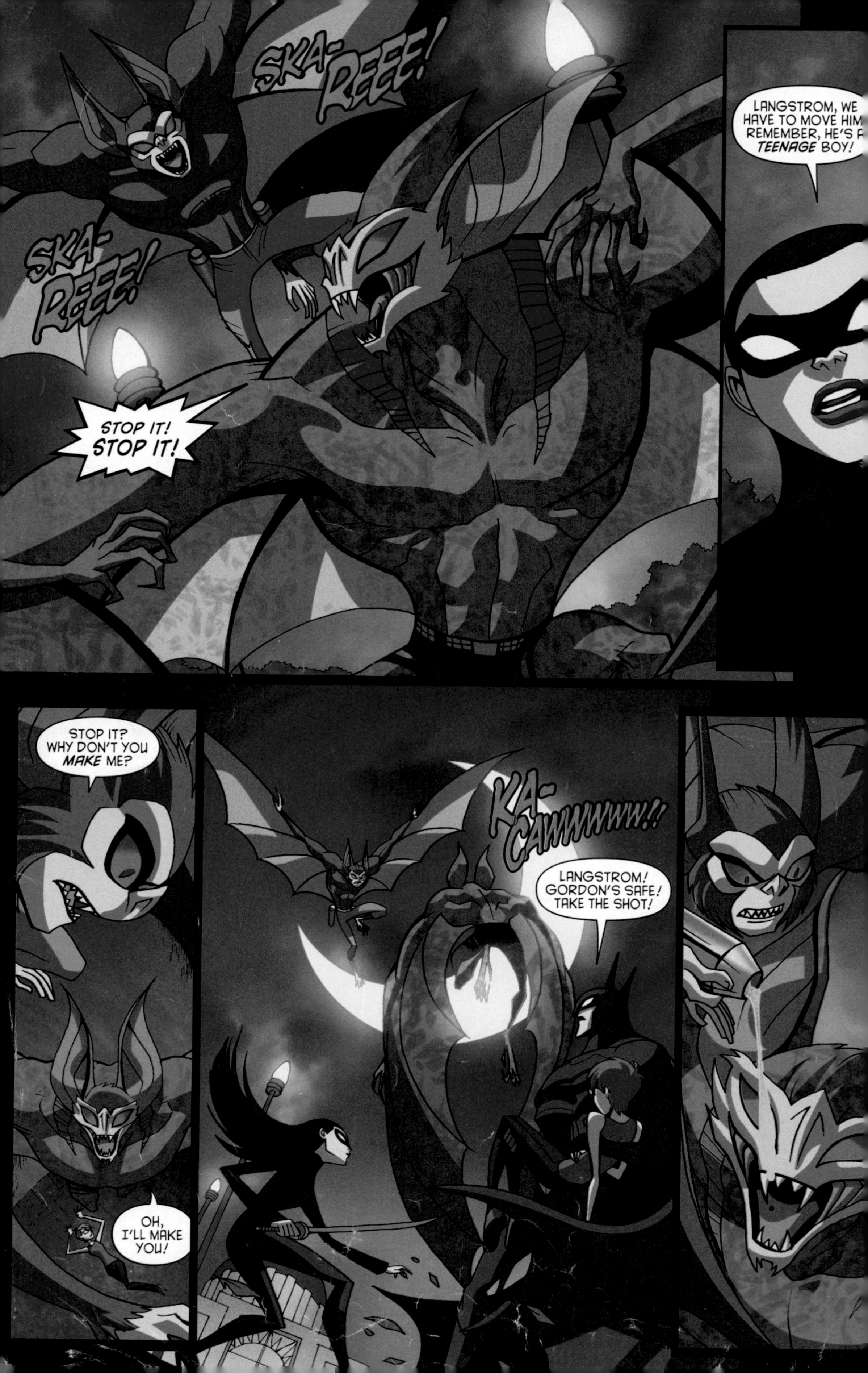
SKA-REEE!
SKA-REEE!
STOP IT! STOP IT!
LANGSTROM, WE HAVE TO MOVE HIM! REMEMBER, HE'S A TEENAGE BOY!
STOP IT? WHY DON'T YOU MAKE ME?
OH, I'LL MAKE YOU!
KA-CAWWWWW!!
LANGSTROM! GORDON'S SAFE! TAKE THE SHOT!

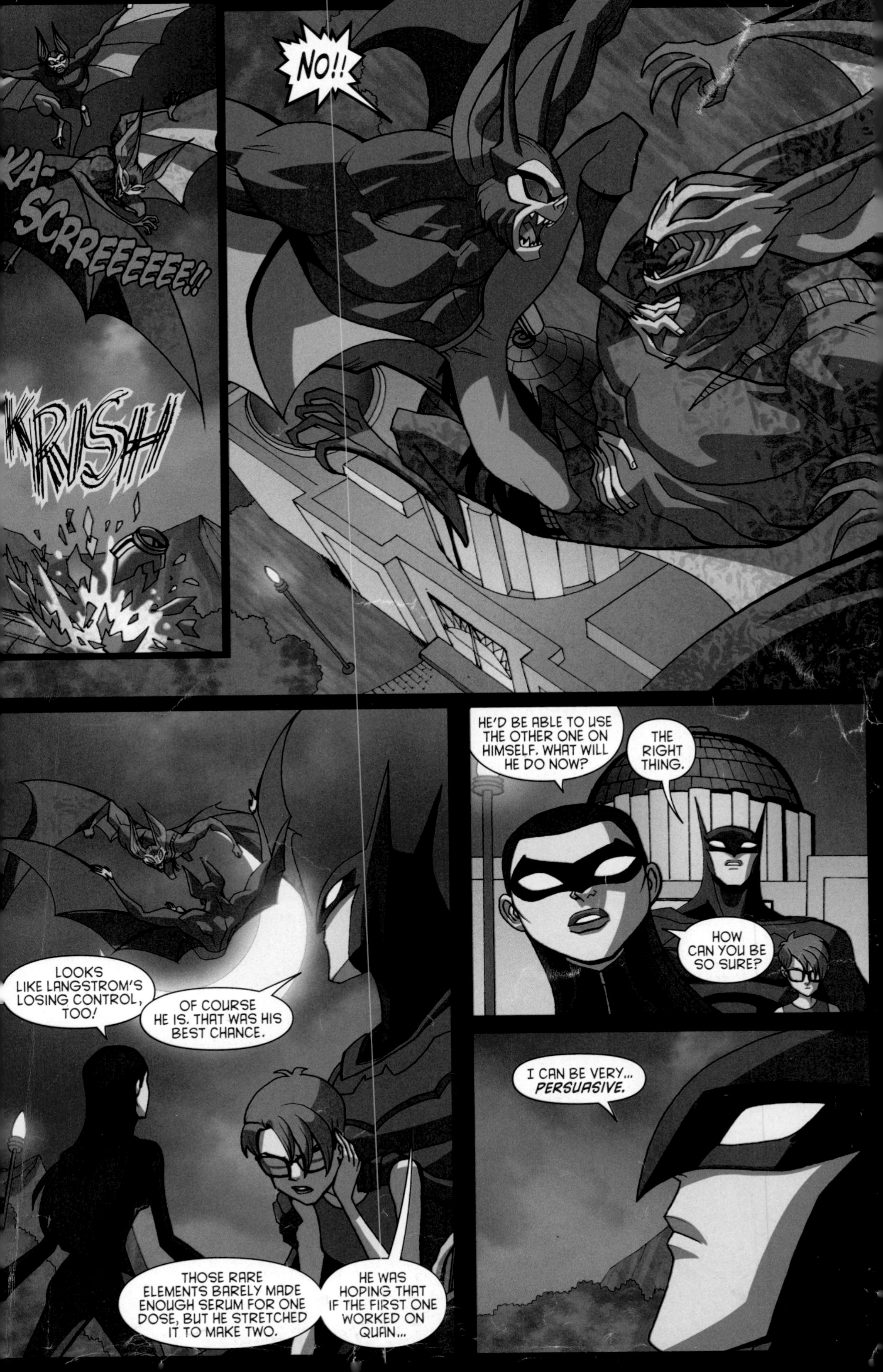
KA-SCRREEEEEEE!!
KRISH
NO!!
LOOKS LIKE LANGSTROM'S LOSING CONTROL, TOO!
OF COURSE HE IS. THAT WAS HIS BEST CHANCE.
THOSE RARE ELEMENTS BARELY MADE ENOUGH SERUM FOR ONE DOSE, BUT HE STRETCHED IT TO MAKE TWO.
HE WAS HOPING THAT IF THE FIRST ONE WORKED ON QUAN...
HE'D BE ABLE TO USE THE OTHER ONE ON HIMSELF. WHAT WILL HE DO NOW?
THE RIGHT THING.
HOW CAN YOU BE SO SURE?
I CAN BE VERY... *PERSUASIVE.*

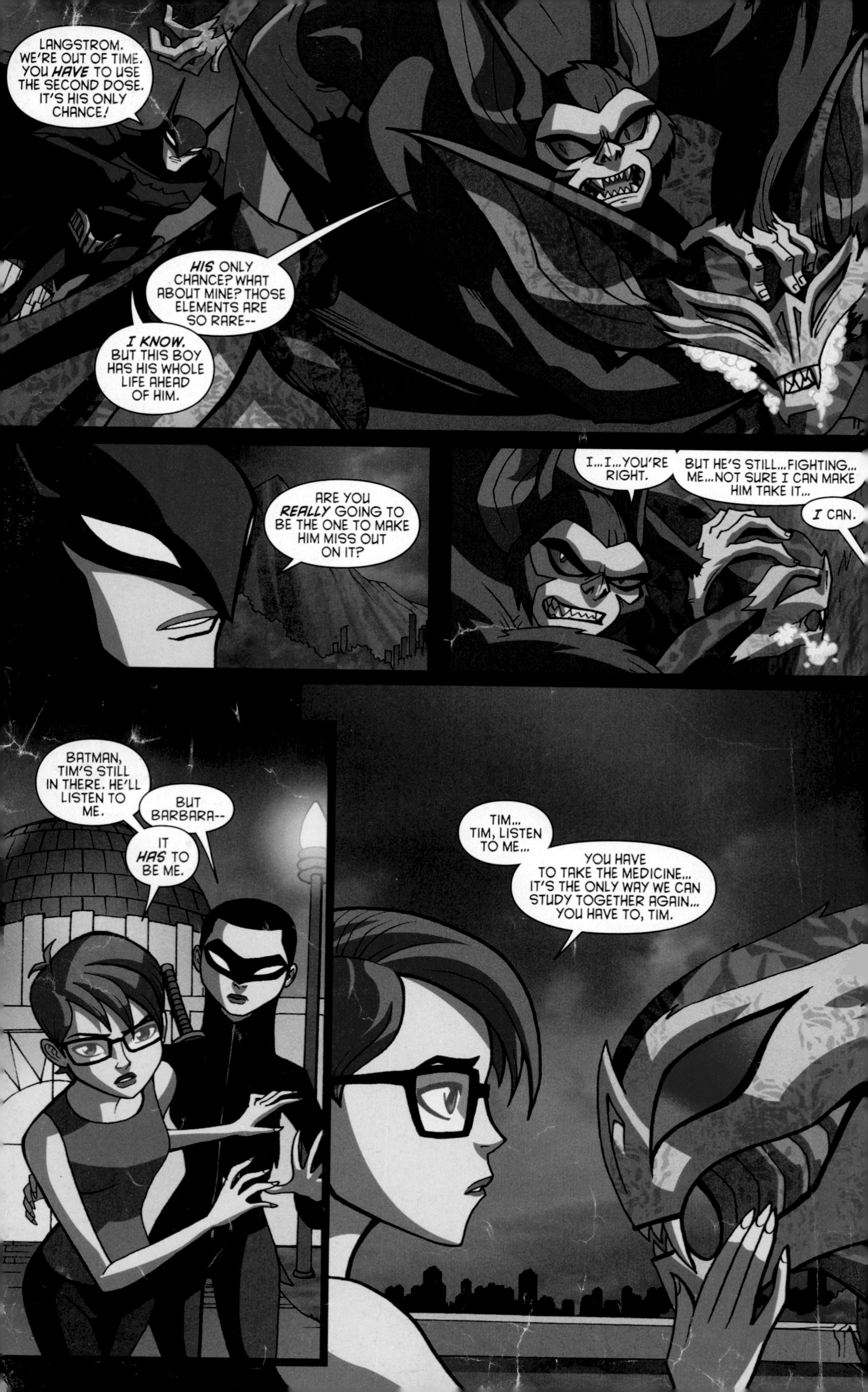
LANGSTROM. WE'RE OUT OF TIME. YOU *HAVE* TO USE THE SECOND DOSE. IT'S HIS ONLY CHANCE!
HIS ONLY CHANCE? WHAT ABOUT MINE? THOSE ELEMENTS ARE SO RARE--
I KNOW. BUT THIS BOY HAS HIS WHOLE LIFE AHEAD OF HIM.
ARE YOU *REALLY* GOING TO BE THE ONE TO MAKE HIM MISS OUT ON IT?
I...I...YOU'RE RIGHT.
BUT HE'S STILL...FIGHTING... ME...NOT SURE I CAN MAKE HIM TAKE IT...
I CAN.
BATMAN, TIM'S STILL IN THERE. HE'LL LISTEN TO ME.
BUT BARBARA--
IT *HAS* TO BE ME.
TIM... TIM, LISTEN TO ME...
YOU HAVE TO TAKE THE MEDICINE... IT'S THE ONLY WAY WE CAN STUDY TOGETHER AGAIN... YOU HAVE TO, TIM.

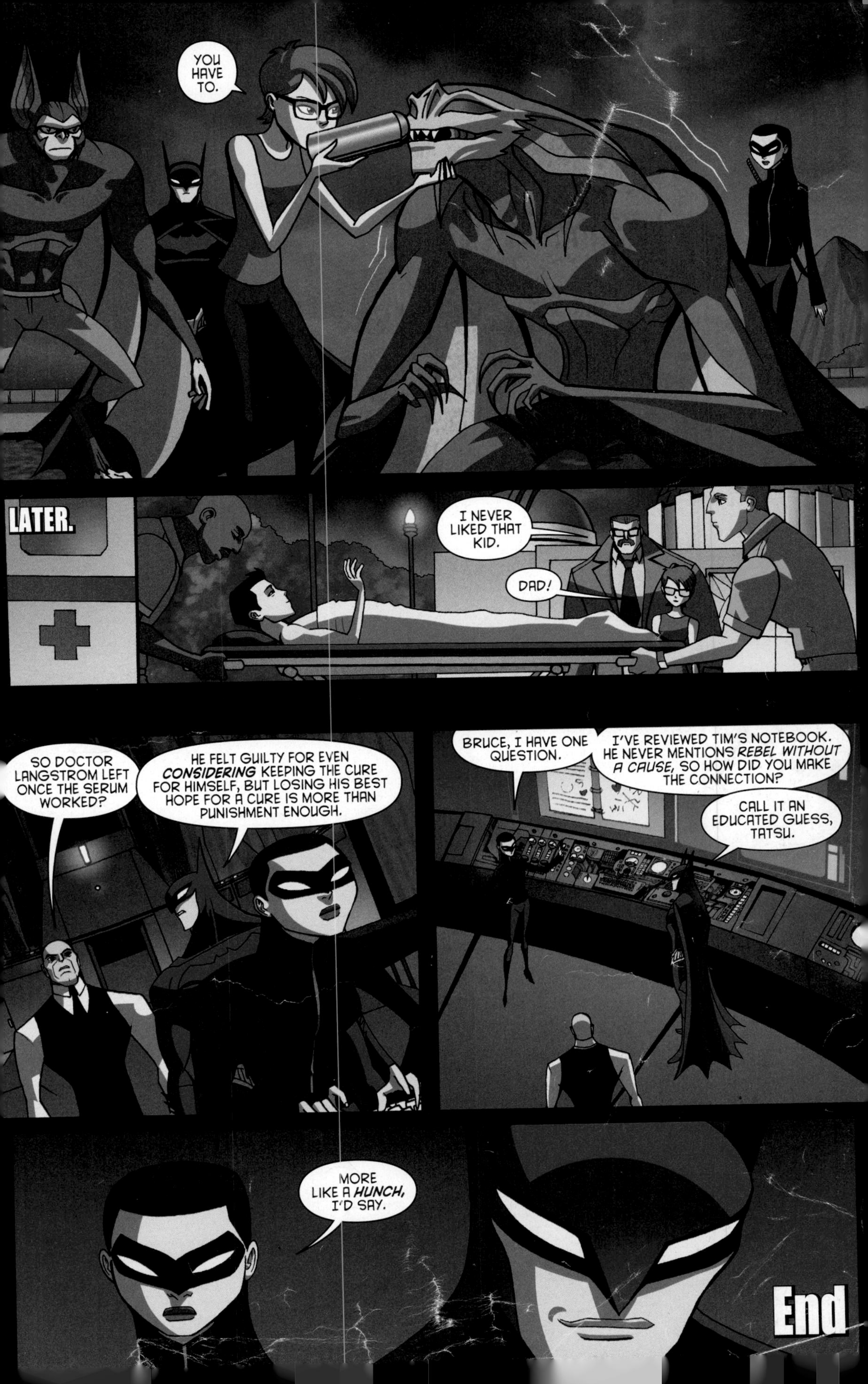
YOU HAVE TO.
LATER.
I NEVER LIKED THAT KID.
DAD!
SO DOCTOR LANGSTROM LEFT ONCE THE SERUM WORKED?
HE FELT GUILTY FOR EVEN *CONSIDERING* KEEPING THE CURE FOR HIMSELF, BUT LOSING HIS BEST HOPE FOR A CURE IS MORE THAN PUNISHMENT ENOUGH.
BRUCE, I HAVE ONE QUESTION.
I'VE REVIEWED TIM'S NOTEBOOK. HE NEVER MENTIONS *REBEL WITHOUT A CAUSE*, SO HOW DID YOU MAKE THE CONNECTION?
CALL IT AN EDUCATED GUESS, TATSU.
MORE LIKE A *HUNCH*, I'D SAY.
End

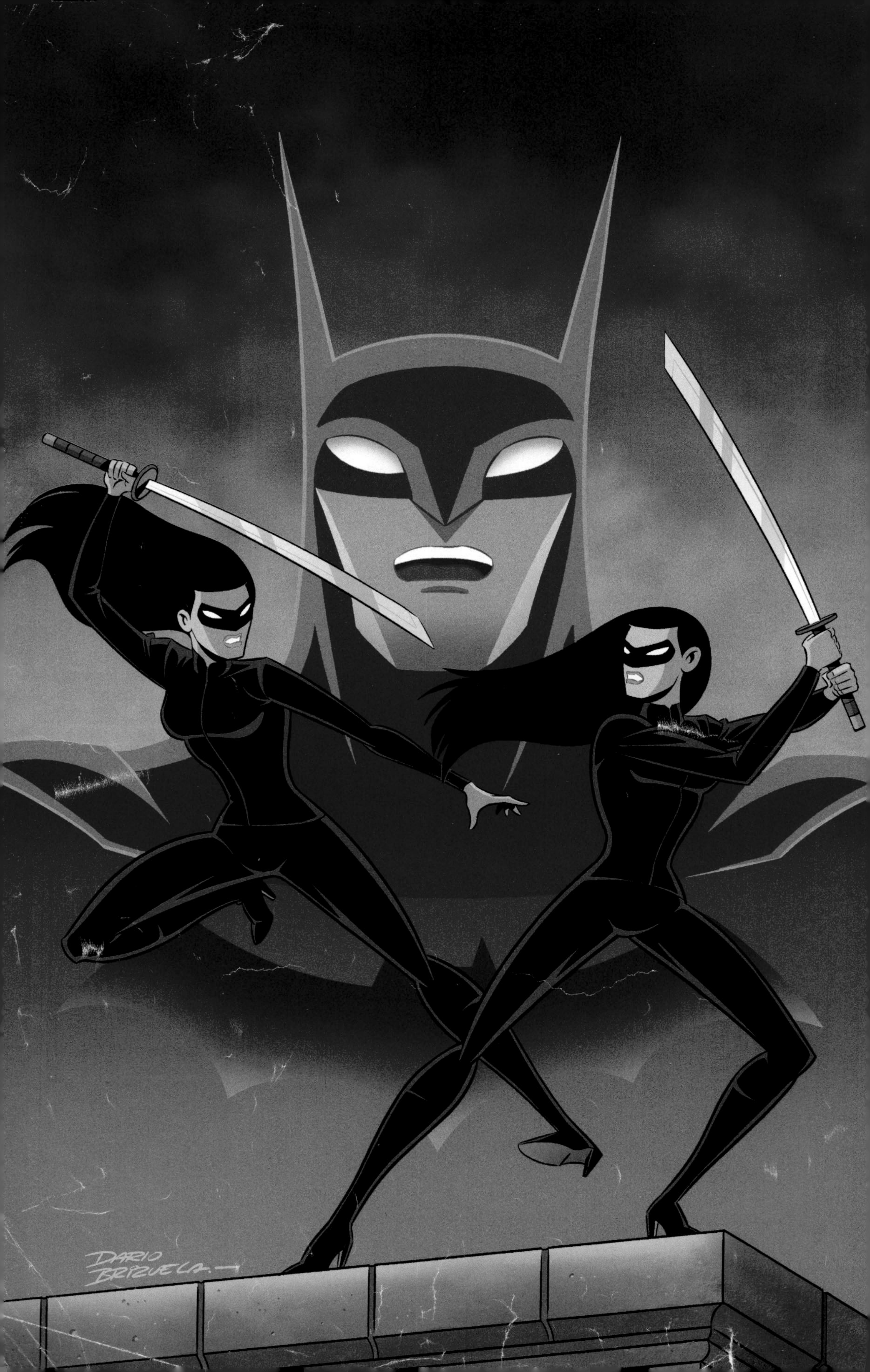
DARIO
BRIZUELA

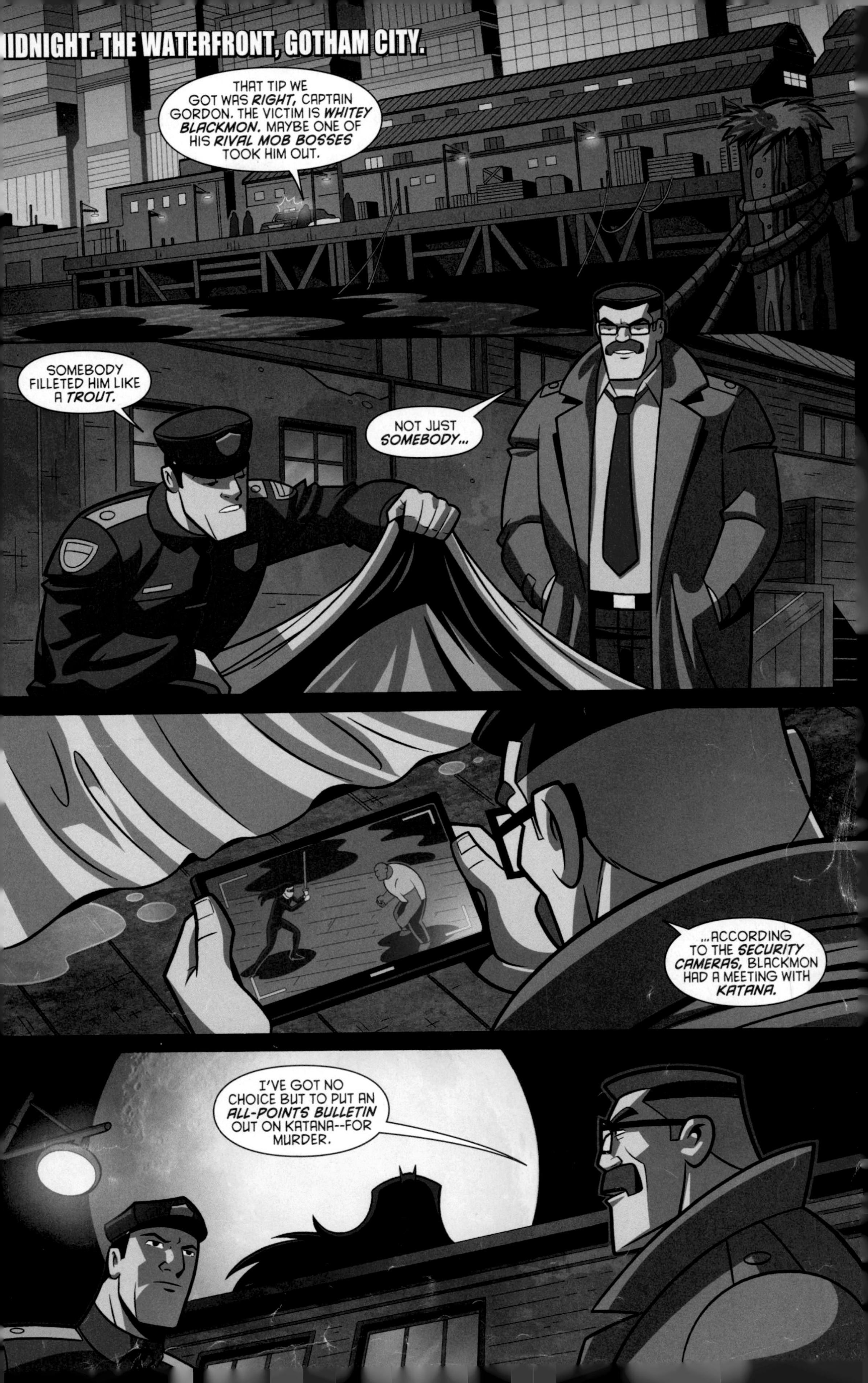
IDNIGHT. THE WATERFRONT, GOTHAM CITY.
THAT TIP WE GOT WAS RIGHT, CAPTAIN GORDON. THE VICTIM IS WHITEY BLACKMON. MAYBE ONE OF HIS RIVAL MOB BOSSES TOOK HIM OUT.
SOMEBODY FILLETED HIM LIKE A TROUT.
NOT JUST SOMEBODY...
...ACCORDING TO THE SECURITY CAMERAS, BLACKMON HAD A MEETING WITH KATANA.
I'VE GOT NO CHOICE BUT TO PUT AN ALL-POINTS BULLETIN OUT ON KATANA--FOR MURDER.

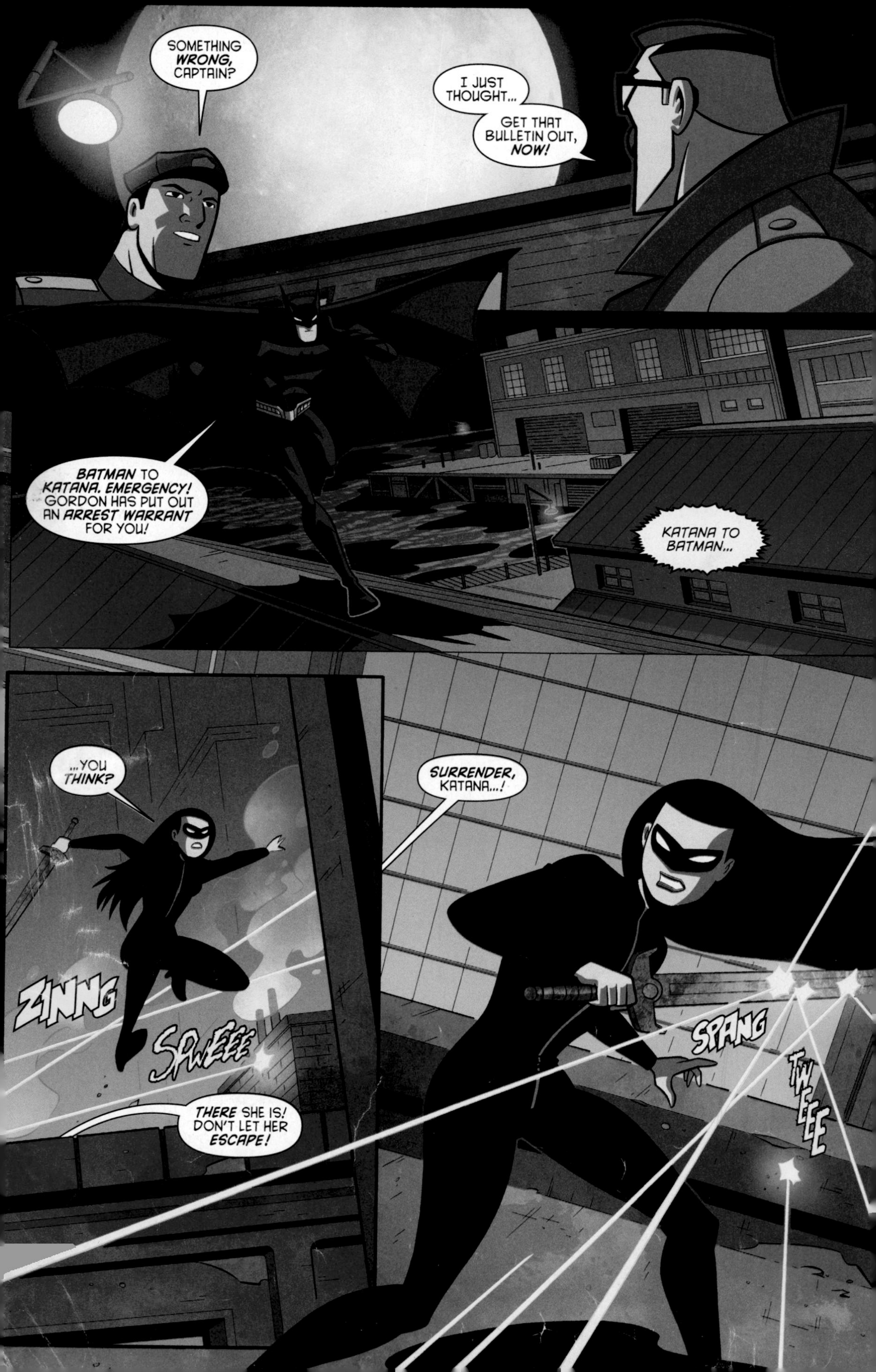
SOMETHING WRONG, CAPTAIN?
I JUST THOUGHT...
GET THAT BULLETIN OUT, NOW!
BATMAN TO KATANA. EMERGENCY! GORDON HAS PUT OUT AN ARREST WARRANT FOR YOU!
KATANA TO BATMAN...
...YOU THINK?
SURRENDER, KATANA...!
ZINNG
SPWEEE
THERE SHE IS! DON'T LET HER ESCAPE!
SPANG
TWEEE

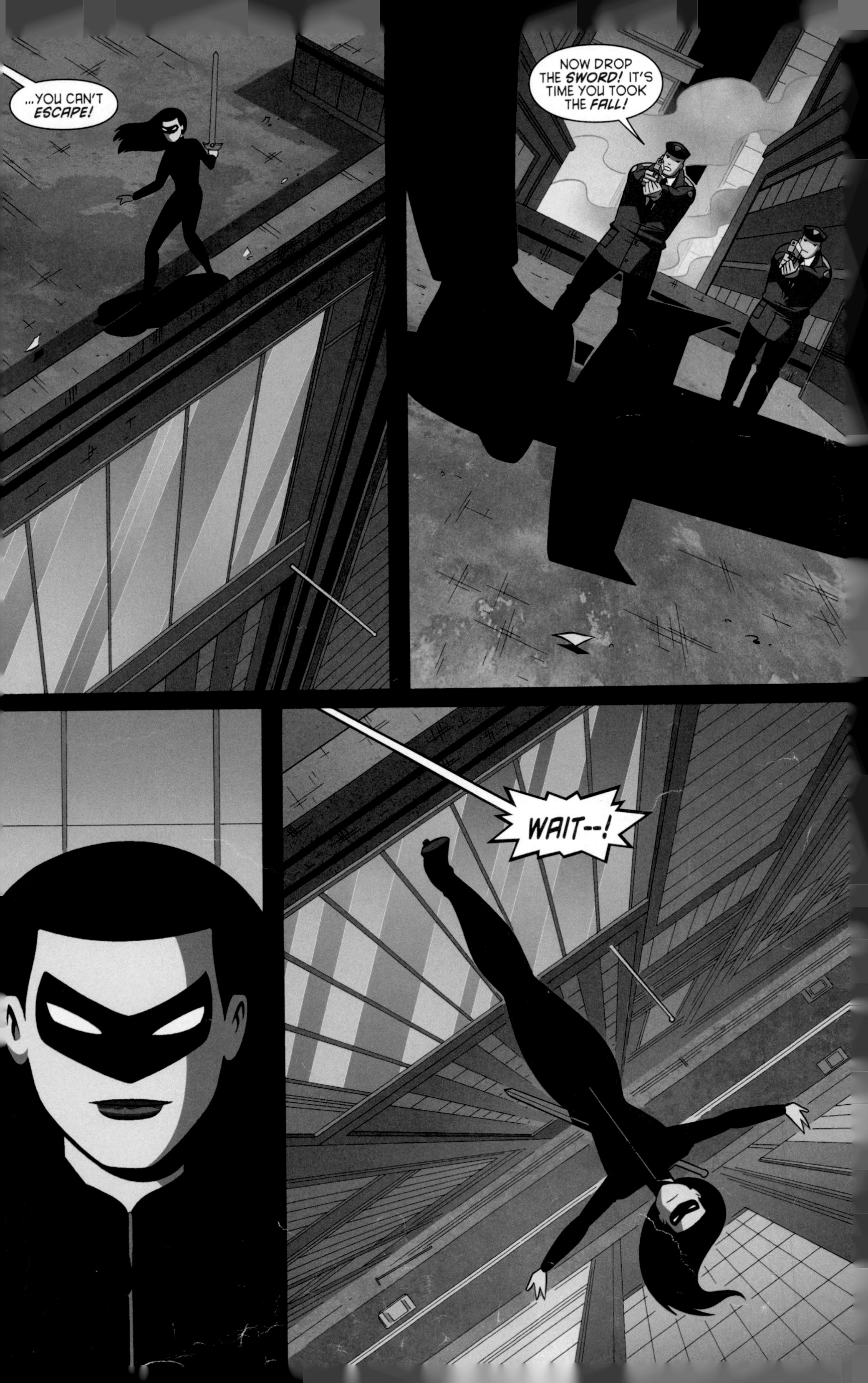
...YOU CAN'T ESCAPE!
NOW DROP THE SWORD! IT'S TIME YOU TOOK THE FALL!
WAIT--!

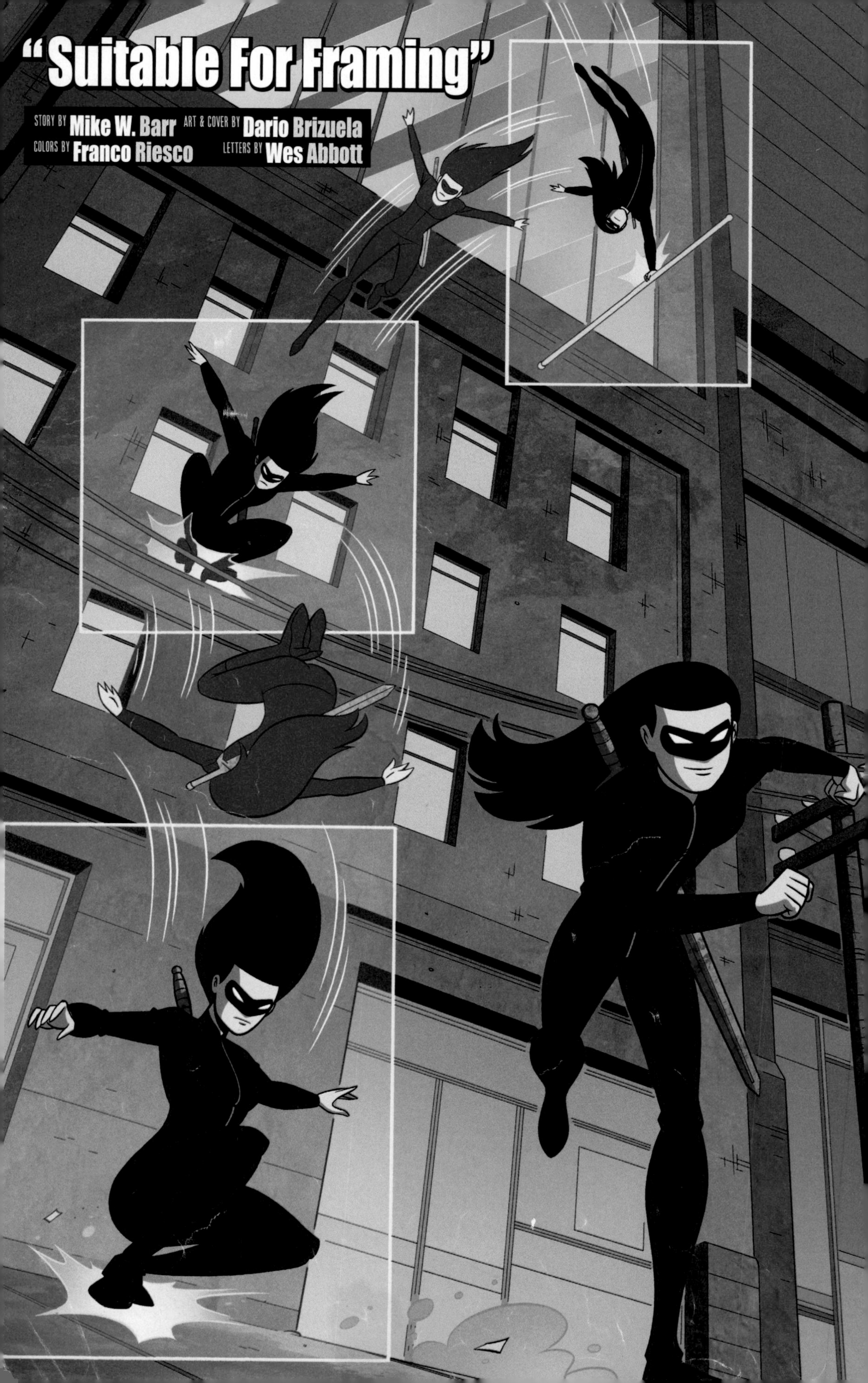
"Suitable For Framing"
STORY BY Mike W. Barr ART & COVER BY Dario Brizuela
COLORS BY Franco Riesco LETTERS BY Wes Abbott

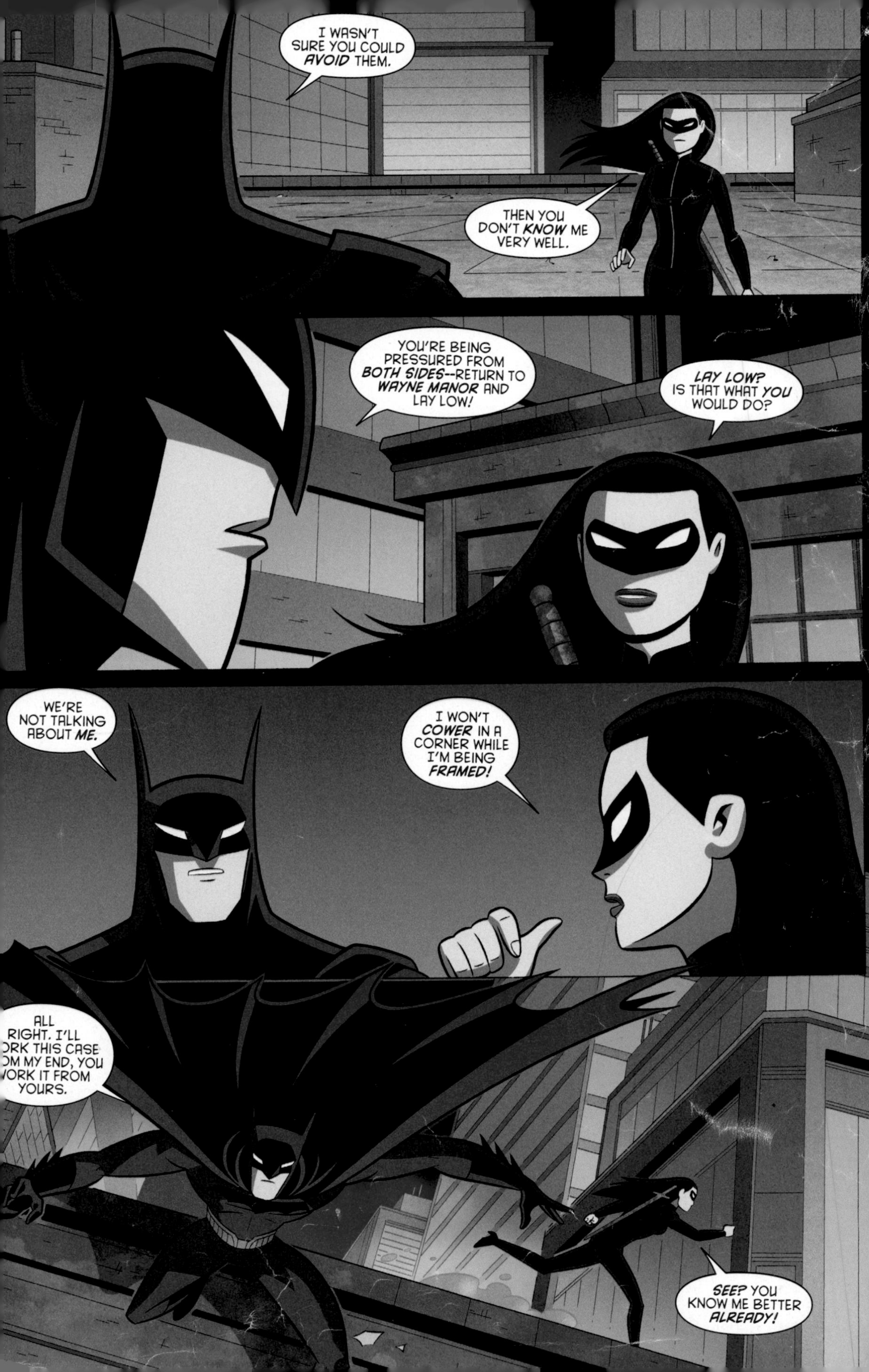
I WASN'T SURE YOU COULD AVOID THEM.
THEN YOU DON'T KNOW ME VERY WELL.
YOU'RE BEING PRESSURED FROM BOTH SIDES--RETURN TO WAYNE MANOR AND LAY LOW!
LAY LOW? IS THAT WHAT YOU WOULD DO?
WE'RE NOT TALKING ABOUT ME.
I WON'T COWER IN A CORNER WHILE I'M BEING FRAMED!
ALL RIGHT. I'LL
ORK THIS CASE
OM MY END, YOU
VORK IT FROM
YOURS.
SEE? YOU KNOW ME BETTER ALREADY!

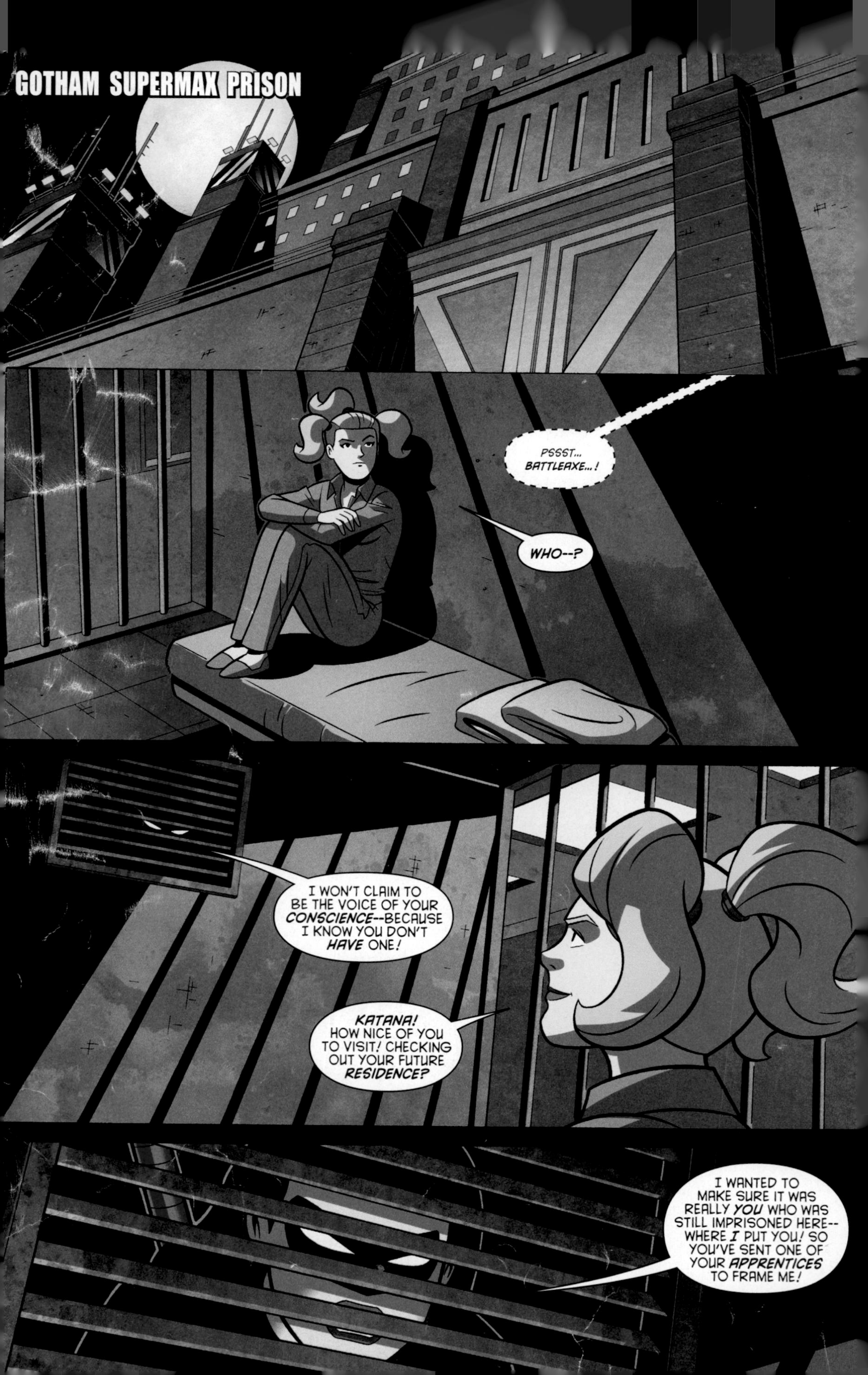
GOTHAM SUPERMAX PRISON
PSSST... BATTLEAXE...!
WHO--?
I WON'T CLAIM TO BE THE VOICE OF YOUR CONSCIENCE--BECAUSE I KNOW YOU DON'T HAVE ONE!
KATANA! HOW NICE OF YOU TO VISIT! CHECKING OUT YOUR FUTURE RESIDENCE?
I WANTED TO MAKE SURE IT WAS REALLY YOU WHO WAS STILL IMPRISONED HERE--WHERE I PUT YOU! SO YOU'VE SENT ONE OF YOUR APPRENTICES TO FRAME ME!

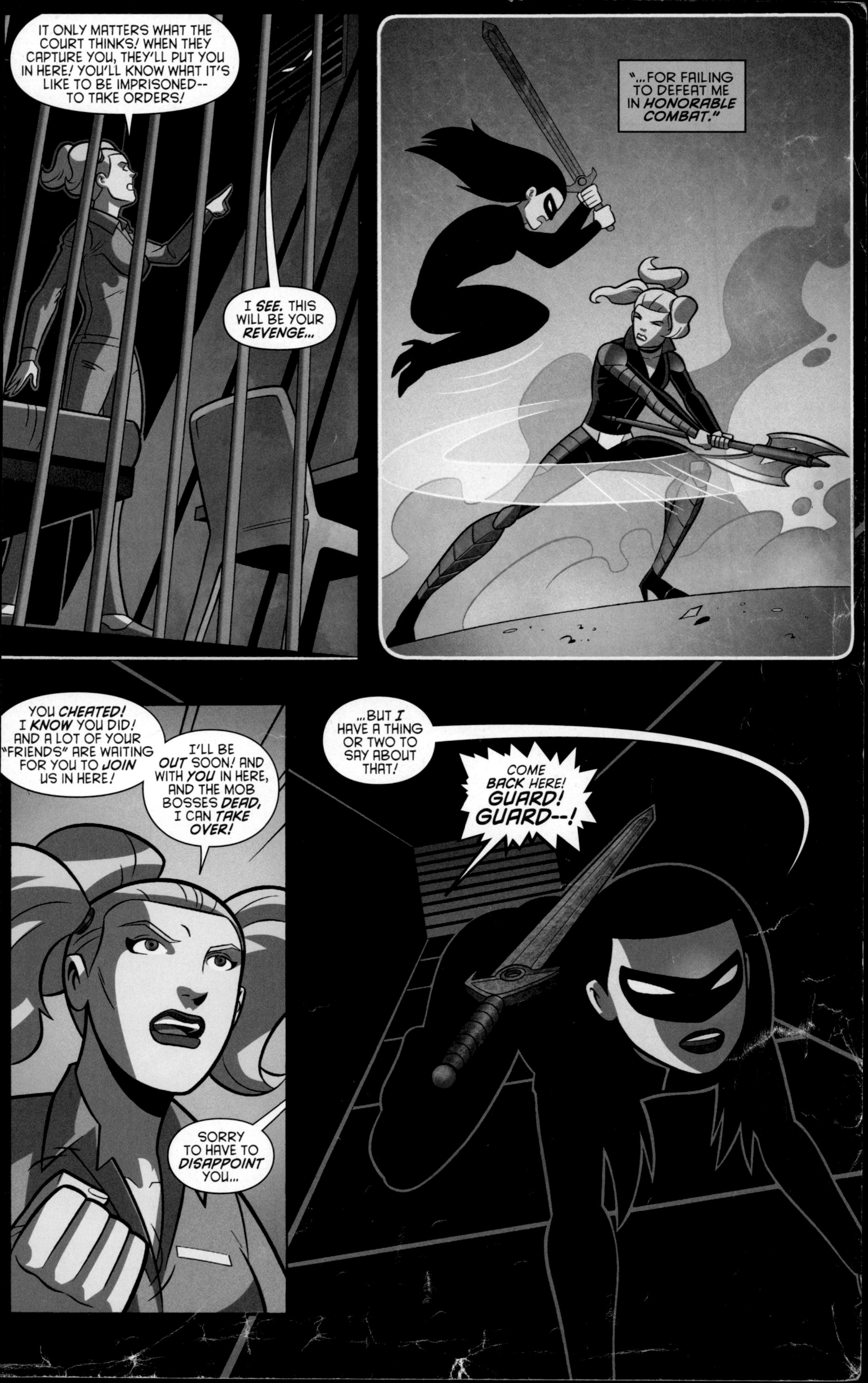
IT ONLY MATTERS WHAT THE COURT THINKS! WHEN THEY CAPTURE YOU, THEY'LL PUT YOU IN HERE! YOU'LL KNOW WHAT IT'S LIKE TO BE IMPRISONED-- TO TAKE ORDERS!
I SEE. THIS WILL BE YOUR REVENGE...
"...FOR FAILING TO DEFEAT ME IN HONORABLE COMBAT."
YOU CHEATED! I KNOW YOU DID! AND A LOT OF YOUR "FRIENDS" ARE WAITING FOR YOU TO JOIN US IN HERE!
I'LL BE OUT SOON! AND WITH YOU IN HERE, AND THE MOB BOSSES DEAD, I CAN TAKE OVER!
SORRY TO HAVE TO DISAPPOINT YOU...
...BUT I HAVE A THING OR TWO TO SAY ABOUT THAT!
COME BACK HERE! GUARD! GUARD--!

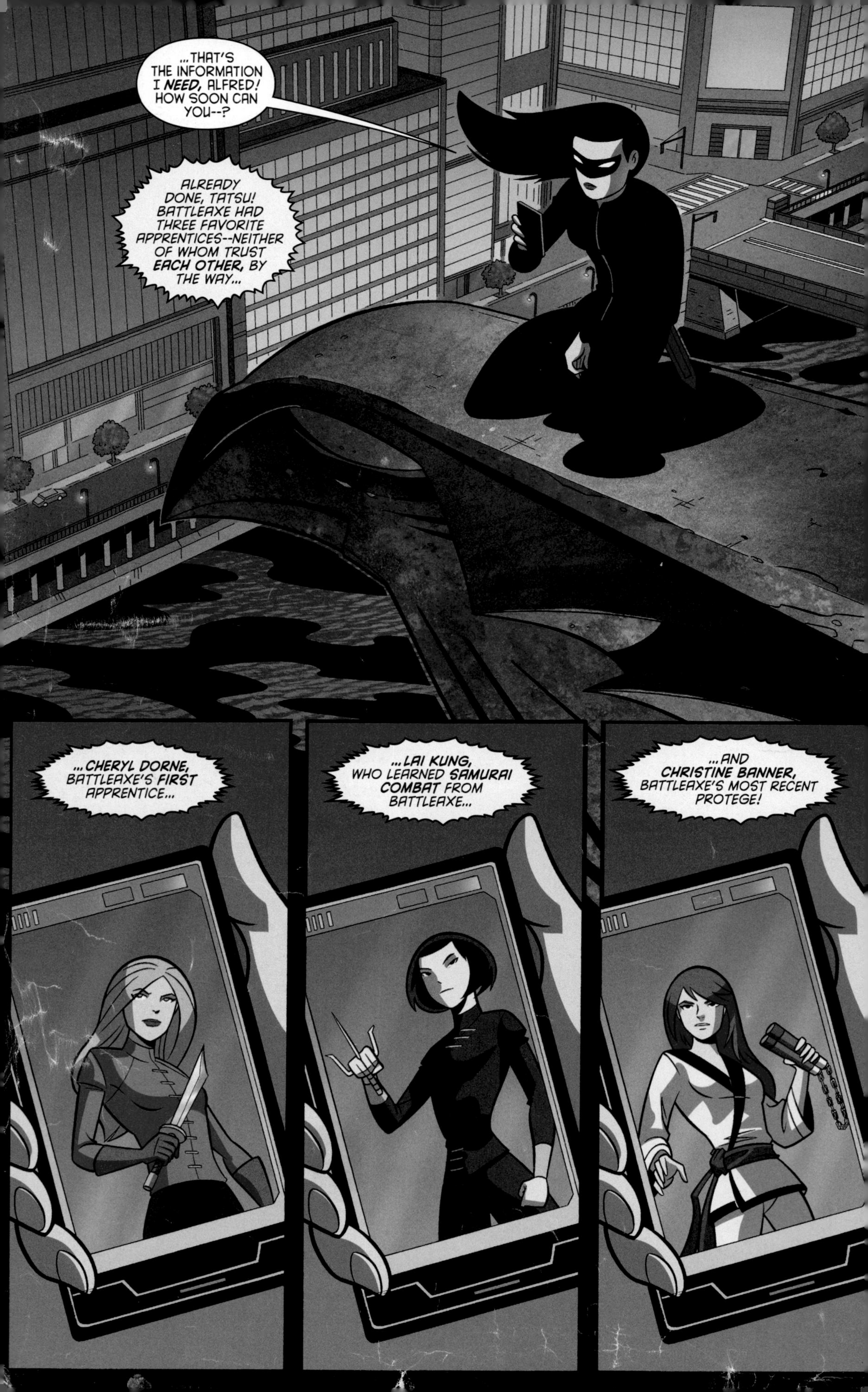

...THAT'S THE INFORMATION I NEED, ALFRED! HOW SOON CAN YOU--?
ALREADY DONE, TATSU! BATTLEAXE HAD THREE FAVORITE APPRENTICES--NEITHER OF WHOM TRUST EACH OTHER, BY THE WAY...
...CHERYL DORNE, BATTLEAXE'S FIRST APPRENTICE...
...LAI KUNG, WHO LEARNED SAMURAI COMBAT FROM BATTLEAXE...
...AND CHRISTINE BANNER, BATTLEAXE'S MOST RECENT PROTEGE!

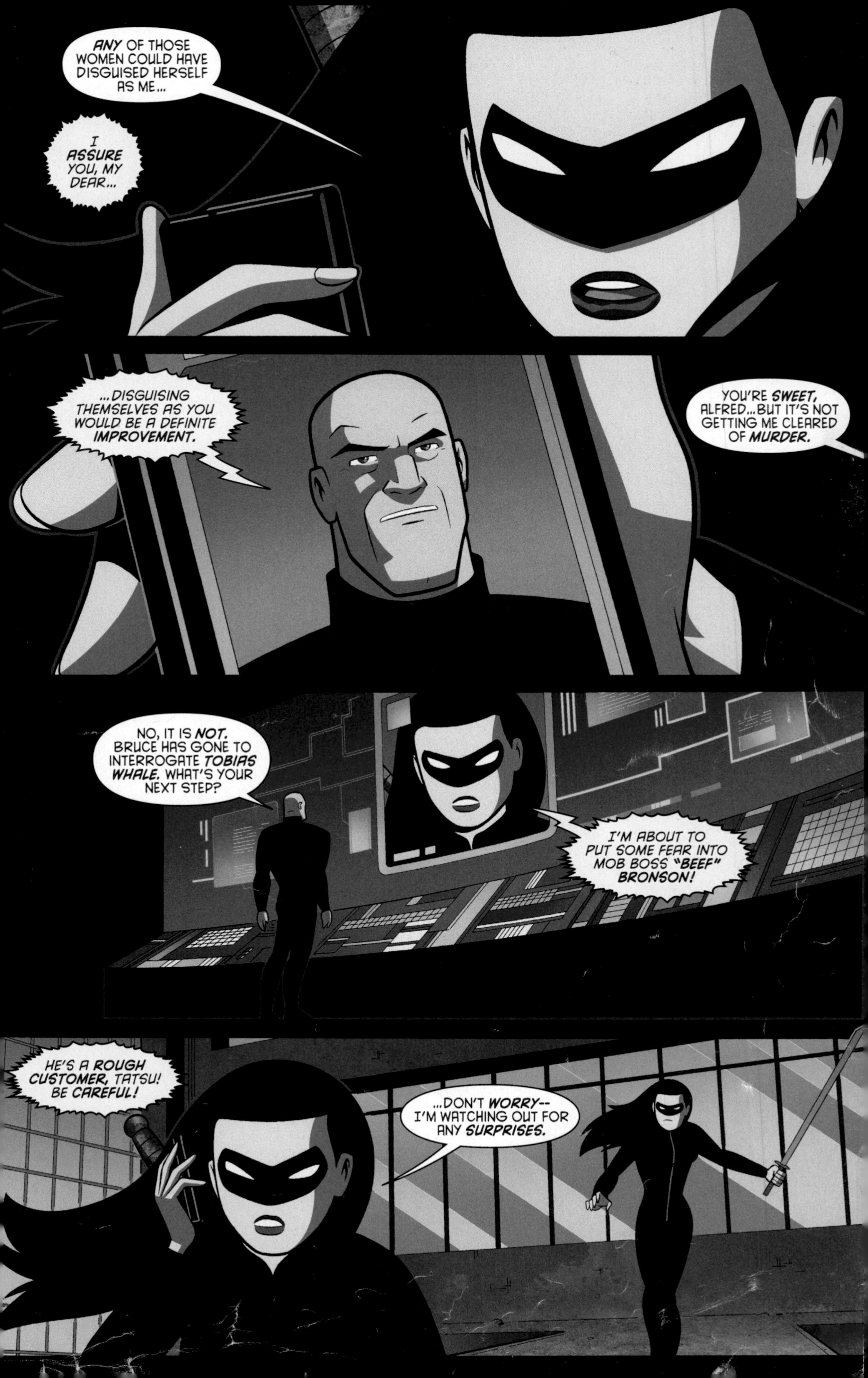
ANY OF THOSE WOMEN COULD HAVE DISGUISED HERSELF AS ME...
I ASSURE YOU, MY DEAR...
...DISGUISING THEMSELVES AS YOU WOULD BE A DEFINITE IMPROVEMENT.
YOU'RE SWEET, ALFRED...BUT IT'S NOT GETTING ME CLEARED OF MURDER.
NO, IT IS NOT. BRUCE HAS GONE TO INTERROGATE TOBIAS WHALE. WHAT'S YOUR NEXT STEP?
I'M ABOUT TO PUT SOME FEAR INTO MOB BOSS "BEEF" BRONSON!
HE'S A ROUGH CUSTOMER, TATSU! BE CAREFUL!
...DON'T WORRY-- I'M WATCHING OUT FOR ANY SURPRISES.

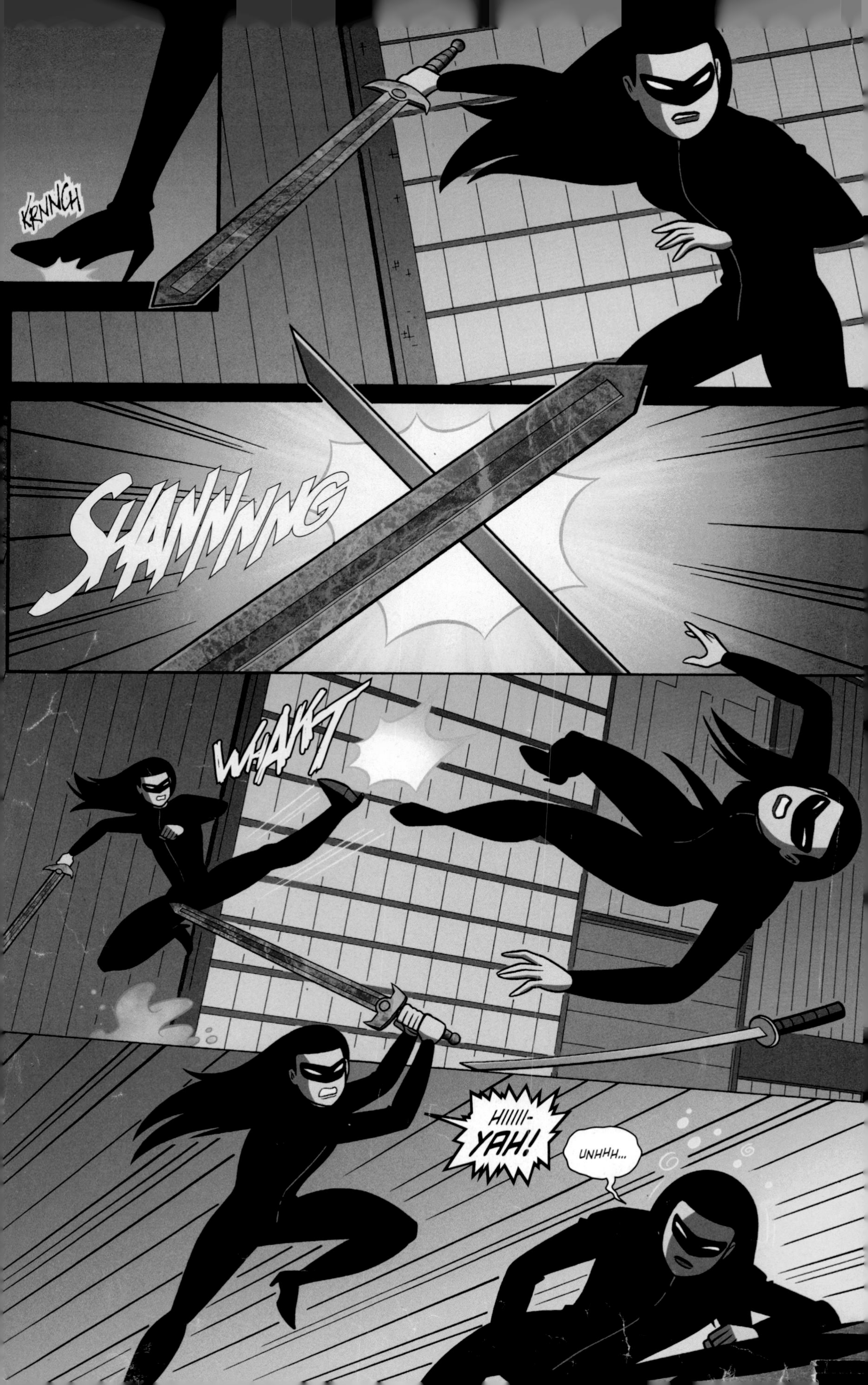
KRNNCH
SHANNNNG
WHAKT
HIIIII-YAH!
UNHHH...

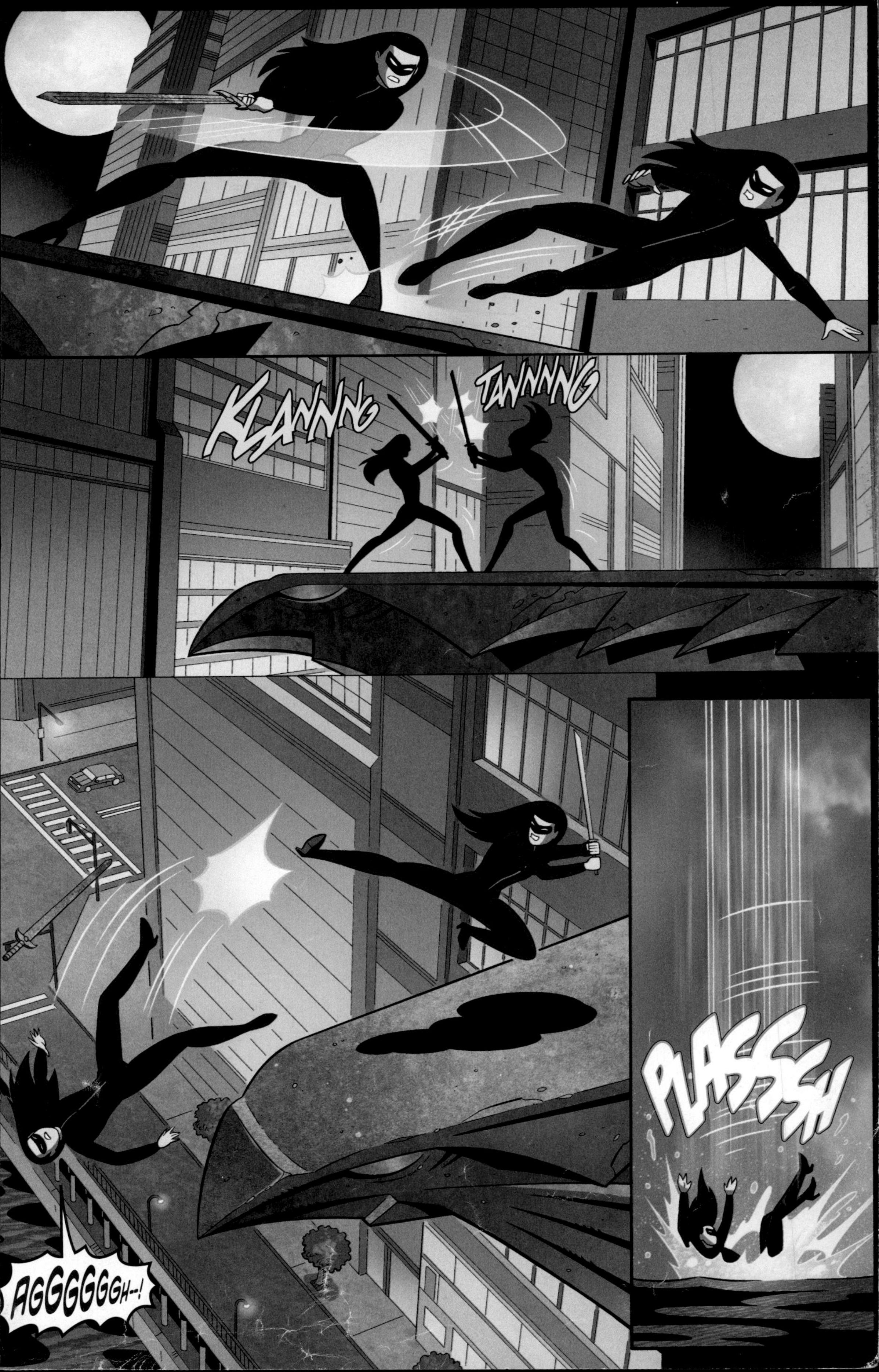
KLANNNG
TANNNNG
AGGGGGGH--!
PLASSSH

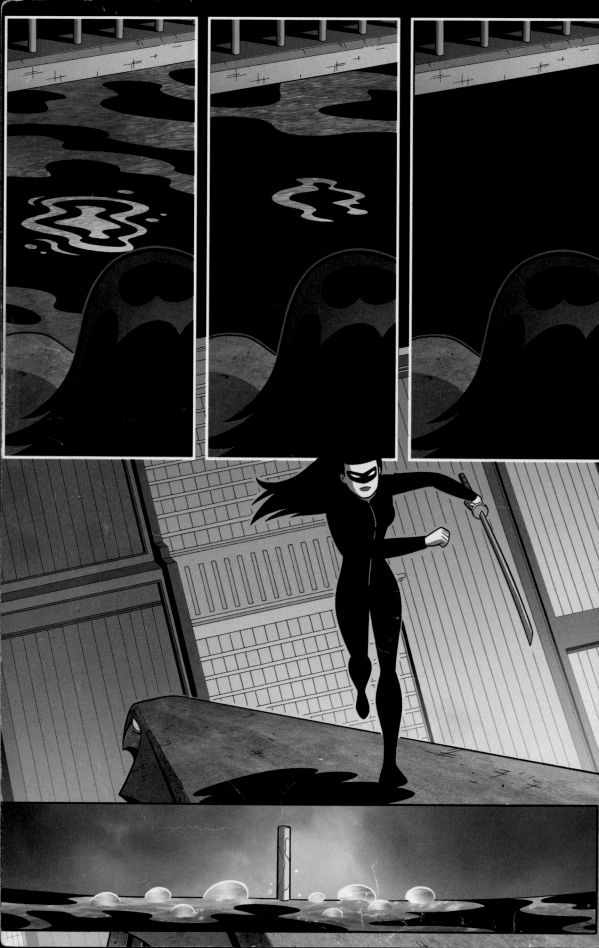

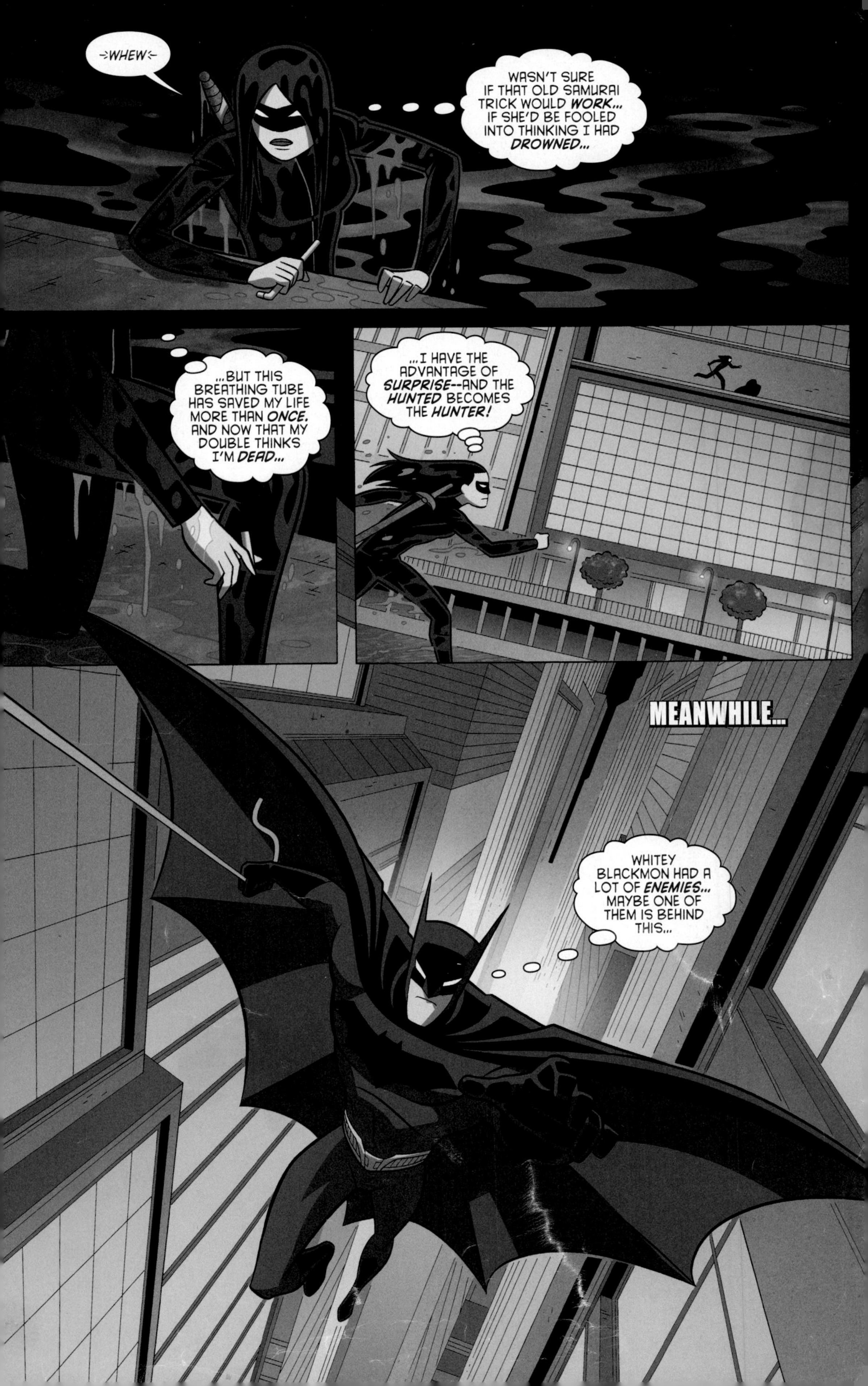
=WHEW=
WASN'T SURE IF THAT OLD SAMURAI TRICK WOULD WORK... IF SHE'D BE FOOLED INTO THINKING I HAD DROWNED...
...BUT THIS BREATHING TUBE HAS SAVED MY LIFE MORE THAN ONCE. AND NOW THAT MY DOUBLE THINKS I'M DEAD...
...I HAVE THE ADVANTAGE OF SURPRISE--AND THE HUNTED BECOMES THE HUNTER!
MEANWHILE...
WHITEY BLACKMON HAD A LOT OF ENEMIES... MAYBE ONE OF THEM IS BEHIND THIS...

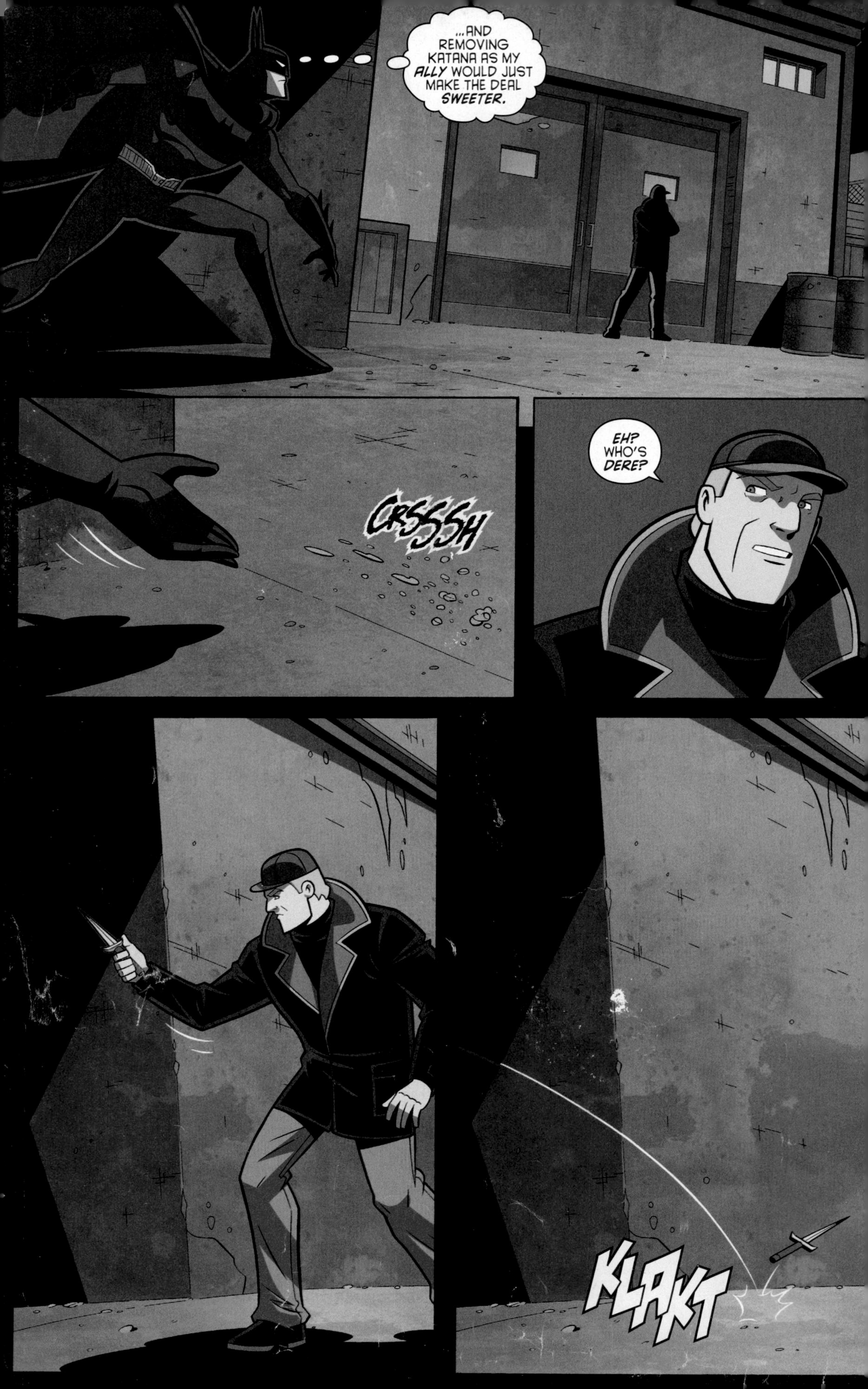
...AND REMOVING KATANA AS MY ALLY WOULD JUST MAKE THE DEAL SWEETER.
CRSSSH
EH? WHO'S DERE?
KLAKT

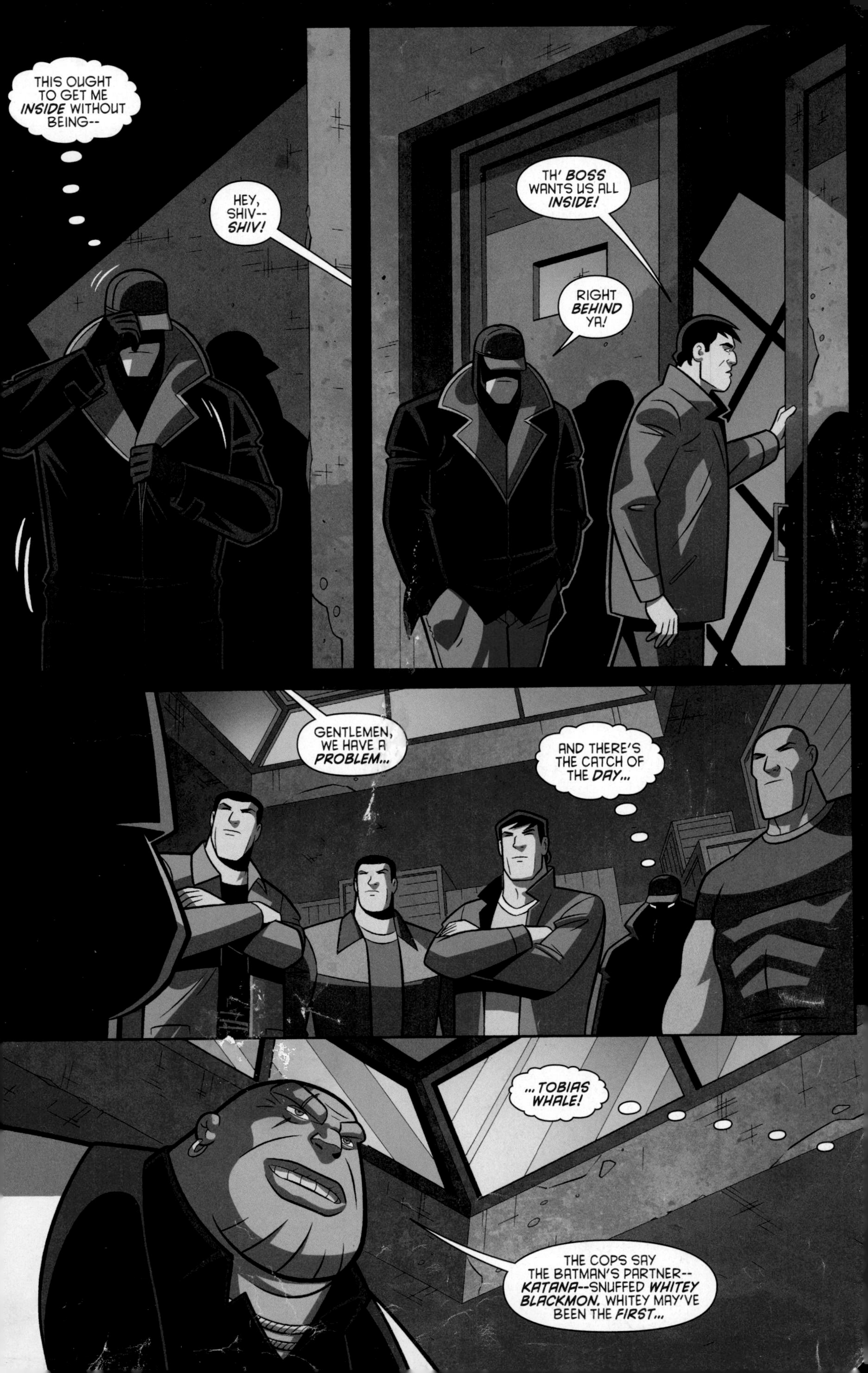
THIS OUGHT TO GET ME *INSIDE* WITHOUT BEING--
HEY, SHIV-- *SHIV!*
TH' *BOSS* WANTS US ALL *INSIDE!*
RIGHT *BEHIND* YA!
GENTLEMEN, WE HAVE A *PROBLEM...*
AND THERE'S THE CATCH OF THE *DAY...*
...TOBIAS WHALE!
THE COPS SAY THE BATMAN'S PARTNER-- *KATANA*--SNUFFED *WHITEY BLACKMON.* WHITEY MAY'VE BEEN THE *FIRST...*

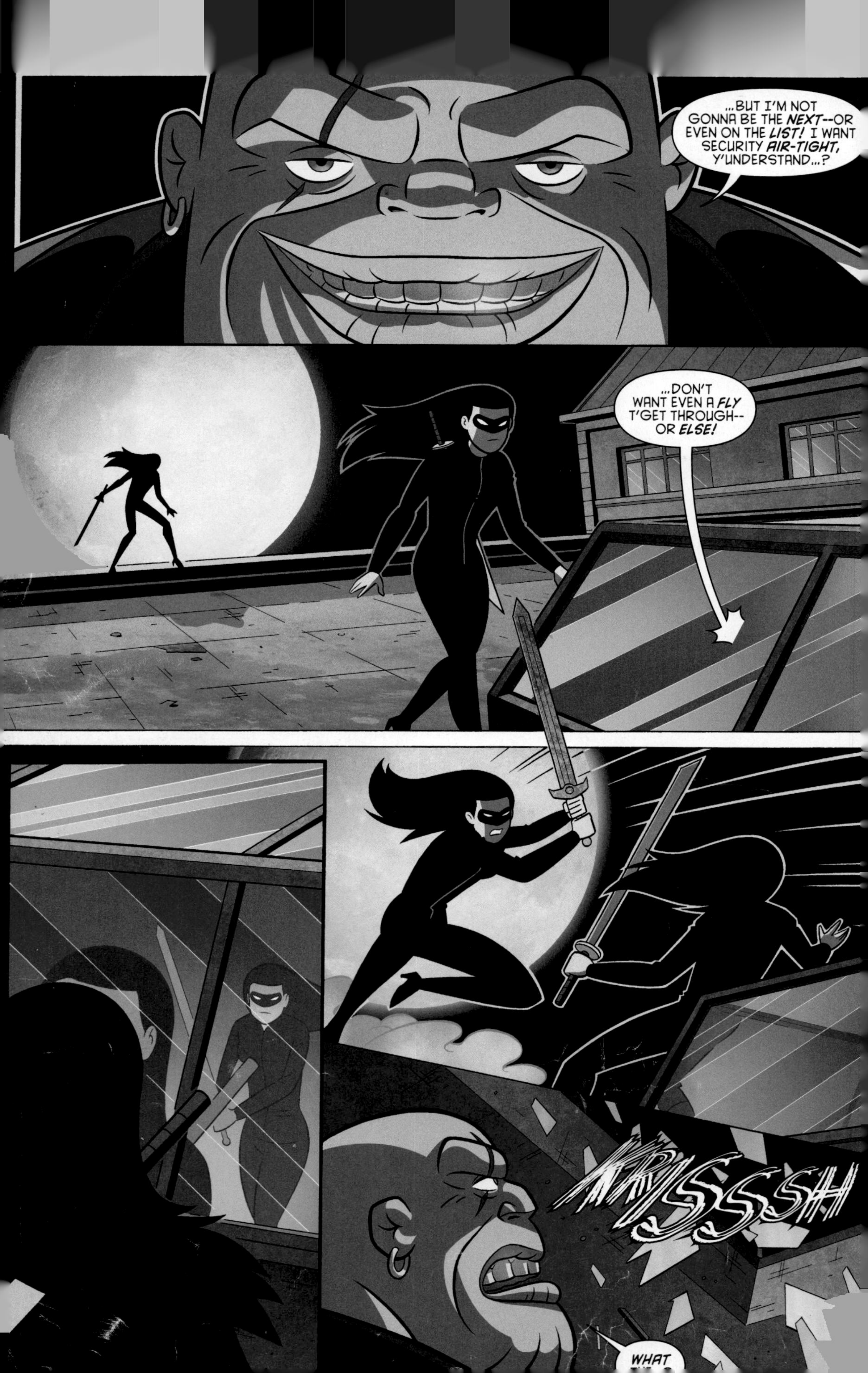
...BUT I'M NOT GONNA BE THE *NEXT*--OR EVEN ON THE *LIST!* I WANT SECURITY *AIR-TIGHT,* Y'UNDERSTAND...?
...DON'T WANT EVEN A *FLY* T'GET THROUGH--OR *ELSE!*
KRISSSSH
WHAT

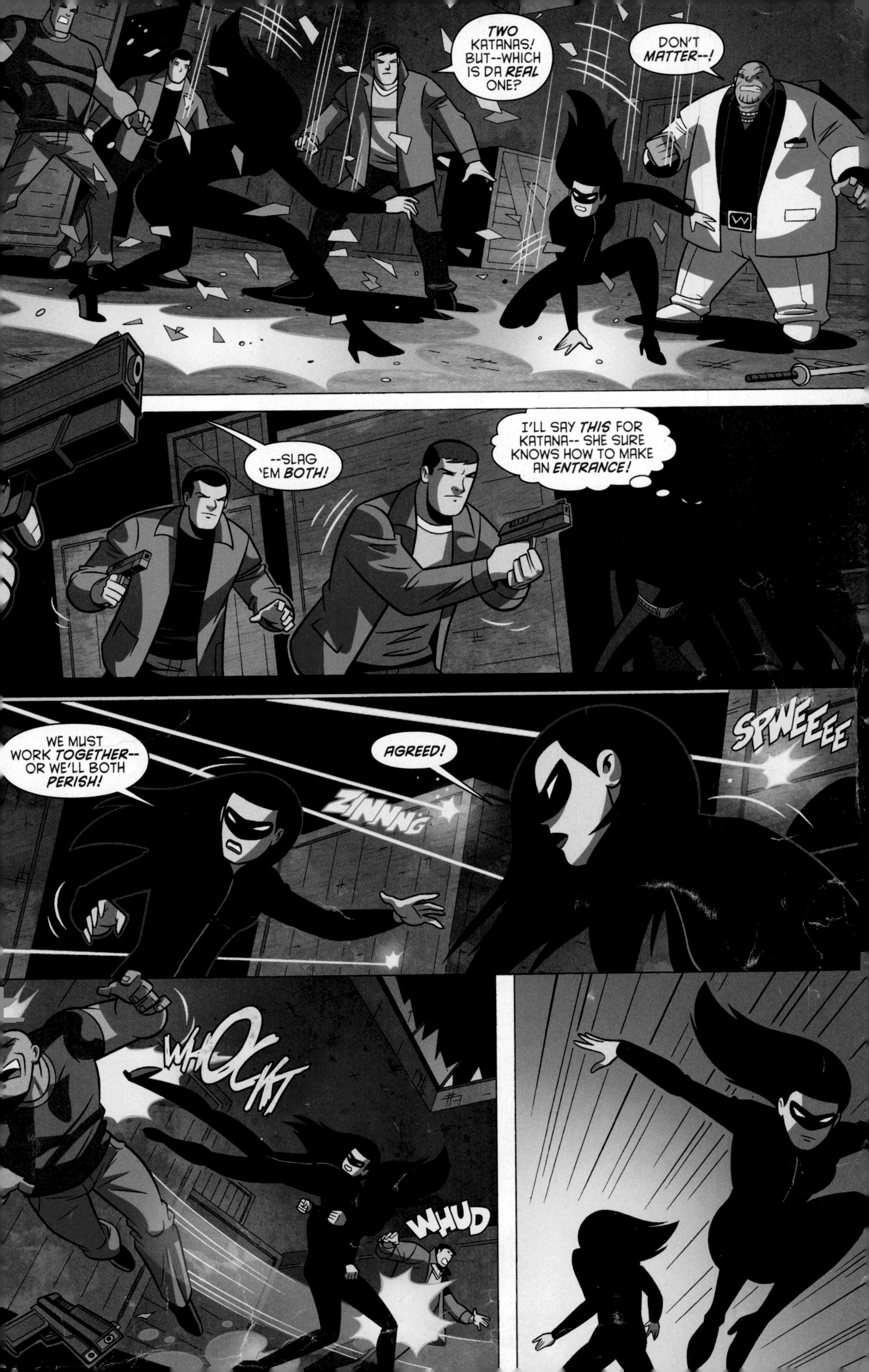

TWO KATANAS! BUT--WHICH IS DA REAL ONE?
DON'T MATTER--!
--SLAG 'EM BOTH!
I'LL SAY THIS FOR KATANA-- SHE SURE KNOWS HOW TO MAKE AN ENTRANCE!
WE MUST WORK TOGETHER-- OR WE'LL BOTH PERISH!
AGREED!
ZINNNG
SPWEEEE
WHOCK!
WHUD

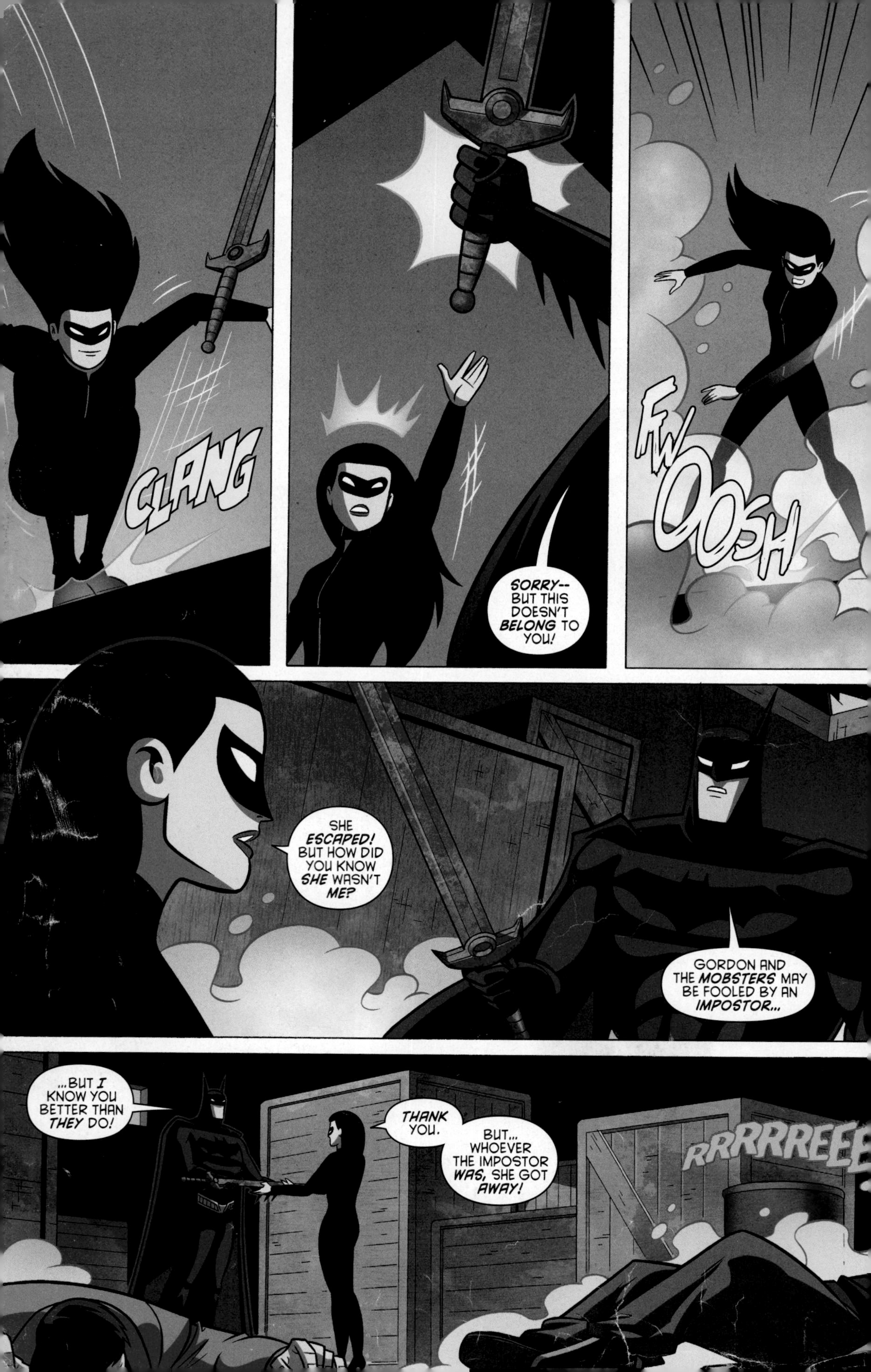
CLANG
SORRY-- BUT THIS DOESN'T BELONG TO YOU!
FWOOSH
SHE ESCAPED! BUT HOW DID YOU KNOW SHE WASN'T ME?
GORDON AND THE MOBSTERS MAY BE FOOLED BY AN IMPOSTOR...
...BUT I KNOW YOU BETTER THAN THEY DO!
THANK YOU.
BUT... WHOEVER THE IMPOSTOR WAS, SHE GOT AWAY!
RRRRRREEE

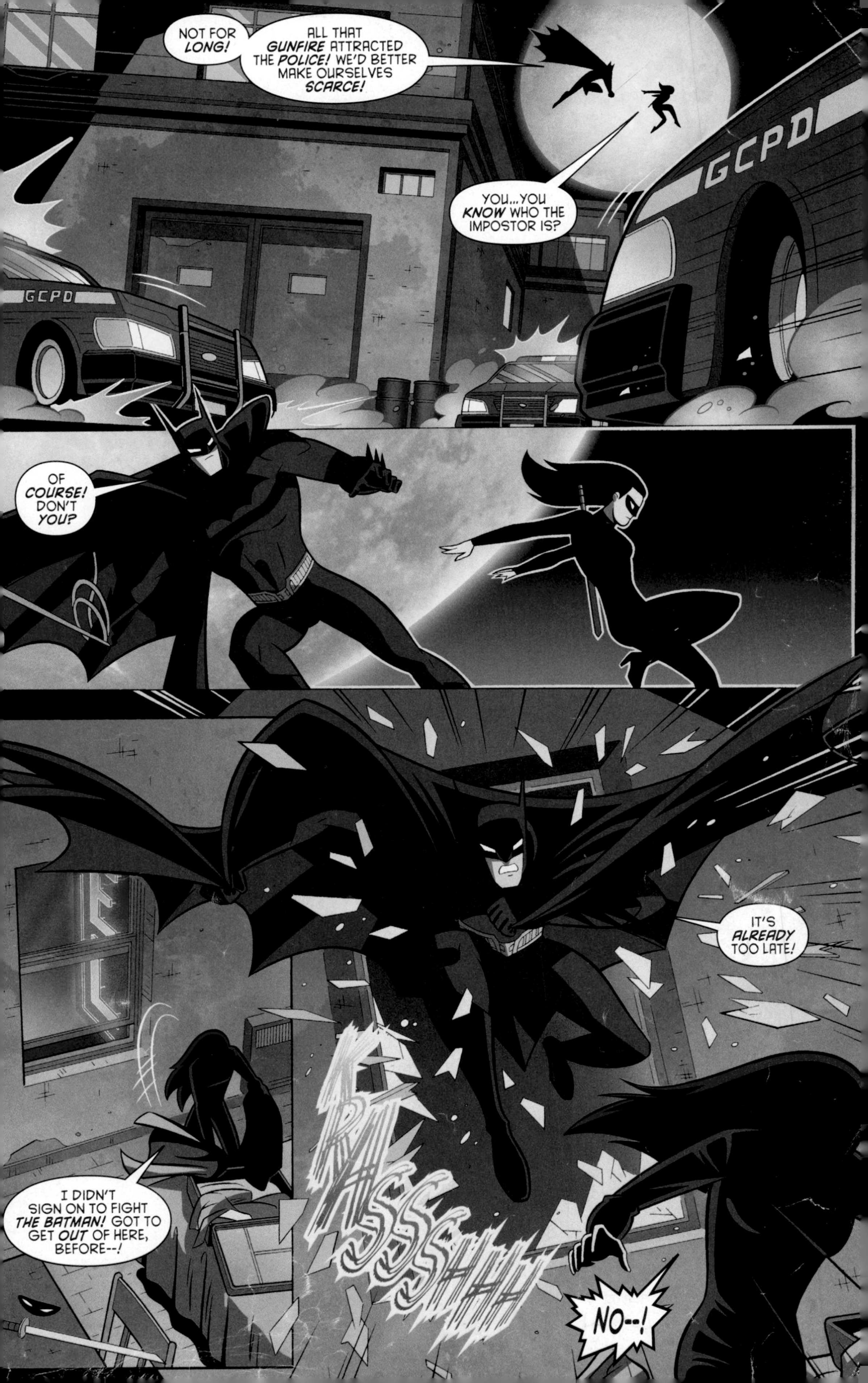
NOT FOR LONG!
ALL THAT GUNFIRE ATTRACTED THE POLICE! WE'D BETTER MAKE OURSELVES SCARCE!
GCPD
YOU...YOU KNOW WHO THE IMPOSTOR IS?
GCPD
OF COURSE! DON'T YOU?
IT'S ALREADY TOO LATE!
I DIDN'T SIGN ON TO FIGHT THE BATMAN! GOT TO GET OUT OF HERE, BEFORE--!
KRASSSHHH
NO--!

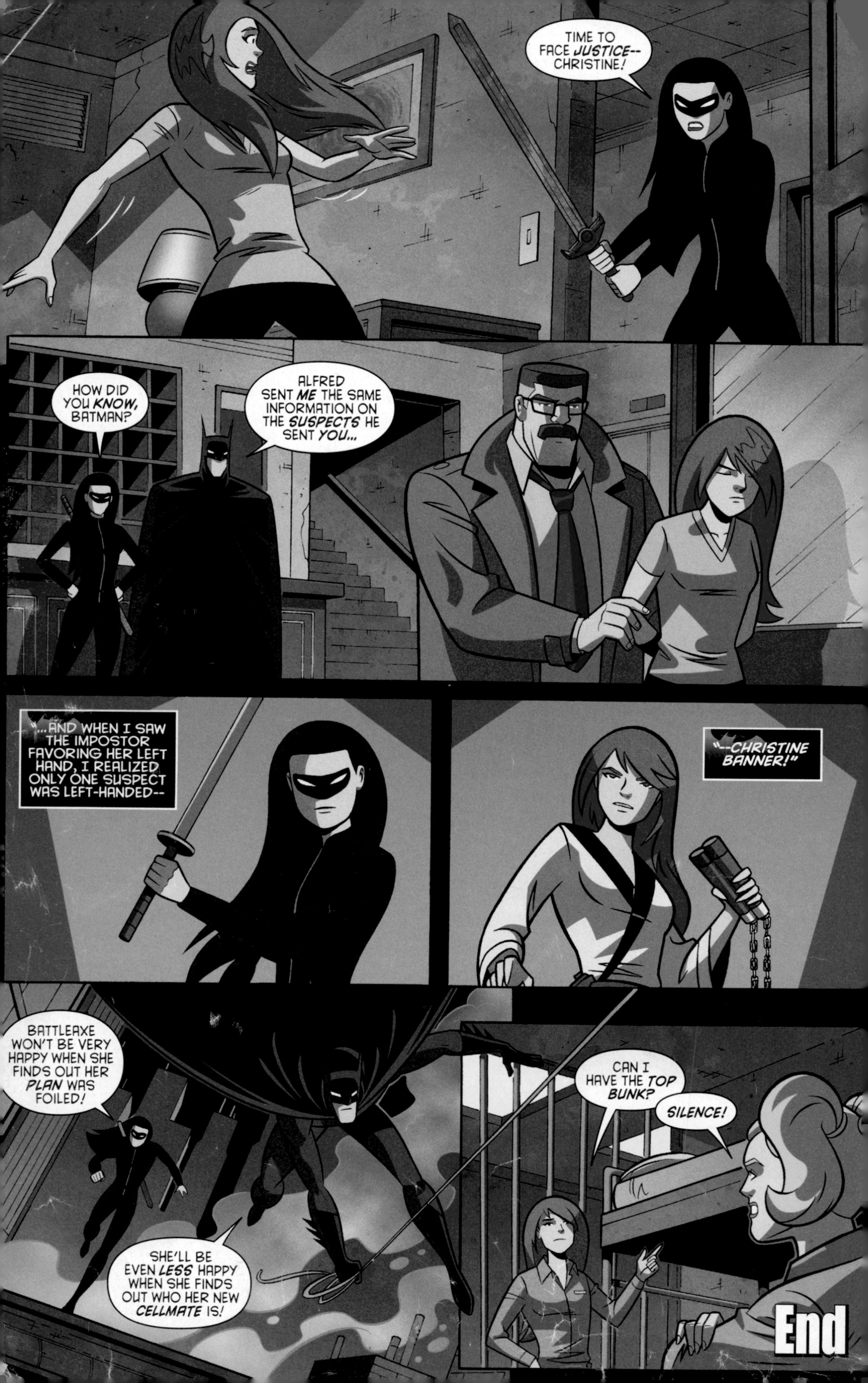
TIME TO FACE JUSTICE-- CHRISTINE!
HOW DID YOU KNOW, BATMAN?
ALFRED SENT ME THE SAME INFORMATION ON THE SUSPECTS HE SENT YOU...
"...AND WHEN I SAW THE IMPOSTOR FAVORING HER LEFT HAND, I REALIZED ONLY ONE SUSPECT WAS LEFT-HANDED--
"--CHRISTINE BANNER!"
BATTLEAXE WON'T BE VERY HAPPY WHEN SHE FINDS OUT HER PLAN WAS FOILED!
SHE'LL BE EVEN LESS HAPPY WHEN SHE FINDS OUT WHO HER NEW CELLMATE IS!
CAN I HAVE THE TOP BUNK?
SILENCE!
End

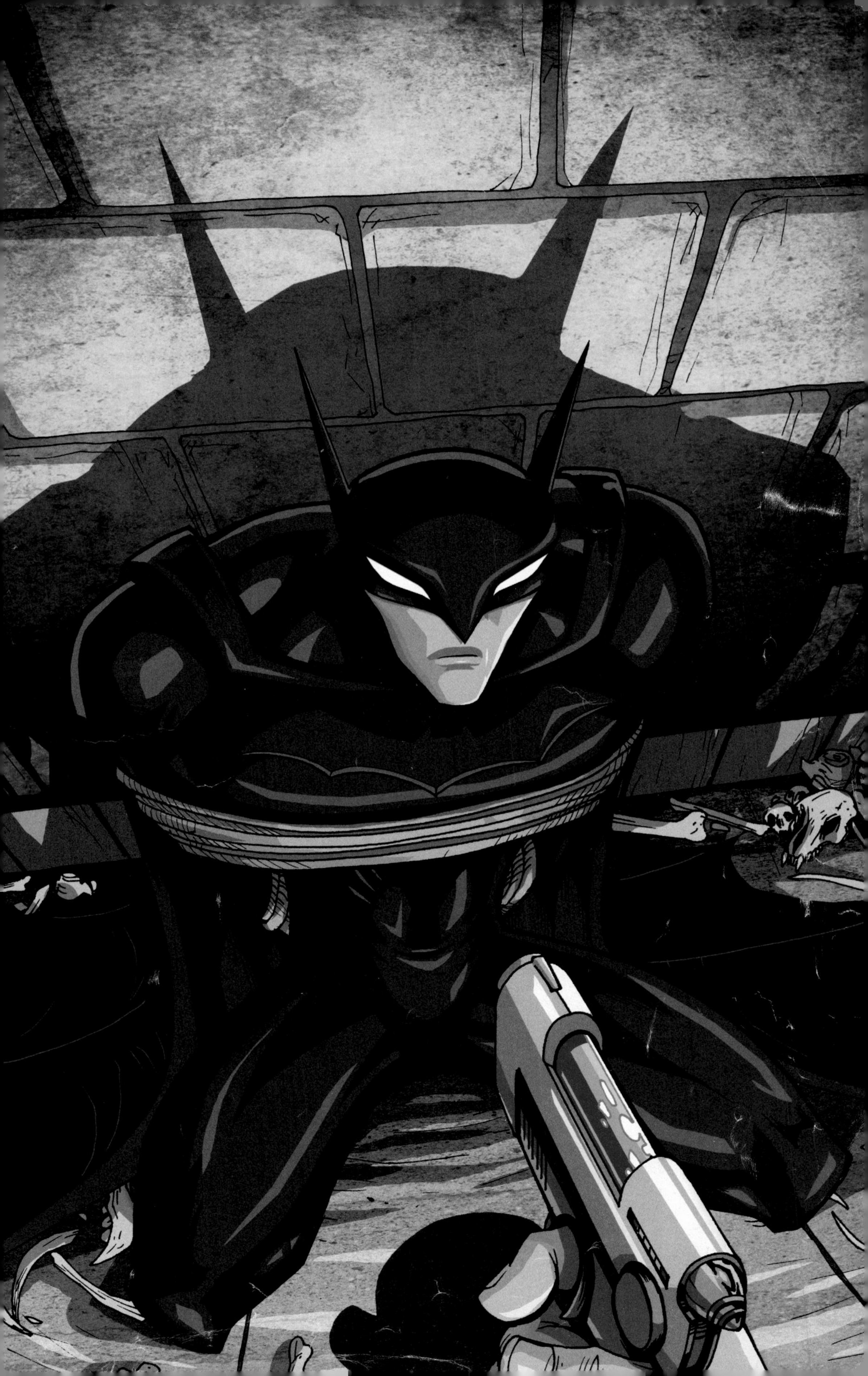

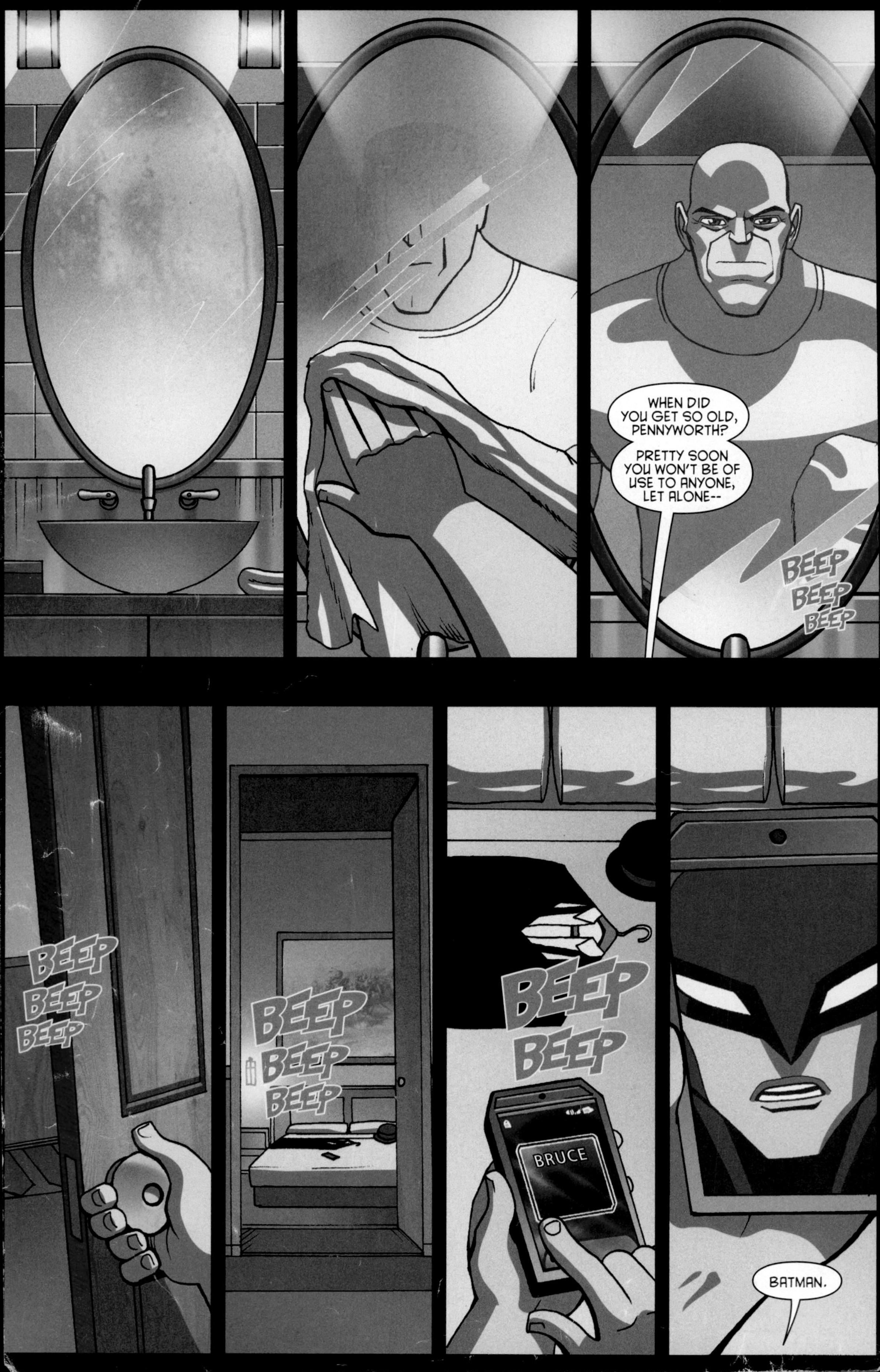
WHEN DID YOU GET SO OLD, PENNYWORTH?
PRETTY SOON YOU WON'T BE OF USE TO ANYONE, LET ALONE--
BEEP BEEP BEEP
BEEP BEEP BEEP
BEEP BEEP BEEP
BEEP BEEP
BRUCE
BATMAN.

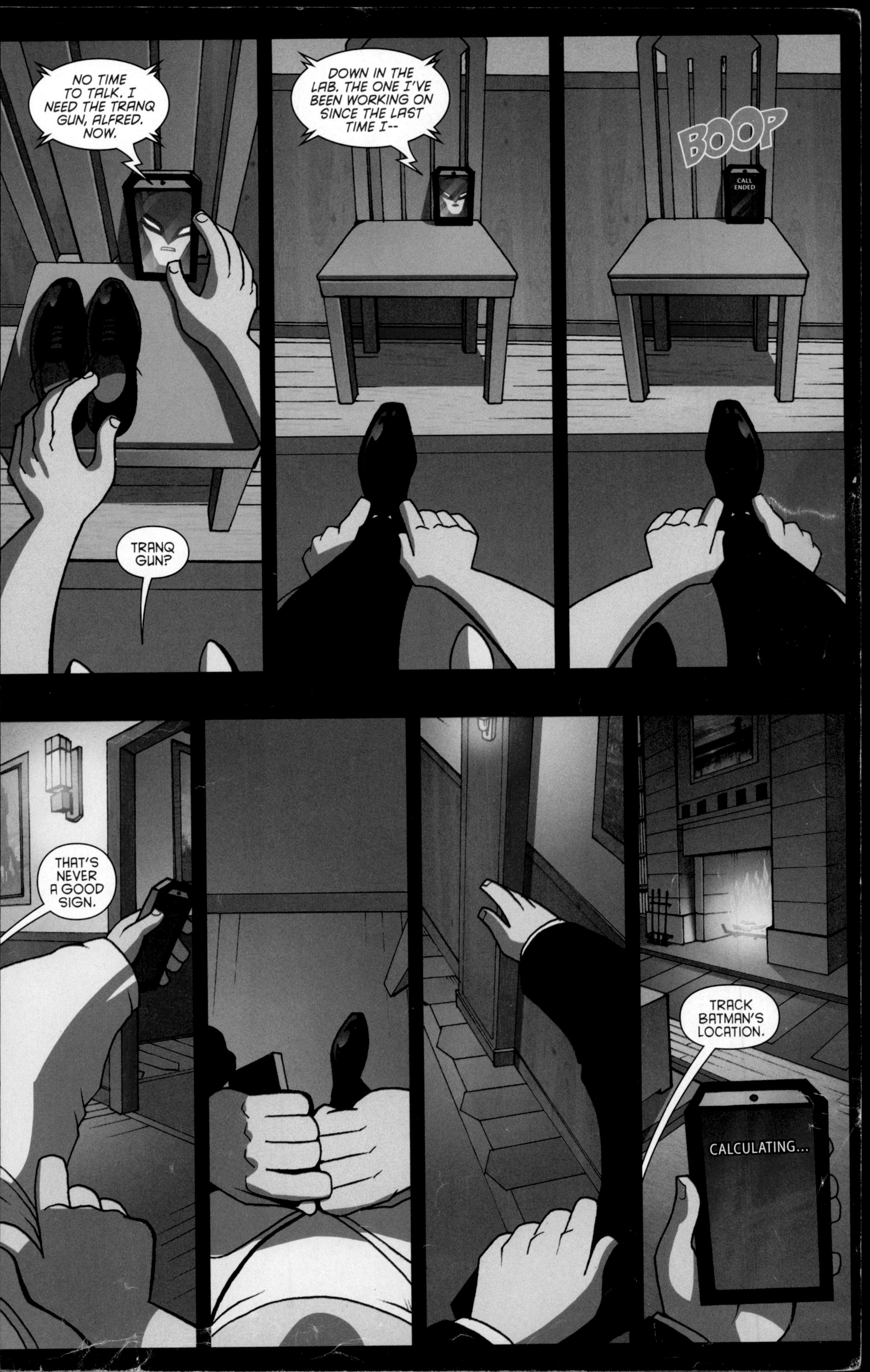
NO TIME TO TALK. I NEED THE TRANQ GUN, ALFRED. NOW.
TRANQ GUN?
DOWN IN THE LAB. THE ONE I'VE BEEN WORKING ON SINCE THE LAST TIME I--
BOOP
CALL ENDED
THAT'S NEVER A GOOD SIGN.
TRACK BATMAN'S LOCATION.
CALCULATING...

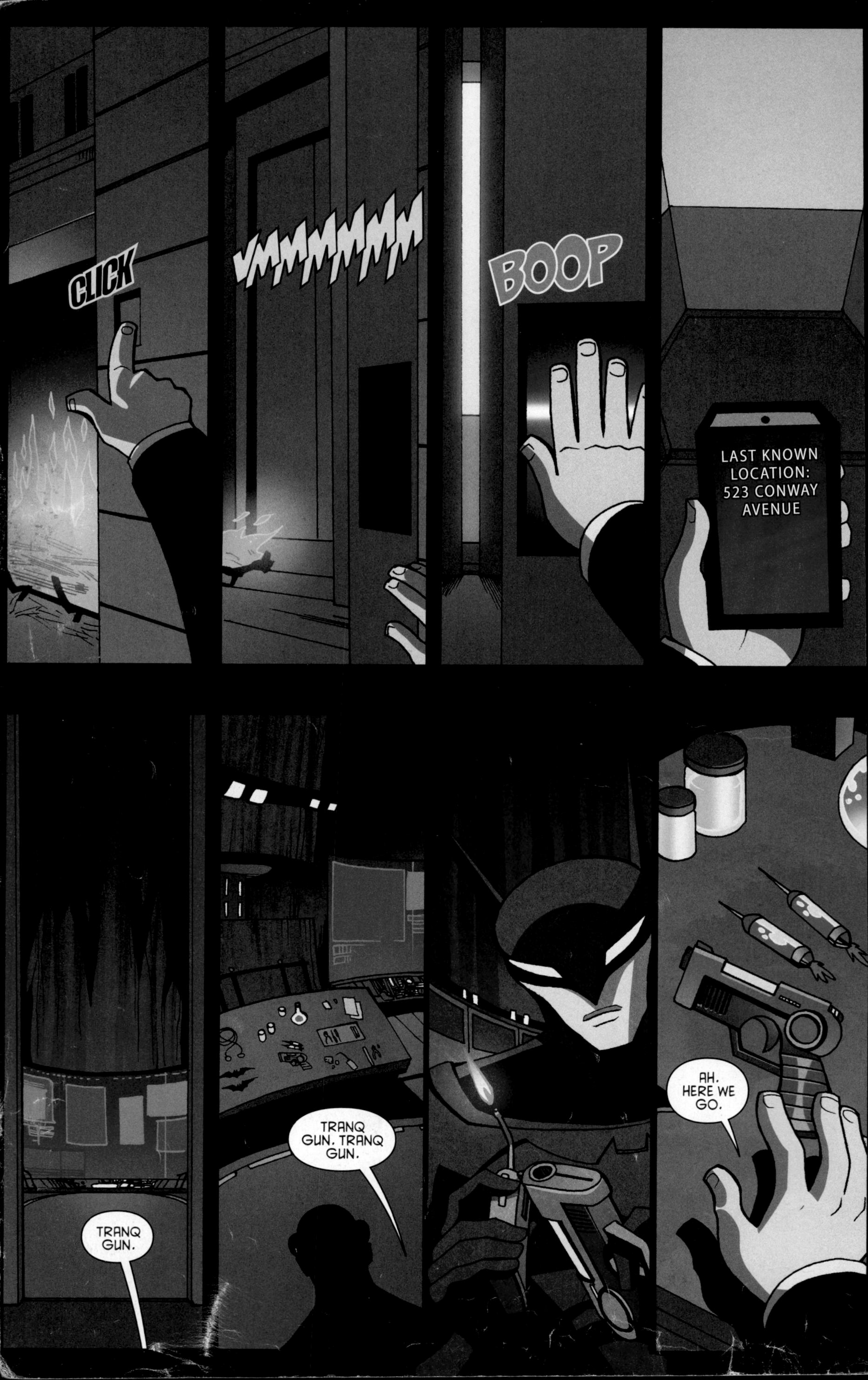
CLICK
VMMMMMM
BOOP
LAST KNOWN LOCATION: 523 CONWAY AVENUE
TRANQ GUN.
TRANQ GUN. TRANQ GUN.
AH. HERE WE GO.

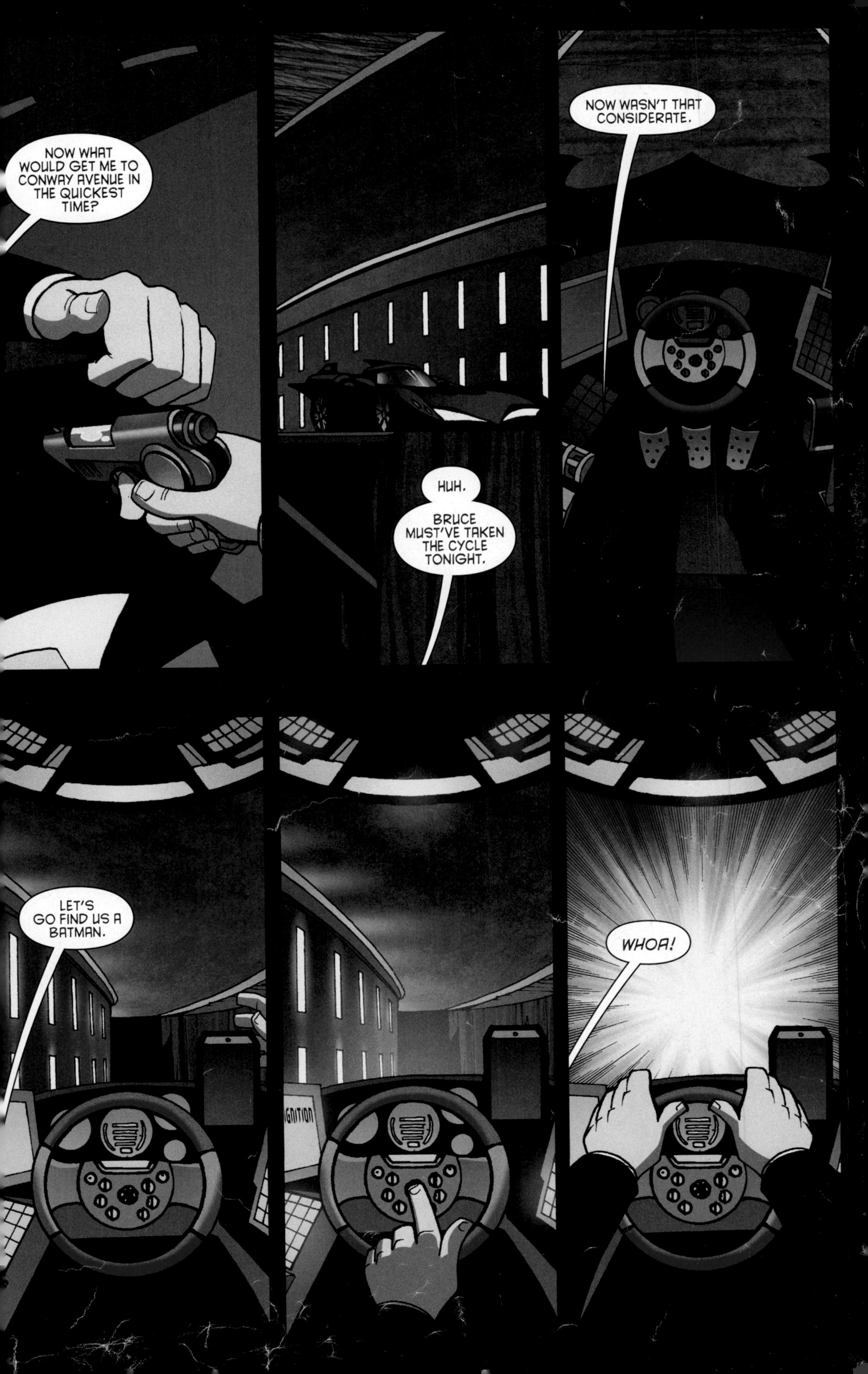
NOW WHAT WOULD GET ME TO CONWAY AVENUE IN THE QUICKEST TIME?
HUH.
BRUCE MUST'VE TAKEN THE CYCLE TONIGHT.
NOW WASN'T THAT CONSIDERATE.
LET'S GO FIND US A BATMAN.
IGNITION
WHOA!

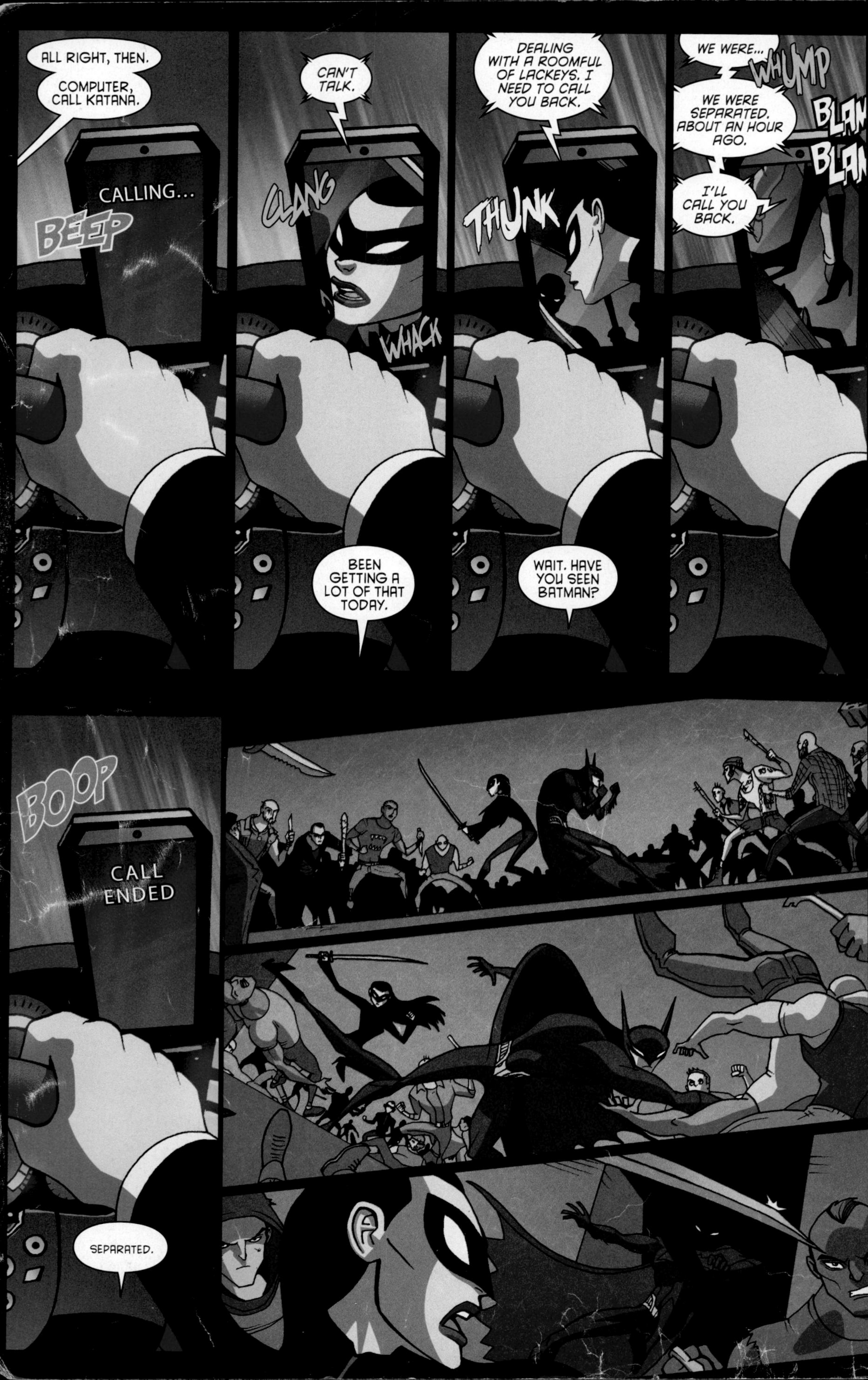
ALL RIGHT, THEN.
COMPUTER, CALL KATANA.
CALLING...
BEEP
CAN'T TALK.
CLANG
WHACK
BEEN GETTING A LOT OF THAT TODAY.
DEALING WITH A ROOMFUL OF LACKEYS. I NEED TO CALL YOU BACK.
THUNK
WAIT. HAVE YOU SEEN BATMAN?
WE WERE...
WHUMP
WE WERE SEPARATED. ABOUT AN HOUR AGO.
I'LL CALL YOU BACK.
BOOP
CALL ENDED
SEPARATED.

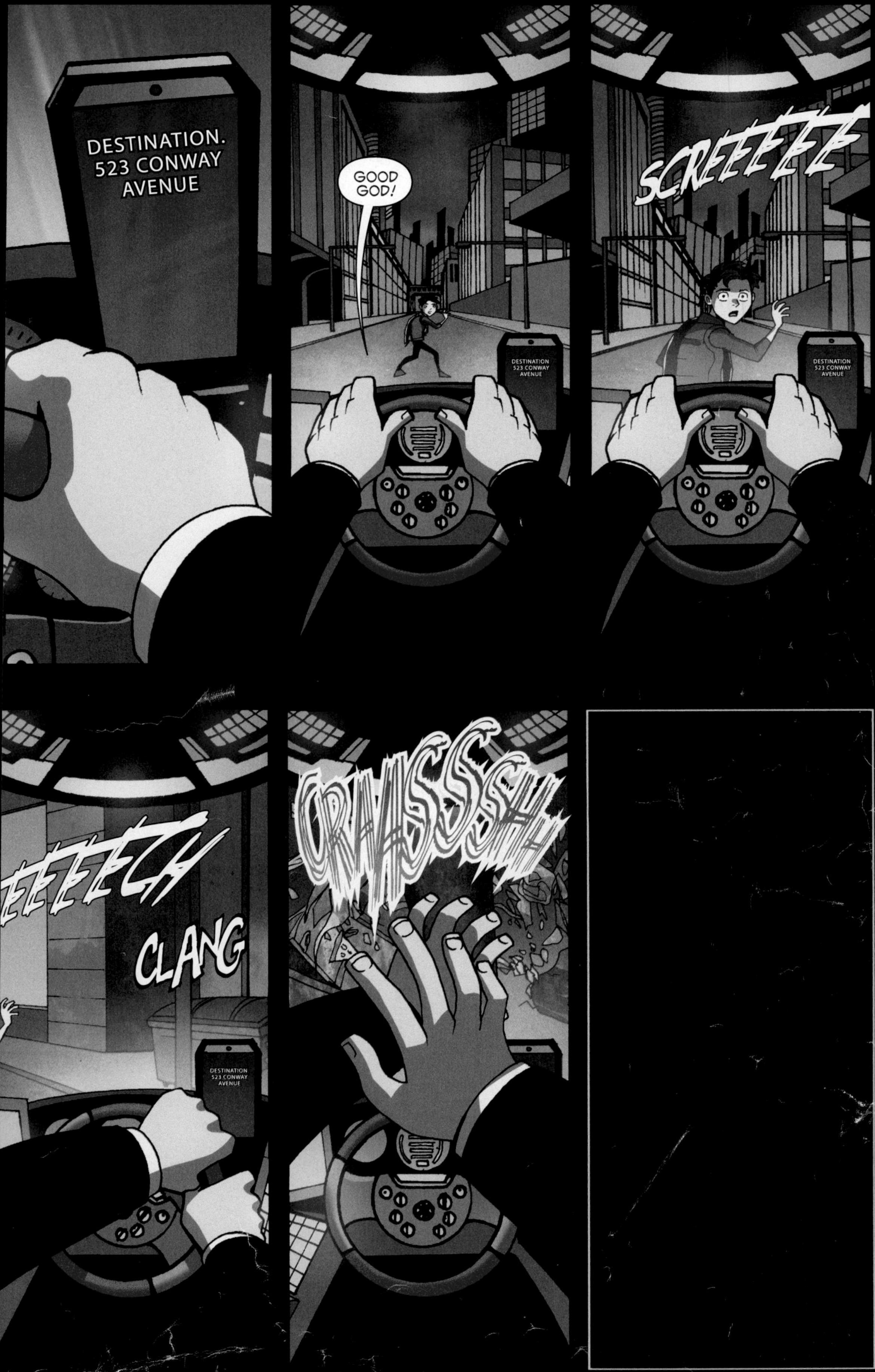

DESTINATION.
523 CONWAY
AVENUE
GOOD GOD!
DESTINATION
523 CONWAY
AVENUE
SCREEEEE
DESTINATION
523 CONWAY
AVENUE
EEEECH
CLANG
DESTINATION
523 CONWAY
AVENUE
CRASSSSH

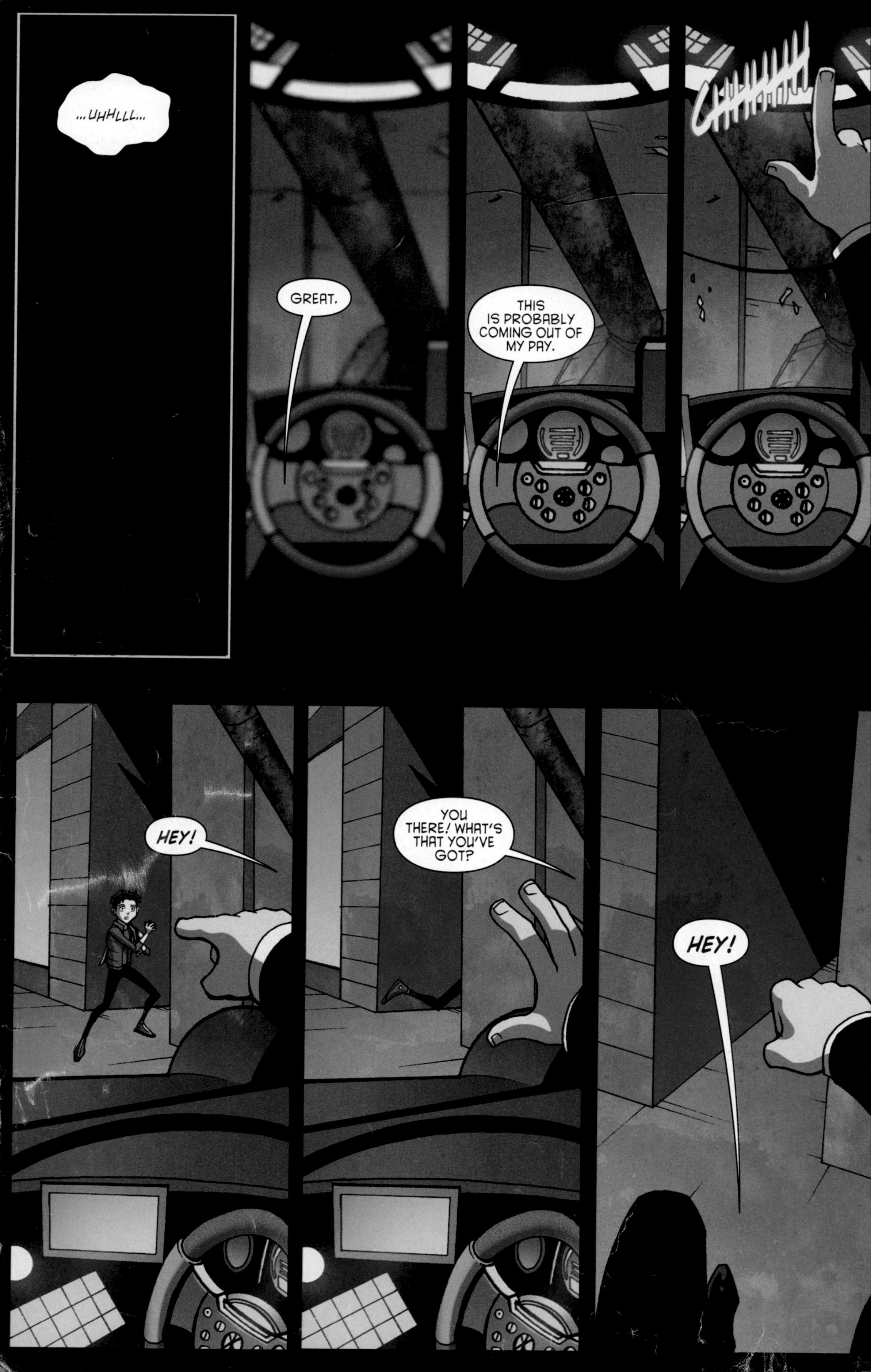
...UHHLLL...
GREAT.
THIS IS PROBABLY COMING OUT OF MY PAY.
HEY!
YOU THERE! WHAT'S THAT YOU'VE GOT?
HEY!

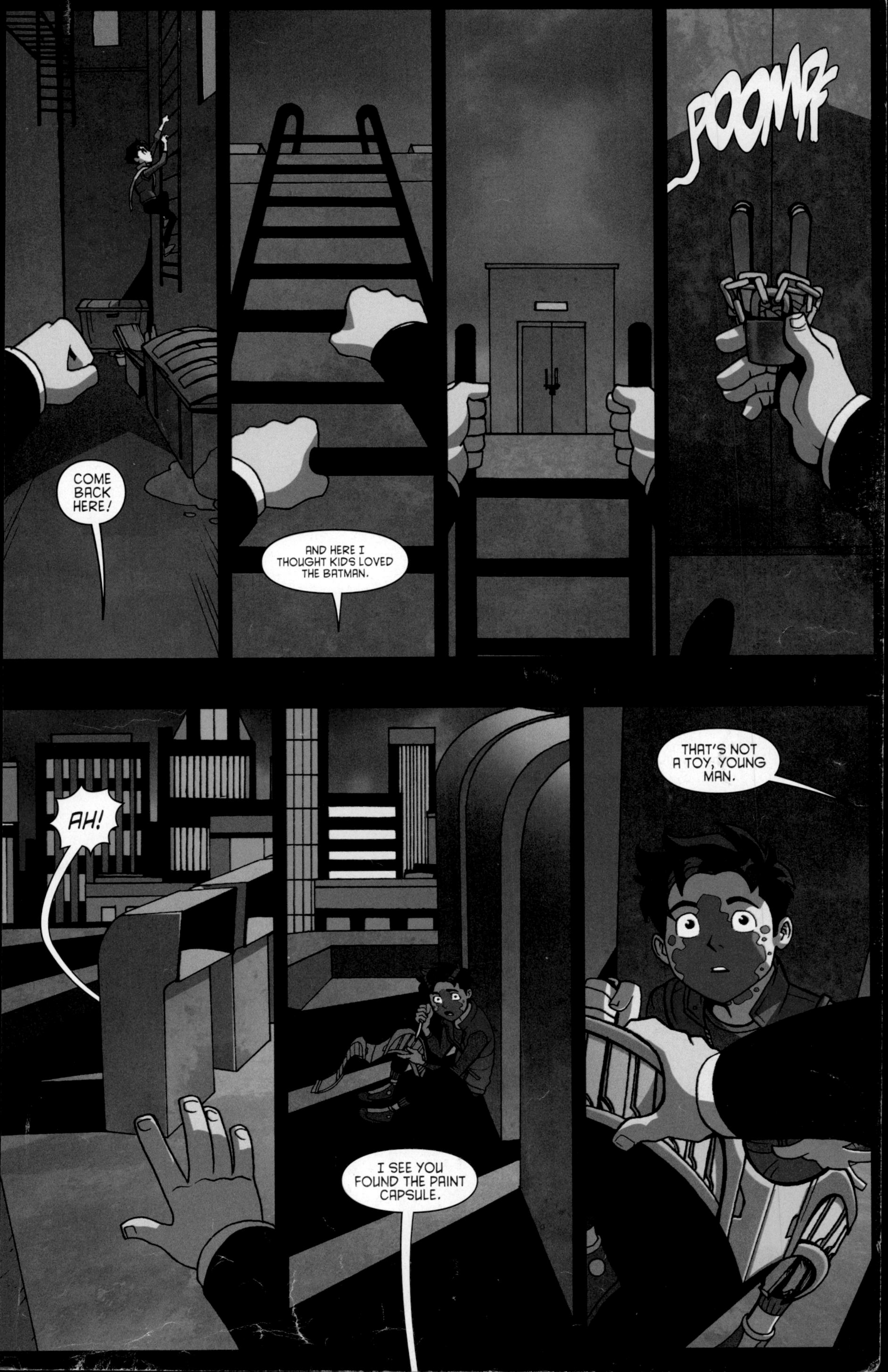
COME BACK HERE!
AND HERE I THOUGHT KIDS LOVED THE BATMAN.
POOMF
AH!
I SEE YOU FOUND THE PAINT CAPSULE.
THAT'S NOT A TOY, YOUNG MAN.

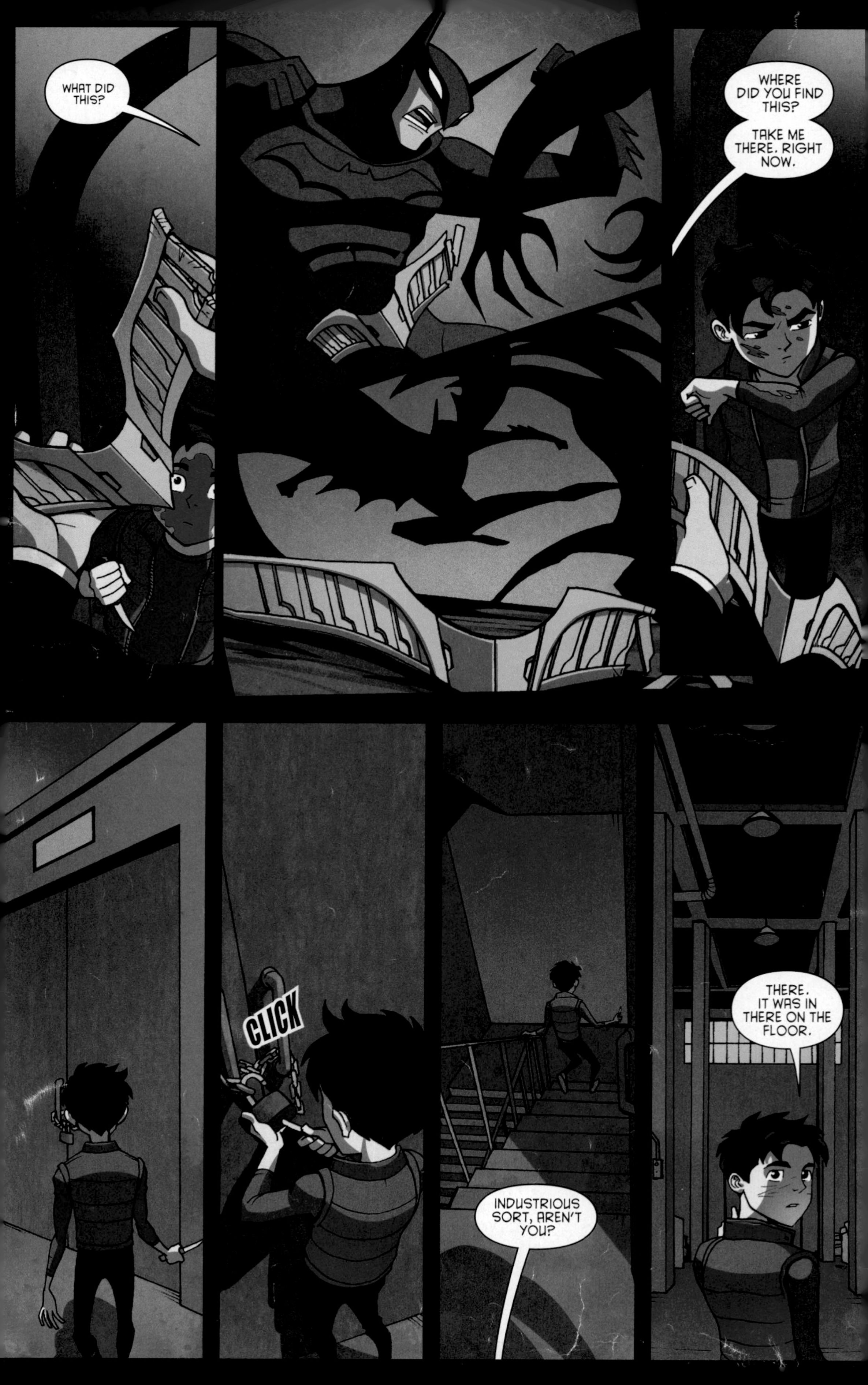
WHAT DID THIS?
WHERE DID YOU FIND THIS?
TAKE ME THERE. RIGHT NOW.
CLICK
INDUSTRIOUS SORT, AREN'T YOU?
THERE. IT WAS IN THERE ON THE FLOOR.

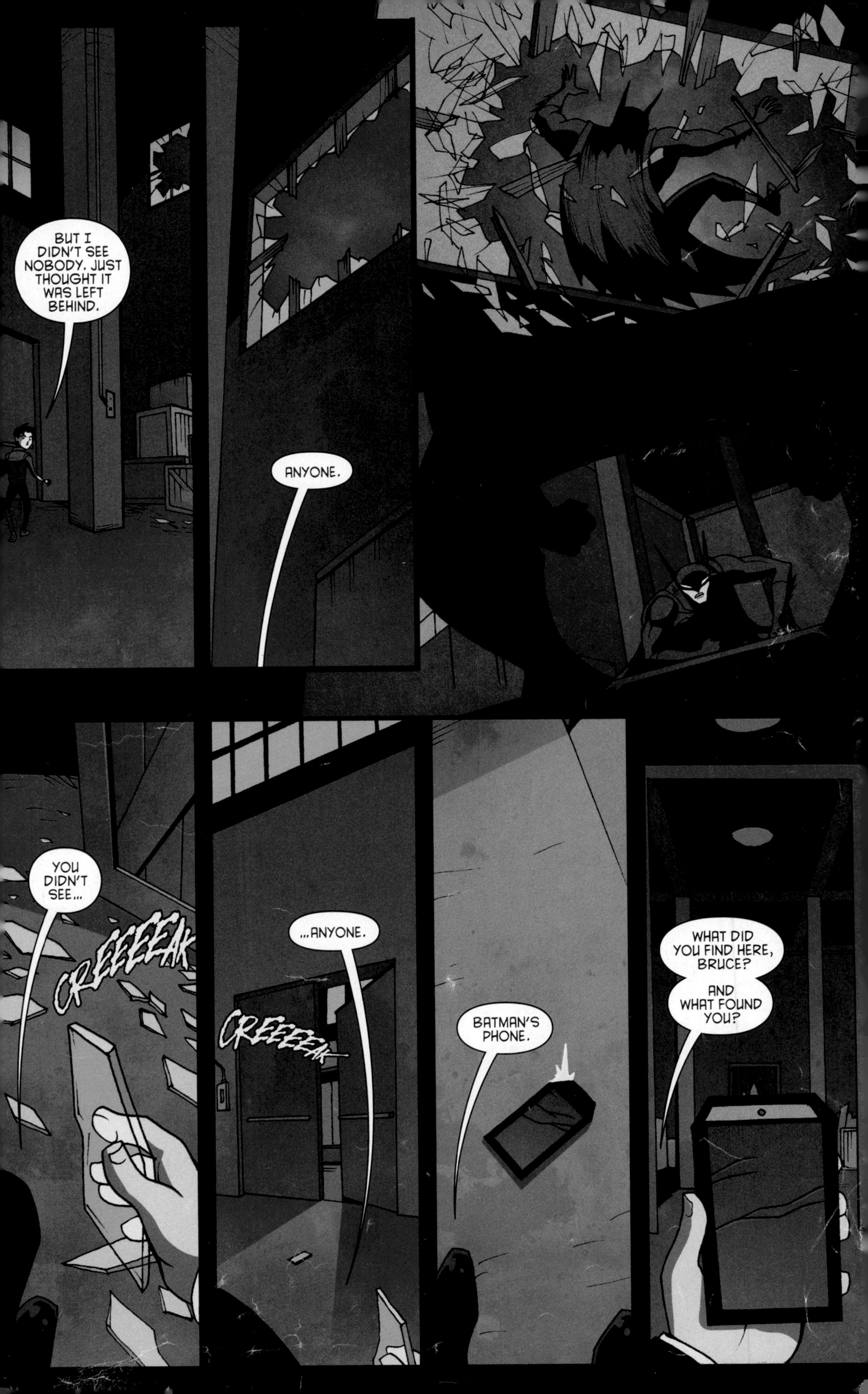
BUT I DIDN'T SEE NOBODY. JUST THOUGHT IT WAS LEFT BEHIND.
ANYONE.
YOU DIDN'T SEE...
CREEEEEAK
...ANYONE.
CREEEEEAK
BATMAN'S PHONE.
WHAT DID YOU FIND HERE, BRUCE?
AND WHAT FOUND YOU?

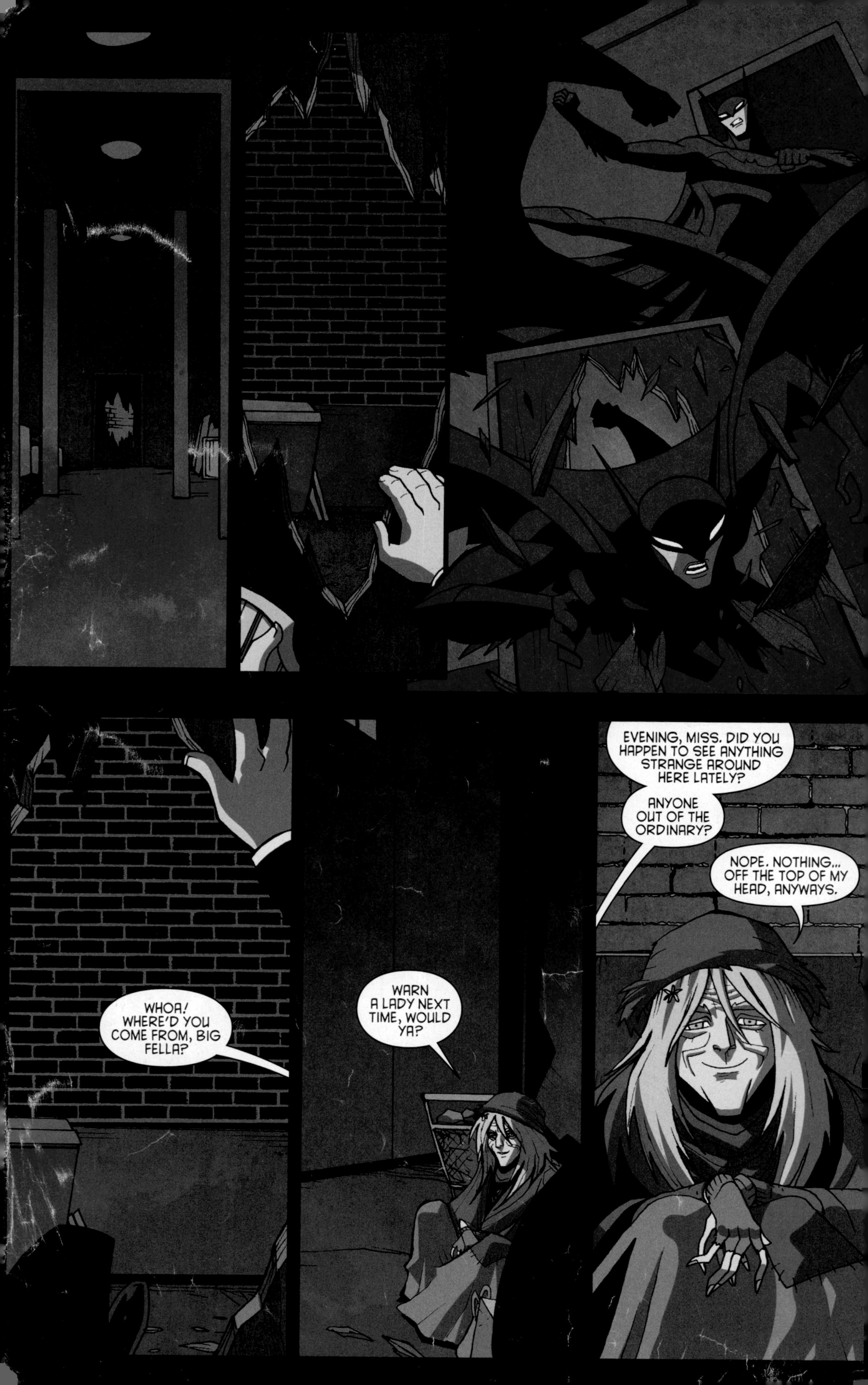
WHOA! WHERE'D YOU COME FROM, BIG FELLA?
WARN A LADY NEXT TIME, WOULD YA?
EVENING, MISS. DID YOU HAPPEN TO SEE ANYTHING STRANGE AROUND HERE LATELY?
ANYONE OUT OF THE ORDINARY?
NOPE. NOTHING... OFF THE TOP OF MY HEAD, ANYWAYS.

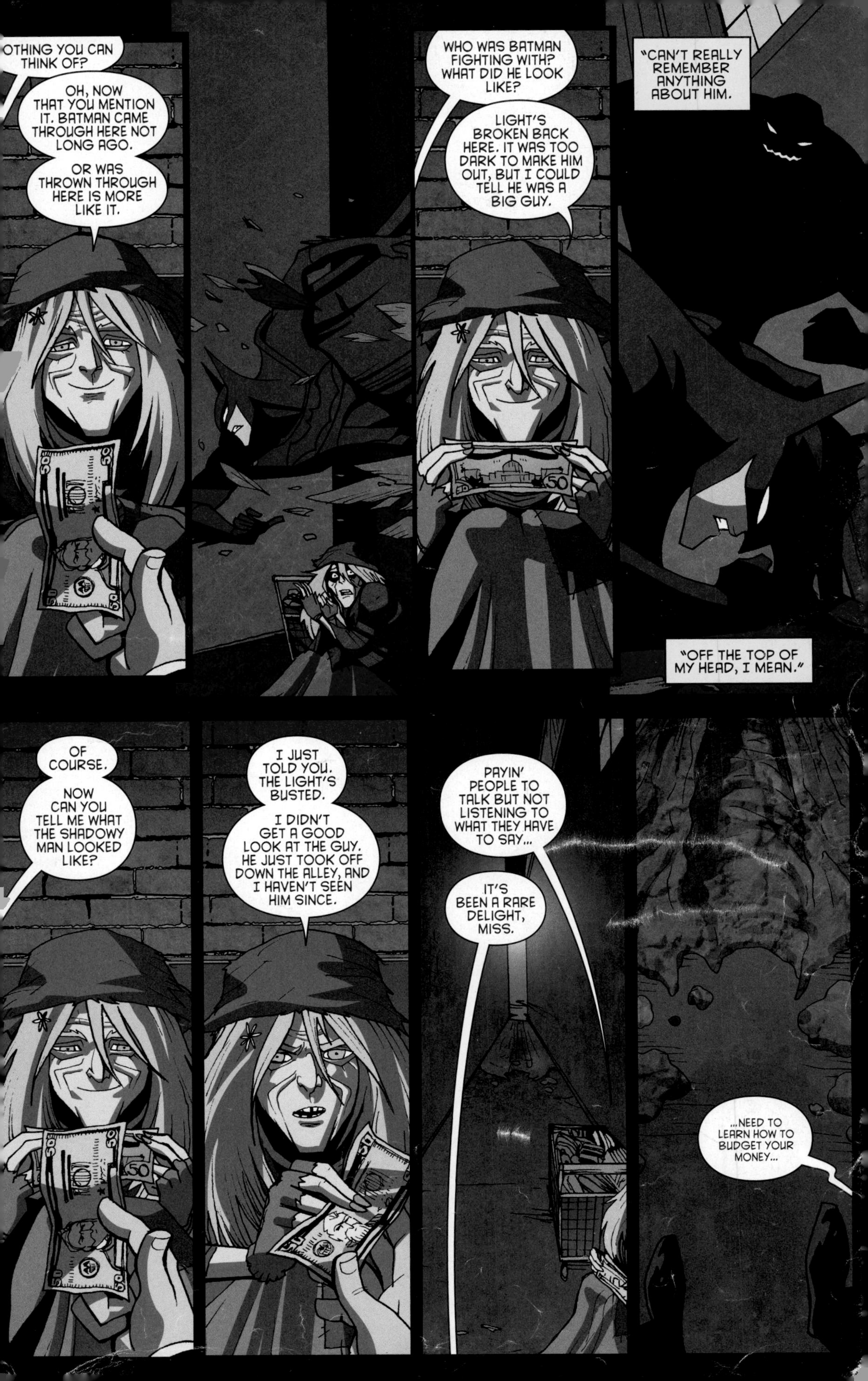
OTHING YOU CAN THINK OF?
OH, NOW THAT YOU MENTION IT. BATMAN CAME THROUGH HERE NOT LONG AGO.
OR WAS THROWN THROUGH HERE IS MORE LIKE IT.
WHO WAS BATMAN FIGHTING WITH? WHAT DID HE LOOK LIKE?
LIGHT'S BROKEN BACK HERE. IT WAS TOO DARK TO MAKE HIM OUT, BUT I COULD TELL HE WAS A BIG GUY.
"CAN'T REALLY REMEMBER ANYTHING ABOUT HIM.
"OFF THE TOP OF MY HEAD, I MEAN."
OF COURSE.
NOW CAN YOU TELL ME WHAT THE SHADOWY MAN LOOKED LIKE?
I JUST TOLD YOU. THE LIGHT'S BUSTED.
I DIDN'T GET A GOOD LOOK AT THE GUY. HE JUST TOOK OFF DOWN THE ALLEY, AND I HAVEN'T SEEN HIM SINCE.
PAYIN' PEOPLE TO TALK BUT NOT LISTENING TO WHAT THEY HAVE TO SAY...
IT'S BEEN A RARE DELIGHT, MISS.
...NEED TO LEARN HOW TO BUDGET YOUR MONEY...

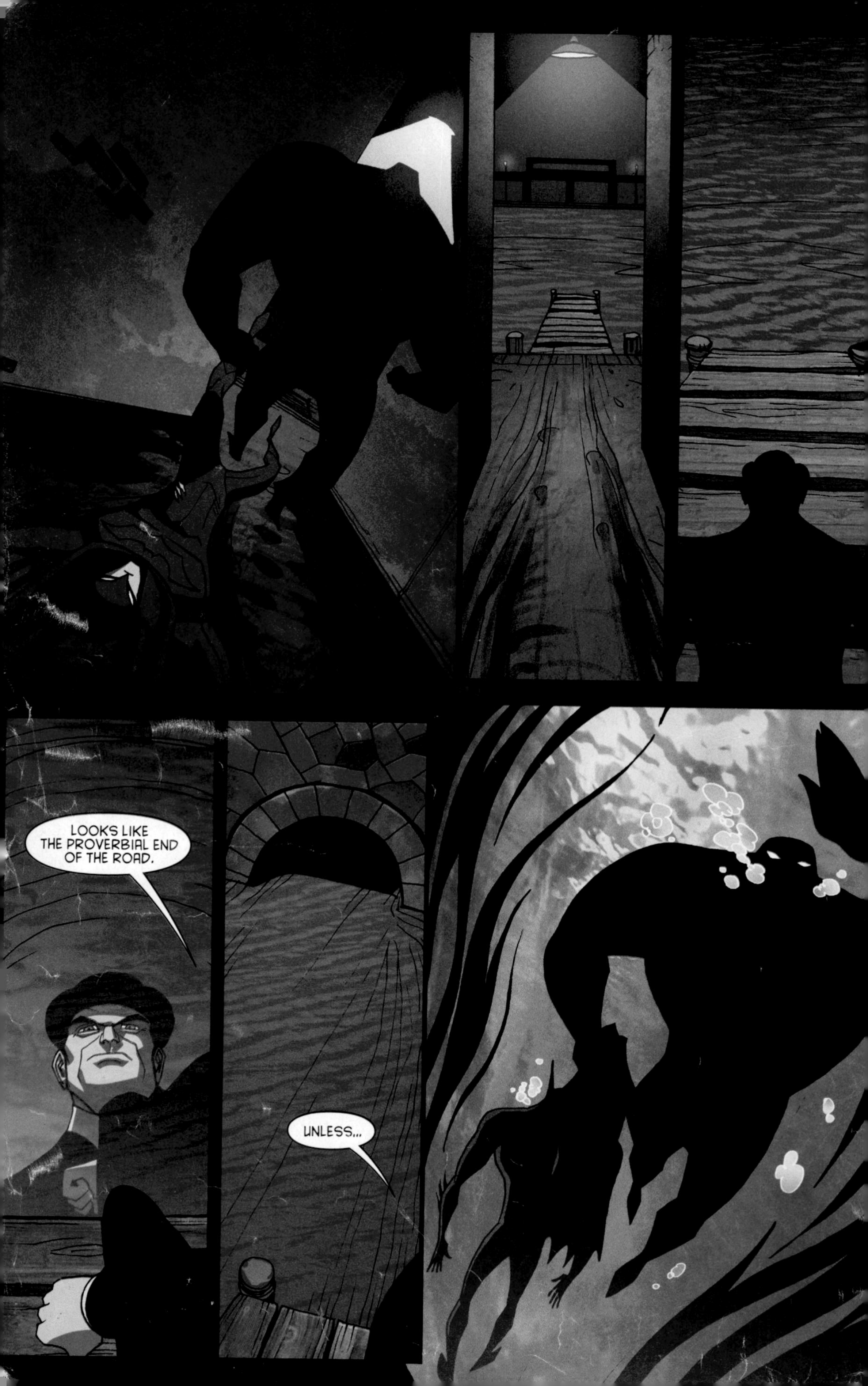
LOOKS LIKE THE PROVERBIAL END OF THE ROAD.
UNLESS...

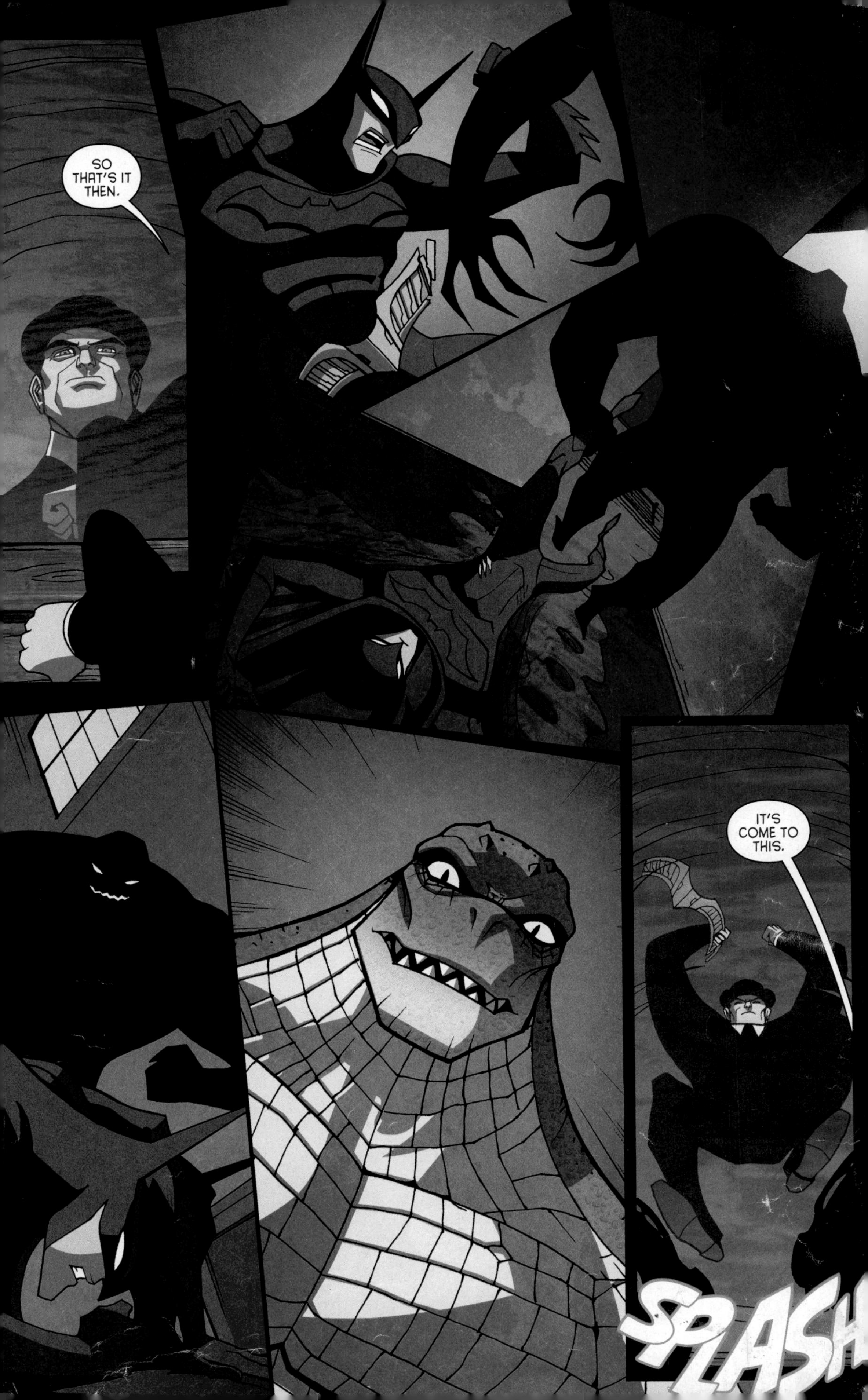
SO THAT'S IT THEN.
IT'S COME TO THIS.
SPLASH

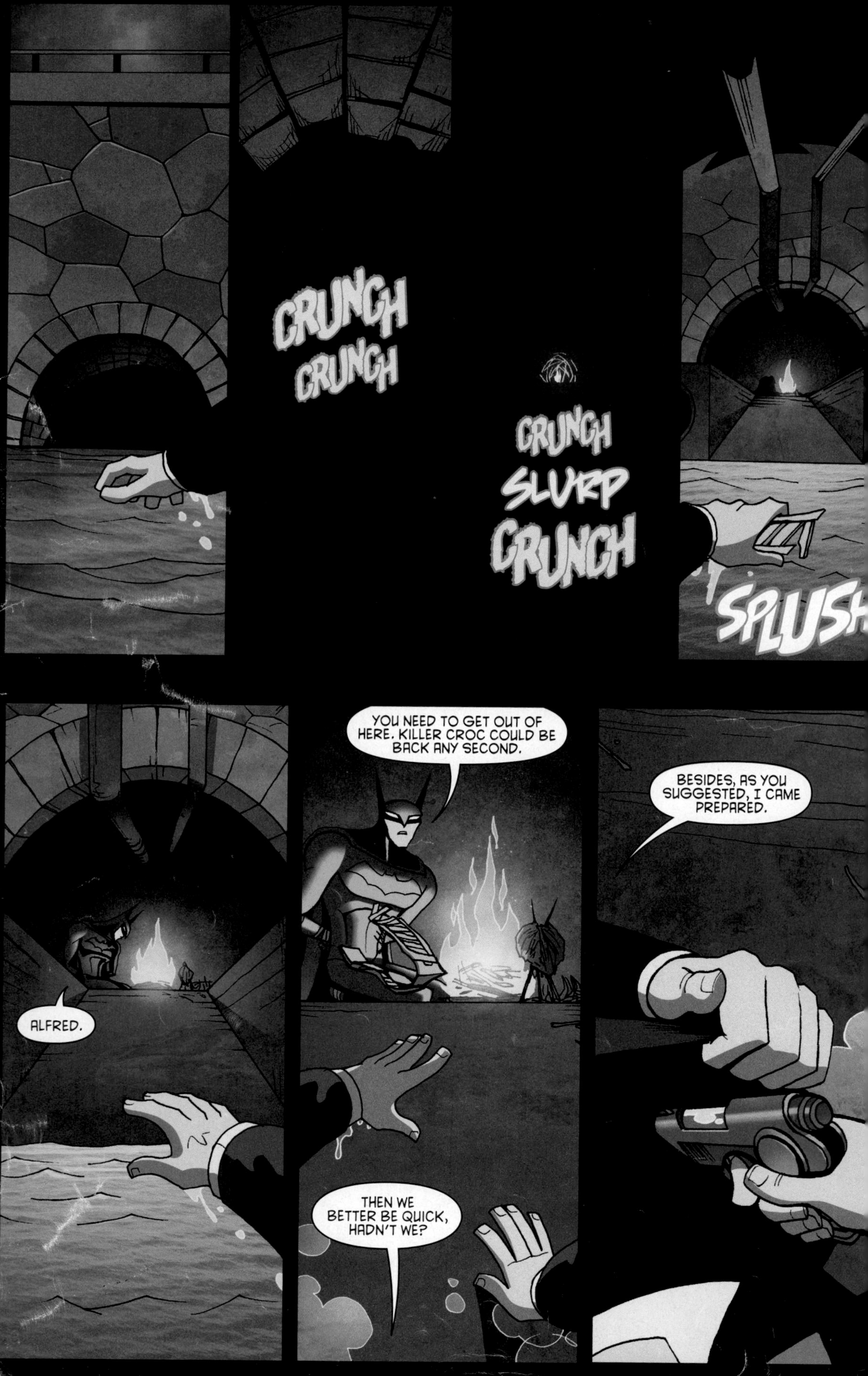
CRUNCH
CRUNCH
CRUNCH
SLURP
CRUNCH
SPLUSH
ALFRED.
YOU NEED TO GET OUT OF HERE. KILLER CROC COULD BE BACK ANY SECOND.
THEN WE BETTER BE QUICK, HADN'T WE?
BESIDES, AS YOU SUGGESTED, I CAME PREPARED.

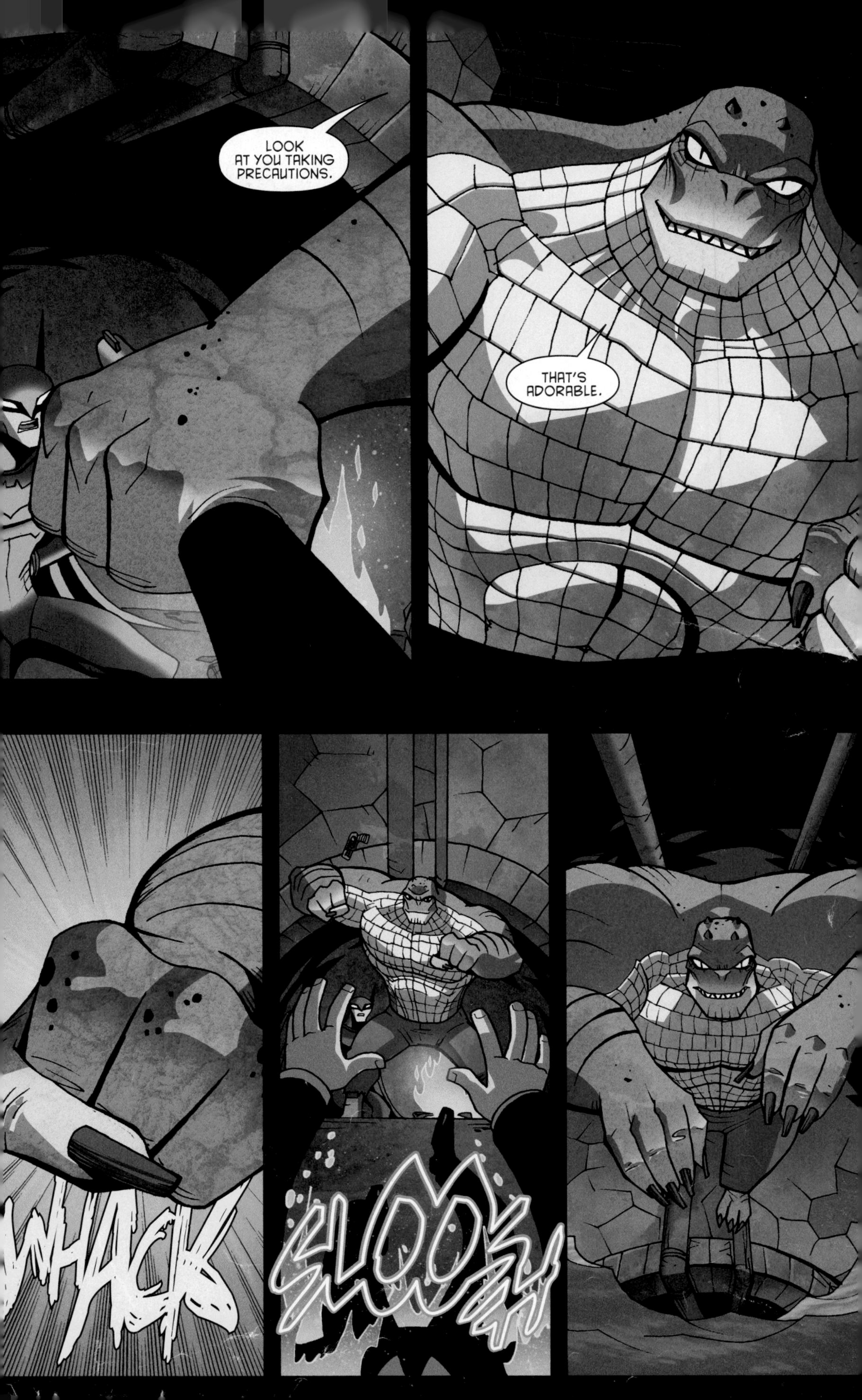
LOOK AT YOU TAKING PRECAUTIONS.
THAT'S ADORABLE.
WHACK
SLOOSH

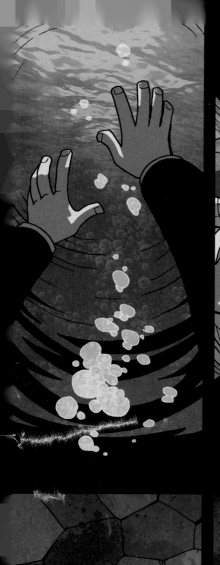

WHUNK

I THINK THAT'S JUST ABOUT ENOUGH OUT OF YOU.

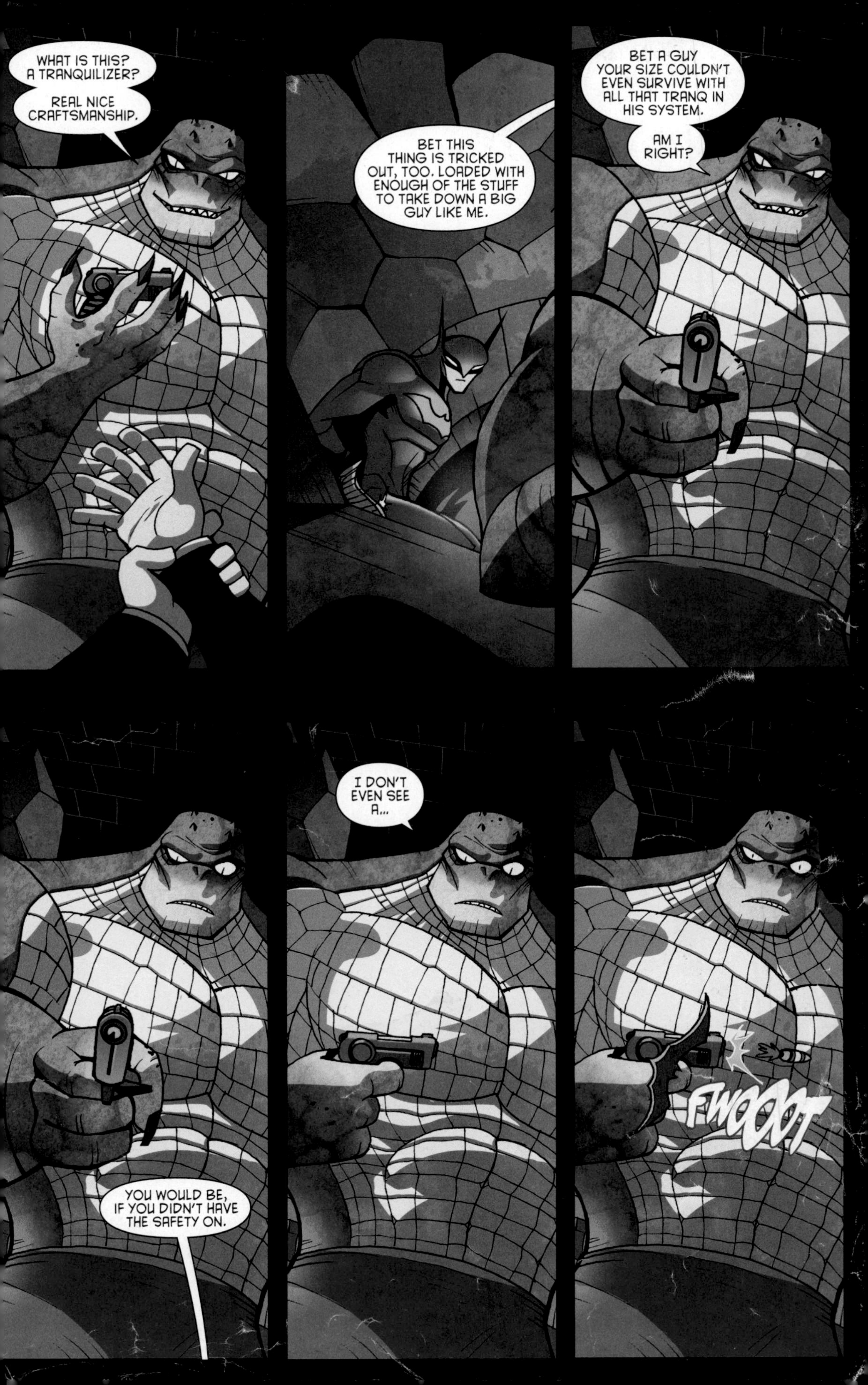
WHAT IS THIS? A TRANQUILIZER?
REAL NICE CRAFTSMANSHIP.
BET THIS THING IS TRICKED OUT, TOO. LOADED WITH ENOUGH OF THE STUFF TO TAKE DOWN A BIG GUY LIKE ME.
BET A GUY YOUR SIZE COULDN'T EVEN SURVIVE WITH ALL THAT TRANQ IN HIS SYSTEM.
AM I RIGHT?
YOU WOULD BE, IF YOU DIDN'T HAVE THE SAFETY ON.
I DON'T EVEN SEE A...
FWOOOT

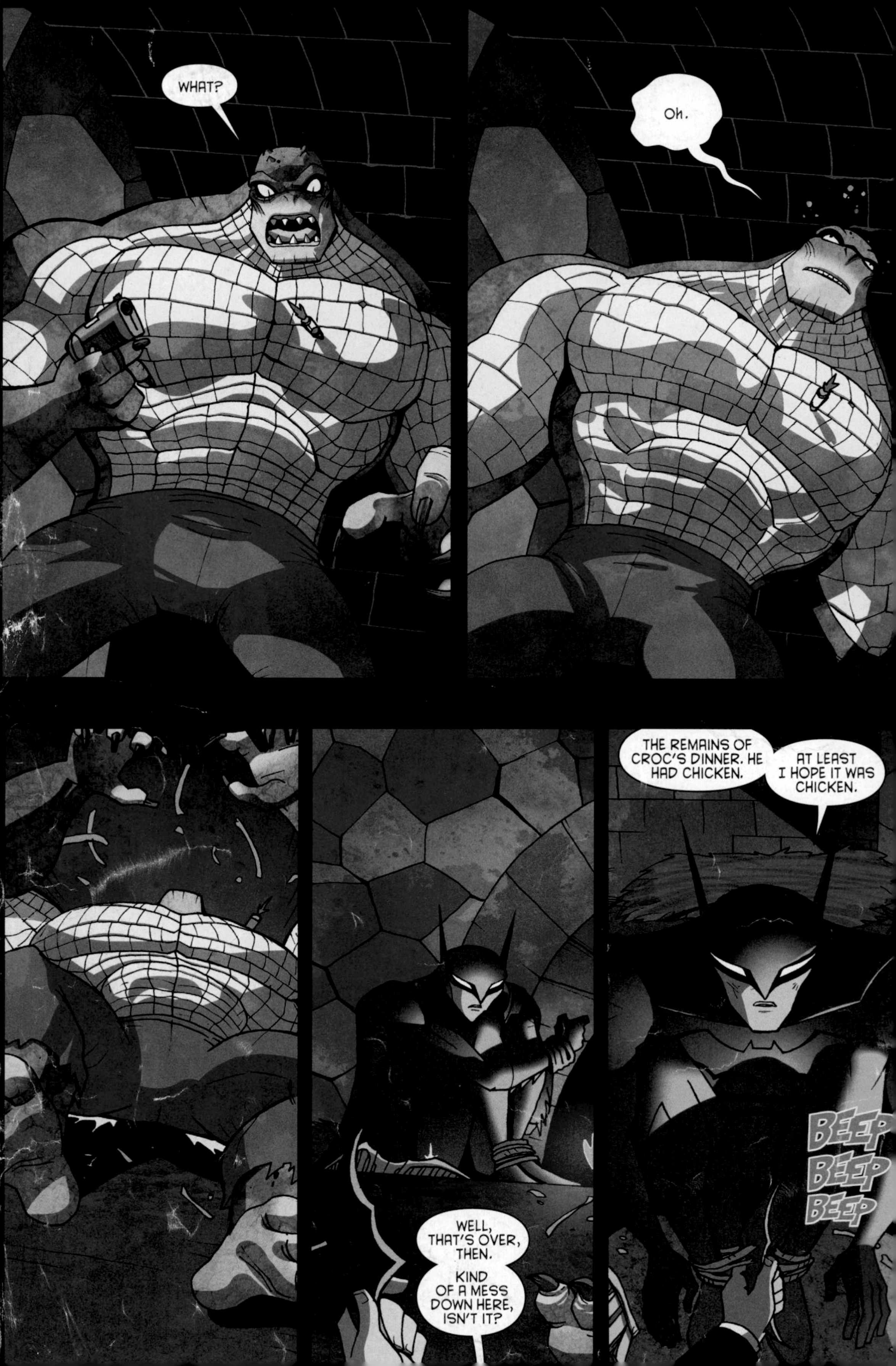
WHAT?
Oh.
WELL, THAT'S OVER, THEN.
KIND OF A MESS DOWN HERE, ISN'T IT?
THE REMAINS OF CROC'S DINNER. HE HAD CHICKEN.
AT LEAST I HOPE IT WAS CHICKEN.
BEEP
BEEP
BEEP

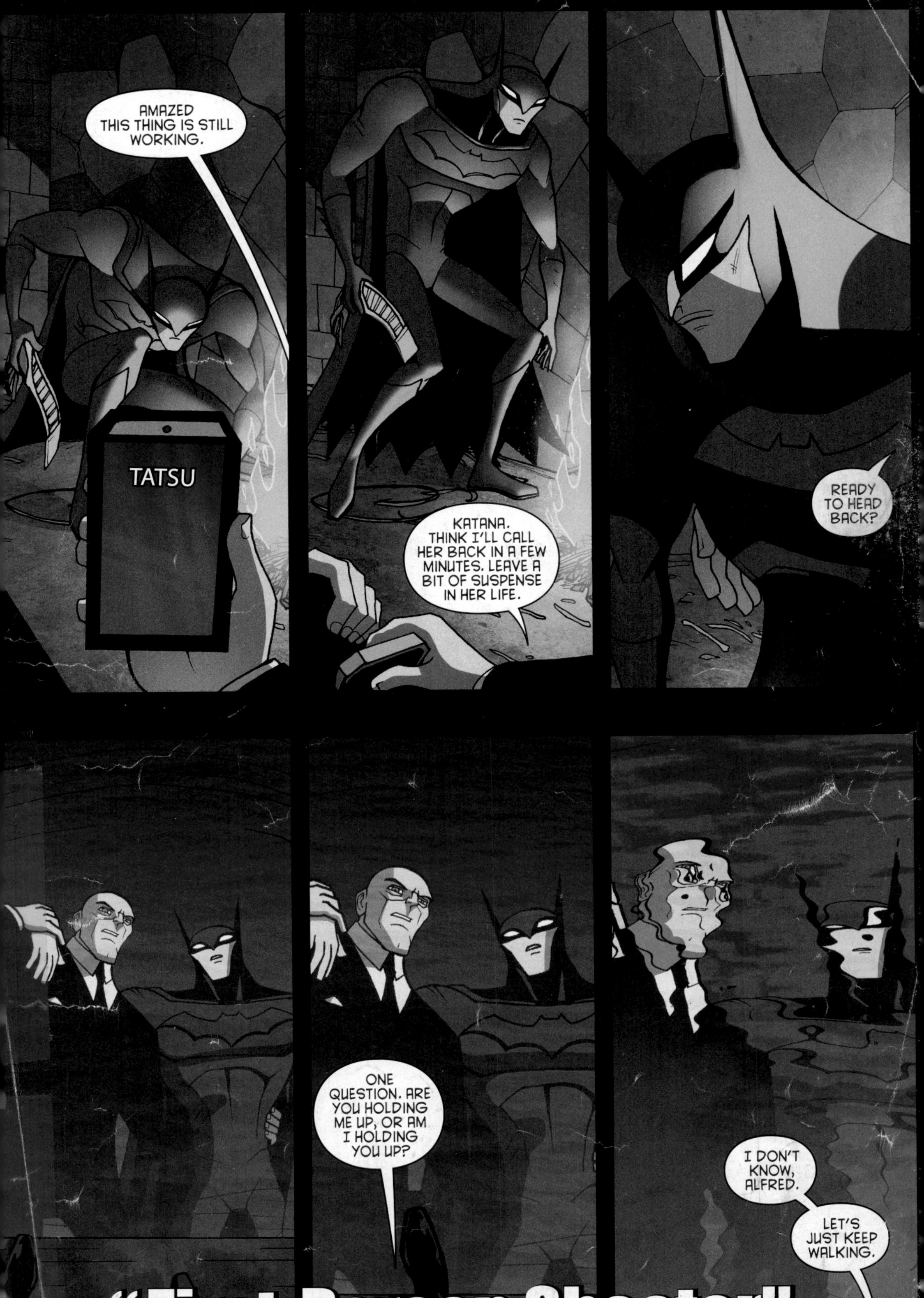
AMAZED THIS THING IS STILL WORKING.
TATSU
KATANA. THINK I'LL CALL HER BACK IN A FEW MINUTES. LEAVE A BIT OF SUSPENSE IN HER LIFE.
READY TO HEAD BACK?
ONE QUESTION. ARE YOU HOLDING ME UP, OR AM I HOLDING YOU UP?
I DON'T KNOW, ALFRED.
LET'S JUST KEEP WALKING.

"First-Person Shooter"

STORY BY **Matthew K. Manning** ART & COVER BY **Luciano Vecchio** COLORS BY **Franco Riesco** LETTERS BY **Wes Abbott**

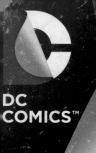

DC COMICS™

"A real treat for any lover of the superhero genre of comics."
—*WASHINGTON TIMES*

"Fans of DC Comics' classic characters will find much to love here."
—*ATLANTA JOURNAL CONSTITUTION*

THE DARK KNIGHT. THE MAN OF STEEL. TOGETHER.

SUPERMAN/BATMAN: PUBLIC ENEMIES

JEPH LOEB & ED McGUINNESS

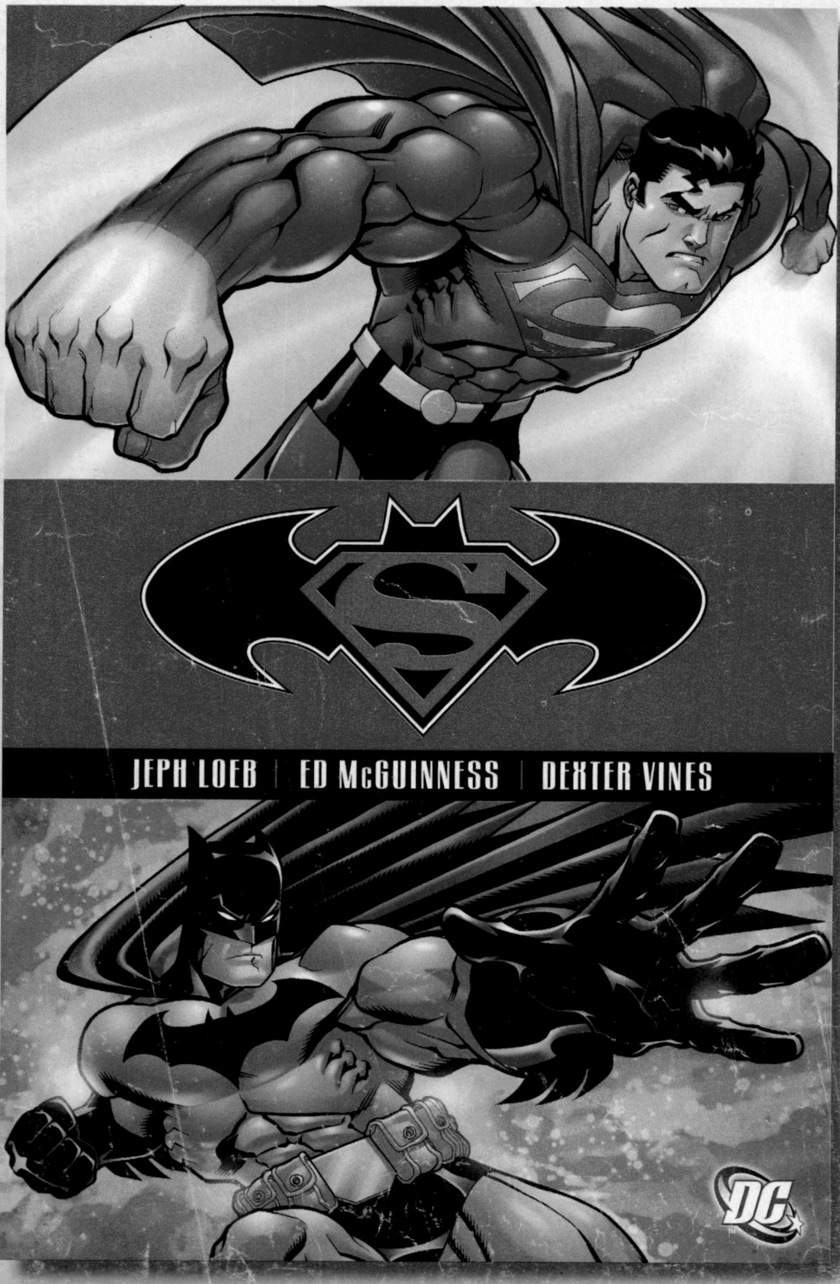
JEPH LOEB | ED McGUINNESS | DEXTER VINES
DC

SUPERMAN/BATMAN: SUPERGIRL

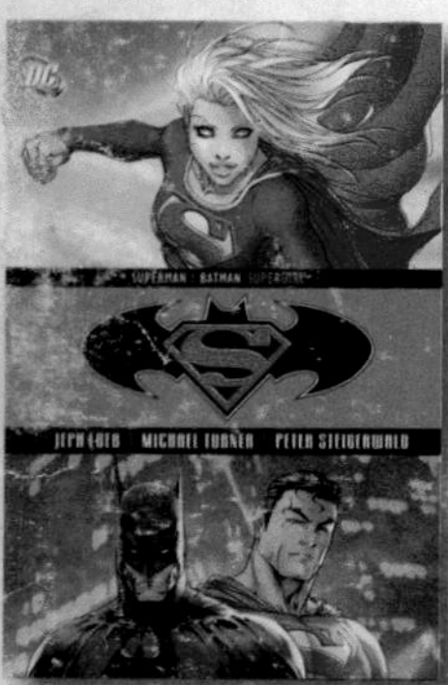
JEPH LOEB MICHAEL TURNER PETER STEIGERWALD

SUPERMAN / BATMAN: PUBLIC ENEMIES

SUPERMAN / BATMAN: SUPERGIRL

SUPERMAN / BATMAN: ABSOLUTE POWER

SUPERMAN / BATMAN: VENGEANCE

SUPERMAN / BATMAN: THE ENEMIES AMONG US

SUPERMAN / BATMAN: TORMENT

SUPERMAN / BATMAN: THE SEARCH FOR KRYPTONITE

SUPERMAN / BATMAN: FINEST WORLDS

SUPERMAN / BATMAN: NIGHT & DAY

SUPERMAN / BATMAN: BIG NOISE

SUPERMAN / BATMAN: WORSHIP

SUPERMAN / BATMAN: SORCERER KINGS